THE BLOOD
OF AN
ENGLISHMAN

THE BLOOD OF AN ENGLISHMAN

JAMES McCLURE

PANTHEON BOOKS, NEW YORK

Library of Congress Cataloging in Publication Data

McClure, James, 1939–
The blood of an Englishman.

(Pantheon international crime)
Reprint. Originally published: New York:
Harper & Row, 1980.
I. Title. II. Series.
PR9369.3. M3B5   1982   823   81-48255
ISBN 0-394-71019-3 (pbk.)   AACR2

Manufactured in the United States of America
First Pantheon Paperback Edition 1982

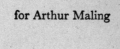

for Arthur Maling

Fee, fi, fo, fum,
I smell the blood of an Englishman.

The Giant in *Jack and the Beanstalk*

CHAPTER ONE

Droopy Stephenson hadn't been a dirty old man all that long. He was still adjusting. He was weighing up the pros and cons, and trying not to allow it to affect his work.

Which wasn't easy.

'What's this I hear, Droopy?' asked Sam Collins, his boss, crouching beside the Land-Rover from which Droopy was removing the sump. 'Man, I'm shocked at you!' And off he went with a laugh, slapping his thigh.

Droopy extended a hand for a No. 8 ring spanner, and Joseph, his intuitive Zulu assistant, wiped the grease from its shank and placed it gently in his grasp. Then for a while Droopy just lay there on his back on the crawler board, staring up at the sump's drain plug.

Three days ago, he had gone into the little fruit shop on the corner, a few yards down the back street from the two-bay garage where he worked, and said to the proprietress, 'Another scorcher, hey, Mavis? Okay if I feels your tomatoes?' He liked his tomatoes crisp. And Mavis Koekemoor, who had known Droopy for years, hadn't even bothered to nod. Instead, she told him that her feet were killing her, and that while the heatwave lasted she had a good mind to get her young niece along to look after the counter side of things. As the shop had only a counter side of things, the idea had seemed promising to Droopy, and he had said as much. He had also asked politely after Mavis's young niece, whom he remembered vaguely as having helped out in the shop during school holidays, and had learned that she was waiting to start a job as a hair stylist. 'Ja, she's a big girl now,' Mavis Koekemoor had observed with satisfaction, giving the bag of tomatoes a quick flip, closing and sealing it all in one operation. Droopy had tried to repeat this neat trick after enjoying two of the tom-

9

atoes with his lunch-time sandwiches, and had lost the rest of them down the lubrication pit.

'The boss wants Number Six?' Joseph enquired uneasily, having heard no sounds of activity from beneath the vehicle.

'Ach no, a Eight's about right.'

After applying the spanner to a couple of bolts, Droopy fell once again into a reverie, going over and over the events leading to his new image of himself.

Two days ago, he had gone into the little fruit shop on the corner to be confronted – there was no other word for it – by a pair of amazing bosoms, and a hair style like an electric shock. 'You know Glenda,' Mavis Koekemoor had prompted from a comfortable seat in front of the fan. 'And will you just look at her? I ask you! That's this young madam's idea of "catching a tan, Auntie"! – she's red all over.' Notwithstanding his normally shy and retiring nature, Droopy was already looking. In fact he was staring fixedly at Glenda, rather less awed by the fiery ravages of the sun than he was by changes of a more permanent order. 'Hi, Droopy,' Glenda had said, with such a sweet, innocent smile. 'Well, do you see anything you'd like?' 'Er, okay if I feels your tomatoes?' '*Really*, Droopy!' And from there it had gone from bad to worse. Much worse. Until Droopy had finally fled, clutching a free cucumber and two oranges, while Mavis Koekemoor had collapsed, helpless with laughter, into the arms of her unscrupulous niece.

'The boss is sick?'

Droopy had emitted an involuntary groan. 'Ach never! Isn't it about time you fetched my tea?'

'Sorry, boss.'

The next day, of course, which seemed like a million years ago but was only yesterday, Droopy had avoided the little fruit shop like the plague, seeking to augment his landlady's idea of a packed lunch by a visit to the cake shop. Ordinarily, the three girls in there seemed to take no notice of him whatsoever, but sold him his confectionery without pausing in their conversations together. A tense silence had fallen the moment he reached the counter, the first giggle had come from behind his back, and then the house had come down when he'd asked, rather crossly, if they had any lemon tarts. 'We never *imagined*,' said the blonde one, as she handed him his change. 'Still waters run deep, hey,

Droopy?' It was enough to make anyone feel confused, baffled and bewildered, and soon it brought on a nasty headache. So, on his way back to Sam's Garage, Droopy had slipped into the chemist shop. The two girl assistants had clung together behind a case of sunglasses, sniggering loudly, and then one, prodded forward by her colleague, had said, 'Just hang on a sec, Droopy, and I'll fetch the manager to serve you!' 'What can he sell me you can't sell me, hey? All I wants is a thingy of Disprin.' Her plucked eyebrows had gone up. 'You're sure? You've not run out or anything?' 'Of course I've bloody run out!' Droopy had snapped, adding immeasurably to their merriment. The last straw had come when, on his return to the garage, the scatty receptionist had looked on him with twinkling eyes and said, 'Oh, Droopy – where have you been all lunch-time? What *have* you been up to?'

Joseph's gape-toed shoes scraped to a halt beside the Land-Rover. 'Excuse, boss. Boss Sam he say does the boss want Boss Sam to put stuff in his tea?'

'What "stuff"?'

'Ungasi, boss. I go ask him?'

'No, just bring me my bloody tea and stop fooling around, man! I've got work to do!'

'Sorry, boss.'

But still the No. 8 ring spanner lay inactive in his hand. Enlightenment had come on his way home, when little Miss Brooks, who ran the Dolls' Hospital round the corner, had beckoned him into her shop and said, 'I just want you to know, Mr Stephenson, that no matter what that hussy is telling everyone, *I* shall never be persuaded you're a – you're a dirty old man.' Droopy had thanked her humbly, and returned to his lodgings, where he'd tossed and turned on the small divan all night, trying to think of ways of killing Glenda Koekemoor stone dead. By the morning, he had admitted to himself that all he could do was brazen this whole thing out, and so, before arriving at the garage, he had called at the cake shop, the chemist shop, the travel agency, the film rental place, and several other businesses, including the little fruit shop. Glenda, Mavis Koekemoor had told him, would be coming in later that morning, and he left a message saying he'd like to see her. Actually, although he had dreaded the idea of doing the rounds, Droopy found that he had enjoyed himself.

In the cake shop, the usual crowd of apprentices and virile young office workers, buying their sticky buns for eleven, had gone ignored the moment he walked in. The girls there had hung on his every word, and he had no need to say anything more than half-funny for them to shriek with laughter, and flaunt their charms at him. Much the same had happened in the chemist shop until the manager had intervened, and Droopy had marched out with the first packet of sheaths he had owned in forty years. As for the red-head in the travel agency, she had titillated him beyond words by insisting that, for a man of his reputation, there was nowhere in the world he should sooner go than Gay Paree – and she would, given half a chance, accompany him. Even walking back down the street had been excitingly different; whereas Droopy had been accustomed to pass by, shabby and unseen, now his progress was the focus of almost limitless attention.

A pair of grease-soaked moccasins came up to the Land-Rover. ''Morning, Droopy!'

It was his fellow mechanic, Boet Swart.

''Morning, Boet. How goes it?'

'So-so, hey? But tell me, how do you do it?'

'Do what?'

'Ach, come on, Droopy – don't play games with me, hey? The word is out – let me tell you that, the word is out!'

'I know,' said Droopy, and surprised himself by quite liking the idea; some of the titillation he'd received this morning was still having a residual effect. 'I heard it off Miss Brooks last night.'

'Oh ja?'

The misgivings in Boet's voice pressed a needle point against the bubble of Droopy's elation. 'Why say "Oh ja?" in that fashion? Surely you would be glad if all the popsies –'

'But Miss Brooks, hey?'

'She calls me into her shop, and she –'

'Hell.'

'She was doing it out of kindness, and what's so wrong with that?'

'Hmmmm.'

Droopy crabbed his way out from under the Land-Rover, and got up off the crawler board. 'That's a funny expression, Boet – best tell me what's on your mind.'

'Well, maybe you haven't heard about Miss Brooks, Droopy

12

old friend. There could be another reason she's suddenly so interested in you . . .'

Droopy cocked his head to one side, waiting. 'What could an old woman like that want with me?' he said.

'Man, it's a question of what *kind* of old woman,' said Boet dolefully, 'and she won't be the only one after you, now the word is out. You'll have them coming for you from every direction.' Then he spun on his heel and walked very quickly away, while the scatty brunette grinned at them from Reception.

Panic rooted Droopy to the spot. Fantasies with nubile young popsies had been one thing, but not for a moment had he considered the possibility of dirty old women getting the hots for him. His brother had been a policeman, and he'd often said he would rather face nine kaffirs armed with cane knives than one determined woman – especially the posh sort, like Miss Brooks, when they were hysterical. Given another second or two, Droopy might have been able to laugh the whole thing off, but he didn't get the chance.

A high, cultured voice rang out from the open workshop door. '*I* don't see what the difficulty is! Why can't I have that one? He doesn't appear to be doing anything at the moment.'

And when he turned round, Droopy saw a tall, skinny woman, with white hair and very red lips, pointing her finger at him.

'Can you come over for a minute?' Sam asked, waiting until Droopy had shuffled over before going on. 'It seems that this lady has a problem you can help her with.'

'Yes, lady?' said Droopy, ignoring Sam's wink and the snorts coming from behind him at Reception.

'My boot's stuck – it's absolutely infuriating. I'd just bought a *mountain* of things to put in it, but I simply can't get the key to work. It won't even go in.'

'I'll leave you to it,' said Sam, turning away to his office.

'Here,' the woman said, handing over her key-ring. 'I've left it over there, and now I must dash, or I'll be late for my hair appointment.'

Droopy wandered out and down the road a short way. The first thing that struck him about the car was that dogs had been peeing all over the back tyres and the back bumper. This was a bit strange, but shouldn't have affected the lock. Then he crouched down and inspected the keyhole.

'Hi, Droopy!'

He jumped. It was Glenda, bursting forth out of a thin blouse and quite unrepentant. His grip tightened on the shaft of the No. 8 ring spanner, which he still had with him.

'You wanted to talk to me, Auntie says. I hope it's not going to be so embarrassing like the last time!'

'Look!' said Droopy, before words failed him.

It was no good, his common sense insisted. There was nothing he could say that would change what she'd done. All he could pray was that something else would come along to take people's minds off it, although that was the trouble with a back street, nothing ever happened.

'Forget it,' mumbled Droopy.

Glenda crouched beside him, nudging his left shoulder with her right. 'What's the problem?'

'You've got eyes, haven't you?'

'Ja. There's a bit of matchstick stuck in there.'

Droopy hadn't noticed that. He squinted, put down his spanner and felt in his pockets.

'Hairpin,' said Glenda, handing him one of her own.

'That's no bloody good.'

'You haven't tried it.'

He tried it. The matchstick only became wedged more firmly. 'Bloody kids!' he grunted. 'Trust them to . . .'

'Oh ja, it's always kids – blame the kids! How do you know?'

'Who else?'

'Let me try, Droopy.'

'You can push off, as far as I'm concerned!'

Glenda stayed right where she was. She sniffed. She wrinkled her nose and made a face. 'Hell, there's a horrible smell around here,' she said, disgustedly. 'Where does this car come from – a farm? Must be stuck to the wheels.'

'I said, push off!'

'Ach, Droopy man, you mustn't be like that, hey?' She laid her soft hand on his gnarled fist, and a tingle shot right through him. 'You must learn to take a joke!'

'What joke?' he scoffed. 'Since when is what you did a joke?'

'You mean me telling everyone about the tomatoes?'

Her audacity took his breath away. 'You need your panties pulled down and your bottom spanked, young lady!'

14

'Are you offering?'

'Glenda Koekemoor!'

'But naturally it was a joke,' she went on blithely, taking the hairpin from his nerveless fingers and trying her luck with the lock. 'It wouldn't have been funny if you was *really* a dirty old man, would it? But you're not – in fact, you're probably the most *unsexy* man in the whole of Trekkersburg.'

'Hey?'

'Do you think anyone would dare to play up to you if you weren't – you know, sort of a nice nothing? They'd run a mile first!'

'I – I –'

'My boy friend could open this easy – he just gives it a boot, and the thing flies up.'

'I –'

'Mind you, it's got him in trouble with the cops before!'

'God Almighty,' gasped Droopy, hurt as he'd never been hurt before, 'who are you calling a "nice nothing", hey? Who are you to judge a man – ?'

'Ah!' Glenda laughed delightedly. 'So you're admitting now that there *was* some guilty feeling in the way you blushed red as a beetroot?'

That did it. Droopy found the No. 8 ring spanner back in his grasp, and all he wanted to do was hit her and hit her, to hurt her just as she was hurting him with every lash of her wicked tongue. More than that, he wanted to smash her whole head to pieces, splattering the brain that could think such things, penetrate so deeply into him, all over the road.

'Droopy!' cried Glenda, jumping up in alarm.

And he struck, delivering a terrible blow to the lock. The boot of the car sprang open, a frightful smell choked the air, and there before them lay what was undoubtedly the dirtiest old man either of them had ever seen. He was covered in mud, excrement and blood, and he had his hands tied behind him in a knot tightened by some hideous strength, for the bones were broken. Lastly, he was dead.

Glenda screamed and screamed and the whole street rushed to her rescue.

CHAPTER TWO

News of the horrifying discovery in Gillespie Street, momentous as it would prove, did not reach CID headquarters in Boomplaas Street as quickly as it might have done. There were several reasons for this. When uniformed officers of the South African Police first arrived on the scene, they were faced by a considerable public order problem. And then, once they had brought the crowd under control, one of their dogs had disgraced itself by biting the sergeant in charge, whose over-excited manner apparently aroused its suspicion. So for a time, while all this was being sorted out and a new chain of command established, it was a case of the *status quo* in the CID building. Some detectives grumbled over their paperwork, others chatted up the typists, and a few doggedly pursued enquiries.

He must have been sitting there so long and so still that the fly thought it would be okay to come and lay some eggs in him. What the hell else was it doing, poking its nose up his left nostril? And then having a dither, none too sure if the other nostril wasn't the better bet. It was in his right nostril that Lieutenant Tromp Kramer, of the Trekkersburg Murder and Robbery Squad, had his cold, and there was certainly less of a draught in there. As a matter of fact, he hadn't breathed through that particular nostril in three days. The fly moved across.

The prisoner plainly found all this fascinating. He sat pretty still himself, and just stared and sweated a lot.

Kramer stared back and didn't sweat at all. His fever had left him overnight, and now his sore throat had almost gone too. He felt the fly move upwards and pause. Paper handkerchiefs, each guaranteed softer than the kinky alternative of a baby's bum, had rubbed his upper lip raw, giving it an unusual sensitivity, and Kramer found it easy to picture what was happening. The fly was

16

standing on five of its legs, scratching its horrible hairy head with the sixth, and wondering if it should toss a coin or something. Another shuffle. It had opted for the left nostril after all, and was tickling its way in against the hairs.

This brought a small, sly smile to the prisoner's narrow face. Meerkat Marais – Mongoose to his English associates – always liked to think he knew more than you did, and it didn't much matter what.

Kramer reached for the tissue box without any hint of this movement reaching his head. He spread the tissue out over his right hand. He pinched his nose suddenly, quite hard, and then blew the dead insect into the exact centre of the paper square.

'It never fails,' he murmured.

Fully five minutes went by before the prisoner finally stopped thinking about the fly, and broke the silence to ask, in a thin, strained voice, why he had been made to sit on top of the filing cabinet.

Kramer shrugged, and dropped the crumpled tissue into the waste-paper bin at his side. 'I heard you have this fear of heights, Meerkat old son.'

'Hey?'

'Ach, I thought we might as well start off in a small way, and see where we go from there. Okay?'

Meerkat went ashen and gave a short, shocked laugh. 'This is too way out for me, man!' he said. 'I don't understand! What heights?'

Across the far side of the CID vehicle yard they were building an eighteen-storey office block for the Mutual Insurance Company, and the top floor was almost finished. Kramer turned away from his window and looked at the flashily dressed figure perched in handcuffs on his filing cabinet. Meerkat understood all right. He was trembling like a church elder unwrapping dirty photographs of himself.

'Come,' said Kramer, getting to his feet. 'I know where there's a nice stiff breeze.'

'No!'

'Pardon?'

'Be fair, Lieutenant,' Meerkat pleaded. 'How many hours have you had me here? Three? And you've –'

'Just the two, Meerkat.'

17

'Two then, but what have you asked me? Nothing! How am I supposed to know what you want? How am I supposed to guess? Hell, it could be *anything*, couldn't it?'

Kramer sat down again behind his bare desk. 'No, man, it couldn't,' he said. 'Personally, I only deal in murders and robbery, so if I bring a guy in to talk to me, the topic's already decided. If I don't say anything, hell, that's just because it's not nice to interrupt.'

'Interrupt what?'

'Your flow, Meerkat. Your outpouring. The cleansing of your soul, your great unburdening. Believe me, Meerkat, you will feel a whole lot better for it.'

Meerkat relaxed slightly. 'I'm supposed to have something to confess?' he asked with a jittery smile. 'This is the first I knew of it!'

'Ja, that's possible,' agreed Kramer.

The prisoner was a proper little psychopath of the kind that starts at three by pissing in his granny's hot-water bottle, and after that there's no holding him. People just didn't matter to Meerkat, and he'd done things to people that didn't bear thinking about, all without turning a hair, sometimes without even noticing.

'You're still not putting me in the picture, Lieutenant.'

'Maybe it's the other way round.'

'Sorry?'

'Archie Bradshaw – tell me about him.'

Meerkat blinked. 'Hell, if you think I had anything to – '

'Tell me!' snapped Kramer. 'Tell me everything you know about Archie Bradshaw or two minutes from now you're going for a ride in a cement bucket.'

Meerkat swallowed hard and squirmed, as though his arsehole was so tight it was pinching him. 'Someone tried to wipe Bradshaw,' he said. 'Six days ago, am I right? He was taking his dog for a walk, up by the race-course, and the shot caught him here in the collar-bone. It stopped inside. He woke up and his dog was licking him. Myself I think it was the blood the dog was – ' He cleared his throat nervously, seeing Kramer's fists bunch. 'Ja, well anyway, he got in his car and went home. It was automatic drive so that was all right. His wife saw all the blood and she asked him what happened. He wouldn't tell her. Even when the doctor came, he wouldn't say. Then they took him to hospital and he had an

18

operation. After he came round, he saw the cop there because they'd found the bullet, and still he wouldn't come out with it. The doctors all said he was in deep shock, most probably. It wasn't till the next morning that his wife heard his story the first time. Bradshaw said he had been walking by the trees when he heard this noise in the bushes. He looked round, and all he caught sight of was this massive bloke – like a gorilla, he said, or maybe a giant – with this silver gun in his hand. He had never in his life seen anyone so huge, he said, and it was such a shock he just stayed turned like that. Then he saw the gun go off, before he had a chance to say anything, and it was like a –'

'Meerkat!'

'Ja, Lieutenant?'

'You're telling me what was in the papers!'

'But – but –'

'Come on, man,' said Kramer, getting up again and walking round to face Meerkat at close range, 'let's hear what the whole town doesn't already know about. Let's hear what you –'

'Now, listen, please listen to me, Lieutenant Kramer sir, all I know about this matter is what I have also read in the *Gazette* – and that's the honest truth.'

Kramer took a small plastic bag out of his pocket and dangled the contents an inch from Meerkat's nose, making his eyes cross. 'What's that, hey? A point-thirty-two revolver bullet.'

'And so?'

'A point-thirty-two isn't really so common, is it?'

'Maybe not, but –'

'Bear that in mind,' said Kramer, and returned to his seat behind the desk. 'There has been talk going round that a certain individual is in illegal possession of a point-thirty-two silver-plated, hammerless, five-chamber –'

'Me?' Meerkat tried to make his laugh sound incredulous. 'Things must be bad if you're looking my way, man! Firstly, I've never even met this bloke Bradshaw, and –'

'He swears he'd never seen this bloke before either.'

'Oh ja? And do I look like a giant?'

'The mind can exaggerate these things, as you can imagine. In my opinion, Meerkat, *anybody* pointing a gun straight at you can look a big bloke. I remember a kaffir that came for me and

Zondi one time, out at Peacevale after an armed robbery, and he was as big as King Kong till we put some holes in him.'

'Even so –'

'He was twelve.'

Meerkat looked at the calendar on the wall with the blood spots. 'Six days ago would be the tenth,' he said. 'I've got a alibi for the tenth.'

'What's her name?'

'Staff Nurse Turner.'

'And where were you and Staff Nurse Turner at the time in question? In the sack?'

'*I* was. I was going to have a wisdom tooth out.'

'Impossible,' said Kramer.

Another fly came to trouble him. He swatted it with the docket on *Archibald Meredith Bradshaw, Attempted Murder*, and wished he had chosen some other way of making a living. In the six days he had been in charge of the case, he had done nothing but chase up one blind alley after another, getting nowhere. Soon his boss, Colonel Muller, would have the right to start asking awkward questions. Had any possible motive for his attack been established? – No. Had anyone been found who had also seen a hulking stranger near the golf course? – No. Had the firearm involved been traced? – No. Had the investigation moved forward one inch since last Friday? – No. Had Kramer begun to lose his grip? – Very possibly, yes.

'Meerkat . . .'

'Ja, Lieutenant?'

'I'm going to be very straight with you. I'm in trouble over this case, and my boss is beginning to say a lot of things that are cruel and unkind. So the best plan for me is just to write out a statement – which you will naturally sign – saying that you sold this thirty-two of yours to a kingsize loony you'd never in your life seen before. I know that's not the whole story, but –'

'*Hey?*' gasped Meerkat, almost toppling from his perch.

'Unless, of course, you can prove in some way that I've got it wrong somewhere.'

Kramer heard running on the stairs and glanced towards the door. Two seconds later, a trim, neatly built Zulu, dressed in a zippy black suit with silver threads in it, and wearing a snap-down trilby, skidded to a halt on the verandah and put his head in the door. It was his assistant, Bantu Detective Sergeant Mickey Zondi.

'Don't tell me,' sighed Kramer, 'let me guess. Her husband came home unexpectedly and didn't believe a –'

'There has been a murder, Lieutenant. The Colonel was trying to get you on the phone, but all the time it is engaged.'

Kramer replaced his receiver in its cradle. 'What kind? Black on black?'

'A white boss – the body has just been found.'

'Where?'

'Gillespie Street.'

Meerkat watched Kramer pick up his jacket and slouch towards the door. 'Just a sec, Lieutenant!'

'Ja, old friend?'

'What's going to happen to me?'

'That,' said Kramer, as he left with Zondi, 'is a question you must ask yourself over and over.'

The traffic was heavy for a Wednesday, and Zondi was forced to keep his speed down. They travelled two blocks without speaking, each man absorbed in private conjecture over what awaited them in Gillespie Street, then the Chevrolet stopped at a red traffic light.

'That reminds me,' grunted Kramer. 'How are you making out on that clown who was knifed down at Mama Bhengu's whorehouse?'

'Not so good, boss. I've found the murder weapon, that's all. It was an old hacksaw blade sharpened up.'

'Uh-huh. At least that's a start. Me, I've got nothing.'

Zondi clucked with his tongue and shook his head sympathetically. 'Maybe I should go to Boss Bradshaw's house again and talk more with the servants.'

'Waste of time.'

'What about that lead on the thirty-two?'

'Waste of time as well. And do you know the only dirt on Bradshaw I've been able to come up with so far? That once he swindled an old lady over some gold coins she had, only her son found out and Bradshaw paid up. Great, hey? Tell me one antique dealer who doesn't try little tricks like that from time to time.'

The lights changed and they rolled forward. 'But what about the silver that Housebreaking traced to his shop, boss?'

'He had a good explanation, they tell me, so they didn't press charges. Make no mistake, Mickey, this Bradshaw's a hard man, and there's lot of people in this city who'll call him a bully, a bastard, but there's not one of them who can say why anyone would want to kill him.'

'And so?'

'And so I'm coming round to the Colonel's idea that it must have just been some loony that took a pot-shot at Bradshaw. You tell me what other theory makes sense.'

'Maybe this man will try again.'

Kramer snorted. 'Christ, have a heart! Haven't I got enough on my plate already, now this new one's come up? No, it was a loony, I'm certain of it, and lightning doesn't strike in the same place twice.'

'Boss Bradshaw is a tall tree,' Zondi remarked primly, 'and there is a saying among my people –'

'Bullshit,' interrupted Kramer, 'you're making this up!'

They laughed together, then peered over the cars in front of them, searching for the lane that provided a short-cut to Gillespie Street. This was nearly always a good moment, Kramer thought, and not unlike the feeling a man had just before meeting a blind date. It carried the same catch clause, however, or perhaps he was simply becoming jaded, but it had been a long time since a body had come up to his expectations.

'You should bloody see it!' enthused Sergeant Bang-bang Bronkhorst, who could swear in court he'd never once hit a prisoner, because he always hit them twice. 'Yirra, Lieutenant, this one is *disgusting* – it could make a hyena vomit.'

'You look all right to me, Bang-bang.'

'Sorry? But as I was saying, this old bloke is covered in his doings, there's blood about an inch thick, and a big hole – same size as my fist – in the back of his head!'

'Uh-huh. Who is he?'

'Hell, *I* don't know, Lieutenant! I'm really a replacement here because Fritz went native and bit old Willem on the bum, and there was shambles till HQ radioed through to me in my van.'

Kramer frowned. He didn't know about the police dog, still

less that its name was Fritz, and his faith in the level-headedness of the uniformed branch was being severely shaken. He started to walk towards the green Rover parked on the other side of Gillespie Street, but Bang-bang caught his arm.

'Can that wait a minute, sir? I thought maybe you'd like to see this witness first, seeing as he's being taken to hospital.'

'What's the matter with him?'

'Deep shock, Lieutenant.'

'Not another one,' Kramer muttered, shaking off the restraining hand. 'All right, where is he?'

They skirted the rear of the crowd and went into a small garage workshop, where a bald-headed, rosy-cheeked man of about fifty was sitting on an upturned oil drum in soiled overalls. Around him hovered a blustery type with a big moustache, another mechanic who was young and mean about the eyes, and a scatty-looking female of eighteen or so. He was humming.

'See what I mean about deep shock?' whispered Bang-bang. 'His name's Stephenson.'

'CID, Mr Stephenson – I'm Lieutenant Kramer, Murder and Robbery Squad.'

'You've come to the right place!' said the blusterer. 'I'm Sam Collins, by the way, and this is my place of business. Droopy here – er, Mr Stephenson – is the mechanic I put on the job, and he's the one who found it, you know! The body.'

'You're going to have your picture in all the papers, Droopy!' giggled the girl.

'I knows,' murmured Stephenson. 'That's what I'll be famous for. It's a miracle.' And he went on humming.

'Can you tell me exactly what happened?' Kramer asked Stephenson.

'Simple,' said Collins. 'I was outside checking the petrol pumps when this lady comes up and says she'd just been to the discount warehouse, and she can't open her boot. You know the discount just round the back of here?'

'Naturally the Lieutenant knows!' snapped Bang-bang. 'He's CID, isn't he?'

'Keep your hair on, hey? I'm only trying to help! So I said to Mr Stephenson here, "Go and take a look, Droopy," and no sooner is my back turned than this lady goes rushing off. To tell you the truth, I thought to myself at the time that her behaviour

23

seemed suspicious. Didn't I even say to you, Doreen, how suspicious I was?'

'I don't – well, I can't remember, Mr Collins.'

Collins patted her shoulder and looked soulfully at Kramer. 'She's in a terrible state, poor Doreen,' he said. 'Terrible.'

'Uh-huh. Then I take it you have no idea who this woman was? She wasn't a regular customer?'

'With a Rover?' remarked the other mechanic scornfully. 'Can't you see all we get in here are old crocks?'

'We get *Land*-Rovers,' Collins cut in huffily.

'That's true,' confirmed Bang-bang.

'Jesus,' said Kramer.

There was a hush, and Stephenson looked up at him with a bland smile. 'The lady's name is Mrs Lillian Digby-Smith,' he said. 'Or at least that's the name inside the leather thing on her key-ring.' He dug the key-ring out of his pocket.

'Evidence!' said Bang-bang. 'Pass it over, man.'

Kramer intercepted the pass, checked the name on the tag, and dropped the key-ring in with his tissues. 'Can you describe Mrs Digby-Smith to me?'

'Tall and skinny with red lips,' said Stephenson.

'Young? Old? Middling?'

'Er, oldish really.'

'Hair?'

'White hair. She said she had a hair appointment.'

'Anything else?'

'No, not really.' And he went back to humming.

Kramer turned to the scatty-looking girl, who was squirming uneasily under her employer's comforting caresses. 'How many places are there for hair near here? Could you give a list of them to this sergeant?'

'Well – er, yes, I suppose so.'

'Good. When the young lady's done that for you, Sergeant, I want you to organise a search.'

'Gladly, Lieutenant,' said Bang-bang, self-importantly. 'Just you leave that to me, sir!'

Kramer thanked Stephenson for his help, received a sunny smile in return, and went to take a look at the deceased, ignoring a curious delaying tactic on the part of Bang-bang Bronkhorst.

24

The crowd, which included an old lady carrying a doll of all things, parted willingly, avid for another glimpse.

'Bloody Bronkhorst,' a young constable was muttering, as he struggled to open the boot. 'Why did you have to shut it again so hard, you old fool? Hell! *Hello*, sir!'

Kramer could see that the battered lock was probably the problem. He took a step closer, raised his right foot and kicked, expertly springing the boot open. Immediately a group of uniformed officers gathered round to screen the boot's contents from the public gaze, and he crouched down to peer inside.

At first, it looked much like any other dead body – breathtaking in its own way, of course, but nothing special, and he had the advantage of a blocked nose. Then he saw that it far exceeded his expectations. He saw the arm bones fractured by a knot that must have been tightened by nothing less than a giant of a man, a human gorilla – the same sort of monster, in fact, as Archie Bradshaw had described.

With an instinctive shudder, Kramer closed the boot, thought for a moment, and then went to tell Zondi.

CHAPTER THREE

After a hectic twenty minutes chasing round all the hair salons within easy walking distance of Gillespie Street, Mrs Lillian Digby-Smith was finally run to ground at Jonty's, a high-class establishment offering a wide range of beauty treatment. It was rumoured that a tarantula had once strayed in there, to emerge three hours later with a blue rinse, eight colours of eye shadow and legs like Betty Grable. It was also rumoured that the husbands of half the socialites in Trekkersburg had received the bill – and, what was more, that they'd paid up without demur, looking grateful.

Kramer liked the feel of the plush purple carpet beneath his feet, the svelte look of the dollies who worked there, and the mildly aphrodisiac effect induced by the smell of hot hair and henna. He especially liked the way one petite red-head studied him with sly approval in a mirror, running her cornflower eyes over him like fingers. Jonty wasn't much to his taste though.

The proprietor wafted over to him. 'So *you're* the detective chappie we've all been waiting for? *Super.*' And he gave the chiffon scarf around his neck a flip with the back of his hand.

'Listen, cuddle bunny,' said Kramer, 'where's the lady?'

'Listen,' lisped Jonty, leaning intimately towards him, 'one more crack like that, you bastard, and you get my knee in your balls.' Then he gave a fairy wave towards the innermost row of curtained cubicles. 'She's down at the end there, poor darling – I *do* hope this is nothing serious!'

Grinning, Kramer continued on his way; he had caught a hint of heartlessness in Jonty that appealed to him. Two uniformed constables slipped out of the last cubicle but one, and gave nervous nods of welcome.

'You haven't approached her yet?' asked Kramer.

'No, sir,' they whispered in unison.

'Fine. Tell you what, go and get yourselves a shampoo or something, but stay on the premises.'

Mrs Digby-Smith was lying on a low couch in the cubicle, leafing through a copy of *Vogue* in search of distraction. Her expression didn't alter one jot when she was told that the body of a man had been found in the boot of her car. She sat up, that was all. But when Kramer added that, to the best of his recollection, the body was that of a man in his late fifties, with wavy grey hair and a big brown mole behind his right ear, fine cracks began to appear in the wax mask she was wearing.

'The point is, lady,' Kramer went on, 'have you any knowledge of such an individual – or of how he came to be there?'

'Who?'

Kramer repeated the description, which was rather a limited one as he wanted the district surgeon to see the stiff *in situ* before anyone touched anything. 'Oh ja, and he has on these beige trousers, sandals, and a sports shirt with an unusual label on it. Let me see . . . St Michael?'

'Dear God . . .'

Kramer waited. He waited what felt like a very long time. 'You know this man?' he asked eventually.

Still Mrs Digby-Smith made no reply. Then she began to weep – not to cry, for there was no sound with it. Her staring grey eyes, fixed on the lilac curtain behind him, simply welled up and spilled over. Kramer had seen this kind of thing happen before; one way or another, it had been his lot in life to go round upsetting quite a few women. Naturally, each time it was slightly different, and this time was no exception. The tears usually brimmed the lower lid, fell, slid slowly down the cheeks, and then slipped out of sight below the jaw-line. These tears, however, brimmed the lower lid, fell, shot off the yellow wax, and made a pattern of splotches in the light green smock protecting her dress.

Mrs Digby-Smith was raining.

'Look, lady,' said Kramer, sitting down on a manicurist's stool beside the couch, 'I can appreciate this might not be so nice for you, but if you know the identity of –'

'No!'

'No, what? No, you don't know his name?'

The eyes went on staring. They dried up and took on a glaze. The mouth, cleansed of lipstick and bloodless as well, set hard in

27

an irregular line across the gap in the wax, like an appendix scar turned sideways. It certainly didn't look any more likely to unseal itself suddenly.

Kramer glanced about him. He noticed, on the little locker at the head of the couch, a pad of air-mail paper, a packet of air-mail envelopes, half a letter and a small pile of colour prints with writing on the back of them. The uppermost photograph had this scrawled behind it in ballpoint: *Bonzo and me in the game reserve – that's Jack's shadow!* He turned it over and saw that Jack, a hunched elongation in the foreground, had been the photographer. Posed against the guest huts of a Zululand rest camp, and squinting into the sun, was a couple in outdoor clothing. The person on the left was tall, skinny, white-haired and immediately recognisable as the woman sitting bolt upright before him. The person on the right was a man in his late fifties with wavy grey hair, the same St Michael shirt, and a pair of very new leather sandals. There was an obvious conclusion to be drawn straight away, but Kramer made a closer scrutiny of the photograph before returning it to the pile on the locker. By then there was no doubt in his mind that the couple shared too many facial characteristics for their likeness to one another to be coincidental.

'I know who the body is,' he said.

Her gaze flicked towards him.

'His name's Bonzo, lady – and he was your kid brother.'

Mrs Digby-Smith said nothing. She swooned. She swayed and pitched forward over the far side of the couch, too unexpectedly for Kramer to catch hold of her. The mask of yellow wax shattered on the mosaic floor, scattering like egg shell, and her upper dental plate fell out.

'Bloody hell,' said Kramer, 'just when we were getting acquainted.'

The telephone rang once again in the district surgeon's household. Anneline Strydom sighed and answered it, anticipating who was at the other end by having in her mind the picture of a tall, broad-shouldered man with fair hair, high cheek-bones, slightly protruding front teeth and eyes like green marbles, although it was those big, lion's-paw hands that really gave her the shivers.

'Now look, Trompie,' she said firmly, anticipating her caller's mood as well, 'there's no point in blasting me if Chris hasn't arrived there yet. I gave him your message – what more can I do?'

'Er, actually it's me, Mrs S – not Lieutenant Kramer.'

'Sergeant Van Rensburg?'

'The same, Mrs S.'

And the picture became one of a mortuary sergeant so grossly overweight that his fingers could no longer squeeze into his tight trouser pockets. 'Don't tell me something else has come in!' exclaimed Anneline, crossly. 'My poor husband doesn't often take the morning off, you know!'

'Hell, we all know he's dedicated, hey?' smarmed Van Rensburg. 'It's just – if Doc hasn't left yet – I wanted to save him from a wasted journey down to Gillespie Street. What's happened is they've decided to bring the whole caboose here, you see, to my mortuary, and I've got the car with the body still intact in it out in my yard.'

'Oh?'

'Ja, they towed it here.'

'Well, I'll look and see if Dr Strydom is about anywhere, although I doubt it. This *is* a white that Lieutenant Kramer's making all the fuss about?'

'Definitely, Mrs S.'

'That's all right then. Bye for now.'

Anneline knew perfectly well that her husband was still out in the garden, looking for snails with Josiah the garden boy. It was just that it was so rare for him to show an interest in anything other than post mortems that she felt extremely reluctant to disturb them again, and for another ten minutes she let the matter rest. Then, anxious he shouldn't slip away unaware of the change in venue, she went out to call for him.

'Chris?' He had vanished. 'Chrissie – where are you, man?'

Finally, way down at the bottom of the garden, behind some large azalea bushes, she found her husband and the garden boy squatting on their haunches, looking more like a couple of kids than two grown men, and paying great attention to something they were prodding about in a big Pyrex bowl. To her astonishment, Anneline realised that the 'something' was hundreds of horrible snails, mixed in with a salad of lettuce leaves.

'My goodness me,' she declared, 'you're not thinking of *eating* those things, are you?'

29

'Hau!' said Josiah, and had a fit of the giggles.

'Ach no, what we're doing is scientific,' replied her husband, airily. 'This is the snail Helix –'

'You don't have to be scientific to those extremes, man! And why use my best mixing bowl? All you need to do is stick some salt in a bucket of water : that'll kill them and no mistake. Van's just been on the phone, and I've come down to tell you –'

'I'm coming! I'm coming! I just wanted Josiah to get the hang of it.'

'The hang of *that*?'

'Certainly. We're preparing an extract.'

'*Hey*? What on earth for?' And she laughed girlishly.

But he wouldn't tell her what for, not while his feelings were hurt. He stumped off up the lawn, with his shirt tail hanging out and his shock of white hair matted, muttering darkly. It was just as well, Anneline Strydom thought, that this person he was going to see had no further use for a soothing bedside manner.

Names like Digby-Smith had always irritated Kramer. They smacked of English-speaking snobs with horse-dung under their fingernails and – after drug-crazed alcoholic clap-struck half-castes – there was no breed of human he distrusted more profoundly. Yet he had to concede that the name Digby-hyphen-Smith had one undoubted virtue. It was listed only twice in the Trekkersburg telephone directory, and to make things even simpler, one entry was marked *Residence* and the other *Business*.

'I'm sorry, sir,' said the secretary who answered his call, 'but Mr Digby-Smith is out visiting a site with a client at the moment. Can I put you through to his junior partner, Mr Wells?'

Kramer sagged fractionally. 'Ach no, that wouldn't be much help,' he said. 'Instead, can you do two things for me? As soon as your boss gets back, can you ask him to come down to Jonty's – you know where I mean, the beauty shop?'

'Er, yyyyes . . . You did say this was the police?'

'CID. Also, will you please give me the number of his family doctor?'

'It's Dr Crickmay. But what on earth – ?'

'Later,' said Kramer, and hung up.

He found and tried Dr Crickmay's number. It seemed to ring an unpardonable length of time for a surgery switchboard. While waiting for a reply, he glanced around Jonty's private office, unable to decide whether it was helluva modern or helluva down-to-earth and simple. The floorboards were bare, the walls a plain white, the desk and two chairs were ordinary, the calendar was a trade hand-out, and that was about it – except for a huge family-sized refrigerator in the far corner which added a nonsensical, baffling touch. Helluva modern, was his verdict.

Jonty slipped into the room and closed the door. 'Any luck with that doctor yet? She's still not quite with us, y'know; keeps mumbling about old Bonzo and then fading out.'

'That's who I'm ringing right now, only I don't seem to – Oh hullo, it's the CID here. Is Dr Crickmay available?'

'Sorry, but Doctor's out finishing his morning rounds,' said the surgery receptionist.

'Hell.'

'Is this something urgent? If so, I could have Doctor bleeped to the nearest telephone.'

'Ideal,' said Kramer, and gave her the salon's number.

Jonty waited until the receiver had been replaced before he asked, 'What exactly is going on here? Did you bring her a bit of bad news or other?'

'Ja, pretty bad.'

'Concerning her brother?'

'How did you guess?'

'Well, from what she's mumbling, I suppose, Mr – er . . .'

'Kramer – Lieutenant Tromp Kramer, Murder and Robbery Squad.'

'*Robbery?*' Jonty's thick eyebrows shot up. 'Poor old sod! Where was this? Here in town? This morning?'

Kramer was about to set the record straight when he realised that the salon owner might be more helpful if he was left holding the wrong end of the stick. Murders tended to be messy, very personal affairs in which other people tried not to become involved, but a robbery on the other hand was close to an Act of God, and nobody minded divulging what they knew of a robbery victim's circumstances to anyone who appeared interested.

So instead he said, 'Bonzo was found about an hour ago in Gillespie Street. You speak like you know him.'

'I know *of* him, certainly,' said Jonty. 'As you can imagine, we get the lowdown on all our clientele and their belongings, one way or another – there's what they themselves insist on boring us with, plus the juicier bits of gossip their best friends pass on. It's a pain at times, but there you go, we're in the ego business.'

'Uh-huh.'

'And so I've naturally picked up quite a bit on Bonzo, alias Edward Hookham, DFC and bar – now there's a thought!' Jonty swung open the refrigerator door to reveal about ten dozen cans of chilled beer. 'What's yours, Lieutenant? A lager?'

'Please,' said Kramer, and felt suddenly very much at his ease, being a man of simple, down-to-earth tastes himself. 'And don't bother with a glass, hey?'

As Jonty removed the cans of lager, Kramer subjected him to a swift reassessment. He could see now that the salon owner was a fairly ordinary sort of bloke under all that rubbish he wore – the wide leather belt, the embroidered shirt and pink jeans – and probably not the least bit perverted. His age was around thirty-five, his build was well above average, and his face would not have disgraced a bulldozer driver, provided something was done about those golden ringlets first. One thing still seemed a little strange though, and that was his accent.

'Right, get that down yer,' said Jonty, handing over the lager. 'Where were we?'

'You were telling me about this bloke Bonzo.'

'Old Trekkersburg family, the Hookhams. Must've been second- or third-generation South Africans by the time our Lillian was born, followed a few years later by Bonzo. Their dad was in the seed trade.'

'Oh ja, Hookham & Bailey, down by the Market Square.'

'Right. Lillian married money – Digby-Smith really only plays at being an estate agent – and Bonzo buggered off to England to join the RAF when the war started. He was in Bomber Command, and that's where he got the nickname Bonzo, apparently, which h⸱s stuck ever since. Then he did the opposite to me.'

Kramer tipped his head enquiringly.

'What I mean is,' said Jonty, 'I came out here five years ago last March from Southampton – I'm an immigrant.'

'Ah. I'd wondered.'

'And Bonzo did things the other way round. When the war ended, he stayed on in England, married an English girl, and built up a small electronics business. His wife died about two months ago.'

'Oh ja?'

'Of cancer. He was left on his tod – their kids were all grown up – and he decided to carry on with the holiday they'd planned for his retirement, which was to come and visit his sister. First proper holiday he's ever taken, she tells me.'

'When did he arrive here?' asked Kramer.

'In Trekkersburg? Oh, I'd say about three appointments ago. That's right, they took him to Hluhluwe Game Reserve last week, and so he must have arrived –'

'– at the beginning of the month.'

'Check.'

Kramer watched Jonty drain a can of lager in one long pull. 'And now the juicy gossip, hey?'

'About the Digby-Smiths?'

'That's right.'

Jonty laughed. 'You've got to be joking! Those two? They're not only past it, I don't think they ever bloody reached it!'

'Tell me more.'

'No kids, two dogs, six servants and a house the size of a sodding hotel. They run on rails. They do the same things year in and year out. They don't care about anything, apart from the fact everyone recognises their *position*, is polite to them at cocktail parties, and keeps telling the old bag how well groomed she is.'

'You sound bitter, my friend.'

'Do I?' Once again Jonty laughed, and went over to the refrigerator to get them each another lager. 'Not really. I've been screwing their kind for years, and I've done all right out of it.'

The telephone rang. Kramer answered it and Dr Crickmay promised to be at Jonty's within the next ten minutes.

'So there's absolutely no gossip on the Digby-Smiths?'

'Christ, no!' snorted Jonty. 'It would kill 'em.'

Kramer pondered that for a moment. 'But does the same apply to Bonzo?' he asked. 'No scandal there either?'

'None so far. He doesn't sound a bad fellow, actually. His sister bitches about how "independent" he is, which probably means that they bore the arse off him, and he goes and does his own thing. Like last night, for example.'

'Oh ja?' Kramer's interest quickened.

'That's what she's been moaning about this morning. It seems Bonzo announced he had an old flame to look up, borrowed her car, said he'd be getting back late, and then left it outside the property with its windows open all night. I spared myself the rest of the gruesome details.'

'An old flame?' queried Kramer. 'Any idea of –'

'Not the slightest.'

'And yet you claim there's been no gossip about him?'

Jonty shrugged. 'Well, I suppose there's been a bit of a flutter in certain quarters. Quite a few of the sweet young things he used to know are divorced now – or widowed – and they're all rich and fancy free, y'know. I suppose I've made a bob or two out of new face jobs!'

'I bet.'

'Mind you, they'd be better off going down to the gym, from what I've heard. If anything comes through loud and clear about Bonzo Hookham, then it's that he's very much the dynamic type – a right little ball of energy!'

'The sort to leave them flat on their backs?'

'Or dangling from the chandeliers! No, to be fair to the man, the talk hasn't reached that stage yet.'

Kramer watched Jonty sink his second lager in another long gulp. 'Do you know of any connection between the Digby-Smiths and the Bradshaws?' he asked.

'Bradshaw?' repeated Jonty, looking puzzled.

'He runs an antique shop in Ballard's Arcade.'

'Oh, you mean the idiot who got shot at last week, and said he'd been attacked by a giant? No, I'm pretty sure there couldn't be one – I mean, the Bradshaws are hardly *society*, are they?'

Kramer rose. 'Can you do me a couple of favours?'

'Let's hear them first.'

'Number One, keep your ears open for any snatches of gossip about Bonzo.'

'Fair enough, not that I see –'

'Number Two, deal with this Dr Crickmay for me when he comes. I've got an appointment at the mortuary, and already I'm long overdue there.'

'If your lads are staying on, I don't mind,' agreed Jonty. 'But

I think in return you might let me in on a few of the details, pal. What was Bonzo robbed of, for instance?'

'His life,' said Kramer.

The beer can crumpled in the Englishman's hand like a plastic cup. 'You're pulling my leg,' he said slowly.

'Not really. He was found shot through the head about an hour ago, trussed up like a fowl in the boot of his sister's car.'

Jonty dropped the crumpled can into his waste-paper bin. Then he opened a desk drawer, took out a perfume atomiser, gave a puff into his mouth, making himself cough, and sprayed a lot more of the stuff over his chest and shoulders, smothering the smell of hops. 'I must be getting back,' he said, holding open the door. 'You really are a right bastard, aren't you?'

'Tip of the iceberg,' said Kramer, and winked at the red-head on his way out.

CHAPTER FOUR

N2134 Nxumalo, the Zulu constable who assisted Sergeant Van Rensburg at the police mortuary, a small, red-brick building half-hidden down in the weeds behind the barracks, always had a welcome for Zondi. He slipped out of the side door, taking care not to allow the fly-screen to bang shut behind him, and wandered over with a big, happy smile.

'Greetings, Sergeant,' he said. 'Many thanks for this.'

'For what?' Zondi echoed, vaguely.

He was watching Sergeant Fanie Prinsloo from Fingerprints examine the interior of the green Rover. The car had been towed to the mortuary by a breakdown lorry from the police garage, and Zondi had hitched a lift on it, hoping to see for himself how tightly the dead man's wrists had been tied. It was just possible, he conceded, that the evidence of enormous strength might look more convincing than it sounded, but he had his doubts.

'Many thanks,' repeated Nxumalo, tearing a cigarette exactly in two – for he was a poor man with several wives – and offering Zondi one half of it. 'Up until now, this morning has been terrible. Dr Strydom was not coming in, so Sergeant Van, the old baboon, decided we must have what he calls "spring clean". Do you understand what "spring clean" means?'

Zondi nodded, having a memory of some such thing from his early days as a domestic servant. 'It is when the whites untidy the whole house, make you wash even the walls, and then tell you to tidy up again.'

'Ah, so it is a custom,' sighed Nxumalo, as though this explained a great deal.

They lit up, sharing the same match, and watched the finger-print expert transfer his attention to the exterior of the car, with special reference to the area around the boot lock.

36

'You's a idle kaffir!' mimicked Nxumalo, almost fondly – he had worked with Van Rensburg for many years. 'What's this arm doing here, hey? How long have we had this arm? Hau, boss, many many months – since the big train crash when it hit the petrol tankers. Don't give me excuses, hey? Chuck the bloody thing out! And this head? What about this head you've stuck down at the back of the fridge here? You thought I wouldn't see it, hey? That head, boss, is the one without a body – you remember, the patrol found the dogs fighting over it in Peacevale township, and Dr Strydom said it was cut off with a penknife. But it's just some idle kaffir's head, Nxumalo! You see what happens to idle kaffirs? I do, my boss, only Dr Strydom said I must not – Look, Nxumalo, this is *my* mortuary, not so? If he wants this head so much, then he can take it home and put it in his deep freeze! Why should I have it cluttering up the place? The junk that man collects! Just chuck it out, you hear me?'

Zondi laughed, and blew a smoke-ring.

'On and on from eight o'clock this morning,' grumbled Nxumalo, 'with not one minute's rest. Kaffir! Yes, my boss? Have you looked down this slit behind the sink, you bloody monkey? There's old blood in there that's *caked*. And what's all these organs doing in these bottles under here? You've not been making bloody preserves for your bloody family, have you? I want this slab so clean I can eat my lunch off it – you hear? Yes, boss; straight away, boss – but where do I chuck these things, boss? Chuck them where you bloody like! Put them in with the stiffs that are being collected this morning, down by the feet where nobody'll notice! Only get your bloody finger out, do you hear me? Yes, I hear you, my boss . . .'

Another smoke-ring. 'And now, my brother?' murmured Zondi, wondering when the car's boot would be opened.

'And now that is all forgotten,' said Nxumalo, sighing gratefully. 'Now all the old baboon can think about is this new body you have brought him. He says it comes of a good family, so we must quickly tidy and get the table set nicely for it. I put out the knives, then he told me to bugger off, the rest he would see to himself.'

'Uh-huh,' responded Zondi, with a little unconscious mimickry of his own.

Sergeant Prinsloo had just laid aside his fingerprint equipment

37

in apparent disgust and picked up his camera. He opened the boot of the car and recoiled, wrinkling his nose, then took a long, hard look that puckered his lips into a silent whistle. This was too much. Zondi sauntered across and stole a quick glance at the body.

'Hey, Mickey, this isn't a non-white, you know!' protested Prinsloo. 'What do you want here?'

'Does the Sergeant want me to hold his flashgun, sir?'

'No, I can manage – go on, hop it.'

Zondi hopped it. He went back to where Nxumalo was standing, gave a shrug and leaned against the wall again. One glance was less than he had hoped for, but it had been enough to give him the same feeling in the pit of his stomach as the Lieutenant had told him about. Whether this was because of the terrifying strength implicit in the tightness of the knot, or because there was indeed a link between the Bradshaw case and this murder, he couldn't tell, yet either way his interest was aroused.

'Nxumalo, be a big friend,' he said, handing over half of a Lucky Strike that he'd tactfully torn in two, 'and get me the telephone directory out of the old baboon's office – there's an address I want to get from it.' Although Zondi didn't know a great deal about white people's surnames, he did know that he'd never heard of a Digby-Smith before, and felt that this should narrow things down a bit. His real problem was hijacking a car.

When Kramer drove his Chevrolet into the gravel car-park outside the mortuary, the only people visible were three youngsters from Forensic, gagging and going green over their minute examination of the Rover's boot. The body had been removed, and they were placing samples of earth and other, less agreeable manifestations of Mother Nature into plastic envelopes; none had anything of particular note to report so far.

'In fact,' said one of them, 'Sarge Prinsloo only managed to lift two sets of prints from the inside, and he says that the ones at the back were all smeared.'

'He's where? Gone into the mortuary?'

'Correct, sir. Doc Strydom started work about ten minutes ago.'

Kramer nodded and went through the double doors, across the lobby where Nxumalo was fiddling with three coffins, and then through another set of double doors into the post-mortem room

itself. He had noticed on previous occasions that the district surgeon bore something of a resemblance to a garden gnome. It was
a description that seemed particularly fitting that morning, for
Doc Strydom was hopping up and down at the side of a dissecting
table exactly like a garden gnome who, after dangling his line in
a goldfish pond for ten years, had just had his first strike.

'Trompie!' Strydom exclaimed. 'Man, this is the most fascinating one you've brought me in a long time!'

'Glad you like it, Doc.'

'Look at these wrist fractures!'

'I've seen them. What else is there?'

'Three bullet wounds and a skull fracture!'

'You don't say?'

Kramer approached over the clatter of wooden duckboards.
Prinsloo, with whom he'd fallen out recently, gave him a nervous
nod, while Van Rensburg turned on his 300 lb charm with a wide,
ingratiating smile, which was like seeing a rent appear in a hot-air
balloon. Regrettably, this was not followed by a sudden deflation,
a loud rude noise, and the disappearance of his rapidly diminishing form out through the nearest window.

' 'Morning, Lieutenant!' they said.

He ignored them and turned to the deceased.

Edward 'Bonzo' Hookham was lying on the first of five ceramic
post-mortem slabs with his head supported by a U-shaped wooden
block. The first and most striking thing about him was his pristine
cleanliness. The filthy clothing he had been wearing was packed
away in plastic bags on the next slab along, and Van Rensburg
had obviously been applying his hose assiduously, flushing away
the last trace of unpleasantness from the naked form. The next
most noticeable thing about him was the relatively small area of
the slab he occupied : Krammer put his weight at about 120 lb
and his height at no more than 5 ft 5 in. As for the overall impression he made, it was difficult to choose between a Siamese cat
and a bar of coconut ice. Three weeks' exposure to the South
African sun had turned Hookham's head, hands and feet (save
for the marks of his sandal straps) a darkish brown, while the rest
of his body was very pale, as became someone from northern
climes. Furthermore, it amused Kramer to observe that Hookham's eyes were a deep blue and frozen in a slight squint. Viewed
another way, however, longitudinally from the feet, Hookham's

right half was white and his left half was pink, giving him that coconut-ice look.

'Hypostasis,' confirmed Strydom prodding the discolouration with his thumb. 'All the blood's drained to the side we found him lying on, so we can draw two conclusions from that. A : That he's been dead at least six hours, and B : That he wasn't left lying around for long before being put in that boot. If you take a look at his shoulder here, you'll see the clear impression of a bolt-head from the car's bodywork.'

The octagonal white shape was as decided as a paper cut-out. Other pressure points along Hookham's left side were similarly free of accumulated blood.

'You say at least six hours, Doc, but what's the upper limit?' asked Kramer. 'You've taken his temp?'

'Ja, but under the circumstances, it isn't much help. It was like an oven in that boot, Trompie, and rigor must have set in damn quick – we've even got decomposition.'

'No time of death then?'

'I'd say within the last twenty-four hours.'

'You'd say right. It happened last night.'

There was very little fat on Hookham, corroborating what Jonty had said about his being an energetic type, although the only energy left in him now was kinetic. The face was rather boyish, quite pleasant, and dominated by a moustache that Kramer recognised as typically RAF, upswept and cocky, while the thin mouth looked made for laconic remarks.

'Which bullet did he get first, Doc? This hole in his head?'

'Possibly. I was just about to try probing these others in his chest.'

'Fire away then.'

Both entrance wounds were slightly to the right of Hookham's breastbone. Each was about three-eighths of an inch across and had a dark collar of abrasion, giving them an overall width of half an inch.

'One thing I can tell you right away,' said Strydom, 'is that the shirt showed no sign of fouling by smoke or tattooing by unburnt powder grains, so all of these definitely came from over a metre away.' He paused and frowned. 'That's funny, I can't seem to find the track on this one . . .' He tried increasing the angle of the probe to the body, and moved it around gently. 'Ah, in we go! It looks as though he took these lying on his back.'

'So the first went through the forehead, and these were added afterwards?' asked Kramer.

'From the angle they went in at, yes, I'd say that was a reasonable assumption.'

'Don't know why anyone would have bothered,' mumbled Van Rensburg. 'The bloke already didn't have any brain left.'

'That isn't a handicap to some people,' snapped Strydom, who detested the mortuary sergeant. 'And it's just as well the killer *did* bother, you clown, because there's no slug for us to recover from the head wound – it went right through.'

'You mean we might have something for Ballistics?' said Kramer, perking up. 'No exit wounds in the back?'

'Look for yourself, Tromp – come on, Van Rensburg, get your finger out!'

While the body was being turned over, Prinsloo cleared his throat in the key of a man hoping to make amends. 'Lieutenant, sir,' he said respectfully, 'can I make a suggestion? There's this talk that you think this business and the Bradshaw case could be connected. Now if that is so, and the killer made a mess of it with Bradshaw because he used only one shot, then maybe he has pumped in these extra ones this time just to make sure.'

'Ja, that's possible.'

Strydom ran his hand lightly over Hookham's back. 'Do you know, I think we're in luck!' he chuckled. 'Put on that rubber glove and feel here, Tromp. Sort of a lump, like a cyst.'

Kramer found it easily. 'That's one of the slugs?'

'Pretty sure it is,' said Strydom. 'As you know, after bone, skin offers the biggest resistance to a bullet – in fact, only about half those who try to shoot themselves in the heart are successful. The bullet just hits the sternum, and skids off round the rib cage under the skin.'

'Scalpel? prompted Van Rensburg, officiously, and held one out to him.

Strydom disregarded it and chose another that was identical. 'How many times have I got to tell you this isn't a bloody operating theatre, Sergeant? If I'd wanted that life – instead of peace and quiet – then I'd have made sure my chief nurse was many times prettier than you!'

Van Rensburg, whose crewcut and everything else about him seemed calculated to underline his strident masculinity, went very red, then purple, and finally a sort of muddy brown. He muttered something about having an idle kaffir to kick, and withdrew.

'Er-hum,' said Prinsloo, clearing his throat again. 'Do you want me to take a snap of this as well, Doc?'

'No, but you can get out of my light if you like.'

'Sorry, Doc! Hell, that was interesting about skin, hey?'

Kramer groaned inwardly. Here they came : Strydom's endless supply of pertinent anecdotes based on the case histories he so avidly consumed – while all that mattered right then was the size of the bullet used on Hookham. The difference between an entrance wound made by a .32 and one made by a .38 was, of course, impossible to judge with the naked eye, especially as calibre ratings were such nonsense anyway. A .38 Special was, in fact, a .35, which was how he came to have Specials in the .357 Ruger magnum under his left arm.

'Let me tell you,' said Strydom, pausing with the scalpel poised in his hand, 'about a case reported by a Dr LeMoyne Snyder in America. This bloke was sent along to him with this swollen scrotum – know what that is?' Prinsloo nodded and pointed to one in a glass jar on a nearby shelf. 'Ja, but just a normal one in other respects, not piebald. Anyway, Snyder feels this hard lump inside, and so he gives him a shot of Novocain and makes a little slit the same as this . . .' The incision opened in Hookham's back like a bloodshot eye with a lead-grey cornea. 'And what popped out? A thirty-eight slug! Hold on a sec, Tromp, let me finish, hey? Well, finally the bloke explained what had happened. It seems that ten days previously he'd tried to shoot himself by putting his gun to his breastbone and pulling the trigger.'

'Yirra!' said Prinsloo.

'And the next thing he knew, he was coming round on the floor of his place. All he had was this small puncture mark, a bit of pain, and that was it. At first he looked all over for the bullet, thinking it had sort of ricocheted, then he gave up and just decided that the Almighty had stepped in and stopped his suicide plan – which was probably true enough. He didn't personally connect the swelling in his scrotum at all, you see, and that didn't start up for nearly a week. What had transpired, however, was that the bullet had been deflected downwards between the skin

42

and bone, it had missed going into the peritoneum – the bag around your guts – and it had stopped in his left testicle.'

'He – he was all right after?' Prinsloo asked.

'Perfect!'

'Now there's a thing! And could the bullet have finished up in his left foot just as easily, Doc?'

Strydom blinked. 'Why?' he said, bewildered.

'Well, because it's a fantastic true-life story to tell my class at Sunday School, only I –'

Prinsloo caught Kramer's glare in the nick of time and shut up. Strydom hastily bent over the body again, stretched the skin around the incision and gave a pleased grunt, nipping up a spent bullet between thumb and forefinger. He dropped it into Kramer's waiting hand.

'A thirty-two, I think, Tromp? Popped out as neat as a pea from a pod!'

'A *soft-nosed* thirty-two,' murmured Kramer, feeling another dull thud in the pit of his stomach, 'just like the one they dug out of Archie Bradshaw . . .' He tossed the slug and the original bullet from his top pocket at Prinsloo. 'Get those to your kids out there and tell them they're to be delivered to Ballistics, pronto! I want a full report by lunch-time.' Then he turned back to Strydom. 'Nice going, Doc – now let's see what else you can find for me.'

Zondi drove into the posh suburb of Morninghill in the Lieutenant's Chevrolet which he had slyly removed from the mortuary yard some fifteen minutes earlier, synchronising his departure with that of a clapped-out undertaker's van leaving with a body He parked the car around the corner from the Digby-Smith residence and proceeded on foot.

The Digby-Smiths lived in a wide, colourful avenue lined by flame trees in full blossom and small, bright notices which warned that burglar alarm systems had been installed in the respective properties. Like all the other houses in the avenue, theirs was set well back in park-like grounds, with lawns, terraces, formal flower-beds, neat hedges and a tennis court. Instead of a swimming pool, however, they had a lily pond surrounded by a rockery, and presided over by curious white piccanins in cement, each pot-bellied and bare-bottomed, holding up heavy dishes filled with soil and flowers. These figures were possibly some sort of fertility

43

fetish meant to encourage growth around them, but as their private parts were extremely vague, he couldn't be too sure of this. There was only one way of reaching the house from the street, and that was up a long, crooked drive that was being resurfaced, so he kept to the verge, exchanged greetings with the workmen, and came presently to a walled yard leading off the garage area.

'Is your madam out?' he asked, when a skinny cook opened the kitchen door to his knock.

'Who asks?' she replied haughtily.

'CID.'

'Hau!'

And from there on the rest was easy. The cook invited him into the kitchen, switched the kettle on for a pot of tea, and listened with rapt attention to the description he gave of a known rapist recently seen in the vicinity. She soon had herself half-convinced that she'd actually seen a glimpse of him near the shops, and promised she would pass the word on among the other women servants thereabouts. By the time the tea had been poured, the conversation had turned to this and that.

'No, the work isn't too hard here,' the cook admitted. 'There is just the master and the madam.'

'And the madam's brother,' added the housemaid, a buxom wench who had just joined them. 'Such a small man!' And she giggled. 'Small with grey hair that will not lie straight, and these brown knobs that grow on his head!'

'Shhhh!' cautioned the cook.

'It's all right, he's still asleep,' said the housemaid.

'Asleep?' Zondi feigned surprise.

'He was very late coming home last night,' explained the housemaid, 'and the madam said we were not to disturb him. Look, there is his breakfast tray still waiting for him to ring his bell.'

The cook tut-tutted. 'He has not rung his bell all morning.'

'I believe you,' said Zondi.

He stirred his tea and looked at the cook, wondering if her skinniness indicated she was bad at her job or whether she had worms.

'These white people,' sighed the housemaid. 'It is a good life they live, is it not? Just because you are out enjoying yourself until one in the morning, you are then allowed to sleep all the next day.'

44

'How do you know it was one o'clock?' asked Zondi, winking at her. 'What was keeping you up so late?'

She giggled, and so did the cook.

'You saw him come home?' Zondi persisted. 'How could you see anything in that position?'

'She goes into the garden with the – ' began the cook, then muffled her own words with a clasp of her hand.

'I had got up from my bed to go to the lavatory,' said the housemaid with ill-kept dignity. 'I heard a car coming and I looked down to the street.' Then she giggled again. 'No, I am only joking with you,' she confessed. 'There was a car that stopped outside here at one, but the man who got out from it was big.'

CHAPTER FIVE

The Last Great Journey into the Unknown had properly begun now for Edward 'Bonzo' Hookham. He lay unzipped from pubic arch to jaw bone, and looked as though he was passing through Customs. Zealous rummaging had left his colourful contents in gay disorder; his heart, lungs, liver and gullet had been seized and sliced open on the sink's draining board, his kidneys rested in a kidney bowl on the third table along, and his intestines awaited further inspection in an enamel bucket.

'So far, so good,' commented Strydom, drawing his knife point over the head from ear to ear, and then tugging free the flaps of scalp down either side. 'Your bone saw, if you please, Sergeant.'

'Oh, so I have my uses after all?' muttered Van Rensburg.

'Don't sulk,' said Strydom, turning aside to Kramer. 'Well, Tromp, have you made anything of that interesting piece of cord?'

Kramer was toying with the length of cord taken from the dead man's wrists. 'The only thing unusual about it is that both ends have been recently severed. You say it wasn't much of a knot under all that muck?'

'That's right. Once over and once under – half a granny knot, you might say. But what about that slightly frayed section in the middle?'

'Ach, it looks like the cord was once looped round – or slung over – something that caused friction.'

'A pulley, perhaps?'

'Ja, I'd thought of that myself. It can't be a sash-cord from a window though, because it's a little too thick really. We'll have to see what Forensic can come up with.'

Strydom nodded. 'Of course, but what's got me going is how strong a man would have to be to cause fractures like that. Could *you* pull so hard?'

'Not a chance.'

'Er-hum,' ventured Prinsloo.

'Go on, Fanie,' sighed Kramer. 'Let's hear it.'

'What if it wasn't so much a case of strength as the bloke having a lot of weight behind him, Lieutenant? If I can make a suggestion, why not get Van here to –'

'Watch it!' snarled Van Rensburg, who was struggling to make both ends of his saw-cut meet.

The telephone rang in the outer office, and Prinsloo slipped away to answer it. Kramer went on examining the length of cord. It seemed logical that one end of it should be cut, because God alone knew how long the thing had been in the first place, but why the other end as well?

'That was Ballistics,' Prinsloo reported back. 'The youngster I sent with the bullet has just arrived.'

'And?' said Kramer, suspicious of a message so inane.

'Well, there could be a bit of a hold-up, Lieutenant.'

'*Hey?*'

'Until they've found their comparison microscope or something. They had a promotion party in the lab for Mitchell last night, and some practical joker –'

'Jesus!' Kramer cut in. 'What sort of delay? If they think I'm going to –'

'They promise some sort of result by tonight, sir, so if you . . .'

But Kramer was already striding across the duckboards, stuffing the length of cord into his jacket pocket as he went. Thanks to the formalin fumes in the mortuary, his sore throat had returned with a vengeance; the feuding between Strydom and Van Rensburg was beginning to make his nerves scream; and now, just as some progress seemed to have been made, this had to happen. He almost tripped straight over a body being removed by a tearful black family.

Nxumalo hastened to his side. 'Boss? Can the boss please ask Sergeant Van to come and give these people the papers for them to put their mark on?'

'In a minute, man! Can't you see I'm busy?'

Kramer went into the office off the refrigerator room and dialled Ballistics. While he waited for them to answer, he explored the cluttered drawers of Van Rensburg's desk, found his half-jack of Cape brandy, and took a nip of it for his throat. Then,

47

having waited a full three minutes – it wasn't his morning for telephone calls – he lost patience, slammed down the receiver and almost tripped over the same family again. They had the body in a long electric appliance carton that they'd salvaged from somewhere.

'Boss?' begged Nxumalo.

'Ja, ja, I won't forget.'

Van Rensburg, who had just completed his chore, was picking pink sawdust from the teeth of his saw. Prinsloo was focusing his camera, and Strydom was easing off the vault of the skull, which came away with a sloppy pop.

'Beautiful!' cried the district surgeon, delving about. 'A classic of its kind! Look how the bullet passed through here like a rock through a trifle, toppling as it went so it hit the occiput sideways on, smashing a big hole in the back. And this fracture's quite a size, too, hey?' He drew up the flap of scalp and looked into the hair. 'Good God . . .'

'What?' asked Kramer.

But Strydom remained silent until he had quickly shaved the area with a scalpel, revealing three round bruises in a row, followed by a fourth, much fainter contusion.

'I can't believe it,' he mumbled. 'The skull is normal thickness, the bone isn't soft . . .'

'Could he have fallen backwards on an exposed tree root?' suggested Prinsloo.

'Part of the car's bumper maybe?' suggested Van Rensburg.

'Or on some stones?' suggested Strydom.

Kramer said nothing. He could see the awe in their faces, and knew what none of them was willing to admit to himself. Those bruises on the scalp looked exactly like the knuckle marks left by a single blow with the fist. A fist so powerful it had shattered the skull beneath it. The fist of a Goliath.

'You know, I think we'd better make an experiment,' Strydom remarked quietly, moving over to take another look at the fractures above the dead man's wrists. 'The difficulty is, just how do we . . .' And he fell into a brown study.

'By the way,' Kramer said to Van Rensburg, 'Nxumalo wants you to get rid of a body for him.'

'And while you're out there,' added Strydom, 'see if you can't find a piece of cord like the one that was tied round here. Okay?'

48

Van Rensburg left with a grunt, and Prinsloo made some close-ups of the bruise marks. Strydom wandered round the room.

'Ah, this should do it,' he said, taking the spring-balance from its peg above the sink and discarding the metal dish for weighing organs. 'If we tie one end of the cord to this hook, and watch where the needle gets to along this scale, then we'll get a reading of the required pull in kilos!'

'Very clever, Doc,' said Kramer. 'Only what is that going to prove?'

'Hmmmm? The *real problem* is, of course, finding something to conduct this experiment *on*. It's a pity both arms have been fractured, or we'd be able to . . .'

'Have you any wog paupers in the fridge?' asked Prinsloo, eager to build on his reputation as an ideas man.

'No such luck, I'm afraid. Still, as Ma always used to say, where there's a will there's a way!'

Kramer had suddenly had enough. Whatever the reading in kilos, it wasn't the sort of data kept on file at the CID – or anywhere else for that matter – so this fooling around wasn't going to contribute a damned thing to the investigation. On top of which, he was sure he'd just heard his car drawing up outside the frosted windows, and that was a phenomenon that required an immediate explanation.

'Hey, hang on a sec, Tromp!' Strydom called out. 'I've just had this inspiration, and it won't take Van two minutes to – '

But Kramer had gone.

There was a decided air of the morning-after in Ballistics when Mitchell, who never suffered hangovers himself, popped in for a quick word shortly before noon. Like in the other offices he had visited on his round of thanks, everyone there looked ready to leap out of their seats at the slightest sound, even that of a pencil dropping, as though it were a pistol shot. In fact, when directly compared, this lot seemed twice as twitchy, tense and sickly pale. A pistol shot rang out from the test-firing bench in the corner.

'Life,' grumbled Johan Botha, shuddering, 'can be very unfair.' Then he bent once again over the comparison microscope. 'What can we do you for, Mitch?'

'I just came to say thanks for a great party!'

49

'Oh ja? I don't suppose you know who took this thing and hid it in the darkroom, hey?'

'As a matter of fact, I –'

'What?' said Botha, looking up and narrowing his eyes.

'No, no, I don't mean it was me, man! I was just going to ask if you'd spoken to Japie from Traffic Enquiries about it.'

'You saw him take it from here?'

'Not exactly, but I did see him go into the darkroom with that new typist from CID, and she's so flat-chested I reckon a bloke might need a comparison 'scope to –'

'*Out*,' said Botha.

'Ja, get out,' agreed the others, for once unappreciative of Mitchell's razor-sharp wit. 'Get out and stay out.'

Mitchell shrugged and turned his attention to the two .32 slugs that Botha had lined up side by side under the twin lenses of his instrument. 'What are these?' he asked. 'Don't tell me Wonder Dog Kramer has come up with a match in the Bradshaw case?'

'Cast your own expert eye, if you like,' Botha invited him. 'Not that anyone would need a second opinion.'

'Really?' said Mitchell, impressed.

Kramer slid down low in the front passenger seat of the Chevrolet and hooked his heels comfortably under the dashboard. With Zondi at the wheel, and in a somewhat exuberant state, it was often more restful not having a clear view of the road ahead. They were doing at least sixty along the crowded freeway back into the centre of town.

'Ja, it's all coming together,' he said, his mood much improved by the contribution that Zondi had made. 'Don't ask me *what* is coming together, but the two cases do seem definitely connected. If Ballistics can give us a positive on that slug we removed, then we'll know for certain.'

Zondi intimidated a five-ton lorry and made a gain of fifty yards. 'And if this man is truly big, boss, that will make our job much easier.'

'Right. None of that Oh-he-was-sort-of-average rubbish! How many times have you and me gone looking for Mr Average?'

'Move it!' Zondi growled at a Mini dithering in front of him, then swept by on the wrong side. 'Sorry, boss?'

Kramer had already gone back to reviewing the known facts so far. 'So you say all the vehicles at the Digby-Smiths' were being parked in the street?'

'Yebo, the men have been working on the drive for a week, they tell me, so the cars must be left outside.'

'How many do they have?'

'Three, boss. There is the Rover, Boss Digby-Smith drives a big Ford to work, and then they have this old one they use when the others are in the garage for servicing. It's a Morris.'

'I see, so it wasn't at all strange that the car should be left outside in the street last night. But what about the ignition key?'

Zondi snapped his fingers in irritation at himself. 'That I forgot to tell you! The cook said her madam was complaining at breakfast this morning because the keys had not been put back on the silver tray in the hall. But her husband told her not to be so stupid, and to use the spare key instead.'

'Uh-huh. Did you speak to any of the other servants?'

'The chief garden boy. He lives at Peacevale, so he didn't know anything of what happened in the night. All he noticed when he came to work was that the dogs from all around were sniffing at the back of the car and peeing on it.'

'Didn't that seem unusual to him?'

'It made him laugh,' said Zondi, grinning. 'He said he had felt that way about his employer many times himself.'

Kramer chuckled. 'But did you think to ask him if he'd seen anyone snooping round the property? The killer must have known about the cars being left outside.'

'Why "must"?' asked Zondi.

'Because – ach, we'll try and sort that out later. Tell me more first about what the housemaid says she saw at one o'clock.'

Zondi throttled back as they approached the first set of traffic lights. 'She saw this car come with only its small lights on. She saw it stop outside the hedge, and a big man get out – the street light over the other side was shining behind him. There were a lot of leaves in the way – I looked from the same place and that is true – so she thought maybe it was a different boss in a different car.'

'At that time of night? Wasn't she suspicious?'

'Boss, boss, boss,' said Zondi, with a doleful wag of his head, 'will you never learn that a black child is only seven years old when he stops wondering at the ways of white persons? They do so many strange things, believe so many strange things, that life is just too short.' Then he caught the green and surged across the intersection towards Boomplaas Street.

'But I *know* I've got one somewhere,' the district surgeon was saying to Van Rensburg, as they came out of the post-mortem room. 'And I'm not taking any excuses – just you find it!'

Nxumalo ran his duster over a mahogany coffin that rested on a pair of trestles near the fridge doors. Generally speaking, the only coffins ever seen in the mortuary were the splintery pine boxes which blacks provided for their relatives, while all white remains were removed by undertaking firms to be coffined on their own premises. From time to time, however, when the white remains in question were in a disgusting state and unfit to be later viewed by the family, it was judged more expedient to have them transferred straight into the chosen coffin and screwed down. This had been the fate of Mr Horace Austin, who'd been reduced – in Van Rensburg's phrase – to 'toast and gravy' by a blazing car, and then placed in the coffin now awaiting removal by Abbott & Son.

'Er, Nxumalo,' said Van Rensburg, crossing over to him, 'there's something I want to ask you.' He glanced at a list on his clipboard. 'Where's the body of Philemon Bapuna?'

'Gone, Sergeant.'

'Ja, I thought so. And Daisy Majola?'

'Gone, Sergeant.'

'Let me see . . . This one is Mr Austin – oh ja, what about Roger Dhlamini? Have we still got him round the back?'

'Gone, Sergeant!'

Van Rensburg's face fell. 'Now are you quite – ?'

'Ach, come on, Van Rensburg!' barked Strydom, who had been at his elbow all the time. 'What has this to do with finding that arm for me?'

'Er, I was only getting some routine matters out of the way first, Doc!' Van Rensburg looked appealingly into Nxumalo's eyes. 'Don't tell me you have actually done what I said you must do this morning?'

'Oh, yes indeed, Sergeant!' replied Nxumalo, showing pride in his obedience. 'I took my finger right out!'

Van Rensburg smiled at him wanly, and then turned to Strydom, whose foot was tapping impatiently. 'I'm sorry, Doc, but I don't think that arm is in the mortuary any longer,' he said. 'I can't remember why I believed this to be a fact, but perhaps you could try your experiment on –'

'Sergeant Van Rensburg, *come with me*,' hissed Strydom, and led the way back into the post-mortem room.

Alone once more, Nxumalo chortled and went on using his duster, pausing now and again to look with amusement towards the foot of the coffin lid.

Kramer had quite forgotten about Meerkat Marais, who was posed on the edge of the filing cabinet like The Thinker, with one fist pressed against his forehead.

'Well, well, my old friend,' he said, as he entered his office with Zondi in tow, 'now you have had a chance to reflect on your sinful past, could it be you're ready to change your tune?'

'For pity's sake . . .' whispered Meerkat.

'Good, now I'll tell you what I want you to do. I've changed my mind about that statement we were going to write, and instead I want you to find out for me how many other thirty-twos have been on the market recently – okay?'

'Anything!' replied Meerkat, in the same strained whisper. 'But can your Bantu go out for a minute while I talk to you?'

'Fine, and I also want you to look round for a very big bloke such as Archie Bradshaw described in the paper.'

'Look, Lieutenant, can I have a word in private? *Please*, man, this is an emergency!'

'I haven't time now,' said Kramer, unlocking the handcuffs. 'There, you can jump down and get on your way.'

'I can't.'

Kramer turned to Zondi. 'Dial Ballistics for me, Mickey.' Then he turned back to Meerkat with a menacing expression. 'Do as I say! Jump down and bugger off! I'll contact you later.'

'I can't,' whispered Meerkat. 'I can't *move*.'

'Hey?'

'I dare not, Lieutenant!'

53

'I'm getting a bit edgy, Meerkat – you know that? What the hell's the matter with you?'

'It's my b-l-a-d-d-e-r,' Meerkat spelled out confidentially, with an anxious glance in Zondi's direction.

'Your what?' Kramer began to grin.

'Shhh! Don't say anything!' implored Meerkat, as though the dignity of his entire race was at stake. 'Just tell your –'

'My God, Meerkat, you're really sitting on a time bomb, hey? Just think what it would do to all those files underneath!'

'I realise that! Why do – ?'

'Criminal damage, Meerkat! Wanton destruction of Government property!'

'It isn't a joke! For four hours I've been –'

'Ballistics, boss,' interrupted a poker-faced Zondi, passing over the receiver.

'Hullo, Botha? Anything for me yet?'

The lab man tried unsuccessfully to keep the excitement out of his voice. 'Congratulations, sir – you've had twins.'

'Come again?'

'The two bullets are identical – or, to put it another way, I think we can be one hundred per cent sure they were both fired from the same revolver.'

Even though he had been hoping for this result, Kramer needed a moment before it sunk in. 'That's the best news I've had all week, man. Next time we're in the canteen together, the double brandies are on me.'

'There's a bit more, sir.'

'Shoot.'

'I've just had a telex back from our top expert in Pretoria. I sent him the details of the first slug last Saturday, and he reports that this kind of soft-nosed thirty-two went out of production in the fifties. He also confirms that the five right-hand grooves suggest that the weapon is a Smith & Wesson. I've sent a copy of his report to the Firearms Squad, and we're putting out a new circular.'

'Beautiful,' said Kramer. 'And that's the lot?'

'Ja, until you find the firearm and want it matched up as well,' joked Botha, and rang off.

Kramer winked his off-side eye at Zondi. 'We've got a perfect match on the bullets, so the show's on the road! But first I'd

54

better go down and tell the boss what the position is.' He started
for the door.

'Not again!' whimpered Meerkat. 'You can't go off and – '

'Sergeant,' said Kramer, without breaking his stride, 'do you
think you could find this gentleman a m-i-l-k b-o-t-t-l-e?'

'Yessir!' said Zondi.

CHAPTER SIX

Colonel Hans Muller, divisional commandant of the CID, leaned his elbows on his enormous desk and made a tent of his fingers. For a while he stared at the darker patch of cream wall where an official portrait of Balthazar John Vorster had hung for many years, and then he explored the ceiling for some sign of his small friend, a lizard that seemed also to have passed into retirement. Gradually, his craggy face assumed a degree of composure, and he collapsed the tent to place his hands a business-like foot apart on his blotter.

'What it all boils down to,' he said, 'is that we've got a madman on the loose.'

'A killer on the loose, ja,' agreed Kramer.

'You must admit he was crazy to return the body like that to the Digby-Smiths'.'

'Not necessarily, Colonel; there could have been method in his madness.'

'Such as?'

'I don't know, but I'd prefer to keep my options open on his mental state. Bringing the body back does achieve one thing, so far as he's concerned : we haven't the slightest idea where Hookham was murdered.'

'True.' Colonel Muller flipped open the docket on his desk. 'While you were out this morning, I had another look at the statement you took from Bradshaw. The description it gives of his assailant is very woolly, Lieutenant, very subjective. All it says here is, "There was this massive bloke, built like a brick shit-house." Am I right in thinking you weren't taking him too seriously at the time? I usually expect my officers to do better than that. I'm also grateful when the wording of a description can be used on a "wanted" bulletin without causing grave offence to the general public.'

Kramer shrugged. 'Okay, so I didn't go into it too deeply, sir, but as we both agreed – '

'You didn't go into it at all, Tromp! Let's be honest about this. What we want is a little more precision. What we want is the best possible description of this suspect! Remember, he's out there somewhere at this very minute, and – who knows? – he could be lining up his next victim!'

'That would depend – ' began Kramer.

'Please, Tromp, no half-baked theories at this stage. If you find a pattern that links Bradshaw and Hookham together, well and good, but until such time, we must view this killer as some sort of maniac working at random. In my opinion, every living soul in Trekkersburg is at risk.'

'You could equally say – '

'And our only means of diminishing that risk is to provide ourselves with a clear picture of the enemy. *That* is your priority.'

Kramer gave up trying to finish a sentence, and reached over for the telephone. 'You want me to see Bradshaw again, sir?'

'Who else? The housemaid's the only other eye-witness so far, but she was too far away.'

'Right, then I'll try and get him before he goes back to the river.'

'What river?' Colonel Muller raised a quizzical brow.

Kramer paused in his dialling only long enough to tap the topmost newspaper cutting in the docket, which Colonel Muller then read while they waited for a reply.

'After discharging himself from hospital yesterday,' wrote the *Gazette*'s Crime Reporter, 'Mr Bradshaw said that he might take himself away for a few days to his fishing cottage. "It's all been a bit of a shock to the system," he told me, "but it's nothing that a day or two with a trout rod can't cure! I just hope my arm will be up to it." It is believed that his son, Mr Darren Bradshaw, will continue to run the family business until his father is properly recovered again. Mr Bradshaw Jnr is a student at the Kritzinger Business Studies College in Johannesburg, and an Old Boy of Trekkersburg High.'

True to form, the telephone in the fishing cottage rang and rang. 'I must have missed him,' said Kramer, 'or perhaps he's taken some sandwiches out with him.'

'Hey? No answer? I'm not sure I like that, Tromp!'

'Ach, I don't think it's anything to worry about, Colonel. If you knew the – '

'But I mean, what the hell's the *Gazette* publishing this sort of thing for? This is what I'm always saying about newspapers! Honestly, they are our number one cause of crime in this country! If our friend was determined to get him, then all he had to do was – '

'It doesn't give the whereabouts of the fishing cottage, Colonel,' Kramer pointed out.

'Would that be so difficult to discover? Don't be damned silly, man! God, if I'd only seen this before, I'd have – '

Kramer killed the call and dialled another number.

'Who are you ringing now?' asked Colonel Muller.

'Bradshaw's house. It's possible that he's come home already.' An engaged tone.

'Why haven't you been keeping a proper check on his movements, Lieutenant?'

'Didn't see the need, Colonel. In fact, not until – '

'But this is ridiculous, man! No answer?'

'They're still talking.'

'Are they?' Colonel Muller snatched up the other telephone. 'What's the number of the Bradshaw house?'

Kramer told him, and listened to the brief exchange that followed with the chief switchboard operator at the General Post Office.

'Lieutenant,' said Colonel Muller, a minute or so later, 'I've got some news for you: *nobody* is talking on that line. Either the receiver's off the hook, or . . .' And he bunched his fists dramatically.

'I'm sure it's nothing to worry about,' Kramer replied, getting up off his corner of the desk, 'but if you like, I'll go down and take a look.'

Zondi nosed the Chevrolet into another small backwater down in the oldest quarter of the city, and Kramer pointed to a street-sign half-engulfed by an unruly hedge. 'Kitchener Row,' he said, relieved they had found it at long last. 'Now what we want is Number Forty-two. It's amazing he'd want to live in a dump like these – he's certainly got the money to be somewhere much posher.' All his previous dealings with Bradshaw had taken place at either the shop in Ballard's Arcade or in the hospital.

'Forty-two will be on that side,' said Zondi.

Kramer scanned the line of dreary orange-brick dwellings that stood so close together that some were almost touching. He had always had a strong antipathy for turn-of-the-century, jerry-built architecture, with its pointed cornices, pretentious Doric columns along the verandahs and steeply pitched tin roofs, and regarded them as the stuff of which bad dreams were made. He'd once had a witchlike aunt who'd lived in one, steeped in her memories and general incontinence, and given to pinching the pink cheeks of any young guest before offering them a biscuit.

The car stopped.

'This shouldn't take long, Mickey,' said Kramer, patting his pockets to make sure he had his notebook, and discovering he was still carrying the length of cord about. 'Here, play with this while I'm inside, and see if you can make out what it's from. Doc Strydom thinks this frayed section half-way along is significant.'

'Why are the ends cut off, boss?'

'To make it shorter, of course! Hell, sometimes I think it must be true what they say about you kaffirs . . .'

Zondi laughed and settled back behind the wheel with the cord. 'Some kind of pulley?' he murmured, becoming immediately engrossed.

No. 42 Kitchener Row was a very small, unremarkable house that nobody would look at twice unless he was trying to find its front door. Kramer found it behind a faded canvas roller blind and knocked twice. When this failed to bring a response, he tried to find a doorbell, couldn't see one anywhere, and knocked again. There wasn't a sound from inside.

He left the verandah and took a narrow footpath running between the left-hand side of the house and a high brick wall that cut off the neighbours. At the far end of the path was a wooden gate with a latch in it. He slipped the latch and stepped into a garden that took him quite by surprise; it wasn't only far bigger than he'd imagined, but landscaped and filled with every tropic-bright bloom he had ever seen. Clearly such a garden could not have been put together in a decade or two, but must have been created by the original owners of the drab little house – all except for the swimming pool beyond the mulberry trees. As he advanced towards the pool, having caught a glimpse of movement there, the high wall all around enveloped him in a sense of total privacy that he coveted.

He coveted even more the stunning if diminutive female form in a bikini who stood with her back towards him at the near end of the pool, adjusting her yellow bathing cap. The legs were long and slender, the buttocks were firmly rounded, the waist was small, the shoulders wide, and from what he could see of the left breast, its perky promise was worth fighting and dying for. It was all he could do to keep walking, and not to throw himself forward, taking her – in every sense of the word – completely by surprise. What a wild, truly magnificent encounter that would be, there among the birds and the bees and the flowers, two strangers locked in lusty celebration of Nature's Way, panting and . . .

'Miss?'

She turned and said, 'Why, hello, Lieutenant Kramer! How nice to see you again!'

This second surprise stopped him in his tracks. He recognised the plain, weak-eyed, rather blotchy face under the yellow bathing cap instantly, but simply couldn't reconcile the rest of Mrs Archie Bradshaw with the dowdy, dull little figure he had last seen beside her husband's hospital bed.

'Very nice!' echoed Archie Bradshaw. 'You're always welcome, Lieutenant! Can I offer you something cold to drink?'

Kramer twisted round. Bradshaw was seated with his arm in a sling under one of the mulberry trees. Leisure clothes did little to make him appear less overbearing; although of average height, there was a bulk and a belligerence about the man that filled the eye. His jaw was heavy, his forehead sloped back sharply, and beneath his door-knob of a nose was a grey moustache of short bristles as abrasive as his manner. But it was with fresh insight that Kramer now regarded the antique dealer, seeing him not only in matters of business – but of the heart and home too – as a singularly successful snapper-up of unconsidered trifles.

'Er, I had a couple of lagers not long ago, thanks,' he said. 'It's just that we rang you a few – '

'Have you met Darren?' asked Mrs Bradshaw, proudly.

Kramer nodded to the head that had just surfaced in the pool and was treading water with its foreshortened body. 'Hullo, Darren – how goes it?'

'This is the detective in charge of your father's case,' explained Mrs Bradshaw.

Bradshaw Junior, a belligerent-looking young man of about twenty with weak eyes, said, 'Really?' And swam away under water.

'Well, um, wouldn't you two like to go up to the house?' suggested Mrs Bradshaw, in the awkward way of an embarrassed parent. 'I'm sure you'd both be more comfortable there!'

Kramer noticed the antique dealer wincing at every other step as they crossed the patch of lawn leading to the back verandah. 'Still giving you trouble, hey, Mr Bradshaw?'

'Damn right it is! Partly my own fault though, thinking I could go after trout in this condition. Hooked a three-pounder, had to use the net, and bloody nearly passed out – rush of black blood to the head, y'know what I mean. Really started playing up yesterday and finally last night I got the hell in, sent for young Darren to come up and collect me.' He stopped and turned. 'Darren? Don't forget we open at two sharp – right on the dot!'

'Haven't forgotten,' came back a bored drawl from the pool.

The back door led into an enclosed verandah off which was the kitchen and a room Bradshaw described as his study. There was nothing whatsoever to study in it, unless one counted the piles of invoices and auctioneers' catalogues scattered about, and there were no antiques either, compounding the impression the dealer was just that, with no finer feelings for the aesthetic side of his trade. The telephone was off the hook.

'Cranks,' said Bradshaw, noticing Kramer's glance. 'We've had the bastards pestering us for days – they even come to the front door, so we've had the bell taken away. Best of the bunch was this funny man who said he'd read about it in the paper, and he'd brought along his Scotch terrier called "Jock the Giantkiller"!'

'Uh-huh, you always get them. So you got back last night?'

'Early hours of this morning, to be exact. Darren came up about ten, ten-thirty, and we had a couple of beers and chewed the fat for a while. Sure about that drink?'

'Perfectly,' said Kramer.

'Then sit yourself somewhere,' invited Bradshaw, lowering himself gingerly into a leather armchair. 'Has something come up?'

61

'Ja, you could say that. It's just the body of a man was found shot in town this morning.'

'Shot dead, you mean?'

'Stone dead. Three shots, a skull fracture, and his wrists had been tied together with such force they'd been broken. He'd been shot by the same gun as you were.'

The heavy jaw went slack for an instant, and the antique dealer swallowed hard. 'The same gun? Where? Did you get him?'

'We haven't a clue where. The body was left in the boot of a car.'

'But – but it was the same gun? You're sure about that?'

'Uh-huh.'

'And the wrists were *broken*?'

Kramer nodded. 'That's right. Like you say, this must be one hell of a big bastard we're looking for. The victim was a visitor from overseas staying with –'

Bradshaw started to laugh, checked himself but couldn't get the ugly grin off his face.

'Sir?'

'Ach, I know it's rough this poor bugger's copped it, Lieutenant, don't get me wrong! But you don't know how relieved I –'

'*Relieved?* In what way?'

'Well, how would you put it? To have this proof that I've not been going out of my bloody mind after all! Christ, how long has it been? Six days? For six bloody days I've had this mental picture of the bastard, towering up above me against the sodding skyline, and I've known bloody well that nobody's believed me, including yourself. And now you –'

'Correction, I've never been so far as –'

'Don't give me any bull, Lieutenant! It was there in your face at the hospital! I knew it'd be, right from the start. I said to myself: Archie, who the hell's going to believe you? Keep this "tall tale" to yourself, man! Why do you think I didn't tell the wife when I got home? Why didn't I tell the quack when he was called? Those clever-dick buggers at the hospital? And then, when I did come out with the truth, Jesus! I tell you, I've been regretting it ever since, what with you lot, the Press and all the cranks ringing up. But the worst part has been not believing myself any longer; the doubts. Did I really see a bloke that size?

Then what exactly did he look like? Did he say anything? What sort of clothes? What height? What weight? Can't you see for yourself what a bloody obsession it's become?'

Bradshaw gestured agitatedly towards his desk. Kramer went over and found a scatter of sketches in black crayon; each was very much like another, and depicted a hulking shape holding a revolver in both hands.

'You drew these, Mr Bradshaw?'

'The wife did – y'know, to my instructions. I can't use my hand properly yet, and, besides, I've never been any good at art.' He extended a limp forefinger from his sling. 'There, that one on top is the best of the bunch so far, but still isn't right.'

'Why's it all shaded in?'

'Because,' replied Bradshaw, with a sigh to indicate his patience was being sorely tried, 'because as I've said umpteen bloody times already, he was against the sun, silhouetted against the sun, and I had only about a split-second before I saw the flash of his gun going off.'

'He's got it in both hands, hey? You never said anything about that before.'

'What's that? Oh, that came out when we were getting the outline right, not that I see it's of any special –'

'But it is significant,' Kramer cut in. 'That style of taking aim is quite recent really, so we can guess that this man was either in a young age bracket or had been taking instruction. Would you hold a gun like that, for instance?'

Bradshaw shook his head, and blustered, 'Well, you know what they say about old dogs! It just hadn't occurred to me –'

'You said you'd been going over heights and weights, sir. Have you got anything there for me?'

'Er, I'd say not an inch under six-four. I'm five-ten and –'

'Weight?'

'You've got the picture there, so your guess is as good as mine.'

'Two-eighty pounds?'

'I'd have said two-seventy. Shall we split the difference? As to clothing, all I'm sure of is that he wasn't wearing a jacket. Probably a short-sleeved sports shirt, dark trousers, dark shoes. Just a *chance* his hair was brown, but that might have been the way the sun was catching it.'

Kramer watched Bradshaw clumsily load his pipe from an

63

ostrich-skin tobacco pouch, and noted how agitated he was just beneath the surface; obviously a hardcase of his type hated to be enfeebled in this fashion. Then Kramer took another look at the topmost sketch.

'This bloke's hair is very short,' he said to Bradshaw. 'And the ears, they're very flat.'

'The wife's theory is that he could have been wearing a nylon stocking over his head, which would certainly explain that.'

'Or he could have been a coon. As you say, we mustn't forget this was a silhouette you saw, and –'

'*No*,' said Bradshaw. 'He was *not* a coon.'

'How can you be so certain, sir? There's nothing in this outline that contradicts the – '

'I'm sure, damnit! Now tell me about this poor sod who got shot.'

Perhaps it was typical of Bradshaw, thought Kramer, to have delayed this question for so long – or until he'd had time to think about someone other than himself for a moment. 'Ach, the bloke who got shot was a visitor from overseas, like I said earlier, who was staying with the Digby-Smiths. Do you know them?'

'Only as occasional customers – their taste is putrid. But just a second, you can't mean . . .' Bradshaw took the pipe from his mouth. 'You can't mean Bonzo Hookham?'

The pit of Kramer's stomach cringed, but somehow he'd been expecting this and the thud never came. 'Edward Bonzo Hookham, DFC and bar,' he said, quoting Jonty.

'I don't believe it!'

'Why not, sir?'

'Why not? Well . . . God, *I* don't know why not! You can't have got it wrong? He isn't strictly a visitor from overseas, y'know, he was born and brought up in – '

'No mistake,' said Kramer. 'So you and Mr Hookham – '

Bradshaw rose and made his way painfully to the door. 'Myra!' he bawled across the lawn. 'Myra! Come here, woman. You won't believe what's happened now!' Then he turned to Kramer and said, 'He was at our flying club social last week, the guest of honour. Naturally, as we'd both been in the RAF, the pair of us spent – '

'In the same squadron?'

'Oh no, nothing like that. I was flying Spits, Hurricanes, while

64

Bonzo – as you might have guessed from his size – was in Bomber Command. Not much elbow space in a bloody Lancaster! So they used to snap up all the little blokes, and the – ' Mrs Bradshaw arrived, dripping, in the verandah doorway. 'Listen to this, Myra. The crazy bastard has shot someone else now – Bonzo Hookham!'

'Who, Archie?'

'For Christ's sake, that Bomber Command chappie we met at the flying club the other night. Short, drank brandy – '

'No!' she gasped. 'Not that nice man! But he was utterly charming, so why would anyone – '

'Let's get one thing straight first,' interrupted Kramer, taking out his notebook. 'Are you saying that, although you both served in the English air force, you'd never come across him before? Or have I maybe – ?'

'Never,' said Archie Bradshaw, 'more's the pity. But there were one helluva lot of us, y'know.'

CHAPTER SEVEN

Zondi was still fiddling with the cord when Kramer returned to the car about half an hour later. He had the thing looped over part of the steering wheel and was working it gently up and down, as though trying to trigger off some association.

'Progress, Mickey?'

'A little progress, boss. With much respect, I think the Lieutenant talks a lot of nonsense sometimes.'

'Oh ja?'

Zondi held the severed ends of the cord together. 'You say this rope was cut to make it shorter.'

'Uh-huh.'

'But this rope *isn't* short, boss! It's a very long rope just to tie a man's hands together.'

Kramer thought about that for a moment. 'How do you know he hadn't intended to connect the hands to the feet or something?'

'You mean with Boss Hookham standing up?'

'I mean – '

'And another thing,' Zondi went on. 'Is it not strange that the rope on either side of the worn section is almost precisely the same length?'

'Is it? Perhaps – '

'I tell you, Lieutenant, the answer is very simple, and somewhere a bell is ringing.'

'Ding-dong,' said Kramer, impatiently. 'Just concentrate on getting me back to the office, hey? And on the way I'll tell you what real progress sounds like!'

Zondi draped the cord around his neck like a tailor's tape measure and drove off. In under a mile, Kramer had covered the main points of what he'd just learned in Bradshaw's study.

'Well, Mickey, what do you think of that, hey?'

'Hmmm.'

'Why the "Hmmm"? There's a link there! The start of a pattern.'

'That both were in the RAF?'

'Uh-huh, all that.'

Zondi gave him a sideways glance. 'How many people were at this party, boss?'

'Bradshaw estimates around two hundred,' replied Kramer, putting on his sunglasses, 'if you count wives and girl friends. These socials aren't formal affairs, you understand. The flying club just advertises in shop windows and the small ads, and anybody who's interested turns up. Generally, it's the same crowd each time : Sunday pilots, kids from the parachute club, a sprinkling of ex-SAAF and RAF officers, plus –'

'So there were more men from the RAF?'

'He's given me the names of six, and is going to check with the club secretary in case there were more.'

'But surely,' said Zondi, throttling back with a slight frown, 'this isn't a very big link, boss? And what is a "guest of honour"?'

'Ach, that isn't to be taken too seriously – they hadn't planned it or anything. Hookham just turned up, and because he was from overseas, they tried to make something special out of the occasion. I suppose basically it meant he was taken round, introduced to everyone, and somebody made a stupid speech.'

The Chevrolet picked up speed again. 'So Boss Hookham and Boss Bradshaw are both ex-RAF and they were both at this party. From what you say, Boss Hookham's link with the other six men is just the same.'

'Ja, but none of them's been shot, hey? I tell you it's a start, Mickey! You can't expect all the pieces to fall in your lap.'

Zondi sucked his teeth. 'And what do they share in other matters? Boss Bradshaw was also born in this place?'

'Trekkersburg? No, he's from Jo'burg originally. His wife explained they'd come down after the war, looking for somewhere there wasn't too much competition. Being so English around here, it's a good place to pick up old bits of furniture and suchlike in house sales, and Bradshaw supplies other antique shops all over.'

'But his wife, could she give you more of a link?'

Kramer shrugged. 'She did her best when I explained about patterns, but no, not really. She said they'd started to talk about fishing and so she'd buggered off quite soon after, leaving the two of them at it. I'll tell you one thing, old son, she's wasted on that bastard.'

'In what way, Lieutenant?'

'The *only* way,' Kramer sighed, winking lecherously, and they both laughed. 'But what's really happened is that now I'm seeing this whole business in a different light. When it was just Bradshaw involved, and we hadn't any idea of the motive, there was always a slight chance of some criminal element behind the shooting. As you said yourself, Bradshaw could have been up to some tricks he wasn't going to tell us about. But you add Hookham to the mixture and all that gets ruled out.'

'You mean Meerkat Marais and –'

'Of course! It isn't their scene! How could a man like Hookham – respectable background, a virtual stranger to the city – be mixed up with them? Okay, I've still got to find out about him properly, but I can tell you now that –'

'What I am thinking about is the killer, boss, and the gun,' said Zondi, turning a crocodile of schoolgirls into kangaroos on a pedestrian crossing. 'Those bullets are very old.'

'And so?'

'Well, as the Lieutenant knows, most of the guns in the hands of people such as Meerkat are guns stolen from –'

'Ja, ja, ja,' agreed Kramer, 'I know what you're going to say: are guns stolen from the tops of wardrobes where they've been lying for years, collecting up the dust. Right?'

Zondi nodded.

'I've been going over that myself, and I'll admit – when we still suspected a possible criminal involvement – that Meerkat's type seemed the most likely source for such a weapon. But since hearing just how old those bullets were, the idea has begun to make real nonsense. Firstly, we have to imagine a killer who is willing to use old ammunition, risking the chance of misfires and so on, when fresh ammunition is always easy to get hold of. Secondly, we have to imagine Meerkat, for instance, selling a gun cheap because its ammunition doesn't look too good. Would he do that? Never! He'd put in some new cartridges himself. And thirdly, if you like, we have to imagine that criminal link-up with Hookham, which is just plain impossible.'

'I see your reasoning, boss –' began Zondi.

'Now what if this man has *no* criminal connections? He wants a gun : the only gun to which he has access is the one on top of the wardrobe in, say, his uncle's house, and he takes it. He doesn't know a lot about guns, and the first time he fires only one shot and thinks that'll do it. But no, Bradshaw lives to tell the tale, so next time he adds two more rounds just to make sure.'

Zondi pouted, silently conceding the sound logic behind all this. He braked and swung into the police vehicle yard.

'Happy now?' asked Kramer, as they came to a halt. 'Not that you bloody look it, hey?'

'My problem, boss,' said Zondi, 'is maybe that I did not speak with Boss Bradshaw myself, because I cannot see how you can be so sure there is a link between these two men – I mean a stronger link than you have told me about already – that gives us the start of a pattern.'

'It's a feeling in my bones, man !'

'Ah,' murmured Zondi who, as the officially more primitive of them, had curiously little faith in such things. 'Hmmmm,'

Niggled, Kramer made a quick estimate of the length of the mystery cord in relation to Zondi's own modest stature as they climbed from the car. 'You can't bluff me that wouldn't be long enough to tie your feet as well,' he grunted. 'Go on, try it.'

Zondi slipped the cord from his shoulders and dangled the loop just above the tarmac.

'You're bloody cheating, kaffir ! Extend both your arms down properly !'

With a grin, Zondi obeyed and the loop lay on the tarmac with plenty of slack to spare. 'You win, Lieutenant.'

'Always,' said Kramer, turning away to hide a smile. 'Now get that damned thing to Forensic right away – there's been enough buggering around with it.'

Kramer had gone several yards before he realised that Zondi was not following his usual pace behind in public. He looked round and saw him still standing beside the car, holding the ends of the cord, and staring at the worn section which rested on the rough surface of the yard.

'Zondi?'

'Hau, so simple . . . We had it upside down.'

'What's simple?' demanded Kramer.

'This, boss !'

And with a sweep of the cord over his head, Zondi came skipping across the gap between them.

Forensic were not to be outshone, however. Within a remarkably short time, they had not only confirmed that the length of cord was indeed a skipping rope, minus its telltale wooden handles, but they'd used the unusual weave of the fibres to identify the brand. It was a Master Skip, large size, with Xtra-Zip thanks to two sets of ball-bearings, and its price was so exorbitant that only flashy gymnasiums, the energetic rich or total idiots ever bought one.

'Ja, but we must try and be more exact than that,' said Colonel Muller, turning from Kramer to Galt from Forensic. 'I hope you asked them at this sports shop to go through their invoices?'

Galt blinked behind his finger-smeared spectacle lenses. 'Oh, I made a special point of it, Colonel,' he replied, and dropped his voice even further to add, 'they're Trekkersburg's sole stockists...'

He always spoke a little as though he were giving away dark secrets, and wrote everything in a very thin hand. Kramer ran an amused eye over the razor cut on his throat, the mud on his shoes, the dried bloodspots on his soiled shirt, and watched him pick another almost invisible thread from the cuff of his lab coat.

'And?' prompted Colonel Muller, tapping his pencil.

'And they'd only sold three of them in six months, sir, and were thinking of putting the rest on their next sale at half-price. One of the Master Skips went to the Aquarius Fitness Centre in Stanley Street, and the other two were cash sales. A young woman bought one of them for her boy friend.'

'No name? Her description then?'

'She had freckles – that's all they could agree on.'

'And the other rope?'

'A blank, but they'll do their best to remember, sir.'

Colonel Muller made a note on his blotter. 'And now, Galt, what can you tell us about the things in the car?'

'Including Hookham's personal effects,' added Kramer.

Galt stopped poking about in the ash-tray and took a minute scrap of paper from his pocket. 'This isn't a list of *results*,' he stressed, 'but just a rough breakdown of what we've got to work on. The deceased was carrying hardly anything: ten rand in notes, thirty cents in loose change, a pen, a pen-torch, his British passport, British driving licence, and what looks like a letter from a grandchild in England. We also have a quantity of soil samples for analysis, some pieces of vegetation, an intriguing variety of maggot, and – '

'Got the documents with you?' interrupted Kramer.

'Fingerprints still has them,' explained Galt, turning his scrap of paper over. 'Let me see . . . Ja, the passport is brand new, the driving licence has no endorsements, and the letter was from someone signing himself "Timmy", who talks about his seventh birthday. Nothing much for you there, I'm afraid.'

'Ah! But who was it addressed to?' asked Colonel Muller.

'To "Gramps", Colonel.'

'No, man! I mean was it still in its envelope?'

'Er, yes of course . . . It was addressed to Mr E. J. Hookham, care of 52 Armstrong Avenue, Morninghill, Trekkersburg, Natal.'

'I thought so!' called Colonel Muller, smugly. 'Now we have established how the killer knew where to return the car!'

Galt looked faintly surprised. 'Or he could have taken the address from the cover of the Rover's servicing booklet in the glove compartment,' he said. 'There was never anything very complicated about that. The real puzzle is why did he return the vehicle? Was it to gain those ten or twelve hours before anyone could realise there was something seriously wrong? Was that why he stuck a match in the boot lock, hoping to cause a further delay?'

'Giving himself time to cover his tracks, hey?' said Colonel Muller.

'And, as I've pointed out before,' Kramer remarked, 'by bringing the car back to Square One, we have been left with no idea of where this murder took place.'

'Excellent,' murmured Galt appreciatively, moistening his thin lips. 'There's definitely cunning at work in all this.'

'Could the soil samples help us here?' asked Colonel Muller.

'Could do, sir. Without microscopic examination though – '

'Then I won't keep your from your invaluable work any longer, hey, Galt?' cut in Colonel Muller, using his smoothy's voice. 'And don't worry, I'll be telling your boss what a good job you've done on this so far!'

'It was the nearest sports shop to here,' Galt whispered modestly. 'Couldn't have been easier.'

Kramer felt a light touch on his shoulder, and saw Galt wander from the room with a long blonde hair, scrutinising it thoughtfully.

'So we've got another little lead, Tromp!'

'Sir?'

'The Master Skip, man!'

'Ignoring the possibility it was bought in some other place – Cape Town, Durban, Jo'burg or Magaliesbergfonteinpoort West – ja, I suppose that's true.'

'No, no!' replied Colonel Muller, snapping his pencil point. 'Forget that side of it! What this *particular* Master Skip suggests to me is evidence of a quick improvisation. Nobody would deliberately spoil a nice, expensive skipping rope like that except in a dire emergency, when they had no other piece of rope at hand. In other words, it wouldn't be something you'd plan to do, would it? I can see him grabbing up the Master Skip, cutting off the handles in case they give him away – or maybe he did that afterwards – and then quickly binding Hookham up with it. Where are those handles, hey? Did he throw them out? Did he hide them? Did you remember to do anything with them? Or are they still lying somewhere?'

'Good point,' said Kramer.

'Find those handles and we have found our man!' Colonel Muller went on, getting a little carried away. 'Is it too late to get this in tonight's paper?'

'The final edition is already on its way up in the van from Durb's, Colonel.'

'Ach well, it can go with the rest of the stuff in the *Gazette* tomorrow morning. Let me see, we're putting in the new description of the suspect, repeating the appeal to find this gun, and – er, what was the other thing? I must write this down.'

'We're also asking if anybody heard four shots last night,' Kramer reminded him. 'No police station in the whole divisional area had any reports of gunfire from the public, they tell me. The trouble is that people just don't notice bangs if they think they know the reason: it's the cops, they say to the kids, or it's a backfire – or, out in the country, it's poachers on their neighbours' land again. Somebody killing a snake.'

'Four shots in a row might produce something though, Tromp.

And talking of shots, how is that list of licensed thirty-two owners coming along? The one Records gave you on Monday?'

'It proved useless, sir – that's why I had Meerkat Marais in today.'

'Useless?'

'Uniform and me have already been through it, and apart from five – who didn't even know their guns were gone till we approached them – the rest were negative. Neither does it cover more than this area, arms illegally held, war souvenirs and so on, and – '

'Okay, man, okay, I've got the picture. I must say I'm glad to hear you're delegating for once! This isn't a case for a one-man band, and as you know, my main criticism of you is that you work entirely on your own too often.'

Kramer nearly said something then didn't.

'Well, Lieutenant, what comes next?' asked Colonel Muller, rising from behind his desk. 'If you're wanting to get going with the Digby-Smiths, I don't mind doing some of the delegating myself. I'll send some men out to do the house-to-house enquiries in and around Armstrong Avenue, just in case someone else was up at one o'clock and saw how the killer made his escape from there.'

'Thanks, sir.'

'And what about an armed guard for Bradshaw?'

Kramer hesitated.

'Ach, don't tell me you hadn't thought of that! If there is this pattern you feel so sure about, and Bradshaw is a part of it, then surely he is in danger of being attacked once again?'

'As a matter of fact,' said Kramer, 'Mrs Bradshaw did ask about police protection, but I . . .'

Colonel Muller wagged a stern finger. 'Up to your old tricks, hey? You're half-hoping this bastard will have another go at him, only this time he'll leave a better set of clues behind?'

'Perhaps if it could be a discreet guard, sir, over on the other side of the road maybe, then – '

'No, Tromp, you can't have your cake and eat it, man! Now you've finally talked me into believing you may have a hunch in this matter, and that you have found the start of some pattern, however nebulous, then you must accept the consequences of that.'

'Okay, sir.'

'And there's one other thing I want to warn you about.'

'Sir?'

'I don't want you to do anything but chase this pattern, hey? We've got the rope and those bullets and what Forensic is going to be able to tell us, which means –'

'They'll all take time, Colonel,' Kramer pointed out. 'If I can crack this fast another way, then it's possible I'll stop someone else being done in – this pattern could include more than two people, you know.'

Colonel Muller sighed. 'Ja,' he said, 'I know.'

Once Zondi had been brought up to date with what had been said in the divisional commandant's office, Kramer itched to begin the investigation afresh. He rang Trekkersburg General Hospital, and was informed that Mrs Digby-Smith had long since been treated and discharged. Pleased to have saved himself a wasted journey, and the loss of time that would have involved, he then dialled the Digby-Smiths' home number to warn of his imminent arrival. His face fell when the cook answered and said that her mistress was upstairs in bed with the curtains drawn, while her master had gone out in his car with the two dogs, giving her no idea of his destination. Nobody had told her to postpone dinner, however, so she was expecting him back by no later than half past six.

'Six-thirty? Then tell your boss I'll be there on the dot,' said Kramer, and turned to Zondi as he replaced the receiver. 'Funny bloke! He's gone waltzing off somewhere and left his old woman alone in that state. How's the time?'

'Just after five, boss.'

'*Five?* Jesus, what am I going to do in the meanwhile? I thought it was much later.'

Zondi shrugged. 'Perhaps the Lieutenant could take a look at the Aquarius gym.'

'And see if they've still got their Master Skip? Hell, you're as bad as the Colonel, man.'

'What if theirs has been stolen?' asked Zondi.

'Fat chance!'

'What if they can tell you who owns such a thing?'

'That's enough, I'll go,' said Kramer, picking up his jacket. 'And you? Are you coming?'

Zondi waved the hacksaw blade used in the murder at Mama Bhengu's whorehouse. 'I think there are some enquiries I must make in Peacevale, boss.'

'Oh ja? Well, if you want a lift later on, I'll pick you up at the usual place, usual time, unless I get sidetracked.'

'Thanks, Lieutenant.'

Left alone at his small, plain table and stool in the corner, Zondi gazed at the wall for some time, nagged by the gravest of doubts. It worried him that the Lieutenant had become suddenly so single-minded about the case, instead of leaving his options open, and he couldn't help thinking of the times when just such an approach had repaid stubbornness with disaster. Then he stood up, checked his gun, and went on his way too.

CHAPTER EIGHT

Still trembling with rage and indignation, despite several hours of hard drinking with a solicitous cronie, Meerkat Marais made his way back to his flat above a dry-cleaning depot on the wrong side of town. It wasn't much of a place, and he didn't spend a lot of time in it – for the last eight days, until rudely awakened by that bastard Kramer, he had been sleeping with a nympho from the telephone exchange – but it was home of a sort. A bedroom, lounge, bathroom and kitchen he could call his own, and somewhere among the general chaos was a clean pair of trousers. He decided against going in through the shop, and took the fire-escape stairs instead, which led up from an empty lot on the far side of the building.

After eight days of fending for itself, Dynamite, his ginger tom with a white tail, was pleased to see him. 'Prooouw!' it said, jumping down from the kitchen window-sill.

Meerkat booted Dynamite aside and prodded the lock with his Yale key. He never got to turn it, for the door simply swung inwards, and Dynamite darted in ahead of him.

'Careful!' hissed Meerkat, and felt instantly rather foolish.

Then he followed in Dynamite's wake, treading every bit as softly, and snatched up a bread knife from the kitchen table before putting his nose into any of the other rooms. He was quite certain he'd not left the door unlatched like that.

Stealthily, he crept from the kitchen to the bathroom to the lounge and into the bedroom, but found no intruders present. He flung the bread knife into the bedroom door, and looked about him, trying to establish whether anything had been disturbed. His clothes were all over the floor, drawers were hanging out, a glass lay smashed on the dressing table, and somebody had scrawled on a wall in lipstick, *Up yours, Marais!*; it was all, in fact, very much as he'd left it.

'Proooouw!' said Dynamite, turning and making a dash for the fridge.

Meerkat took a closer look at the rumpled grey sheets on his divan, and found some semen stains he didn't remember making. Of course, he said to himself, that was it: his landlord, Fat Solly Wynberg, king of the premature ejaculation, had been bringing girls up from the shop again, as per their agreement. Probably the skinny brunette with boobs like ice-cream cones, who'd reduced him to such a shambles that he'd just managed to stumble out, forgetting to pull the door tight shut behind him. All the same, Meerkat decided, it would be as well to check on his merchandise, and then to get rid of it pretty damn pronto.

Dynamite was waiting expectantly at the fridge door. 'Prrr-rouw!' said Dynamite, leaning ecstatically against his ankles. 'Miaow?'

'Here, dammit!' snapped Meerkat, scooping out a curl of ancient luncheon meat, and then, very casually, he opened the ice compartment at the top. 'Jeeeeeeesus!' The second ice-cube tray, which should have contained a .32 five-shot Smith & Wesson revolver, was gone. 'I've been done, Dynamite! Bloody burgled, hey?'

Dynamite paused, eyeing Meerkat warily because of the soft voice he was using, and prudently dragged the luncheon meat out of reach beneath the sink unit.

'Bloody burgled . . .' muttered Meerkat, stunned and hardly able to comprehend what this meant, although the act itself had been second nature to him since the age of nine. 'But who would dare do such a thing to me, Dyna? How many were there? Where did they come from?'

The steady green eyes gave nothing away.

'Kids? Those kids from the flats opposite?' It was unthinkable that anyone aware of Meerkat's violent reputation would attempt such an outrage. 'Ja, it was them, am I right? Are you in the mood for some nice fresh meat? Because when I'm finished with those little . . .'

Not a whisker twitched.

'But kids would have fed you from here, wouldn't they? And what kids would ever think to look in a fridge? It couldn't have been kids! – never in a million years. This was a real pro, hey, Dynamite?'

A slow blink.

'Doesn't he know what I'll do to him?'

Another slow blink.

'Kramer!' said Meerkat, grabbing at a roast chicken wrapped in silver foil. 'So this is where that psychopathic dog turd got to while I had to sit all – ' But even as he leapt to this inspired conclusion, he knew that the logic didn't follow right the way through.

It wasn't simply that he was at home and a free man, instead of in Boomplaas Street lock-up having his ribs kicked in; it was also the fact that his personal firearm, a 9 mm Walther PPK semi-automatic pistol, just like that cocky black shit Zondi carried, fell out of the roast chicken at the very first shake.

Trembling violently, now with almost ungovernable fury and in total confusion, Meerkat staggered through to his little gold-painted bar in the lounge, frantic for a stiff drink. Why anyone would want the .32 with its faulty barrel and doubtful ammunition, when they could just as easily have taken the super-efficient PPK – or both! – was more than he could imagine. Then he noticed something else.

The top was off the Johnny Walker bottle, its level had dropped at least three inches, and right beside it stood two tumblers with heeltaps of whisky in them. What was worse, he could plainly see greasy fingerprints on the tumblers gilded by a glint of fading sunlight coming in off the roof of a dry-cleaning van parked round the back. Fingerprints that mocked him, jeered and taunted him, egged him on to call in the cops, just as any other outraged citizen would do in a similar predicament.

With a snarl, Meerkat Marais dashed the tumblers to the floor, grabbed the bottle of Scotch by the neck, and took it through with him into the kitchen, there to calm himself down and plan his terrible revenge.

CHAPTER NINE

A shrewd black beggar, with wasted limbs and his head twisted round to face the wrong way, lay sprawled at the entrance to the lane leading to the Aquarius Health and Fitness Centre. There was nothing quite like a heightened sense of physical well-being, he'd discovered, for making passing whites feel compelled to shower him with coppers.

'God blessing you, my baasie, God blessing you,' he chanted as Kramer approached, but didn't put too much into it as they usually paid better on their way out. 'God bring you much happiness, my baasie . . .'

'How's it, Backchat?' grunted Kramer, pausing.

'Hau! Is it you, Lieutenant?'

'You're not blind this week as well, are you?'

Backchat had a good cackle over that. 'And what does the Lieutenant come seeking today?' he said.

'Seen any giants lately?'

'Four,' replied Backchat promptly, grinning up at him.

'You know what a giant is?'

'Ungasi, Lieutenant, but I do remember you telling me that the police pay well for any information!'

Kramer laughed and poked the old rogue with his foot. '*Reliable* information, hey? A giant in this case is one hell of a big bloke with arms like bloody tree-trunks. Don't tell me you've sat here on your bum all day and you haven't a thing to tell me.'

'Maybe.'

'Such as?'

'There is a good price offered for the man who can find a volovolo size number thirty-two.'

'Oh ja? When did you hear this?'

'Monday, Lieutenant.'

'Who from?'

'The talk was all around.'

'And who's doing the offering?'

'Ungasi, Lieutenant, but maybe I can find out.'

Kramer stood undecided for a moment. This could be something or nothing; it was difficult to tell. Backchat could simply have picked up a garbled story based on the efforts Zondi and he had been making over the last six days to trace the firearm used on Bradshaw. Yes, he must have done because, setting aside the criminal involvement aspect, the time factor wasn't right.

'Which do you mean, Backchat,' he asked as a double-check on this, 'Monday two days ago, or the Monday before that?'

'Hau, *this* Monday of *this* week, Lieutenant – and the news was very fresh.'

'Ja, it's okay, I know about that,' said Kramer, dropping some silver into the collecting tin. 'But you keep your eyes open for a giant, you hear me?'

'God blessing you, Lieutenant!' chuckled Backchat, and quickly emptied out the tin behind his chest.

Kramer strode on up the lane. The Aquarius Health and Fitness Centre looked nothing too special from the outside, which was contrary to what he had been led to expect: it was just a long stretch of whitewashed brick wall punctuated by little windows like portholes and by the backs of three large air-conditioners, struggling hard to remove the smell of rich man's sweat. He pushed open the big black wooden door, in which someone had wasted a great number of huge nails to no obvious effect, and found the reception area equally disappointing. For a start, it was a large room with very little in it, and what there was seemed very makeshift and cheap. The walls were covered in planks that nobody had bothered to paint, the floor was tiled in cork in the manner of an old-fashioned bathroom, and the furniture had been made out of chrome tubing that looked suspiciously like second-hand motor-bike exhausts, necessitating some very uncomfortable-seeming designs. As for the ceiling, it was stuck over with sacking of all things, and the pictures almost defied description, having no doubt been splattered together by somebody's two-year-old. He, for one, would definitely ask for his money back.

In his second glance, he took in a small glass tank filled with tropical fish on the reception desk, and behind it, putting down a red telephone, was a buxom young woman with a thick blonde plait, flatish features and big Afrikaner-blue eyes. Glad to find something in the room that didn't seem alien, he warmed to her instantly and introduced himself, for the first time that day, in his mother tongue.

'I am sorry,' she said shyly. 'I am not long from Sweden. You speak English?'

'Ja, when I have to, miss,' he sighed. 'I'm from the CID, the police – I'd like to see your boss.'

'One moment, please,' she lisped, pressing a hidden buzzer.

There was an awkward silence. Kramer stooped over the fish tank and pretended to admire its inhabitants. 'I like your aquarium,' he said politely.

'I am sorry?'

It was hopeless.

Then the boss arrived, all two hundred and fifty pounds of him, dressed in white slacks, a singlet and white tennis shoes, walking with a spring in his step that looked very tiring. His big round head was notable for its glisten of sweat, its high pink colouring, and some of the most horrible blackheads Kramer had ever seen on a face that size; it was like starting a conversation with a slice of water melon.

'Glad to meet you, Lieutenant Kramer!' the owner of the gym said. 'Jimmy Winters is the name, health and fitness is my game! You'll find everything here to keep you in tip-top shape, right on your toes, ready for anything that comes up!' And all the time he went on shaking hands, trying to demonstrate his crushing grip.

'Do you do skipping then, Mr Winters?' asked Kramer.

'Skipping! Weights! Isometrics!'

'I'm interested to know if you have such a thing as a Master Skip skipping rope,' said Kramer, quite prepared to go on shaking hands if it made the man happy. 'I'm working on a murder case where one is involved, you see.'

'A Master-what? I don't know, to be honest, but would you like to take a look?'

'Please.'

'Well, shall we . . . ?' Winters had gone right up on to his toes, and seemed to want his hand back. 'I mean . . .'

'After you, Mr Winters.'

A girlish giggle, Kramer decided, as he followed the great oaf

81

down a narrow passage, could sound just as nice in Swedish, and he wondered what her name was. Then the passage ended in a dazzle of white light and gleaming equipment.

'Not bad, hey?' said Winters, proudly. 'What you saw when you came in cost me a pretty penny, but this! – this is nothing but the latest, nothing but the best.'

'Uh-huh.'

'And look at the clientele . . .' Winters whispered behind a raised hand. 'All the top-notch, the cream. You won't find skolly boys in here pumping iron!'

It was certainly an educative and engaging sight to see so many of Trekkersburg's leading citizens stripped down and running over. What Kramer enjoyed most was the Supreme Court's most pompous and self-righteous judge, so paunchy he looked pregnant, using a vibrating-belt machine with every indication that he hoped, with so much bouncing about, to procure an illegal abortion.

'The skipping ropes are kept over here,' said Winters, leading the way across to five pegs in the wall. 'Probably what you're after is this newish one – am I right?'

It had Master Skip imprinted in both handles, and that was it. Kramer gave the rope a turn around his left wrist, explained the business of the fractures to Winters and asked his professional opinion, not expecting very much.

'Well, anything's possible, isn't it, Lieutenant?'

'Have you anybody coming here who has a pull like that?'

'I couldn't say for sure, but I doubt it.'

Bradshaw's description of his attacker fell on equally stony ground. Finally, Kramer asked if any member of the regular clientele had expressed an interest in the Master Skip, and may in fact have purchased one for himself.

'But why should he buy equipment?' said Winters, very puzzled and finding a small area of hair at the back of his bald head to scratch. 'That's why they come here, Lieutenant.' He thought for a while, and then added, 'Isn't it?'

Kramer flipped the skipping rope back over its peg, and turned to take his leave.

'Hello, there!' said a voice under some form of press. 'I was wondering when you'd notice us.'

By crouching down, Kramer was able to see Jonty the hairstylist flat on his back inside the gadget, straining at it with bulging arms. 'I hadn't noticed you actually, but tell me, have you got anything to report yet?'

'There's been a little cracker in the salon asking questions about someone all afternoon.'

'Oh ja? About who?'

'You, old cock. Know who I mean? The red-head?'

'Ach, what I'm more interested in is –'

Jonty laughed. 'You amaze me, Lieutenant! How can you ignore the sort of invitation I'm about to make? Come up to my place about ten and she'll be there. There's a crowd of us getting together after the drive-in.'

'Uh-huh, but nothing on where Hookham could have got to last night?'

'And this new bird out front, she'll be there too. You know, that cracking Swedish piece – I fancy a bit of smorgasbord!'

'I can't believe there wasn't talk in your salon this afternoon,' persisted Kramer, bringing an edge to his voice. 'Or are you trying to bugger me about?'

Jonty sat up then, looking hurt. 'Christ, no need to get your knickers in a knot, chief! If there had been anything worth passing on, don't you think I'd have contacted you by now? All I know is there's been a big ring-round on the phone, lots of excitement, but nobody had Hookham visiting them last night – or else they're not coughing to it.'

'Thanks,' said Kramer, getting up.

'But what do I tell Trish? That you'll be over at ten?'

Kramer left the question unanswered. He also left the Aquarius Health and Fitness Centre quite convinced that, just as he'd expected, his visit there had been a complete waste of time and he hadn't learned a thing.

Mama Bhengu stood with her arms folded at the front door of her whorehouse, doing the work – in terms of sheer physical obstruction – of four grown men. Her enormous dress hung partly unbuttoned from a pair of sloping shoulders rather like a polka-dotted bell tent, and peering out through the flap at the bottom, so to speak, was an evil-eyed billy-goat. Zondi made reasonably sure it was clamped tightly between her fat knees before advancing a step nearer.

'Greetings, Mama Bhengu,' he said, lifting his hat most politely. 'All goes well with you?'

She spat to her right.

'All does not go so well?'

She shrugged.

'The murder here has been bad for business?'

She stared at him for a time, and the billy-goat grew restless. Zondi decided to come straight to the point. 'See this, Mama? I have in my hand the weapon that was pushed into Jackson. Smith on these premises last Thursday night. Have you perhaps ever seen anyone with it?'

'Never.'

'You answer very quick.'

'And why not? I answer quick, you go quick – it is *you* who is bad for business, Michael Zondi.'

'My heart weeps for you, Mama Bhengu,' he replied, and drew his Walther PPK. 'Of course, if you wish to see something *really* quick, then all I have to do is fire one shot in the air, and your customers will join us from every window.'

She threw back her head and laughed so heartily that the goat's head shook up and down. 'Come inside, Michael,' she said, shuffling backwards into the hall. 'Come inside, and we will have gin together, son of my soul! What else is it you want?'

'To ask the same question of your nieces,' said Zondi, 'if that is agreeable to you.'

'All are at work except my new niece.'

'Their work never takes very long, so I will wait – I am in no hurry.'

'Come, let us go through to the back room.'

Mama Bhengu took the goat by the horns, dragged it out from under her, and then led the way, keeping the animal firmly in check until she could tether it to a table leg in the back room. Half a dozen drunken customers were seated there on stools made from condensed-milk crates, exchanging lewd predictions while they waited their turn; each seized up as he became aware of Zondi's presence, but nobody made a move to run. Zondi put away his PPK and took a look at the new niece, who was perched on the arm of a sagging settee. Mama Bhengu ran one of the best brothels in the township, so he had been expecting another of her true Zulu beauties: a sturdy young heifer with golden-brown

84

skin, full breasts, wide hips and big strong thighs with plenty of lift in them. The new niece had a golden-brown skin, but for the rest she was as skinny, flat-chested and narrow-hipped as a white woman, and topped it all off with an absurd yellow wig. He wasn't in the least surprised to find her unoccupied.

'What do you think?' whispered Mama Bhengu, tipping her head toward the girl. 'I tell you she is making me plenty, plenty money that one.'

'It does not look like it, Mama!'

'Huh! What do you expect on a Wednesday night? All these men here, what are they? Factory workers, labourers, loafers from the streets. But on Saturday night, Sunday night, those who find work in houses, cook boys, garden boys, drivers even, they all want to try out Missy Madam! Here take your glass and finish that while I fetch another bottle.'

Zondi tipped the dregs of the half-jack into the glass and sat back, keeping his shoe-laces out of reach of the goat. The back room, as Mama Bhengu called it, was really a large, lean-to shed with walls and a roof made of corrugated iron, and a floor made of crumbly concrete. The waiting area occupied a narrow strip nearest to the house itself, and the remainder of the floor space was divided up into curtained cubicles that ran across his line of vision from left to right, totalling eight of them in all. Someone with especially good hearing could probably pick out various sounds coming from behind the curtains, but the record-player on the table drowned most of them in a never-ceasing tumult of loud music, which was something to be grateful for. Zondi noticed that the last cubicle on the left, in which Willie Jackson had died, was empty and had its curtain pulled back.

'Are people afraid to go in there?' he asked Mama Bhengu when she returned with a full bottle of Gordon's.

'Of course. The funeral is not until tomorrow, and his spirit is still so strong in the place. Such is always the way when a man is murdered.'

Zondi felt a tap on his shoulder and turned to face a wheeze of cane spirit. 'What do you seek, brother?' he asked.

'Wunsh particle of information, Mr Detective sir,' slurred the drunk, a degenerate Indian with red eyes and red teeth. 'Wunsh small ray of kind enlightenment . . . You are willing for me to say?'

'Say on,' invited Zondi.

'That most terrible weapon you are displaying on your arrival in our humble midst, can it be a revolver size thirty-twos?'

'Nine-mil automatic; the size is the same though.'

'Ah!'

Then Zondi steadied the man with one hand, and asked, 'Why the interest, my friend?'

'Interesh?' The drunk frowned in thought. 'To know, to acquire most telling information for which I am thinking Mr De–'

'Yes, but why? What for?' Zondi rapped out.

'So I will know what I see when I see it, my goodness me, yes! But that one is no good, not automatic wanted – revolver.'

'Wanted by who?'

'Ah!' said the Indian, and looked blank.

'Mama, can I borrow that cubicle?' asked Zondi.

'Just to talk?'

'Just to talk, Mama.'

She gave her reluctant consent, hastily poured out free tots of gin for her other waiting customers (which stemmed a rising panic), and took the further precaution of turning the music up even higher.

Kramer coasted into another tree-lined street on Morninghill, having about nine minutes still to kill before he was due at 52 Armstrong Avenue.

His mood was brittle, far darker than it should have been, notwithstanding the skipping-rope fiasco, and he pondered the reason for this.

Eight minutes.

Finally, he had to admit to himself that it'd rankled when Zondi had decided to go back to the Willie Jackson case for the time being. Not that he could question the expedience of the move : Zondi was fluent in Afrikaans, English, Zulu, Xhosa and Sesuto, yet some levels of investigation were, for obvious cultural reasons, not open to him. Neither could he question Willie Jackson's posthumous right to have his murderer brought to justice without delay, and if anyone could solve that particular puzzle, then it was Zondi. What troubled him was that, in deciding not to go along with him in a literal sense, Zondi might also be making one of his mute, more figurative protests.

Seven minutes.

And that led inevitably back to the hunch which had given Kramer his impetus – an impetus that, for want of any outside support, was beginning to flag slightly. He reached the end of a cul-de-sac and began to retrace his meandering route.

Six minutes.

Yet the feeling was still there. Not as strongly, perhaps, as when it had first taken hold of him, back in Bradshaw's study after Mrs Bradshaw had arrived all dripping, but it remained a sure sense of unexplained, inexplicable certainty none the less.

Five minutes.

It was impossible that Zondi, despite all his talk of putting plodding police work before flashes of intuition, had a hunch of his own about this, and that was what made him so damned stubborn. Kramer smiled to himself. Yes, that was indeed a possibility, and it'd place them on an equal footing : one hunch against another, and may the best man win! He checked his watch again.

Three and a half minutes.

'Ach, bugger this for a joke!' said Kramer, opening the throttle and arriving at 52 Armstrong Avenue in little more than a matter of seconds.

He parked in the street and picked his way up the verge of the newly surfaced driveway, shuddering at the ornamental statues around the lily pond. Anybody who enjoyed looking out of their windows, and seeing little kids stuck there in the garden forever, holding up things that were obviously too heavy for them, was just a bit sick in his opinion. It was not until he had climbed the steps to the front verandah of the house that Kramer realised he had seen only one car, and that a Morris Mini, parked in the street outside.

'The master not home,' a giggly housemaid informed him, peering round the edge of the door. 'Madam fast-fast asleep.'

'CID, hey? I spoke to the cook girl on the phone.'

She nodded vigorously.

'Has Mr Digby-Smith rung up to say he'll be back?'

'No, the master not ringing.'

'Okay, then show me where I can wait for him.'

The house had a heavy scent of wax polish, lavender and boiled vegetables – plus a pronounced hint of long-haired dog – that summed up several of Kramer's ethnic prejudices in one.

'Here all right?' said the housemaid, then fled.

Kramer found himself in what had to be Digby-Smith's study. A real study this time, with rows and rows of books, an orderly desk, plenty of leather, plenty of soft light, and a great big oil painting of an English sea captain in knee-breeches, scratching himself under his smart blue tunic. Pride of place in the room, however, went to an enormous collection of bottles lying on their sides with little ships somehow shoved into them. The only thing these ships had in common was that they were all battling through stormy seas; in every other way, they were as different from one another as they could be, and the mystery of how the masts fitted through the necks of the bottles temporarily defeated him.

Then through the big side window, he glimpsed something going on under an apple tree that mystified him even more. But, unless he was very much mistaken, the Digby-Smiths' garden boy was digging two graves.

CHAPTER TEN

Mama Bhengu's five customers had taken their pleasure and gone by the time Zondi emerged with the Indian from the last cubicle along. They had been replaced by an even more ill-favoured crew, including a leprous albino, who were all so drunk that seeing two men come out together only made them snigger. The Indian smiled back in a dazed sort of way, and meekly rejoined the end of the queue.

Mama Bhengu raised her eyebrows in surprise at this. 'How is it that you have not lost me that miserable rand's worth?' she asked. 'Truly, I never thought he would stay long enough for me to see his ugly face again!'

'It was nothing,' grunted Zondi, sitting down and reaching for the bottle and his glass.

'*Nothing?* But how? You must tell me!'

'Am I a man to ruin your business? I just made it clear to Mr Govender that tomorrow I might change my mind about going easy on him, and if he didn't have one now, then it could be the last chance he'll ever get.'

Missy Madam, who had come to sit at the table too, shared in Mama Bhengu's delighted laughter. Then she leaned over and took the end of Zondi's tie to play with.

'Your little talk was good?' she asked.

'It was – no, you could not say good.'

'You talked very softly,' she said.

'This one?' chortled Mama Bhengu, nudging Zondi with an elbow the size of a knee. 'You know how he talks so softly? He talks with his hands!'

'Mmmmm,' murmured Missy Madam, opening the front of her blouse to him and shaking her small breasts free. 'Will you say something to me?'

'Uh-huh- I also talk with my feet,' rasped Zondi.

Then he closed his eyes on the whore's uncertain mirth, tipped his hat forward, and concentrated on getting half a glass of neat gin inside him. As it burned down his gullet, set fire to his empty stomach, and seemed to pass straight to his brain, he went over what he had managed to extract from one Jiji Govender. It amounted to very little : someone, somewhere in the town, had put out the word on Monday that a good price would be paid for a .32 Smith & Wesson revolver. Govender was such small fry, a mere scavenger snatching crumbs from bar counters, street corners, flop houses, that the task of tracing this information back to its original source through him was impossible. And would it be worth it? Govender insisted there had been not a whisper of such a thing before Monday – *this* Monday nine days ago – which came too late for the attack on Bradshaw, and made nonsense of the time factor. Perhaps a few enquiries could be made elsewhere, but on the face of it everything pointed to Govender having simply picked up a garbled story based on the efforts the Lieutenant and he had been making to track down the weapon since Saturday. No, it had been Monday before they'd really got down to that. How sweetly the gin was beginning to ease his acute disappointment.

He felt the clink of Mama Bhengu refilling his glass, and nodded his thanks to her. And yet, just like the Lieutenant, he had this feeling deep inside him, a feeling that criminal involvement could not be ruled out of the case, even if Hookham made it seem incompatible. Or was it that he knew too little of this kind of white man? Was he also being swept away by his imagination? Perhaps the best plan was to sleep on it, and to keep to what he said he'd set out to do.

Zondi opened his eyes and smiled at Mama Bhengu. 'I have something to show you,' he said. 'Not the hacksaw blade again, but something new. I have just found it.'

'Hau!'

'But first, Mama, a serious question. Is it true that nobody has been in that cubicle since Willie Jackson was stabbed there?'

'As true as I sit here, Michael Zondi.'

'Then maybe my time has not been wasted.'

'Why?'

'While I was talking in there, my eye saw this rolled into a corner, and I cannot say I looked everywhere last Thursday night;

90

there was that niece of yours under the body to remove, together with many other distractions.'

'Indeed it was terrible! I thought she was dead as well, not only fainted!'

'But can we see what this thing is?' begged Missy Madam.

Zondi opened his fist and an aluminium object, rather bigger and rounder than a thimble, closer in shape to an acorn cup, tinkled on the table top, rolled round in a half-circle and came to a stop. It made both women gasp very loudly.

Rupert Digby-Smith was a man with a smooth, almost glassy exterior, storm-grey eyes, and a sharp chin that jutted out, dividing the way before him. He was dressed in a silk cravat, white shirt, fawn slacks, desert boots and a double-breasted blazer with brass buttons and a bowls club badge. His voice came from far back in his mouth, rounding its vowels into plum puddings of over-rich sound, and his handshake was like testing the weight of a seal's flipper : cold, damp, quite impersonal.

'I saw you at the window, officer,' he said, opening a small liquor cabinet. 'Wretched business, but it had to be done. My wife is quite beside herself at the thought of her brother being the object of their attentions this morning, and insisted I had them put down without delay. The vet was very good about it.'

'You'd had the two dogs long, sir?'

'Since pups. Fine animals both of them, and I dare say I'd have forgiven and forgotten soon enough, but . . .' And he sighed with restraint. 'I can offer you brandy, whisky, gin, rum – or would you care for a beer?'

'A brandy and orange juice.'

'What you people call a "dop en dam", I believe?'

Kramer tried not to allow his hackles to rise. 'And what you people call a "ghastly concoction", I believe?' he replied.

Digby-Smith stared at him. 'Ah! Very good!' he said, noting humour rather than appreciating it.

Down under the apple tree, the garden boy was refilling the dogs' graves, working slowly and apparently enjoying himself. Probably, to judge by Digby-Smith's slow, stiff gait, it had been the servant's job to take the big Irish Setters for their walk every evening.

'Your glass, officer.'

'Cheers, sir,' said Kramer, turning round. 'Now I wonder if we can – '

'Ice?'

Kramer accepted two lumps of ice, and watched the muscles in the angle of Digby-Smith's narrow jaw bunch up and set hard. They stayed that way for several seconds, went down again, there was a moment's delay, then the action was repeated.

'Now, sir, as I was about to say, there are a lot of questions I must – '

'What I dread,' said Digby-Smith, taking a sip of his brandy and water, 'is telling the servants. They were fond of my brother-in-law, he spoiled them, treated them quite wrongly; he'd been away too long, y'know. God, what a scene.'

'How long exactly had he been away, sir?'

'Oh, years and years,' Digby-Smith replied, taking the high-backed chair behind the desk. 'Do sit down, officer, there's a good chap.'

Kramer pulled a chair up to face him on the other side of the desk, and took out his notebook. 'He was in the RAF during the war? Why was that?'

'Wanted to do his bit, I suppose – fiery little devil Edward, of course. Couldn't wait until we had got things sorted out here, so off he went. Joined the RAF in Rhodesia, got his wings and that was the last my wife's family saw of him; rather selfish, I thought. Still, even some of your people got the same bee in their bonnet, didn't they?'

'Sir?'

'You must have heard of Sailor Malan, surely? Afrikaner like yourself; finished up the top-scoring RAF fighter pilot in the war, friend of Bader's, came back here and blotted his copybook by starting the Torch Commando.'

'That would be before my – '

'War veterans, y'know. It'd all gone a bit to their heads, this business of having blacks out there in the desert with them, doing the cooking and the ambulance driving and that. They tried to nip the Nats' plan to implement apartheid in the bud, but not too surprisingly came unstuck.'

'Uh-huh. If we could – '

Digby-Smith narrowed his eyes distrustfully. 'You may have been too young then, as you say, but surely you must have read about Malan when he died? Parkinson's disease? There were headlines in all the papers when the Government refused him a military funeral on the grounds that he'd fought for – what was by then – a foreign power.'

'It wasn't headlines in the Afrikaans press, I don't think,' said Kramer, curbing his impatience but only just. 'I'm really more interested in Mr Hookham himself, sir, and in what you can tell me about him. I notice you don't call him "Bonzo" the same as your wife does.'

'Don't I? Well, perhaps that's because I regard that sort of thing as fractionally childish. Got saddled with that after his squadron's fox terrier was run over by a drunken wing commander, y'know; they were due to fly on a raid again that night, hadn't time to find a replacement, and so they decided – on account of his size, I believe, and his snappy, terrier-like temperament – to adopt him as their lucky mascot. Rather rash of them, in the event: he only survived three more raids before they were faced again by the same problem. Settled for a greyhound that was a damned sight faster than the wing commander's Austin.'

Kramer underscored the one phrase in all that he'd copied down. 'Do I understand you to mean, when you say he "only survived three more raids", that he was shot down or something?'

'Over France,' confirmed Digby-Smith, smiling slightly. 'Which was, on reflection, a lucky-ish thing. Yes, our young hero found himself up to his neck in a midden in Normandy, surrounded by grinning peasantry, and was duly marched off to a POW camp. Had that midden been in Saxony, I dare say the peasantry there would have continued to heap ordure upon him until he suffocated or whatever – if he hadn't had a pitchfork through him before then. You know what the Germans called them? "Terrorflieger" – hated, loathed and feared them like nothing on earth; would butcher them on sight.'

'Oh ja?'

'Oh yes,' said Digby-Smith. 'And if you've ever read an account of what happened to places like Dresden, who could really blame them?' His slight smile twitched at the corners. 'Ironic that – no, never mind. He was a prisoner of war for only six months, escaped with two others and, helped by the French underground, made his way back to England. In fact, the girl he married came from one of the French families who'd hidden him in their attic for a time.'

Kramer looked up from his notebook. 'She was French? I'm sure I was told English by someone today.'

'It's a common assumption people make,' replied Digby-Smith, shrugging. 'They hear he married and settled down in England after the war, and – well, need I go on? You can't have got that from anyone we know intimately.'

'And so that's why your brother-in-law stayed on in England?' said Kramer, sidestepping the question implicit in that last remark. 'He didn't want to take his wife too far away from her family?'

'Not quite, old chap,' murmured Digby-Smith, patronisingly. 'Alice – he always called her that, although her real Christian name was Alloise – had become an orphan by the time he got back to France. Some bother with the Gestapo.'

'Oh ja? Then what was the reason for him staying on, sir?'

'The village pub, if he's to be believed. Cricket on the green, *The Times,* his circle of friends, something nebulous he calls "civilisation", while damning trade unions as "the new barbarism". However, the truth probably lies closer to the fact his ex-navigator, Hampshire born-and-bred and totally unwillingly to move, had this brilliant idea for some form of electronic gadget, and asked him to make up a partnership. With his approach to life, Edward did rather well on the business side.'

'His approach?' repeated Kramer, detecting a faint echo of Bradshaw in this. 'Are you saying that Mr Hookham was a hard-headed bas–, um, businessman?'

Digby-Smith considered his reply carefully, swilling a mouthful of his drink round and round before finally swallowing it. 'If required,' he said, 'to provide a thumbnail sketch of my brother-in-law's chief characteristics, then I'd possibly describe him as resolute, impetuous, unforgiving and an aggressive little bore at times. But I'd rather you didn't put that on record for my good lady's sake.'

God, thought Kramer, why this bugger keeps ice for his drinks, I'll never know; he's so cold that all he needs to do is stir the stuff with his finger.

'Well, officer, have we finished with the biographical background? I've had an afterthought, actually : possibly the fact his wife was known as Alice led to the confusion in the mind of that person who thought she was English.'

'Uh-huh,' said Kramer, almost certain the man was fishing. 'She died of cancer, I'm told.'

'Like his mother.'

'Sir?'

'Left her with us, you see. I had to feed, house and maintain her, put up with her whining, listen to her eternal stories about her golden-haired boy. The most abominable woman.'

'I see, and – '

'Well, you don't think he'd have honoured us with this visit had she still been alive, do you?' Digby-Smith laughed then, but his laughter was completely silent. 'Always a chap to look after his end of things is Brother Edward.'

'*Was* Brother Edward,' Kramer corrected him.

For upwards of a minute, Digby-Smith stared straight back over his desk, not moving a muscle. Kramer held the stare, trying to see in beyond the cool, calm façade confronting him; never before had he conducted an interview quite like this one.

'You must think it odd ...' began Digby-Smith.

'What, sir?'

'That I have spoken to you so frankly. You should perhaps be made aware that my opinion of Edward Hookham has never been a secret. I have made it known to him personally on several occasions, just as he has informed me of what a dull, stuffy, wet and thoroughly gutless specimen I am. I may yet, of course, come to moderate my views somewhat, to feel a degree of remorse, to even enumerate his undoubted virtues as a self-made man – who knows? But not until I have finally convinced myself.'

'Convinced yourself of what, Mr Digby-Smith?'

'Why, that he's well and truly dead, of course!'

It wasn't an easy line to follow. Kramer stood up, took the man's glass over to the liquor cabinet for a refill, and returned it to him without speaking. Then he gave the big globe of the world a spin, and tried to pick out the area of England called Hampshire.

Digby-Smith came round to stand beside him. 'Ah, I see what you're at! Take a line directly just to the east of it – yes, about there. A lovely thing, a globe.'

'True,' said Kramer. 'And the fact of the matter is, sir, that your brother-in-law has departed this one forever. I would now like to hear about the last three weeks, dating back to his time of arrival.'

'He came, he saw, he didn't care much for it.'

'Pardon?'

'Things here had either changed too much or they hadn't changed enough,' said Digby-Smith, adopting his icy, nonchalant manner again. 'But shall we leave out the politics? Lillian – my wife, y'know – tried to find things to amuse him. The trip to Hluhluwe Game Reserve was a partial success, in that he managed to capture on film the rare sight of a rhinoceros mating, but otherwise our idea of entertainment seldom seemed to suit him. Then again, how does one entertain a man whose wife has just died? Hardly with bawdy song and dancing girls.'

'Ja, I see the problem,' said Kramer, wondering how soon the tense would switch from the past to the present again. 'You reckon he was quite upset then?'

'Liked to go off on his own, moped a good deal, was liable to bite one's head off for practically nothing. Neither of us had seen him for ages, of course, but yes, I think it would be fair to say that at least some of his behaviour can be attributed to his recent bereavement.'

'And last night? Do you know where he went?'

Digby-Smith returned to his chair. 'Not the faintest idea – neither has Lillian. It's almost become a regular routine in this house : he disappears after dinner, comes back at an unearthly hour, and the servants are under instructions to allow him to sleep-in the following morning. Come to think of it, the only evening I've actually known his whereabouts was at the start of last week, when I suggested he might like to gate-crash the flying club's monthly social.'

'You're saying that was your idea, sir?'

'Entirely,' said Digby-Smith, lighting a cigarette without thinking to offer one first. 'It seemed to buck him up a bit. I thought it might – birds of a feather, y'know! Wings?'

'Ah, very apt,' Kramer replied, finding a half-smile. 'It bucked him up in what way?'

'Became livelier, more attentive to our idle conversation. Oh, it lasted until last Saturday, when the paper arrived with that tale about that swine Bradshaw – no doubt up to his devious tricks again, and somebody with enough decency and nerve tried to put an end to it. Damned shame they missed.'

'You've had dealings with Mr Bradshaw?'

'Dealings singular,' said Digby-Smith, bitterly. 'I thought it might be amusing to put one of my small creations on the market, just to see what sort of price it could fetch, and he swindled me completely.'

Kramer looked across at the little ships. 'So those are your handiwork, hey? I'm impressed. Where did you learn how to do it, sir? Were you in the navy?'

'I regret to say I have never served in any of the armed services, old chap; Royal, Republican or otherwise.'

'Really? You were saying –'

'Black-outs, y'know; don't remember a damned thing.'

'Shame, hey? This newspaper report . . . Did Mr Hookham have some reaction to it?'

'Fright,' said Digby-Smith, twisting his thin smile.

'He looked scared, you mean?'

'Shook like a leaf and we had to ask him what the matter was. Told us he'd only just met the chap, former RAF type and so on. Lillian disagrees with me, mark you. She says our little hero looked absolutely furious at the thought that an old comrade-in-arms had been attacked in such a cowardly fashion. Again, in an effort to be fair, his reaction probably lay somewhere between those two extremes – shall we say he was merely startled?'

Kramer nodded. 'Ja, maybe we'd better, sir – unless you can suggest a reason for it frightening him. Without there being more of a connection between him and Bradshaw, why the hell should it?' Then he gazed intently at Rupert Digby-Smith, who appeared as glassy smooth and suave as ever on the surface, yet seemed to have all manner of tempestuous things bottled up inside him.

'Maybe that was a big mistake,' Mama Bhengu confided in a mumble, having second thoughts as she watched Missy Madam lead a swaggering youth with one eye into the middle cubicle. 'Maybe I should have said to him, "No! You choose another girl!" You can plainly see he isn't a house boy, so for him to – well, he could be not straight in the head. He could have strange prac-tices . . .'

'He could just have a lust for young girls before they become

97

proper women,' sniffed one of her nieces, whose own charms were bountiful. 'She is not a woman that one. Where are her breasts?'

'Such jealousy . . .' murmured Zondi.

Mama Bhengu laid a hand on his arm. 'You will stay five minutes more, Michael Zondi?'

'Why sound so worried, Mama? You know how to handle these guys if they get rough.'

'You have not finished your questions. Look, Gertrude has just come out.' She beckoned to the slut. 'Here, Gertrude, the detective sergeant wants to ask you something.'

Gertrude, a dull-skinned, sour-faced frump, whose one redeeming feature was that she didn't mind lying with dirty old men and other undesirables like Jiji Govender, slopped over, buttoning up her blouse.

'What is it?' she whined. 'I have not done any –'

'Just look at that and tell me if it means anything to you,' said Zondi, pointing to the table in front of him.

The prepuce-cover still lay there on its side. Once such an object was all that a Zulu needed to wear to consider himself fully dressed, and although modern society demanded rather more of him, the traditions of encasing one's foreskin in this fashion persisted beneath even some quite sophisticated trousers. Not that anyone bothered to have it woven out of palm leaves any longer, when various sizes were available cheap and ready-made at most trading stores.

'Um-ncedo,' said Gertrude, like a child in class.

'That is its name,' agreed Zondi. 'Now its owner's name?'

'Banjo Nyembezi.'

'And why?'

'Because it is the only one I have seen made in that kind of metal.'

Zondi grinned and slipped it into his pocket. Without exception, every other niece in Mama Bhengu's house had made the same response, and so it looked very much as though Banjo Nyembezi was on his way to being restrung in the gallows room at Pretoria Central.

'Mama, I have to meet my white boss at ten,' Zondi began apologetically, 'so sadly I must –'

There was a terrible whimper from the middle cubicle.

'I'm ready, Mama!' whispered Zondi, leaping to grab the curtains. 'Go, Mama, go!'

Mama Bhengu moved with astonishing speed. She freed the billy-goat, swung it round in the right direction, and gave it a mighty slap on the rump. The goat charged straight through the gap in the curtains that Zondi provided for it at the very last moment, and its lowered horns caught a pair of sadistic buttocks right in the act, so to speak.

CHAPTER ELEVEN

Kramer glanced at his watch. It was almost twenty to ten, and soon he would have to make a decision : Zondi was expecting him then, so was Jonty, while his visit to 52 Armstrong Avenue had still a few minutes to run. He clenched his teeth on another boiled-cabbage burp and took a final look at the diary he had found in the drawer beside Bonzo Hookham's bed.

The entries were no more than jottings, not literary efforts but appropriate to the nature of the diary itself, which was the sort businessmen carry to remind them of appointments. The nearest it came to having any character was when Hookham had apparently added a comment or two in brackets when checking what lay in store for him the next day.

November 6: *Will arrive Louis Botha Airport, Durban, 1100 hrs – Diggers and Lil to pick me up, whisk me to Trekkersburg.*
(I think he'd gladly have put me down again)
November 7: *Lunch with D & L and one of their Best Friends at the Albert Club, 1230 hrs.*
(Preferred walk with dogs)
November 8: *Lunch with another BF at the golf club, 1300 hrs.*
(Dogs win yet again)
November 9: *Sundowners with the Postlethwaites, ex-Kenya, 1700 hrs. (More English than I'll ever be – or any Englishman! What are these people doing here? Bigotry would amaze the dogs – sorry, lads, I'll time things better tomorrow)*
November 10: *Dinner at Basil Strongpiece's, 1930 hrs.*
(A.K.! How extraordinary)

Kramer pondered this parenthetical aside, skipped the pages covering Hookham's stay in the game reserve, and stopped at an entry made soon after his return.

November 18: *Flying Club 'do' at 2000 hrs, dress casual – Diggers. (Unbelievable, I've met the swine! – goaded Diggers, said what a fine fellow he seemed – Diggers had a rant – all part of some grand design? – poor old Diggers, and it's him I really have to thank for this stunning evening – I feel alive again!)*

There were other entries to follow, many detailing appointments Hookham would now never keep, but his habit of adding comments ended at that point. It was as though a man who'd been living inside himself a lot, talking to himself and comforting himself, had suddenly turned outwards on the world again. To check his theory, Kramer leafed back through the pages for April and May, and found that Hookham had used brackets only very occasionally. One entry stood out from all the others.

May 27: *Mr Tullerby, Cancer Research Unit, So'ton Gen. at 1400 hrs. (Says it's hopeless. But we'll fight! Dear God, hasn't my poor Alice suffered enough in her life? Albert – her family, now this!*

Such had been Hookham's agitation that he'd not closed the brackets again, and like the entry for November the 18th, his handwriting showed evidence of heavy drinking. Kramer shut the diary with a snap.

'What have you got there?' asked Digby-Smith, coming into the guest bedroom. 'Don't tell me Edward kept a diary!'

'Do I need to?' said Kramer, with a flash of insight into Digby-Smith's earlier remarks about the beneficial effects of the flying club social. 'Businessmen like Mr Hookham surely get in the way of writing down lunch dates et cetera?'

'Oh, is that all it's got in it?'

'Have a look if you like, sir.'

Digby-Smith flicked through the diary in a too-uninterested way. 'Hmmm, not very inspired, I must say. More importantly, have you managed to get anything useful from it? Apart from the fact he took to consorting with lower forms of canine life in the late afternoon?'

'Ach, you could say I've built up a better picture of the deceased, sir – attitudes, things like that.'

Digby-Smith coloured very slightly. 'But no riveting clues?'

'Only one,' said Kramer, taking the diary and going back to

November the 10th. 'Or should I say, only one reference that doesn't explain itself. Can you suggest who this "A.K." person is?'

After looking at the initials, Digby-Smith cross-checked them with a list of names that he and his wife had been compiling in her bedroom. 'We've included here every single friend or acquaintance of his that comes to mind, but I'm afraid if it's an A.K. you want, you're out of luck. Perhaps something will occur to us overnight, but my good lady has had quite enough of this for one day, and I'm becoming a trifle worn-out myself.' He handed over the list and glanced meaningfully at the door. 'But naturally, if you feel this extremely long interview could be prolonged even longer to your advantage, then –'

'I'm just on my way, sir,' said Kramer, pocketing the list and picking up a small suitcase. 'I'm taking various papers, his shoes, odds and ends for our laboratory – there's a receipt on the dressing table. Oh, and this diary as well.'

'Excellent. Shall I show you the way down?'

Kramer waited until they had reached the front door of the house before putting his final question for the night. 'About this phone call for Mr Hookham, the one when the bloke spoke with a funny accent . . .'

'Yes, I answered that not last night but the night before, just as I've already said at least three times.'

'The exact words again, please?'

Digby-Smith glared. 'Good God, you're not trying to trip me up, are you, officer? Anyway, a half-witted child could get it off pat! He said, "Can I speak to Bonzo Hookman, please?" I said, "No, he's out, I'm afraid, and I don't know where." Then he said, "Will he be there in the morning?" To which my reply was, "You are sure to get him then, but don't ring before eleven as we generally allow him to sleep-in." He said, "Sorry to trouble you, just say it was an old school-friend who wanted to surprise him – no, better say nothing, or that will spoil it." My answer to that was, "Very well, I won't, good night." "Good night," he said.'

'Ja, I was trying a trick,' Kramer admitted unashamedly. 'I hoped you might slip into imitating the accent this time – sometimes that happens, you know. It's the funny accent that really interests me, you see.'

'Not funny – *strange*,' snapped Digby-Smith, putting up a hand to close the door on him. 'It wasn't foreign, it wasn't local – it was, at best, a mixture of both.'

'Someone trying to sound foreign then?' asked Kramer.

'Yes, or even vice versa.'

'Pardon?'

'Caesar would despair of you, officer! What that means is this fellow could just as well have been a foreigner trying to sound local.'

'Uh-huh, I follow,' said Kramer, nodding.

'But let's not make too much of that phone call – well, not tonight if you please! I really must leave off now, as I've the news still to break to his offspring in England, and dialling those endless codes – '

'You've not told them yet?' said Kramer, taken aback. 'I thought it'd been arranged with you at lunch-time – you know, that it would be better than doing it through us and the English police?'

'Quite,' replied Digby-Smith, closing the door. 'But you've been here all evening and, as you know, it's cheaper after six.'

Anneline Strydom switched off the television set in the living-room and looked in on her husband in the kitchen. 'Still playing with those horrible snails? Yiggg!'

The snails were distributed all over the enamel working surface of her smaller table, and Strydom was scraping at their slimy trails with a glass slide. Once he had a little of the slime collected, he transferred it to a small test-tube kept upright in a teacup, and then sought some more of the stuff. Even amassing as much as a thimbleful was obviously going to take all night.

'You're not intending to – '

'Don't start your nagging!' he growled.

'Chris, have you seen what time it is? It's after ten.'

'And so? Am I a man of science, or aren't I? Does Einstein have his wife telling him when to go to bed?'

'Maybe that depends,' said Anneline coquettishly, 'on what mood Mrs Einstein is in. Come on, Chrissy, put your snails away and – '

'Ach, I'm fed up with today! I've got nothing finished I wanted to do! First my snails got interrupted, then I couldn't find an arm anywhere! You'd think one arm wouldn't be asking too much! But no, not one morgue in the whole district has got an arm for my experiments. For weeks my fridges are full of paupers, unknowns, little bits and pieces, then suddenly – poof! What's happening? Aren't we meant to be in a recession?'

Anneline came up behind him and massaged his shoulders, bringing the smell of her bath salts well within range of his sensitive nose. 'Now, now, my little lion, don't roar and show your teeth to your Annetjie, hey?' And she planted a tiny kiss in his shaggy grey mane. 'How long is it since you last said to me, "Come, my beloved, my queen of the veld, let us go into the long grass?"' The muscles in his shoulders lost some of their tension. 'Tell me,' Anneline murmured, 'has Mrs Einstein long shiny black hair such as mine? Long enough for her to sit on it? Do you want to undo my bun?'

'How should I know what her hair is like!' muttered Strydom. in slow pursuit of a really slimy snail. 'Hell, I don't even know what *he* looks like!'

'Hey? But you said you'd met the new Jewish doctor at the medical centre.'

'Bernstein! Bernstein! Don't you ever listen?'

'I like that!' Anneline stepped back and stood with her fists on her hips, looking daggers at him. 'I've spent the whole evening listening to you moaning about that stupid arm of yours! You know your trouble? You're obsessed with bodies!' A sob caught her throat. 'Oh, Chrissy, why does it have to be dead bodies all the time?'

'Anneline!' cried Strydom, coming slowly up out of his chair with a radiant smile. 'Come, let me give you a big hug for that! Of course it doesn't have to be a dead body – just so long as the arm is dead, that is all I ask!' Then he hurried through in his slippers to the telephone.

Kramer ducked his head, noted that the lights above Jonty's salon were on, caught a glimpse of the man himself at a window, and then allowed the Chevrolet to pick up speed again. Two blocks further down, he braked outside a small park and looked to see if the statue of Queen Victoria had a white man's burden in its vast maternal lap. But Zondi had already jumped down from his accustomed resting place, and was at the kerb almost before the car had stopped.

'Hullo, Lieutenant!'

'Hullo, Mickey, old son!'

As their greetings had been strangely effusive, perhaps a touch embarrassed somehow, neither said anything until on their way out of the city. Then Zondi began by showing the prepuce-cover to Kramer, and a sketchy plan was made to bring in Banjo Nyembezi next morning.

'And now you, boss?' said Zondi. 'Have you also had good hunting?'

'So-so, Mickey. I've been up at the Digby-Smiths' nearly all night – Jesus, their cook is bloody useless, hey? – and I've learned quite a lot. I also think that some of the time Mr Digby-Smith was trying to play games with me.'

'Hau! On the day his kin is found murdered?'

'You've heard nothing yet, just wait . . .'

Kramer went back to the beginning and repeated all the main points of the interview, before, during and after dinner. By the time he had finished, they'd passed through the high security fence surrounding Kwela Village township, and were dodging pot-holes in the grid of dirt roads that divided up the thousands of identical houses.

'A strange, strange man,' murmured Zondi, shaking his head. 'But tell me again the part when he said Boss Hookham was made frightened by the newspaper.'

'Ja, I cornered him on that,' said Kramer. 'I asked him why, if there was no special connection between his brother-in-law and Bradshaw, that he should be scared when the bugger got shot. He just shrugged. So then I asked directly. I said to him, "Can you connect these two shootings in any way?" What I didn't realise at that stage was Digby-Smith had no knowledge of it being the same gun used each time. No, he couldn't connect them, he said – after all, Hookham only knew Bradshaw because of the party, and it'd been him, Digby-Smith, who'd suggested it.'

'What happened when you did tell him about the bullets coming from the same gun?'

'He went almost human for a while.'

'He was surprised?'

'Very.'

Zondi touched Kramer's arm and they came to a stop outside a house indistinguishable from any other in the street; once there had been a path edged by condensed-milk tins, but they had rusted away. Kwela Village had no electricity – apart from that supplied to a few street lamps and the white superintendent's house and offices – and a small, friendly candle glowed at the kitchen window. Kramer switched off the engine.

'In what way human?' asked Zondi, as they lit up their last smokes of the day.

'Well, first he said that Hookham was almost bound to react with the shakes to the news of Bradshaw getting shot – after all, the bastard had very nearly been killed, and Hookham was in a highly sensitive state concerning death and people he knew.'

'Only very slightly, Lieutenant.'

'Ja, but I think there's a lot in that. Do you remember when Gawie Willems got his head blown off last year during that drugs raid up near Bergville? Hell, I hardly knew old Sarge Gawie, but I got the twitch in the mortuary next morning, and there wasn't one corpse there that I knew.'

Zondi conceded the point with a nod and flicked his ash out of the window. 'But still I wish to know why he said such a thing about Boss Hookham. There is malice in it.'

'Oh, definitely. I think he's taken a hammering all his life about his hero of an in-law, and it amuses him to say he looked scared. He gets some sort of kick out of it.'

Again Zondi nodded, satisfied with that reply, yet ready with another question. 'Okay, he has explained all this. Now how did he describe the time after the newspaper, up until last night?'

'Haven't I told you?'

'No, not with details, boss.'

Kramer sighed but didn't much mind repeating the whole thing again blow by blow. Having gone to a mission school which shared about ten textbooks between two hundred pupils, Zondi had cultivated for himself a photographic memory, and this facility had extended itself to conversations as well. Telling Zondi something was, in effect, as good as feeding it into a small brown computer; it freed one's own mind to deal with the broader issues, while every snippet was reliably retained, ready to pop up at the appropriate moment – or, and this no computer could do, at an imaginatively inappropriate moment, which was often just as effective in solving a crime.

'Well, after Hookham had seen the newspaper, he took the

dogs out for a walk. He had lunch with the D-Smiths and a friend, spent the afternoon reading in his room, writing to his grand-children, and then, after a light supper, he went out again. On the Sunday he read the papers, and D-Smith and him laughed at Bradshaw's "giant" story, which Colonel Muller had released by then. He seemed in a much happier mood all round, then there was a row with his sister over various arrangements they'd made for the following week – this week, in fact. It ended up with her saying he should just please himself what he did, and she cancelled a bridge party and all the rest of it. On Monday two of the ex-RAF blokes came round to see him, and they ended up very drunk on the lawn. On Tuesday he complained of a hang-over – that would be yesterday – and stayed in his room nearly all day. Digby-Smith says his manner at table last night was a bit jumpy and peculiar, and he kept looking at his watch. He also apolo-gised to them for being "such a bolshy guest" and admitted that leaving familiar surroundings so soon after his wife's death had probably been a mistake. The truth of the matter, he also told them, was that he was homesick, disoriented and miserable. Finally it came out that he wanted to cut short his stay and go back home to England this coming Saturday – or sooner, if he could change his ticket. Mrs Digby-Smith got very upset, and said it was all her fault, and what would her friends think of her if he walked out. Digby-Smith – ach, in a way, you've got to like him for what seems his honesty – told Hookham that he thought it was a perfect plan. Never mind about anything else, he said, any man takes a chance with his happiness when he tries to revisit his past. And that's how they left it, although Mrs Digby-Smith was determined to make him stay, and this morning she was writing to tell the family what a good time he was having. End of story.'

'Did you speak with her again?'

'No, she was a bit too upset, and I accepted that.'

Zondi chuckled. 'You're a bad bugger, boss! You must have given that woman a terrible shock this morning.'

'Expedient at the time, kaffir! We white men don't like to sit around all day on our bums like *you* people, hey?'

They laughed together, and Kramer was reminded of the con-versation he had had with Backchat outside the Aquarius. Zondi matched it with Jiji Govender's tale, and after turning the information this way and that, they agreed that it must have been a rumour started by their own activities that week.

'So forgetting all that,' said Kramer, 'what are we left with, Mickey?'

'Indubitably some progress, Lieutenant.'

'Oh ja?'

'We have learned much about Boss Hookham, as to his character and his heavy heart.'

'Is that all you can say? Christ, do you want me to spell it out for you?' Kramer started counting on the fingers of his left hand. 'One: we have some initials that are a mystery. They could be part of the same mystery as where Hookham went to on his own at night.'

'That doesn't connect the cases.'

'Two: if that bloke on the phone was our man,' Kramer went on, gritting his teeth, 'then we know it was premeditated, and we know how the killer learned that nobody would expect to see Hookham until late in the morning. Added to that, whichever way you think about the "strange accent", it must have been fake.'

'That doesn't connect the cases.'

'Three, you cheeky bastard: there was a significant change in Hookham after he attended that party where the RAF were – he says so himself in the diary. There also seems to have been a change in him after seeing and talking with those RAF who visited him.'

'Hmmmm.'

'You can't see that the RAF connects everything?'

'With respect, boss, I see nothing in Boss Hookham's behaviour that would have been different if *Boss Bradshaw* had *not* been in the RAF, but just a man he met first time that night.'

Kramer flicked his cigarette into the road, and searched his jumble of thoughts for the right answer to that. 'It's what got them talking together, man!'

'And what did they talk about? Fishing? Weren't they fishermen, too?'

Kramer slumped. The rats of sweet reason had enjoyed a field day with this hunch of his, nibbling and gnawing and shredding it until very little remained. Now Zondi had gone and added another cageful, and he'd had enough.

'Look, you can't bloody argue that the bullets don't connect Bradshaw and Hookham!' he said angrily.

'The bullets are the connection between the man with the gun and the people he shot,' said Zondi. 'They prove nothing else. God gave us both red blood in our veins, but that does not make us brothers.'

Such dispassionate logic was irrefutable. 'You win,' sighed Kramer, his voice tired and dull.

'No, Lieutenant, maybe you are right,' said Zondi, as he slipped out of the car and closed his door quietly. 'Tomorrow we must check those initials,' he continued at Kramer's window. 'I cannot explain it either, for there is so much more we must have in our heads first, but I am beginning to have that same feeling you spoke about.'

Strydom's Thursday also seemed to hold fresh promise from the moment he snatched up his hall telephone at its very first ring. 'Hello? Dr Meyer? Don't say it! You've rung back so quick because you can't – *you have?* Gas gangrene? And when are you going to amputate? Hell, that's marvellous, hey? No, no, don't get anybody to deliver it, I'll come round myself personally. Ja, it could be crucial to the case. Leave no stone unturned, as they say! No, what I'm actually doing is confirming an expert opinion. Mine. Ja, ja, absolutely! Can't be too careful – it's a thing laymen never appreciate. And many, many thanks again, you hear? Good night!'

Euphoric, he tugged undone his dressing-gown cord, tiptoed down the passage to the bedroom, and paused just inside the door to give a low, rather regal growl. And from the long grass, a delighted lioness coyly answered him back.

CHAPTER TWELVE

By midnight Meerkat Marais had beaten up three people whom he considered retarded enough to have entered his flat while he was away having his oats with the nympho. People that stupid were in a decided minority, and no matter how much thought he gave to the matter, he just could not think of a fourth. This was very upsetting because, as he knew from the blubberings of the ones he had put in a confessional mood, he was no nearer to finding the culprit and exacting his revenge.

Except that he had, to all intents and purposes, eliminated complete idiots from his list.

'Ja, that's a start anyway,' he consoled himself, as he crossed Leeman Street and approached the dry-cleaning depot. 'I wonder, I wonder . . .'

A flash of inspiration struck him outside the wig shop. What would Kramer do in this situation? How would he begin to solve a puzzle like this? With a lot of boring, routine questions, no doubt. But it was late, and there didn't seem to be anyone left around in the innocent-bystander class.

Dynamite was skulking in the tall weeds on the edge of the empty lot leading to the fire-escape stairs. For a cat that had made off with an entire roast chicken, Dynamite still had a lean and hungry look, which was both lacking in gratitude and deceitful. Meerkat kicked out as he went by, and Dynamite protested. Over against the far side of the vacant patch, someone grumbled in his sleep.

'Ho, ho!' said Meerkat, coming to a dead stop.

The epileptics: he'd forgotten about them. Five women and two men, old to middle-aged, all black, who had been discharged from hospitals and left to fend for themselves. They had somehow grouped together on the lot five months ago, and had dwelt there quietly ever since, rain or shine, with the crippled woman tending the fire while the others scavenged in garbage bins for food. They would almost certainly keep a sharp eye on anyone who came near them, fearing eviction or something worse.

Meerkat stumbled over the uneven ground towards where they lay huddled round their dying fire, clothed in sacks and rags. The legless man was clutching an iron pipe – perhaps he was good at throwing – and one of the women, not the cripple but the defective, was cradling a crazy sort of doll made out of a nylon stocking and stuffed with black horse-hair. Meerkat's first thought was to kick over their eating tins, and wake them up that way. His foot, however, stopped just in time.

It wasn't that he feared them in the slightest, but he did have a horror of unwanted publicity and, for the last three days or so, these horrible objects had been very much in the news. Some Christian kind of black or other had discovered them, told his minister about their way of life, and since then the *Gazette* had been digging up all sorts of excuses to drag the thing out. Even after the city council and the Bantu Affairs office had both said they weren't responsible for them, some people hadn't been satisfied. Yesterday a city businessman had offered them accommodation in Peacevale, provided he could be assured they were 'genuine cases', and in the meantime a smart lady from Morninghill way was coming down each day with a hamper of food. That was the snag : no doubt she was the type who would make a fuss if she found them a bit stiff in the morning, and he would have to tread lightly, no matter how difficult it might prove to make them remember things.

'Wakey, wakey, my friends! Wakey, wakey!' said Meerkat, very sweet and low indeed. 'Would you like some cigarettes?'

Dynamite, who was poised to retrieve a chicken bone out of a crumple of tin foil, and looking fairly self-righteous about it, flattened his ears at that hiss of sound and fled.

CHAPTER THIRTEEN

Thursday dawned bright and clear, bringing a zip to the morning
in two houses out of three.

Zondi woke at six, shook his head to see if Mama Bhengu's gin
had done any damage, felt nothing, and slipped out of the double
bed that he shared with his wife Miriam and their three youngest.
Placing his feet carefully, for the next ones up had graduated to
sleeping on mattresses spread on the rammed-earth floor, he made
his way over to the door leading into the other room of their
house, the kitchen. The twins, so big and strong now, were
stretched out one under the table and the other on the settee that
the Widow Fourie had given them. She had also given them an
old electric kettle and an old electric iron; only the latter was any
use – although it didn't retain heat too well, it could be warmed
up on the stove – but they had not returned them for fear of
hurting her. It was really, mused Zondi, as he glanced at them
with Bradshaw on his mind, a little like displaying upside-down
antiques. Then, humming to himself, his mood sweetened and
made proud by the beautiful faces of his sleeping children, he
gave the Primus stove a few pumps and lit it. Miriam, who had
worked as a housemaid for many years, knew no better treat than
to be served a cup of tea in bed.

What a morning! thought Kramer. Sun streaming in; the smell
of bacon frying; the Widow Fourie just in her bra and pants
bending over him. Bliss.

'Trompie,' she said, shaking him by the knee. 'Trompie, it's
after eight and even the kids are out of the house – I've sent them
to school with the maid this morning, just so I could make sure
you ate your breakfast for a change. Trompie?'

A gentle snore.

'Ach, stop fooling, hey? You're the one who woke me up to
say you'd a lot to do today!' She leaned over to blow in his ear,

and her long blonde hair tickled his bare chest excruciatingly. 'Tromp! Now listen! Time to get up!'

'Time to get up?'

'Ja, I – Trompie Kramer!'

'Orders are orders,' he said, pulling her struggling form down on top of him, and then rolling over to sink into a pneumatic heaven. 'I'm yours to command, hey?'

'You don't,' she giggled, 'have to take me so literally!'

'Lady,' replied Kramer, 'I'm going to take you right now, any way I want, so you better grab hold of the bedposts!'

But it wasn't like that. It was slow and gentle and, above all, familiar.

'Chrissy!' said Anneline Strydom, stripping the sheet off his unaccustomed nakedness. '*I want you, Chrissy!*'

His eyes opened, blinked at the strong sunlight, and then widened in disbelief. 'Not again,' he mumbled. 'Not when there are servants – '

'Servants! And what do you think those servants are doing? You want to know? Get your dressing-gown on and I'll show you!'

Strydom suddenly realised his wife was in the most terrifying rage. He cupped a hand over himself and hopped smartly out of bed, getting his slippers on the wrong feet at first, and putting on his dressing-gown inside out, so that he couldn't find the cord. Out of the corner of an eye he noticed the time on their dressing-table clock was eight-twenty.

'Look at the time!' he gasped. 'Why haven't I been woken up before? Dr Meyer is operating at – '

'Christian Strydom, say one more word and that will be *it*,' Anneline warned between clenched teeth, and gripped him firmly by the elbow. 'You and me are going to take a look at my kitchen.'

Strydom stood in the kitchen doorway and looked. He looked left, he looked right, he looked at the floor and at the ceiling. In fact everywhere he looked there were snails, and behind each snail was a long, silvery trail, making the room appear, if you weren't a conscientious housewife, surprisingly pretty and unusual. The cook and the garden boy were going round with wet cloths and a bucket.

'Never, never again!' said Anneline Strydom.

And he was a little too apprehensive right then to ask her exactly which of two dire possibilities she meant by that.

Kramer's second start to the day was every bit as satisfying as his first, and again he had the Widow Fourie to thank.

'Can I see that list of names of his friends?' she asked, setting down a huge plate of fried eggs, farm sausages and tomatoes. 'You say there's nobody called "A.K." on it?'

'It's in my top pocket in my jacket over there,' replied Kramer, tucking in hurriedly.

The Widow Fourie looked through the list and set it aside while buttering herself a ladylike small piece of rusk. 'I know where you should begin,' she said. 'You should ring the Digby-Smiths and ask them if they've been able to –'

'Done that, while you were in the bathroom.'

'And?'

'Digby-Smith claims that the list contains every single acquaintance, friend, companion et cetera that Hookham ever had. His wife couldn't sleep last night, so she got out all his old school photographs, the letters of congratulation her mother received when he won the DFC, everything; and she went through the lot. Net result was those nine new names on the bottom.'

'Ah, I wondered why they were in your handwriting.' She crunched into the rusk. 'There could be a simple answer, you know, Tromp. These letters "A.K." could stand for the name of a place or a thing, instead of for a person.'

'Uh-huh, that's not bad.'

'Haven't you done any thinking about this yet?' she teased, and poured him his coffee.

'None. I'm starting fresh this morning, and I'm taking one thing at a time.' He wolfed down his second sausage. 'As for "A.K.", it could be also the initial letters of two words he didn't want someone else to poke their nose into, or even a mixture of words and names.'

'Like "Alert Kramer"?'

Kramer laughed; the Widow Fourie often surprised him with her quickness and, as in this example, her command of English. 'But I still go for it being a name,' he said. 'My hunch tells me I'm right. And, besides, Hookham uses initials for names in his diary in other places.'

A shadow passed fleetingly over the Widow Fourie's face. 'So you're working with a hunch this time? Be careful about that, Tromp – it's got you into trouble before.'

'Zondi agrees with me.'

'Well, a native would. They're full of that kind of thing.'

Kramer's involuntary expression was less fleeting.

'All right,' agreed the Widow Fourie, puzzled but making her voice jolly again, 'let's say your hunch is right about this being a name. Whose name? The name of the person he went to see the night he was killed?'

'It's as good a guess as any, my girl.'

'And you've not one clue who it was? Even what sort of person?'

'Through Jonty the hair man I heard that Mrs Digby-Smith thought it was an "old flame" of his, but she won't repeat the same to me.'

'No, not now she knows he's been murdered,' said the Widow Fourie. 'We get her kind in the shop sometimes, and they can't take any sort of scandal. An "old flame" is an old girl friend in Afrikaans, isn't it?'

'Correct.'

'And Hookham left here when he was only a teenager?'

'Correct.'

The Widow Fourie picked up the list again, trying not to get butter on it. 'One, two, three, four – hmmm, there are nine names starting with an "A"; take away the men and you are left with four again. It could be one of those, you know.'

'Hey?'

'Well, doesn't it stand to reason, if he's been out of touch for so long, that he'd know her by her maiden name? People didn't get married as teenagers in those days, hey?'

'Phone,' said Kramer, sinking his coffee at a gulp.

The Widow Fourie followed him through into the sitting room and unearthed the Trekkersburg and District directory.

'Er, 'ullo, lady,' Kramer said, when there was a reply to the first number he dialled. 'Ah's giving you a bell about your income tex form, hey? Certain irregularities.'

There was a giggle behind him, and the Widow Fourie, who had never heard his civil servant routine before, which was an Afrikaner speaking English with a terrible accent, bit on a thumb.

'Ja, income tex office – tex, same as you puts in carpets to keep them flat. You got it. Now Ah'll jist come rart out with it, hey? You's has totally failed to print in your maiden name in block capital letters. Hell, Ah should know what's on the blerry ding! Come again?'

Kramer clicked his ballpoint pen, and scribbled quickly on a message pad. Then he nudged the Widow Fourie, and she read out in an excited whisper, 'Angela Elizabeth Kendall!'

'Ach, that's all rart, lady! Heppy to oblige, hey? Bye-bye now . . .'

'We did it!' whooped the Widow Fourie. 'First shot too!'

'Ach, it was a four-to-one chance,' said Kramer, going back into the breakfast room for his jacket. 'And who knows? We could easily be wrong still.'

Zondi lounged against the side of the Chevrolet and waited to see whether curiosity would compel Mrs Westgate's gardener to find some excuse for conversation.

It was a curious garden, come to think of it. From a distance, as he and the Lieutenant had bowled along through the dry, yellow scrub to the south of the city, it had looked like a green mat left lying on the sear hillside. There was this definite edge to its regular shape, a sharp contrast of gentle growth against harsh survival, which could be simply explained as the difference between irrigation and the mean annual rainfall. And yet, when one arrived at the conventional small bungalow, with its pink brick, corrugated asbestos roofing and burglar guarded windows, there was something else about the garden that seemed to cut it off even more. Zondi looked carefully at the arrangement of meandering, stone-flagged paths, at the various kinds of trees, and at the choice of well-tended plants, flowers and shrubs. It seemed slightly strange to see a willow tree so far from running water, and there were some clumps of bullrushes too, but quite a few whites appeared to regard such things as essential, without ever using them to weave something useful. He also noted there were very, very few weeds. But further than that, never having been a garden boy himself, he felt too ignorant to venture. Until he looked again at the rockery a few yards in front of him, and realised that, quite unlike any other rockery he had ever seen, this one had no little cacti growing on it. There were no saw-toothed aloes with their fine yellowy-red flowers in the garden either – although they grew wild on the slopes all around – and no rose bushes. Never, on reflection, had he ever come across a garden of this type without rose bushes. And then it dawned on him : what made this garden so subtly at odds with its thorn scrub surroundings was that, as far as he could tell, there wasn't a prickly thing in it.

Driven by his own curiosity, Zondi flicked away his cigarette and went down some steps into a sunken area to where the gardener was working, still with his back turned, in blue overalls and a huge, floppy straw hat. He was seated on his haunches, apparently weeding, and kept right on humming even when Zondi's shadow had fallen over him.

'Greetings, my brother,' said Zondi.

The gardener turned and looked up. 'Hello, Mr African,' he said in English, quite unperturbed.

It was Zondi who felt mildly startled. The gardener was a white man with the face of a slanty-eyed, small-mouthed child, and he had a friendliness that was like a rush of oven air.

'Hau, sorry, my boss ! I did not mean to disturb you !'

'Are you looking for work?'

'No, boss. Look, I – '

'I can ask Mummy to give you work if you're hungry.'

Zondi smiled and squatted down a few feet away, alert now to the sort of simple, kindly mind he was dealing with. 'Many thanks, sir, but I am not hungry for I have work already.'

'Is that car yours, Mr African?' The heavy work glove pointed back over Zondi's shoulder. 'Mummy's car isn't like that.'

'What is Mummy's car like?'

'Smaller, and it's azalea colour, not geranium.'

Zondi raised his brow. 'But I was told,' he said, 'that your mummy's car was a big green one called a Rover.'

'Then you *are* silly.'

'Why, my boss?'

'Because the big green one is Uncle Bonzo's.'

Mrs Angela Elizabeth Westford, *née* Kendall, went to stand gazing out of the window overlooking her front garden. Against that background, and framed by the curtains and pleated pelmet, she reminded Kramer of an oil painting he had seen quite recently, during an enquiry at the National Heritage Museum in Oak Street. The painting had been done from inside an ox-wagon, and it had shown a pioneer mother looking out from beneath a tattered canvas tilt at new pastures green – so green, in fact, that they owed more to the fertility of an artist's imagination than to anything else, and everyone knew what terrible buggers artists were for spreading bullshit. Mrs Westford, despite her obvious English ancestry, seemed to be of the very same stock as that Voortrekker vrouw : she was sturdily built, plain in feature, proud in carriage, and gave an immediate impression of steadfastness, devotion and courage. Yet she could never be painted properly in oils, being nearer to a water-colour in the translucent quality of her skin, the washed-out blue of her eyes, and the runny splotches of red on her neck and chest and upper arms, while the shape of her head showed plainly beneath a thin swirl of prematurely white hair. She wore stout leather sandals, a mustard-coloured smock, and had a man's watch with a wide strap on her left wrist.

'I'll be all right in a minute,' she said.

Trust me, thought Kramer, to come barging into a home, where they didn't get newspapers and hadn't a radio, and then to come straight out with a leading question which had rocked Mrs Westford on her feet. 'That's fine – I understand, hey? I'm in no hurry.'

'I see Timmy's making a new friend,' she said, smiling. 'He loves Africans: I think it's their openness and joy at living – neither do they have some of the prejudices we go in for, which makes things so much easier for him.' She turned round and invited Kramer to sit down with a gesture of her hand. 'My son's a mongol, you see, Lieutenant Kramer, and a haemophiliac. Wouldn't you be more comfortable on the sofa?'

'Honest, this chair is ideal, Mrs Westford,' said Kramer, staying on the wooden upright at the table. 'Like I say, you must forgive us for thinking you knew already about Mr Hookham.'

'Nothing to forgive; you weren't to know what an isolated life Timmy and I have chosen to live out here. Quite the worst part – which you couldn't have known either – was that I'd half been expecting something awful to happen. Nothing something – well, quite as . . .'

Kramer waited until she had stopped biting her lip and had

looked back at him again. 'Was this just a feeling you had, Mrs Westford? Or was it something more specific?' With an intelligent witness, it was often possible to rely on their own analytical powers.

'Timmy started me off thinking like that. Last week some time, he came to me and said that Uncle Bonzo wasn't so sad any more. I think it was on Wednesday, but I can't be certain.'

'Not the day after he'd been to the flying club social?'

'Yes, now I come to – but how would you know that?'

'Tuesday,' said Kramer, making a note.

Mrs Westford walked over and sat down on the edge of the sofa. 'In fact, now I've had a chance to think, Lieutenant Kramer, how did you discover that Ted was visiting us?'

'Was it such a secret?' asked Kramer, lightly.

'No, I shouldn't have thought so, but for my sake he'd probably not want the Digby-Smiths to know, and you don't seem to have spoken to anyone else we have in common.'

'For your sake, Mrs Westford? What exactly – ?'

Her smile had a kink in the middle. 'It's one of those silly private things that take an awful lot of explaining, and even then I'm not sure you'd understand. There are two things I detest in this world, Lieutenant: one is being patronised and the other is being pitied. Between them, Rupert and Lillian Digby-Smith are very good at doing both.'

'That I can believe,' murmured Kramer, with a kinked little smile of his own.

'Can you? Of course, you're Afrikaans! How silly of me!'

They shared smiles then, and their rapport, which had been building up surprisingly quickly, was completed.

'Well, where does one start, Lieutenant? I don't want to bore you with sordid details! Very simply, Ted and I were sweethearts when the war broke out – I'm not sure if we weren't actually in love, but it's so difficult to tell at that age. One feels everything so *passionately* as a teenager, doesn't one?'

'Ted's what you used to call him then?'

'I still – ' She swallowed. 'Yes, that's right. Timmy calls him Uncle Bonzo, because Bonzo is – was – which is it? – a name he's awfully proud of. The King actually said to him, "Well done, Bonzo Hookham!" or something like that, when he went to Buckingham Palace to be decorated. But I was . . .'

'Saying about passionate ideas, Mrs Westford.'

'My undoing, when I look back on it. War came into them, of course, and I absolutely loathed the whole business. I couldn't see any excuse for people killing each other and all the rest of it. Ted took the opposite view, told me all sorts of things about fascism which I didn't understand then, and we ended up having a terrible row. I stopped seeing him and started going out, really to be spiteful, with Rupert Digby-Smith who was a pacifist. Or claimed to be one, until social pressures made it time for him to enlist, and then he invented this story about black-outs which I've never quite believed. The point of all this, however, is that Ted was so hurt that he disappeared overnight, and the next thing I knew, he'd joined the RAF – this country wasn't properly in the war then, and I'd not expected a move like that.'

'Hell, that was tough luck, hey?'

'I've only myself to blame,' replied Mrs Westford, and wound up her watch. 'I've always had myself to blame, one way or another. I got rid of Rupert immediately – although he made a tremendous fuss, and wanted to get engaged right away – and did what I could as a nurse to help the war effort here, not being able to leave a pair of aged parents and follow him to England. Oh, Rupert went on pestering me, and when news arrived that Ted had married some Alice or other, he was round like a shot with his final proposal. Out of sheer perversity again, I accepted another proposal I'd had from a Scottish doctor, a man very much older than myself, which is possibly why it was disastrous when Timmy arrived as his sole heir. Rupert told me I'd live to regret the day – he was perfectly right for once – and Lillian Hookham, a dreadful little social climber who had been hovering in the wings, sank her claws into him. They were married the very same week.'

'That was deliberate, hey?' wondered Kramer.

'Oh, I think one could be quite sure of it. And then, of course, when I became pregnant before she did, a mutual friend tells me there was a fearful to-do, with her blaming him and –'

'Vice versa?' Kramer cut in.

'Precisely – and you're right to smile, that part of it was mildly hilarious. You can, however, imagine the I-told-you-so smugness I had to endure when my baby turned out to be – well, as I've described him. This reached new heights when Hugh – Dr Westford – found he couldn't bear having Timmy anywhere near him, and decided to desert me.'

'He just ran off?'

'Not quite. He bought me this house and garden – it was a farm manager's cottage going cheap, but I loved it from the first moment – and saw to things like providing proper protection for a woman living on her own in the country.'

'Ja, I noticed what good burglar guards you've got on the windows,' said Kramer, nodding at them. 'Then what?'

'He went, went back to Scotland. Our divorce came through sixteen years ago, but I'll say one thing for him, he's always been very good with his maintenance payments. Timmy and I are very happy here, and we want our world just to stay the way it is. If Ted had told the Smiths that he'd been visiting us, that would have been a marvellous excuse for them to insist on having us over for a meal, just to see if Timmy eats with his hands, or to drop in unexpectedly with snippets of news about Ted when he'd gone home to England. That's rather a long answer to a short question, I'm afraid, but I find living virtually on one's own can make one appallingly talkative!'

Kramer wished her laugh hadn't been so embarrassed. 'Ach, no, Mrs Westford, the point is that I totally agree with you and Mr Hookham in saying nothing about this. And you're quite right, you know, they haven't forgotten you. Your name appears nearly at the top of a list of friends and acquaintances they gave me, only I must quickly add that they themselves hadn't worked anything out. After all, you and Mr Hookham hadn't parted on the best of terms, hey?'

'Then how did you work it out, Lieutenant?'

'From some initials in his diary,' replied Kramer. 'I wonder if we can now turn to when you two met up again, and to anything you remember about Mr Hookham after that flying club social?'

'Can I ask one more little question of my own first?' said Mrs Westford, looking at him with a keen twinkle in her eye.

'Please! Go right ahead!'

'Since when, Lieutenant, have Ah bin required to prints my maiden name in a blerry income tex form? Do you know, I'd been puzzling over that all morning until you arrived with your bombshell.'

121

CHAPTER FOURTEEN

The heat haze held the garden in a shimmer, making Zondi and Timmy Westford, who were chatting away as they pulled up weeds together, look like wobbly projections against a corrugated backdrop of green. Kramer had a shrewd idea what was making the sly little bugger look so well contented : for once he was getting his next instalment in the Bonzo Hookham saga ahead of time. It would be interesting to see how they compared.

'A penny for your thoughts, Lieutenant.'

He turned and saw that Mrs Westford had taken up some embroidery. 'Ach, nothing specific – just like this weird feeling of anxiety you felt building up. I mean we've been through all the main points once already, and yet that remains unexplained.'

'Don't you ever feel something *instinctively*?'

'Ja, but there's usually some reason, some little thing that triggered it off,' he replied, quoting the Widow Fourie's parting remark that morning. 'Do you think we could go through it all once more, please? What you tell me could be very important.'

'I don't really see how, but I don't mind,' said Mrs Westford, shrugging. 'The only condition I make is that I must be free to start Timmy's lunch at half past twelve. Not having servants is a blessing if one values one's privacy, but at times like these it can be a bit of a snag.' Her eyes welled up then, for the fact of Hookham's death had broken through her self-protective layer, and she bent quickly over her sewing.

'Right, there's no need to repeat the first part – the part, that is, before the flying club social. He heard your name mentioned at the Strongpieces', as per diary, and –'

'Please – let's not, if we don't have to.'

Kramer sat down at the table and opened his notebook. 'So we'll start with the day after the party, when Timmy said he didn't seem so sad any more. Why should that worry you? Wasn't it good news?'

'It was – well, rather sudden. There were logical reasons for a change, I realised that. He had been lifted out of himself, put into company with people who spoke the same language – about aeroplanes anyway. And, of course, he loved teasing Rupert about supposedly being so taken by Archie Bradshaw.'

'Did you think there was some truth in that?'

'Heavens, no! Ted saw right through him.'

'Oh ja? This is new.'

'Not in certain circles, it isn't!' said Mrs Westford, almost managing a laugh. 'Everyone knows how that vulture swept down from Johannesburg on the Ye Olde England pickings he could make among the innocent old dears of Trekkersburg. He even descended on us when our marriage broke up, and tried to convince me that the extremely valuable chair you're sitting on wasn't worth a penny. Only greedy, rather stupid people like Rupert are blind to that old rascal's wiles – or the doddery, as I've said – and Ted's view was that he wouldn't trust him further than he could spit. We had a giggle about Rupert, and that was it.'

'Uh-huh. The change was too sudden.'

'Or to put it another way,' said Mrs Westford, 'I suppose I was frightened he was on an "up" that would have its "down" soon enough. Grief is filled with these – what, hazards?'

'Ja, I know. Could it be your feelings were based on the fact that "down" never came?'

'Where do you – ?'

'I get that,' said Kramer, 'from everything you say after that point.' And he checked with his notes. 'You use words like "lively", "excited", "stimulated" et cetera.'

'How odd!'

'Let's go on,' Kramer suggested. 'Mr Hookham didn't come by this way again until the Saturday night, after the first story had appeared in the papers about Friday's near-fatal shooting.'

Mrs Westford nodded. 'Timmy and I were disappointed, of course, but I was glad for his sake that he wasn't having to rely on our company any longer. He said he'd been looking up two of the ex-RAF chaps he'd met – not people I'd have heard of, because they lived quite a way out in the country.'

'It's a pity I haven't addresses to go with these five names I've got,' Kramer grumbled, annoyed with himself for having not delegated the job to someone.

'But I'm sure he didn't mention names.'

'What I meant was the addresses will help me to narrow this down,' explained Kramer. 'Now was there an inconsistency in Mr Hookham's behaviour that also boosted your anxiety?'

'In what way?' she asked, surprised.

'A few moments ago, Mrs Westford, you said that Mr Hookham had complete contempt for Bradshaw, right?'

'You're putting words into my mouth, Lieutenant!'

'Ach no, all I –'

'All you're doing is wording it too strongly. Ted just didn't think much of Mr Bradshaw, and felt sorry for his little wife, who seemed rather nice. When he feels contempt for someone, Ted makes jolly sure that they and everyone else know it!'

'Okay, he didn't think much of him. And yet, if Mr Digby-Smith is to be believed, he reacted very strongly to the news Bradshaw had been shot. Did this jar with you?'

Mrs Westford frowned. 'No, and I still can't see why it should. In fact, I found it reassuringly *consistent* with his character. As surprising as it might seem to us, Lieutenant, I sincerely believe that Ted Hookham underwent some form of "culture shock", as they call it, when he returned to South Africa. He repeatedly said he couldn't adjust to the level of violence, and when a violent thing was done to someone he knew, even a chance acquaintance like Bradshaw, it epitomised the whole thing for him. It wasn't Bradshaw he cared so much about, but the *idea*.'

'And he said all this is to you that Saturday night?'

'Ted didn't have to, Lieutenant,' she replied quietly. 'We had become very close.'

Kramer had already had a taste of her powers of insight, but he still wasn't getting the answers he wanted. 'Sticking just to what *was* said,' he stressed gently, 'can you remember anything to do with the RAF?'

'No, not apart from his usual chit-chat with Timmy, who dotes on some war comics he's had for years. They made a practice of – wait a moment! You've just brought it back for me, word for word. Do you know that first story in the papers?'

'Ja, just saying Bradshaw had been shot, and before he started talking about a giant.'

'That's right. Well, after the three of us had discussed it, Ted ended up by saying, "It's a devil of a thing to survive what we did, and then to end up darn nearly catching a packet like that! Jerry must have come at him from out of the sun, Timmy!" Then I spoiled his joke by saying it'd more likely have been Nemesis, and Timmy didn't understand that.'

'Christ,' said Kramer, under his breath. 'Just hold on a sec while I get that all down.'

'What's so significant about — ?'

'The way he worded it!'

'But that was for Timmy's benefit, Lieutenant. Ted had been explaining to Timmy that a fighter pilot's weak spot was — '

'Ja, consciously maybe, but subconsciously — listen, did Mr Hookham make any other jokes?'

Mrs Westford's smile was bitter-sweet. 'He was always joking! Although perhaps it isn't surprising that Rupert didn't tell you that.'

'You saw him the next night?'

'Timmy did. I was lying down in my bedroom next door with a dreadful migraine, and the pair of them sat in here making aeroplane noises.' She laughed softly. 'Then Timmy found the Sunday papers which Ted had brought me with that ridiculous "giant" story in them — a man like Bradshaw would obviously have to be attacked by someone bigger than him! — and Timmy became so over-excited, jumping about and pretending to be a giant himself, that I had to call out and ask Ted to go home. He was awfully apologetic when we saw him next on Tuesday night.'

'Can you remember any funnies from then?'

'None. As I've told you, it wasn't a very funny occasion. I thought I'd never see him again, and . . .' She bit her lip hard.

'But if you could tell me again, in more detail, it might — '

'I really can't see the point, Lieutenant.'

'Ach, *please*, Mrs Westford,' said Kramer, although he disliked causing this woman any pain.

She kept her head well down over her embroidery as she spoke. 'Ted broke it very gently to us that he had decided to cut short his stay and return as soon as possible to England. He said he should never have come at a time when his mind was in such a turmoil, and then, suddenly, he was saying good-bye. Timmy went absolutely to pieces. He knows people tend to reject him, and he blamed Ted's wanting to leave on himself. I told Ted to go and sit on the bed in my room, and I took Timmy on my knee, here on the sofa. I told him all about Uncle Bonzo's garden being in desperate need of watering, and we tut-tutted over how long he had left it to bake in the sun, and finally Timmy was quite happy again. Then Ted came back to join us, and we took him to the door and – goodness, do you know, you've just done it again! I'd heard about your methods, but I thought you used hose-pipes and bright lights and things.'

'Was it another joke?' urged Kramer. 'Did he – ?'

'Ted looked at me and his last words were, "Well, old thing, perhaps I'll risk a final sortie. I could be back here on Thursday." That would have been tonight.'

'Hey? What's a sortie, Mrs Westford?'

'You really ought to ask Timmy that, but it's a sort of flight somewhere, a journey – I took it to mean he'd be making one last call on us, and you'll see I've bought some wine specially. A sortie is, well, a mission over enemy territory, or even . . . Oh my God, now I see what you're driving at!' She stood up and her embroidery fell to the floor. 'Look, you've only said that Ted had been shot, but now I want to know where and how!'

'It's twelve-thirty, Mrs Westford,' said Kramer.

N2134 Bantu Constable Nxumalo had a remarkable physique beneath his khaki uniform. He had never been in a gym, neither had he subscribed to any course involving dynamic tension. But he had spent a decade or more lifting and carrying some extremely dead weights about, and this had put considerable muscle on him, particularly in the region of his shoulders and arms.

'Er, Nxumalo,' murmured Strydom, appearing without warning in the refrigerator room.

'The doctor boss wants me?'

It alarmed Nxumalo to turn about and find himself being surveyed like something on a slab, for truly the district surgeon seemed to be looking right through his clothes. Then he saw a gleam of admiration, which was gratifying, and also a hint of surprise.

'You're even better than I thought, hey, Nxumalo? It's amazing the things you find right under your nose.'

'Boss?'

'Ach, just put the girl down and come this way.'

Nxumalo found a spare trolley to dump her on, and went through into the post-mortem room, where his lord and master, Sergeant Van, was standing red-faced and sweaty beside a strange contraption attached to an unattached arm.

'Hau!' exclaimed Nxumalo, breaking out into a sweat himself, then he realised to his great relief that it wasn't the arm about which his conscience was bad.

'What I've done so far,' explained Strydom, 'is I've ruled out the possibility that weight alone is sufficient to cause fractures of the ulna and radius bones at this point in the human arm.'

'What "weight alone"?' protested Van Rensburg. 'How could I pull if I didn't have a terrifying grip?'

'Now what I want you to try,' Strydom said to Nxumalo, who was trying to pick out Afrikaans words that he knew, 'is to apply maximum force to –'

'It can't be done,' said Van Rensburg, sniffing. 'I tell you, Doc, with all respect, it's just impossible.'

'Quiet, please, Sergeant – you have had your chance. Do you see these ropes, Nxumalo? Do you understand what they are designed to do?'

Nxumalo saw a piece of rope knotted around the arm, just below the wrist, and that one end of the rope was loose. The other end of the rope was attached to the hook at the bottom of a spring balance, and there was a second piece of rope, to provide him with something to pull on that side, attached to the ring on the top of the spring balance. If he took the two free ends and tugged, the amount of force would register on the spring balance's scale in between.

'Not understand, boss,' said Nxumalo.

'Well, that doesn't matter, hey? Just do as I say. Take that end and that end and pull like hell!'

'Hau, but I break these bones, boss!' warned Nxumalo, in a state of confused alarm.

'You do that, hey, and I'll give you one rand for each bone you snap! Ready now?'

'The rope's wrong,' objected Van Rensburg. 'I've heard it was a special kind of skipping rope with fancy handles.'

'This *is* that kind of skipping rope,' said Strydom. 'I personally went into the shop this morning and bought one.'

'They rooked you, Doc. This one's got no handles, hey?'

'I *cut* them *off*,' growled Strydom, implying a great deal more than he said, should this go on any longer. 'Take hold, Nxumalo.'

Having thrown his inhibitions to the wind, and agog at the thought of how many cheap cigarettes he could buy for two rand, Nxumalo flexed his pectorals and took up the strain.

'The arm's wrong,' objected Van Rensburg. 'That's a young arm, it can't be more than twenty, and so it'll break by sheer fluke after I've been weakening it up for an hour.'

'Stop!' Strydom ordered Nxumalo, then took a very deep breath. 'My patience, Sergeant, is close to the end of its tether. A young arm will, in actual fact, be harder to fracture than one belonging to a fifty-year-old man, and you, you great clown, have weakened nothing *except* your facile case with that stupid observation!'

Van Rensburg went his predictable purple, but less predictably, stood his ground. 'Oh ja? Let us see . . .'

'On your marks, Nxumalo!' snapped Strydom. 'Get ready! Go!'

Nxumalo applied a sudden violent jerk to the ends of rope in his iron hands. What happened next was over in an instant: the arm leapt up from the slab, the spring balance's hook straightened out, and the spring balance itself went whizzing just over Strydom's head, shattering a bottle of stomach contents on a shelf.

'Now *that* was clever!' chortled Van Rensburg. 'Hell, that was a fantastic trick, Doc! Why not do it again?'

'There's no need to do it again,' Strydom replied smugly. 'The measurement doesn't matter – the proof is enough.'

'Hey?'

'Look for yourself – both bones fractured, and in a manner identical to Hookham's!'

Nxumalo wiped his right palm in readiness to receive those two rand notes. Perhaps he would keep only the one, and present the other to his wife.

'The experiment's wrong,' objected Van Rensburg. 'In Hookham's case, the rope was knotted round two wrists, not just one. That's why I couldn't put my heart into it.'

Now Strydom started going purple. '*Wrong?*'

'By some fluke, Nxumalo has been able to break this set of bones,' conceded Van Rensburg. 'I'll even say, for the sake of argument, he used x amount of strength. But has he got twice x in his arms, Doc? Because, unless I'm very much mistaken, so far he has, as usual, only half-done a proper job.'

'It wouldn't take twice –'

'But there would be a difference, Doc! As a man of science, you can't deny that.'

Perhaps, thought Nxumalo, who couldn't follow a word of all this incessant arguing, he would keep fifty cents for himself, give forty cents to his wife, and distribute the remainder among his many children.

'Nxumalo?' said Strydom gloomily.

'Two bones broken, boss!'

'No, forget that now and go back to work, hey? It looks like I'm going to have to start this whole frustrating business back at Square One again.'

The Chevrolet's tyres squealed as Kramer swung from the dirt road out on the high-speed carriageway from the south leading back into town. In under a minute he was passing everything before him, and making up for all the time lost by the briefing he had given Zondi after leaving Mrs Westford and Timmy at their gate. Mother and son had stood together, hand in hand, not waving, and the memory of that made him sick to the stomach.

'But,' said Zondi, looking at his watch, 'it is only twelve-thirty now, boss, so why did you tell a lie to that woman?'

'I was trying to get out of telling her any of the details, Mickey. She was not to be fooled so easily, but I didn't mention about the rope and the car boot and all that. I just said he'd been found in Gillespie Street.'

'Then she will *know* you are a liar!'

'They don't get the papers, hey?'

Zondi used one of the two knives he carried in his trouser-tabs to clean the sand from under his fingernails. 'You seem to like this woman, boss.'

'Very much.'

'How was it exactly that Boss Hookham started to go to her place?'

'Remember his Basil Strongpiece entry in the diary? He went there without the Digby-Smiths, and naturally these people tried to fill him in on all that'd happened since he left for the war. Obviously people who weren't friends of the Smiths had a ball telling him about Rupert and his love life, and Hookham suddenly wanted to see his old girlfriend again. The Digby-Smiths had never mentioned in their letters that she'd had such misfortunes – I suppose they didn't want him to try and help her or something. Anyway, he made contact again, and that place must have become sort of an escape hole for him. At least he could talk about his wife to someone – nobody else wanted to listen, they said he mustn't dwell on it or he'd become morbid – and with her knowledge of suffering, Mrs Westford was just the right person. She thinks he was missing his grandchildren too, and Timmy was a bit of a substitute for that. Personally, I think it all went deeper than she lets on, but I'm not saying they were sleeping together or anything like that.'

'No, they did not,' said Zondi, with a grin. 'That is one of many, many things that I have learned this morning. Hau, I am ready to be a garden boy. Lieutenant! I know now the names of every flower! I also have learned the meaning of the word "flak" and what is signified by "coming out of the sun".'

Kramer nodded. 'And the bastard did come out of the sun, Mickey! Old habits die hard, perhaps! But Hookham could only have guessed that – all right, all right, subconsciously – if his mind had already started to put things together.'

'Hmmmm.'

'Look, man, this new "hmmmm" habit of yours is beginning to get right up my nose, hey?'

'I was just wondering if Boss Hookham would not automatically say that, because as Timmy has taught me, that was the *only* easy way of attacking a fighter pilot.'

'Okay, I'll accept that,' said Kramer, handing Zondi one of two cigarettes he had just lit. 'But let's go on from there. He also spoke of risking a "final sortie", and when you take that with the various descriptions of his behaviour, how do you read it then? Do you think that flying club social simply "lifted him out of himself"?'

Zondi remained in silent thought.

'And remember, Mickey, his thoughts of his bereavement seemed pushed aside. Clear your mind of everything else! In a nutshell, from then until he suddenly decided to get far away from here, how did he seem to behave? Ach, what makes *you* feel very alive?'

'Danger, boss,' replied Zondi without hesitation.

'Exactly, hey? Hookham smelled danger at that social! He went looking for these two other men, perhaps to find out if they felt the same way, and then he could be right when Bradshaw was shot. That's what made him shake a bit! Probably it was the same men he saw again on the Monday night, and by the Tuesday he was wanting out. Then he saw how upset he'd made Mrs West-ford and Timmy, and must have wanted to stay a little longer. So what does he propose? That he will *risk* one more sortie! He will take one more look and see if a theory of his is correct.'

'And if it is wrong after all, then he need not escape a danger which isn't real,' continued Zondi, nodding. 'But one thing strikes me which is strange.'

'Uh-huh?'

'Why didn't Boss Hookham come and see you, Lieutenant? There was an appeal in the Sunday papers he took out to that house, and Colonel Muller had stated clearly that we knew of no motive.'

'Put yourself in his shoes, man. If he suspected some ordinary motive, okay! But what sort of motive connects two men whose only link is their membership of the RAF? A pretty crazy one, if you ask me!'

'But Boss Hookham wasn't alive to make the –'

'Ach, Zondi, don't start buggering me around, hey? I'm saying Hookham smelled a motive when he smelled danger, but it all seemed so fantastic he couldn't be sure he was right, even after Bradshaw was shot. In fact, he was *never* sure, hence the final sortie which could have put his mind at rest, dispelling his fears and letting him stay on here.'

'Would a brave man run though, Lieutenant?'

Kramer grunted irritably. 'He didn't in the end, did he? He bloody took that risk, my friend, and it didn't come off! Now he'll never run anywhere. But there's another thing about even brave men that you should remember : we can all fight an enemy if he is clearly marked out to us; only, when we can't be sure who he is, whether he's even real or not, then we can run away from our own imaginings, cursing ourselves for fools. Have you never been a child in a dark room at night?'

'Such poetry, boss,' chuckled Zondi. 'What is the next step? The two men Boss Hookham went to see?'

'Damn right,' said Kramer, overtaking a traffic cop.

Zondi winced and slid down in his seat with his feet propped on the dashboard. 'I feel very much alive, Lieutenant,' he murmured. 'And you?'

CHAPTER FIFTEEN

Colonel Muller had reached the point where he needed every square centimetre of space on his enormous desk-top, simply to do his job. Information had been flooding in from all directions, sparked off by his brilliantly worded appeal in the *Trekkersburg Gazette* that morning, and he had enough stuff about gunshots, guns and giants to keep him busy for a week. That was the big snag, of course. None of the information had something so conclusive about it that his team of detectives had put a mark beside it in red. A typical example of this inconclusiveness was a report from an up-country farmer who had heard four gunshots on the night in question, only there had been a ten-minute interval between the first shot and the other three, and anyway, the first had sounded more like a rifle, while his wife was sure it was only three shots, fired at irregular intervals, and his son, a neighbouring farmer, had claimed to have found some guinea-fowl feathers on his land. If one multiplied this sort of thing by fifty – and more reports were coming in all the time – the mind boggled at how long it would take to check all these stories out. And as for the tall tales of giants he was receiving, there the mind *cringed*; some people had quite missed the fact that the actual description was not bizarre at all, there were plenty of good, strong South African men that size. Yet the phones were constantly ringing with anonymous tips about gargantuan malcontents, rugby-players who could tear the head off an ox, and one meter maid in Durban had been the subject of several more obviously malicious calls. That left the great pile of stuff on .32 Smith & Wesson revolvers, most of it plainly from people who didn't know a revolver from water pistol, and many of them seemed to have very dubious reasons for suggesting searches under so-and-so's bed. Colonel Muller had, in fact, also reached the point where he was looking for an easy way out of all this – and for somewhere to put his tray, simply to have his lunch.

Galt appeared at just the right moment. 'Allow me, sir,' he whispered, and lifted a pile of papers aside. 'Curry and rice, sir? You have no idea how that stuff stains the stomach walls.'

'I'm glad I haven't,' said Colonel Muller, sitting down and tucking the paper napkin into his collar. 'I would also be glad, unless this is very important, to get my meal out of the way before you go any further.'

'Well, it *might* be very important, sir, provided we can support the notion with enough other factors.'

'What's the topic, briefly?'

'Vegetable matter, sir.'

'Ach, then that's okay, hey? You just fire away.'

Galt produced a number of small labelled packets. 'These are all little snippets of things I have found on Hookham's clothes,' he explained. 'Of particular interest, are the samples taken from here and there under the straps of his sandals where they attach to the sole. I have identified soil, dry horse manure, grass seeds and fragments of the wattle-bark chips they use on the soft-track around the race-course. None of which is conclusive in itself, of course, but taken together they suggest something rather interesting. Now do you remember there was a little stream running near where Bradshaw was shot? My prize exhibit, Colonel Muller, is this.' And he handed over a tiny packet with a minute green speck in it.

'Salad?' speculated Colonel Muller, jovially.

'A water plant, sir – portion of its leaf. Moreover, from the condition of this specimen, we are confident that it was alive and growing within the last forty-eight hours. Had the period been any greater, then ... Well, it wasn't.'

'And you are certain of that?'

'Totally.'

Colonel Muller bit a chunk from piece of cheese, studied the even grooves his teeth had made in it, and willed himself to proceed with great caution. 'They've got wattle-bark chips down at the show ground,' he said. 'Horse manure is used on a lot of gardens, and soil – well, soil lies around everywhere. Is this water plant special to the stream by the race course?'

'It's very common, Colonel – found in streams, dams and rivers all over the province. But, when all these things are taken in conjunction . . .'

'They suggest Hookham was down at the race-course on Tuesday night – the night he got murdered?'

Galt closed his eyes and opened them again.

'Well, there were one or two reports of gunfire around the course,' said Colonel Muller, digging back into a stack. 'No, I'm wrong : three reports. A single shot heard in each case, and attributed at the time to some kid with a two-two after wood pigeon.'

'The ground on that side is very uneven, Colonel. We might have a little acoustic problem there.'

'Ja, but . . .' Colonel Muller frowned at his plate. 'I can't understand what would make Hookham go there at that time of the day. Nobody has reported seeing his car or anything.'

'After dark,' replied Galt. 'Has Lieutenant Kramer picked up anything that might make this seem more likely?'

'He could've done, I suppose,' Colonel Muller replied, getting up to pace restlessly. 'I'll just see if his car's in the vehicle yard.' He peered out of the window. 'No, dammit! Still not back. But I'll grab him the moment he comes in.'

'Thank you, sir. I'd like to think my hunch is justified.'

Colonel Muller waited at the window for a little longer after Galt had left. Then, taking a grip on his impatience, he went back to finish his lunch. The curry and rice were excellent, the bowl of fruit salad wasn't bad, but hunt as he might, he couldn't find his piece of cheese anywhere.

The honorary secretary of the Trekkersburg Flying Club was a very businesslike young man. His name was Robert du Plooi, and when he wasn't flying a Tri-pacer at the weekend, he managed a firm that hired out 'bleepers' to people who were still on the long Post Office waiting-list for telephones of their own.

'Our phone number is their phone number, in effect,' he explained, as he took Kramer through into his air-conditioned office. 'If somebody wants them, the call comes into our control room, which is manned twenty-four hours a day, and we "bleep" the client. After we have passed on the caller's number, the client then uses a call box or the neighbours' phone or what have you. Couldn't you blokes use something like it?'

'Ach, not really, Mr Du Plooi.'

'But surely it's time the South African Police started carrying personal radios?'

'Ja, there's a pilot scheme going on up in Johannesburg, but I sort of prefer my freedom.'

Du Plooi barked a short laugh. 'I'm with you, Lieutenant! End of sales-talk. You want this list of names given their addresses?'

'If possible, hey?'

'Find a seat then, and I'll run through it.'

Kramer sat down and watched Du Plooi pick up a gold Parker ballpen and start to write. He was a good-looking young Afrikaner; sandy hair, bottle-green eyes, dimpled chin, new suit, and his left ankle had a creak in it. The chrome-framed photograph on his desk showed a very pretty girl holding a baby.

'There, Lieutenant,' said Du Plooi, briskly, handing the list back. 'They're all our ex-RAF members, I notice. This can't be connected in some way with poor old Bonzo Hookham, could it?'

'Why leap to that conclusion, Mr Du Plooi?' asked Kramer, checking the addresses and finding that three men lived in outlying districts.

'Why not? Blokes with something in common, up to a point.'

Kramer looked up. 'Up to what point, exactly?'

'Well, Hookham was one of the glory boys we always hear about. You know the kind of thing : operating from an airfield in the English countryside, back to base in the morning, beer in the pub at lunch-time, a WAAF in a haystack before supper, cosy billets, all the home comforts. Four of the five on your list – that's excluding old Ernie Wilson – were with 104 and 142 Squadrons of 205 Group. Not in Lancasters either, but Wellingtons.'

'Oh ja?'

'Sorry, I'll explain properly. They carried on their offensive from Africa, lived in tents, had quite a rough time of it while they hammered away at Italy, Greece, places like Hungary and Yugoslavia, not touching Northern Europe. Ja, I'm sure I'm right in saying they never went anywhere near Germany, for instance. They did a fantastic job but, as you've shown yourself, hardly anybody seems to have heard of them.'

'Uh-huh, that's often the way,' murmured Kramer, tightening up. His mind had just been infected by the germ of an idea, and he needed a moment to run tests on it. 'You've seen some service yourself?'

'A little. I flew a helicopter gunship in Rhodesia for a while, donated a foot to the cause and landed up here. If you're wondering why we have this gang of 104 and 142 blokes on our doorstep, there's a little story to go with that. They all seem to have got a taste for Africa, like lots of people do, and –'

'This Ernie Wilson,' Kramer broke in, 'where was he based?'

'Scotland, I think.'

'But bombing Germany as well? A "Terrorflieger"?'

Du Plooi laughed. 'Good God, where did you pick that one up? Have you been reading Deighton's novel?'

'I got it from a man,' replied Kramer, 'who told me that Germans would butcher a "Terrorflieger" on sight.'

Young Du Plooi was no fool; he sat forward in his chair and the lobes of his ears went white. 'All right,' he said, 'Ernie flew over Germany, and so did Hookham and Bradshaw. But if you're trying to tell me that there's a link between that fact and what's happened –'

'Since your club social?' said Kramer.

There was a bemused silence while Du Plooi tried to adjust. A copy of that morning's *Gazette* lay on his desk, and he turned it round to read the main headline: *WAR HERO SHOT BY 'MAD GIANT' – Random Killer At Work, Warns Police Chief.* Then he sank back into his black leather, executive's swivel chair and shrugged.

'You obviously know far more about all this than I do,' he said apologetically. 'I just thought it was a bit of a fluke, that's all. Perhaps you'd better just ask me questions – if you've got any more to ask.'

'Can we start with the social, Mr Du Plooi?' said Kramer, more certain than ever now that no fluke was involved.

'I didn't see much of that. As secretary, I'm organising a lot of the time – seeing the drinks don't run out, that sort of thing.'

'Ja, I can appreciate that. But what about Mr Hookham? Have you any – ?'

'Hardly said a word to him, which I was sorry about – and I've been even sorrier since I read this. They can be a bit of a pain, his type, but he struck me as a nice guy and I'll always listen to their stories once. The first chance I got was when Bradshaw was monopolising him. They were talking about the best places to take dogs for a walk, comparing notes on it, and I tried then to break in. But Bradshaw was soon off on one of his amazing yarns about how he'd shot down half the Luftwaffe single-handed and I gave up.'

'So they spoke about the raids they went on?'

'Naturally! With sound effects and all the usual trimmings.'

'People standing near them could overhear this?'

'When the band wasn't playing, they must've done. Both were ticking quietly by this time, of course.'

'They'd been drinking for how long? Was this near the end of the evening?'

'Oh no,' said Dù Plooi, 'about half-way through. I tried again on my way back from the bandstand, where I'd been making some announcements, and by then they were swapping Stalag numbers. That could have been quite interesting, because I'd already heard that Hookham had escaped from his POW camp and made it right back to England, using disguises and all sorts. But Bradshaw was holding the floor about his own escape, and – '

'So that's something else they have in common?'

'Well, yes and no,' said Du Plooi, grinning. 'Archie didn't tell you he'd been a POW? I'm not surprised, really, because it wasn't one of the more glorious pages in his history! He can't avoid the subject quite so easily among the sort of people the club collects, so he tries to make a joke of it. His bunch were picked up in France in about two minutes flat, when one of them, he alleges, dressed up as a nun, let go a fart in a railway carriage. If that's true, I think we've all got a shrewd idea who that might have been!'

'Ja, no prizes for that one,' laughed Kramer.

'And I'm pretty sure Hookham didn't miss it either! But after the laugh had died down, I could see Bradshaw's never-ending blah-blah-blah was making our guest of honour's smile wear a bit thin, so I found an excuse to take him across to meet Ernie and the others. On the way over, I suggested to Hookham that he should come out and meet the family some time, and he seemed very grateful, so we left it that he'd give me a call when he had a Sunday free. Then Ernie and the others took over, practically carried Bonzo back to the bar, and they all had such a fantastic time there were complaints from two of the ladies that I had to cope with. Ja, I suppose if I must find a silver lining in all this, then it's how over-the-moon Hookham looked when Ernie and his pals carried him out and took him home.'

Kramer frowned. 'He didn't appear excited? Nervous?'

'I defy *anybody* to look nervous after what he'd put away that night!' chuckled Du Plooi. 'He was gurgling like my young son over there.'

Drank very heavily, Kramer added to his notes. *Obvious reaction to stress.*

'But if you're trying to push this "things in common" business any further, Lieutenant,' said Du Plooi, 'you come unstuck when you get to Ernie Wilson. In a literal sense, he never set foot outside England.'

'No, that non-active service side is irrelevant, thanks. What I want to know is, did you see Hookham speaking to anyone else, apart from his RAF colleagues, at any stage in the evening?'

'Umm, no, I can't say I did. But as I've already explained, I was running about and –'

'Fine. Now these guests were a mixed bunch?'

'To a degree – club members, regulars at our socials, parachute club kids trying to fix up free drops, one or two strange faces – but all loosely connected with flying, I'd imagine.'

'Different races?'

'Hey?' said Du Plooi, baffled.

'Ach, I meant nationalities, different nationalities,' said Kramer, then decided to cut a corner by being less subtle. 'Any Germans or people of German origin?'

Du Plooi reddened. 'That could depend – my mother's family are from the Lutheran community at Leeukop.'

'I'm making a fool of myself, hey?' said Kramer. 'So I might as well go the whole hog: any ex-Luftwaffe belonging to the club or at the social?'

'Not that I'm aware of,' replied Du Plooi, losing his look of annoyance and smiling. 'I see the line you're taking, but again I think you could come unstuck. The Luftwaffe dropped a few bombs themselves, you know – think of the Blitz, Liverpool, Coventry – and could have some, er, sympathy? Flying is its own brotherhood in a way.'

'Okay, but you agree it's feasible that this conversation could have provoked someone listening in?' persisted Kramer.

'It might have done, Lieutenant. I've known similar sorts of talk start a punch-up, but here I'm thinking more of rivalry between different air forces, that kind of thing. What I've certainly never come across is someone being provoked into – '

'A bad war experience could do permanent damage to the mind,' Kramer pointed out. 'Who knows how long it might simmer away inside until something goes snap?'

Du Plooi reached for his memo pad. 'What you want the committee to do is draw up a list of people at the social – am I right?' His quick, efficient mind was a tonic.

'Please, man, and as soon as possible.'

'Can't be done before tomorrow, I'm afraid!'

'Oh?'

'The chairman, John Hill, is crop-spraying in Zululand, and Dawie van Niekerk, he's the treasurer, is negotiating a deal in Port Elizabeth overnight. We do have a club guest book, of course, because of the licence, but – between you and me, and don't tell the Liquor Squad – things tend to get a bit sloppy on these occasions. The three of us will have to put our heads together, and even then you may find one or two names missing.'

Kramer stood up. 'I'll be grateful for anything. But how about a short list meantime? Leaving out people you are sure of?'

'Would that be wise, Lieutenant?'

It was a sound observation and, despite his extreme frustration, Kramer settled for the best list they could manage by two o'clock the next day. There were, of course, plenty of other things he could do in the meantime, including trying to cheat the killer of his next victim.

'Not so fast,' objected Colonel Muller.

It seemed the most ludicrous thing anyone could think of uttering after nearly two hours had been squandered in bringing the old stick-in-the-mud up to date with the investigation.

'But, sir,' said Kramer, who had just looked up Ernie Wilson's telephone number, 'I feel there's some urgency involved here! By five o'clock, Wilson could have left his work, and it might be difficult to contact him with our warning.'

'*Your* warning, Lieutenant.'

'Sir?'

'For a whole two hours I have listened to your theory and the evidence you claim supports it. A marathon session which began, let me make it quite clear, with me having no strong views one way or the other. Perhaps I was even a bit biased in favour of this hunch of yours, because a detective always likes to find a pattern.'

'Then surely, Colonel, you –'

'One moment, please! It is my turn to talk. Everything you learned from Mr Digby-Smith, give or take a few details, can be dismissed as background.'

Kramer bristled. 'Really? Are you dismissing the man's demeanour in that? The diary entry when he says he's feeling so alive? The man on the phone with a strange accent?'

'Hookham's reported demeanour was always in keeping with the straightforward and sympathetic explanations offered by two people who knew him well, his brother-in-law and his old girlfriend,' replied Colonel Muller, firmly. 'It is only when passed through the sieve of your personal theory that they take on qualities that are no longer humdrum.'

'What sieve?' began Kramer, growing angry.

'This idea of yours with all the holes in it, Tromp. The man goes out, has a hell of a thrash at the flying club, comes back so drunk that his writing in the diary is all over the place when he does his "comment", as you call it, and you can't accept he's just alive with happiness. Do you see? A piece of logic is missing there. And another piece then goes missing when we come to speak of the "strange accent". Which is more likely? Digby-Smith's belief that it really was an old school chum wanting to surprise Hookham? Or your processed version, in which we are meant to believe that a killer rang up to talk to his victim?'

'Perhaps he was just trying to discover Hookham's whereabouts that night, Colonel.'

'Ach! There you go again!'

'But what about Mrs Westford and what she had to say?' asked Kramer, digging his heels in. 'What about those "jokes" of Hookham's? Many a true word is spoke in –'

'Tromp, Tromp, Tromp,' sighed Colonel Muller. 'I've already touched on all that. Mrs Westford thought she understood both remarks – and so she probably did! – until your RAF obsession started twisting them for her. Tell me, after you reached that point in your interview, did she come out with anything else which seemed of importance?'

'Er, not that I remember, Colonel.'

'That proves my point. Don't get me wrong, hey? I listened to all that in high hope of hearing something to our advantage – I was on your side! But I ended up very disappointed. There was always a reasonable explanation for everything.'

'Which proves my point,' countered Kramer. 'I can't see how my deductions could be anything but reasonable, given the facts, and – '

'Lieutenant!' snapped Colonel Muller. 'Now don't you start trying to twist *my* words! Your explanations are nowhere near reasonable – they exist on a plane of total fantasy!'

'Oh ja? What's so fantastic about – ?'

'Germans taking revenge on these "Terrorflieger" blokes? The Second War World still going on in Trekkersburg? You seriously have to ask me *that*?'

Kramer shrugged. 'It was your idea in the first place, Colonel. You started off this case by saying the killer had to be mad, and what world do the mad live in, if it isn't a fantastic one?'

That put Colonel Muller back in his seat, but his head came up again just as quickly. 'That I admit,' he said. 'But I'll bet you right now that *his* fantastic reason for shooting these two is nothing so fantastic as the one you've dreamed up! Honestly, I find it embarrassing . . .'

'Embarrassing?' Kramer echoed in total disbelief. 'And that's why you don't want me to alert Ernie Wilson to the fact he could be next for the chop?'

'Do you want me to look a complete laughing stock in Pretoria? First we have bloody giants, next it's Germans on the warpath – what next? Homicidal gorillas from Mars?'

Hearing it summed up like that, Kramer's own sense of the absurd took the wind out of his sails momentarily, and his hunch – being, like most hunches, a fairly frail craft – drifted dangerously towards the jagged reef of self-doubt.

Colonel Muller struck. 'If you had found me one piece of corroborative evidence from *outside* your highly personal interpretation of all this, then you could do as you like, Lieutenant. But, before any more time is frittered away, there are these items of physical evidence to be examined, checked, double-checked, accepted or eliminated. You still haven't bothered to say what you thought of Galt's highly significant deduction.'

'Ach, that fits in with my theory too, Colonel,' said Kramer, rallying his reserves. 'Do you recall the part when Hookham went on a "final sortie" looking for this bloke? It's just possible he found him at the very same spot as Bradshaw was – no, what most likely happened is that he was bound up and taken there to be executed. In a crazy way, that could seem very fitting.'

'No, I'm not listening to any more of that rub –'

'Can you suggest how he got there, sir?'

Colonel Muller faltered for only a moment. 'Yes, he was taken there, like you suggest,' he said. 'What I'm disputing is the *motive*.'

Then Kramer had a sudden, quite brilliant idea.

CHAPTER SIXTEEN

Kramer's idea was this. If Bradshaw and Hookham had provoked someone with their boisterous reminiscences of death and destruction, and if Hookham had noticed this someone looking less than amused by their talk, then it stood to reason that Bradshaw might have noticed that someone too.

'I don't call that a brilliant idea,' grunted Colonel Muller. 'I call it further time wasted.'

'I only said a "quite" brilliant idea, sir – not a "very". In a way, it's a self-evident idea at this stage of the investigation.'

'Only if you subscribe to the lunatic link you've constructed between these two blokes. Why, for example, hasn't Bradshaw come forward with such information himself?'

Kramer smiled. 'Well, for a start, he's one hell of a thick-skinned bugger. I'm sure angry looks just bounce off him unnoticed.'

'Then what is the point in going to see him?'

'Prod his memory a bit, sir.'

'Oh no,' said Colonel Muller, wagging that hairy great finger again. 'I think you've fed enough people their lines so far, Lieutenant Kramer. Does he know about your RAF theory?'

'No, not since I've developed it. When I saw him yesterday, I just asked him and his wife to go over every factor they might have in common. Look, I promise I'll – '

Colonel Muller stood up. 'Promise nothing, Lieutenant. You still feel this is worth putting other things aside for? That this Mr Wilson could be in danger?'

'I do, Colonel.'

'Okay, then I'll tell you what : we'll give this old cat one more swing by the tail. But if you don't get your corroboration, then that whole avenue of enquiry is closed forthwith.'

'Fair enough,' agreed Kramer. 'I'd better get a – '

'Not so fast,' Colonel Muller again reprimanded him. 'I said *we'll* do this – together, hey? I'll do the talking, and you will just sit there, shut up and, let me warn you, don't try any hypnotism!'

What it was, Kramer thought, as they went down the stairs, to be trusted.

Zondi, who had been included in the party as its official driver, which lent the divisional commandant's descent to the remote back streets a degree of dignity, crouched beside the big, flashy Ford and watched a stag beetle trying to right itself on Kitchener Row.

'Uh! That's better – God, I was going mad in that place.'

Detective Constable 'Stormtrooper' Schoeman, who was so lightly built he appeared to go everywhere on tiptoe, had come out on the pavement outside the Bradshaws' house to run on the spot, swing his arms, and do some smiling. He was a good sort, young Schoeman; never familiar, never ill-mannered, and in a tight spot he had fists on him like a trip hammer.

'Hello, boss,' said Zondi, standing up. 'How long is your shift?'

'Ach, the usual, Zondi. I'm on two-to-ten, then that new bloke does the ten-to-six. At least by then this boring old bugger has gone to bed, and you can read or listen to the radio. If his son and him had one argument last night, they had about twenty, so I'm going to try and sell him the idea of going to the drive-in. Hell, I'll even fix him up with a popsie!'

Zondi laughed. 'Good luck, Boss Schoeman! Hau, once I had such a job – they made me this important man's house boy – and I nearly used my gun on him, I tell you! This is not policeman's work.'

'How long's Lieutenant Kramer staying? Have I got time to get some smokes from the shop?'

'Let us quickly drive there,' suggested Zondi, who liked not being ordered to go and buy them. 'Okay?'

'Ja, let's do it in style! Why not?'

They sneaked the car away from the front of Bradshaw's house, and then shot round the corner.

'The Lieut's going well on this case?' asked Schoeman.

'Very well, boss,' said Zondi. 'Moving very quickly.'

But, from what he had overheard of the Lieutenant's latest

notions about vengeance-seeking Germans, he was beginning to doubt seriously his sense of direction.

Mrs Bradshaw was in shorts and a low-cut blouse, and Colonel Muller, rather touchingly, couldn't keep his eyes off her. It was the one saving grace of an interview which had done nothing so far to confirm any of Kramer's deeper and more pressing suspicions.

'You realise why I must keep on about this social?' the Colonel said to her. 'We in the CID have our methods, you see, and establishing the pattern of a crime is most important. Not only does it help us to piece together what has gone before, but it allows us to predict the future.'

'Goodness!' exclaimed Mrs Bradshaw, plainly flattered by his kindly attentions. 'Isn't that marvellous, Archie?'

'I see nothing marvellous in having to repeat myself forty times over,' muttered Bradshaw. 'What am I supposed to have said anyway, that might've made somebody look threateningly at me?'

'Before I answer that, Mr Bradshaw, I want you to pause a minute – close your eyes even! – and cast your mind back one final time. You're standing talking to Mr Hookham, you two are laughing together, and suddenly you see these eyes on you! You feel somebody is staring at you from behind somewhere! Or later, as you're moving round, socialising, somebody cuts you dead.'

Kramer winced.

'Close your eyes, Archie!' commanded Mrs Bradshaw.

Bradshaw cast a despairing glance at Kramer, and flopped back in his study armchair, closing his eyes as requested. Colonel Muller's eyes then met Mrs Bradshaw's eyes, lingered, and reluctantly moved back to the witness under interrogation. Bradshaw had apparently dozed off.

'Er-um, Mr Bradshaw, sir?' said Colonel Muller.

'Mmmmm . . .'

'What can you see now? In your mind's eye so to speak?'

'Faces. Happy, smiling faces. People laughing at my jokes. My wife's face when I'm talking about fishing.'

'Good, good! Now think of another topic you discussed with Mr Hookham.'

'There's a lady present, Colonel.'

'Oh Archie!' giggled Mrs Bradshaw, but looked sad.

146

Colonel Muller flushed. 'Ja, no, that wouldn't be relevant,' he reassured everyone hurriedly. 'Perhaps it would be all right for me to prompt you a little at this stage.' He caught Kramer's baleful stare. 'And I'll tell you how I'll do that : I'll say what you *weren't* saying at the time that interests us.'

'God,' sighed Bradshaw, very quietly.

'You weren't, for instance, telling Mr Hookham about the time you were a prisoner-of-war and escaped dressed as a nun.'

Bradshaw's eyes shot open and he looked directly into Kramer's delighted gaze.

'Funny you forgot to mention that before, hey?' said Kramer. 'Mind you, there are the different versions.'

'Lieutenant !' snapped Colonel Muller.

'Sorry, sir. I hope I haven't broken the trance.'

'Eyes closed again, Archie !' ordered Mrs Bradshaw, who shone with gleeful, if suppressed, enlightenment. 'I'll make Colonel Muller promise this *will* be the very last time.'

'I promise,' he said, unbidden. 'And do you remember talking about the best places to take a dog for a walk? Did you tell Mr Hookham about the side of the race-course? Well, not that conversation either.'

Bradshaw gave Kramer an ugly look, then sank back, knitting his fingers together. 'If it wasn't that, then it must have been . . .' He smiled cynically to himself, as if he had become reconciled to this ridiculous game. 'Bonzo told me about his factory, his flight out on South African Airways, his time in the Raf . . .' Then the smile vanished and was replaced by a blank, faintly sour expression.

Kramer leaned forward.

'Shhhh !' cautioned Colonel Muller.

'Think hard !' urged Mrs Bradshaw, whose instincts were good. 'Think hard, Archie !'

It became so silent that the muted hum of the swimming pool's filtration pump grew quite distinct.

'No good,' said Bradshaw, opening his eyes and sitting up. 'I had a damned good time at that social, swapped stories with Bonzo, ran over a few dogfights, the big job I acted as pathfinder on, and that's it. I can't remember causing any upset to anyone, and if I'd seen somebody looking at me aggressively, then I'd have punched the bastard on the nose.'

'He would,' confirmed Mrs Bradshaw, with another of those giggles that had a sad ending. 'My husband always stands up for himself! It's his motto.'

Colonel Muller turned away from Bradshaw's self-satisfied smirk and looked at Kramer, who was feeling sick and defiant all at the same time. That wasn't the only fish he had to fry.

'Can I speak now, Colonel?'

'Oh, before you do, Lieutenant – if you'll excuse me butting in,' said Mrs Bradshaw, laying a hand on Colonel Muller's hand on the armchair beside her, 'I want this gentleman here to explain how the "pattern" idea works.'

'It doesn't always work,' replied Colonel Muller, with a shrug of his shoulders. 'Without going into all the tedious details, in this instance Lieutenant Kramer's theory was that the killer was taking his revenge on former members of the RAF who bombed Germany during the last war.'

'But Archie has never bombed anyone!' she said indignantly. 'How very unfair!'

Bradshaw snorted scornfully. 'That's a bit bloody far-fetched, isn't it? I mean – oh for God's sake!' And his laughter hurt his bullet injury, and he sucked in his breath.

'Does it hurt?' Kramer enquired, glad that it did. 'But what you can't deny, Mr Bradshaw, is that you assisted those bombers to carry out their raids, and so carry the same amount of blame in the eyes of someone who suffered. You could even say they regarded it as a war crime.'

'Rubbish!'

'Say what you like, Mr Bradshaw, you and Bonzo Hookham are linked by bombing for the RAF. One man shooting at both of you proves that.'

'Even greater rubbish, Lieutenant! It's a sheer coincidence, just like our meeting up was a coincidence! Haven't you got something better to base your "pattern" on?'

'We have, as a matter of fact,' Colonel Muller intervened. 'Forensic evidence suggests that Mr Hookham could have been killed near where you were shot. A piece of water plant presumably from the stream there confirms as much – and it ties in with the time of death as well.'

Mrs Bradshaw blinked. 'I can't see the pattern in that,' she admitted, seeking out Colonel Muller's deep grey eyes. 'Is there one?'

'Why, of course, my dear! The killer favours that spot!' And Colonel Muller continued in a positive flood of inspired guesses, if only to hold her gaze, perhaps. 'He favours that spot because it's lonely and *yet* it's also handy to the suburb of Six Valleys built on those hills to the east of it. He is aware that gunshots are not infrequently heard coming from kids with two-twos, and perhaps he picks his victims from among the people who walk their dogs there. Who knows? Mr Hookham could have tried it out himself last week, and while he was away from the car with the dogs, the killer could have seen the service booklet through the window, noted the address, and made his plan. We must all remember we're dealing with a diabolically clever mind here!'

'True,' remarked Kramer, very softly, but his resolve was weakening again. There had been a lot of sound reasoning in that. 'There is one other – '

'Ooooo!' exclaimed Mrs Bradshaw. 'You *have* frightened me, Colonel!'

'Ach no,' he comforted her, 'don't you worry, madam!'

'Myra.'

'Myra then, we'll – '

'To get back to the pattern,' harrumphed Bradshaw, giving his wife a terrible scowl, 'and here I mean the *plausible* pattern, what are your predictions, Colonel Muller, if I may ask?'

'Ah.'

'That the next attack – if there is another attack – will come in or around that area?'

'Exactly,' said Colonel Muller, rising imposingly to his feet. 'If this is only the beginning of several attacks, as are characteristic of this type of criminal, my prediction is as you have so intelligently guessed.' Then he looked sharply at Bradshaw to gauge the mollifying effect of his words.

Mollified to all appearances, Bradshaw rose as well, but his sling hampered his attempt to reach his full height. 'I take it that this little chat is over? Can I offer you gentlemen a drink, perhaps? A sundowner?'

'Well . . .' Colonel Muller sneaked a peek down Mrs Bradshaw's cleavage, pretending to check on the shininess of his shoes.

'Ach, why not? We're not in any hurry any longer, are we, Lieutenant?'

'But how many attacks are there going to be?' lamented Mrs Bradshaw. 'What you've said still makes me shiver all – '

'My prediction is one more,' said Kramer. 'And I'd – '

'Ja, possibly only one more,' agreed Colonel Muller, with another look of sudden inspiration. 'And shall I tell you how I work that out?'

'Fascinating,' encouraged Bradshaw, pulling his wife to her feet. 'Get the drinks tray, dear – and a jersey, maybe?'

'Let me hear this first, Archie!'

'I base my assumption on another assumption, I grant you,' declared Colonel Muller, with a wary eye on Kramer, 'but here goes. Everything indicates this five-shot Smith & Wesson was stolen – that's Point Number One. Point Number Two is that the ammunition being used is very old. Point Number Three is the clear indication that the killer has only the ammunition that was in the gun when he stole it, and – '

'Point Number Four,' said Mrs Bradshaw, excitedly, 'is he's fired four shots and so he can have only one left!'

When Colonel Muller looked at her then, it was clear to everyone else in the room that she was, most definitely, a woman after his own heart. 'Did you hear that?' he said to Kramer. 'Can you fault such reasoning, such perfect logic?'

'I think so,' said Kramer, but had to think hard before coming up with the answer. 'For someone so short on ammo, he wasn't fussy about wasting two more than he really needed on Bonzo Hookham, sir.'

'Heat of the moment, Lieutenant! He didn't think!'

'Why, what's your theory, if it keeps clashing?' asked Bradshaw, poking Kramer in the chest. 'Is your prediction, of one more, different?'

For a wild moment, Kramer felt almost like hugging the bastard. 'Firstly, I don't think he'd have started this campaign of revenge without enough ammo, even if it was old. And – '

'For the last time, dammit! – ' began Colonel Muller.

'No, let's hear him out,' insisted Bradshaw. 'The way your ace detective's mind works is fascinating to a mere layman.' The type of fascination it had for him was implicit in his evil little eyes, which twinkled and sparkled.

You son of a bitch, thought Kramer, but remained in his debt none the less. 'Mr Digby-Smith reports having received a telephone call,' he said, 'which purported to come from an old school friend of Bonzo Hookham's. I want to know if possibly there's another link here.'

'No old schoolmates of mine have rung up recently, if that's what you mean!' laughed Bradshaw, hurting himself again.

Kramer turned to Mrs Bradshaw. 'What about these crank calls? Anyone you noticed with a strange, foreign-sounding accent?'

Mrs Bradshaw jumped. Then she looked wide-eyed at her husband.

'No, no calls anything like that,' he said brusquely. 'What about those drinks I offered you just now?'

'But, Archie . . .' she said reproachfully.

'Myra, didn't I ask you to fetch the tray?'

'I think you ought to tell them, Archie. I always said you should.'

'Then *I'll* get the bloody tray!'

Kramer watched Bradshaw leave the room, then turned to see how Colonel Muller was enjoying this turn of events. 'A definite link of some kind here, sir?'

Mrs Bradshaw could not endure the silence that fell between them at that moment.

She rapped her fingers on the desk top.

She crumpled up one of her sketches.

She inhaled a very deep breath.

'It was one of the first things Archie told me at the hospital the morning after,' she began in a rush. 'Do you know when I mean? When he started speaking about what'd happened. He said that he could have sworn the man called out to him, attracted his attention, made him swing round to face the gun. He sort of thought the man had said, "You're my first" – but that sounded so silly. What made it harder to be sure, he said, was that the man had this funny accent. Not exactly foreign, sort of a mixture. Then he said he had been dreaming about the thing all night, having those terrible nightmares that drugs in hospitals give you after an operation, and he could really have imagined that part. I went on at him to remember which it was, and the more he thought, the more uncertain he became, until finally he was sure it must have been just a dream. I still wanted to tell you, but he made me promise not to – he was going to look a big enough fool already, he said, and then he didn't want to say a word about how big this man had been. I won him over on that score, but – until you said that a few moments ago, about Digby-Smith – I had dismissed it from my mind.'

Bradshaw came back in at that moment, carrying the tray so awkwardly that she hastened across to help him.

'Thanks,' he said. 'And thanks also for what you've just done to me. They'll think I'm a proper old fool now.'

'Do you realise,' flared Kramer, 'that if we'd known this bastard had said, "You're my first," then people could have been warned – Bonzo Hookham could be alive now?'

'Hold on,' said Colonel Muller, grabbing his elbow. 'That remark could fit a maniac doing it once and once only! He didn't say, You're *the* first.'

'He's done it twice, that's all that I know!'

'But how could we have – ?' asked Colonel Muller.

'My pattern was there from the night of the bloody social,' Kramer retorted. 'But not having Hookham's death to throw attention on – ' True, there was nothing he could have done.

Bradshaw slapped his good hand down hard on the desk top. 'I've had enough of this!' he said. 'Will you stop going on about that pattern? Even if I did hear a foreign accent – and I'm not bloody swearing to that in a statement even now! – who is to say that telephone call wasn't genuine?'

Kramer started for the door. There was something he could do about Ernie Wilson though, provided he hadn't already wasted too much time.

'Hey, wait for me, Lieutenant!' ordered Colonel Muller. 'Now don't worry,' he said quickly to the Bradshaws, patting Mrs Bradshaw on the bare forearm. 'You're quite safe with young Schoeman to look after you, and, anyway, I personally feel there's been no need for all this shouting. If you'd never been in the RAF, Mr Bradshaw, the only "link" would be the link there is already in the bullets – namely the link created with the killer when he turned his gun on you. Okay?'

'Oh thank you,' said Mrs Bradshaw, who had become a little tearful. 'If I thought I could have prevented . . .'

'No, no, I'm sure you'll find it's my theory that proves right in the end,' added Colonel Muller, risking a reassuring wink. 'Just give it a few days and you'll see.'

Zondi waited anxiously in the passageway beneath the stairs that led up to Colonel Muller's office. The silence in the car all the way back from Kitchener Row had been deafening; it had pressed in on his eardrums until his brain had been fit to burst with wild speculation. One thing had been tacitly obvious, and this was that the Lieutenant and Colonel Muller had emerged from the Bradshaw house at complete loggerheads with one another. Given the Lieutenant's present mood, which was as difficult to deal with as a friend infatuated by obviously the wrong woman, he could only hope that the outcome would not be too difficult to live with. Once or twice the Lieutenant had spoken of resigning, usually in situations like this one, and his streak of stubbornness might carry him over the brink this time. If the Lieutenant left the force, life would be – Zondi stopped thinking, lit a cigarette, and started to pace again.

CHAPTER SEVENTEEN

'Coming?' said Kramer, reaching the foot of the stairs. 'Or have you better things to do?'

Zondi fell in step with him, and they crossed the hall of the CID building together, took the steps down into Boomplaas Street and turned towards the vehicle park.

'He's given me one last chance, Mickey.'

'To prove your theory is right, boss?'

'He wasn't so specific,' said Kramer, tossing over the car keys. 'But I tell you my theory *is* right, and with a little luck I'm going to prove that to him tonight!'

'How can you be so sure?'

'I can't be – that's where the luck comes in. But the way I read it, the heat's on now and this crazy bugger could be rushing to finish the job and get away before – as he thinks – the pattern becomes clear to us.'

'The pattern, boss?'

'The link between these bomber blokes. He's had a go at Bradshaw and at Hookham, that leaves ex-Squadron Leader Ernest Wilson for the chop.'

'We are being sent to warn this Boss Wilson?'

'To protect him, Mickey,' said Kramer, waiting at his car door for it to be unlocked. 'And, of course, to bring this bastard in if he shows up.'

'Just you and me?' asked Zondi, surprised.

'If you're wondering where the rest of the police force has got to, they're up to their necks in skipping ropes, bits of fluff and horse manure. Head out of town along the Ladysmith road.'

After fifteen minutes of hard driving, Kramer noticed that Zondi had slyly adjusted his rear-view mirror so that he could study his face. 'What's on your mind, kaffir? Besides all those nice nieces you're missing out on?'

'Are you David, Lieutenant, that you are sent all by yourself to fight a giant?'

Kramer grinned. 'So you're not just an ugly face,' he said.

'I've decided that Tromp needs a bit of a hand,' Colonel Muller told Lieutenant Frans de Klerk of the Housebreaking Squad, after calling him into his office. 'He has been overdoing things lately in every sense of the word. It isn't just the hours he puts in, but the effect this strain is having on his police–public relationships at certain sensitive levels. Only a few hours ago, for example, he went to town on a very lovely lady, and I think there is every chance that her husband will be sending in a written complaint.'

'Oh ja?' said De Klerk, whose sole vice was his elusive prurience. 'Anything I can do to straighten something out between us and this lovely lady?' He winked.

'No, I've seen to that personally, thanks,' said Colonel Muller, reassured by the wink that De Klerk was prepared to be discreet. 'What's happening is this : I'm putting Warrant Officer Oppenheimer in charge of Housebreaking for a while, and I'm transferring you to Murder and Robbery on a temporary basis. I'm not asking you to take on more than one job, mark you! Your role is to be clear-cut and circumscribed.'

'Ouch!' said De Klerk, crossing his legs and squirming. 'Actually speaking, wouldn't Solly Oppenheimer be better equipped for the job, sir?'

Such modesty pleased Colonel Muller. 'Let me be the judge of the best man to second to this investigation,' he said. 'I've been watching you closely for some time, De Klerk, and I have yet to catch you out even once.'

'It's my lightning-fast zip, Colonel!'

'It's more than your zip, De Klerk – it's the way you handle yourself. And don't try smiling as if I don't know what I'm talking about, because the statistics are there for all the world to see : a full three per cent rise in the detection rate for housebreakings since you took over. Now I want to apply that same eye for detail, that same love of hard facts, to the Bradshaw–Hookham case.'

'Hell, you mean I'm to work on a major investigation? Not just fill in on the more minor – '

'Now perhaps you see why I'm keeping you from the bosom of your family at this hour!'

De Klerk quite forgot himself, missed a cue and said eagerly, 'When do I start, Colonel?'

'Right away,' replied Colonel Muller, nodding at the piles of reports in front of him. 'I'll give you a rough idea of the situation, and then Tromp can brief you fully in the morning, once he has had time to have a decent sleep for a change and has got rid of a stupid obsession of his.'

'You mean – '

'I mean that I've sent Tromp back to that boarding house where he lives, with strict instructions to forget about squadron leaders, bombs, vendettas and all the rest of it. He's to have two brandies, a hot bath and – '

'But I thought I saw him and that Zondi – '

'Correct,' said Colonel Muller. 'I told Tromp to get Zondi off the premises as well, and to dump him down somewhere he can start nailing one Banjo Nyembezi. Shall we make a start now?'

It was one of those all-night service stations that could no longer sell petrol after five because of the government's Save Fuel policy, but the café attached to it was open for business. Kramer directed Zondi to park on the café forecourt, where they made a careful check on who was about.

A large and obviously farming family from the Orange Free State sat at four tables in the café, waiting for their food to be served. Over against the juke box, moodily twisting paper straws, slumped a hitch-hiker with the Israeli flag on his haversack, looking as though he wished he'd never wandered. The only other customer, a hefty, fair-haired man in a bush shirt, sat with his back to the road, dividing his attention between his newspapers, his cup of coffee, the clock on the far wall, and the pair of telephone booths half-way between the side entrance to the café and the petrol pumps. If Kramer remembered correctly, the café had a big-busted, black-haired manageress with a sultry appeal, so presumably a fifth reference point might be added to these at any moment.

'All is quiet,' repeated Zondi.

'If you want to back out, Mickey, I won't think any the less, hey? I could be putting your head right in a noose if I'm wrong about all this, and the Colonel finds out where we've been tonight.

156

I'm not guaranteeing this bloke will show, although it does stand to reason.'

'You could be putting my head right in a coffin if you're *not* wrong about all this, boss!' said Zondi. 'So now you know the meaning of Black Man's Choice, which is a saying among my – '

'Bullshit!' said Kramer, and they both laughed. 'All right, so you want to be stubborn. Let me give you a quick run-down. Do you see the dirt road going off down the side here?'

'Check.'

'Only about four hundred yards along it is Ernie Wilson's small-holding. I've seen the layout dozens of times, because it's that place you glimpse as you're travelling towards Trekkersburg round that top bend back there, and – '

'One shed,' said Zondi, confidently. 'One garage, two thatched rondavels, one with a lean-to kitchen – he must sleep in the other hut. Also a chicken run.'

'Check,' confirmed Kramer. 'What is strategically on our side then?'

'No trees, hedges or bushes, boss. The homestead is almost totally exposed.'

'Not easy for a "giant" to approach unnoticed, would you say?'

Zondi smiled. 'Not easy for anyone, Lieutenant – except, perhaps, a small dark man.' He was right out ahead.

'Good, you've got the picture, Mickey. The only place for me to hide is in the main hut with Wilson. That's fine, it'll give us odds of two against one, but the essential thing is we get warning of his attack. When did you last – ?'

'Share a perch with a chicken, boss?'

'Ach no! But there must be an irrigation ditch or something you can get into. I'll go now and you can follow five minutes after.'

Zondi stroked his chin. 'How do you know this person isn't already at this place, boss?'

'Because I've checked on all the cars here, and they're accounted for by the people we can see sitting around. My bet is that this is where he'll leave his own vehicle, because any car or truck stopping near Wilson's small-holding at night is bound to attract his attention. Any more objections?'

'One more question, Lieutenant. How long are we going to lie in wait? If there is so much doubt about – '

'Not too long, I hope! See you, old son, and keep your fingers crossed.'

Then Kramer was gone, striding away through the slant of shadow thrown by the big truck abandoned under the KWIK SNAX sign, and without anyone in the café noticing a thing.

The two Zulu waiters appeared, heavily laden with fried eggs, salad and rump steak. They served the family from the Free State and stood back in polite astonishment while a white-bearded patriarch first said Grace. The hitch-hiker unfolded a limp road map, yawned, and looked at the clock. The fair-haired man with big shoulders looked away from the clock, down at his newspaper, and then out at the pair of telephone booths, which were flimsy affairs standing side by side. He ordered another coffee.

Zondi looked at the clock. Sixty seconds.

If only he still shared that feeling with the Lieutenant which placed the RAF at the heart of this mystery. But it had been crushed out of him by the weight of too many assumptions, and every atom of his being was convinced that no killer would appear that or any other evening at Ernie Wilson's small-holding. Even so, when the time came, Zondi opened his car door and stepped out, closing it again quietly.

Colonel Muller washed his face and hands, dried them thoroughly and returned refreshed to his office, where he had left De Klerk sorting out the various reports on his desk. They were already in a number of smaller piles, clearly arranged according to some rather clever system.

'You've been amusing yourself, I see!' he said heartily. 'That's the style, Frans – just carry on and don't mind me.'

'Sorry?' said De Klerk, cupping a hand behind his ear.

Colonel Muller smiled indulgently. 'Didn't catch what I said? There's concentration for you! I must say you picked up the main points of the case remarkably quickly, and as soon as – '

'Sir?' said Detective Sergeant Bateman from the doorway.

'Ja, what is it, man? Lieutenant De Klerk and I are – '

'There's just been this weird phone call, Colonel. It came in on the duty officer's phone a minute ago, and I thought that in the light of – '

'Out with it, Bateman!'

The detective sergeant took a pace into the office. 'Er, it was this bloke with a strange sort of accent, Colonel. He asked if this was the CID, then all he said was, "Don't worry, I get my third and last tonight, then I'll be happy." '

Colonel Muller looked at De Klerk, who snatched up a pad and pencil.

'Have you any idea where the person was ringing from?' asked De Klerk, quickly copying down the message. 'Private line or call box?'

'Call box, sir, but it was all over too fast for me to –'

'That's all right, Bateman,' said Colonel Muller, cutting him short. 'The fact he said "get" and not "got" is the vital part. We'd better get some men out there fast, Frans – where do you think would be our best bet to stop something happening?'

De Klerk hesitated for only a moment before placing his finger on the wall map, and then describing a tight circle around the area where Archibald Meredith Bradshaw had been shot.

'I agree,' said Colonel Muller. 'I'll start by telling the Six Valleys patrol to hurtle down there, and then we'll have Uniform and dogs seal off the entire race-course. Let's hope our guess is good and we're in time, hey?'

Former Squadron Leader Ernest John Wilson was not the easiest of men to convince that his life could be in mortal danger. He sat in open-toed sandals in a deckchair, sipping rather than smoking his briar pipe, and now and again he wiggled his grey moustache from side to side like a mildly astonished rabbit.

There was quite a lot of rabbit in Wilson, Kramer had decided, if the old bugger's main rondavel was anything to go by. He had filled it with so many books, articles of unused furniture, magazines, bags of fertiliser, cardboard boxes, fencing poles and egg trays that, in order to be able to move about, he'd had to burrow out a warren of narrow paths through which, by stepping sideways, a man could just fit. His deckchair was placed to the rear of all this, in a small semicircle of uncluttered floor space. The wall above him was decorated with photographs, the one in the middle was a group portrait taken beneath the wing of a Lancaster bomber, while around it were a dozen or so snapshots of smiling women, some with modern hairstyles and others typical of the forties. This display served to encapsulate the paradoxical quality of the rabbit which also seemed to lurk within him: although his broad face was gentle, his manner charmingly vague, and his gaze so innocently steady, he could no doubt pack a nasty kick in those hindlegs of his, and as for lady rabbits, well, they had a surprising lot of fun. But it was not an analogy to be taken to extremes, because as Kramer could see for himself, looking like a frightened rabbit just wasn't Ernie Wilson's style at all – and never would be.

'Jolly decent of you, old boy,' the veteran airman said to him, 'popping out all this way to give me the gen. Like to offer you a spot of something – or must you dash?'

'Nothing right now, thanks,' said Kramer. 'I was wondering, sir, if we could move this cupboard across the window?'

'Interesting,' murmured Wilson, relighting his pipe.

'What is, sir?'

'All this. What sparked it off?'

'You mean the idea? The basis I'm working on? I thought I'd explained that already.'

'Formed a notion of my own, y'know. Listening to you; turning things over in the old noggin. Weak link somewhere.'

Kramer moved the cupboard, then started picking up the avalanche of things that had fallen off it. 'I notice you don't seem to keep a watch-dog, Mr Wilson.'

'He left me, old boy. Not much to watch, I suppose – went off with a family of gadabouts he met up with at the garage.'

'Where do you keep your gun?'

'Good God, haven't the foggiest. Somewhere under all that clobber, but I doubt anyone would ever find it. Can't see old Bonzo upsetting a soul, y'know. Weak link that.'

'Bradshaw reinforces it though!' retorted Kramer.

'Poor old Bradders . . . You do rather base everything on the sort of anti-feelings the chap produces in strangers. Touch of prejudice there.'

'Not just my prejudice,' said Kramer, giving up his hunt for the gun and leaning against a wash-stand out of line of the door. 'In fact the only thing most people like about that man is his nun joke.'

Wilson wiggled his moustache. 'There you go, you see! No attempt to get under the skin. Great friend of mine was in the same show – terrible business. Shot the lot of 'em bar Trigger

Stevens and old Archie, who has the luck of the devil, y'know. Take what happened to him last week : if that'd been a few other chaps I know, wallop! a bullet straight through the head. Not easy to live with, that kind of luck, y'know. Keeps a fella wondering what the price will be.'

'Ja, it must be hell,' murmured Kramer, listening hard to the night outside. 'But if it was such a terrible business, why make jokes about it?'

'Come, come,' chided Wilson. 'Don't you ever do that sort of thing? Don't mind admitting I do! Always best if you can see the funny side of appalling things that have happened to one. I've laughed on the spot, old boy. Nervous reaction.'

Kramer had laughed at the first dead body he had ever seen. that of a janitor who had impaled himself on a broom handle left carelessly propped against some banisterless stairs. 'Uh-huh,' he conceded. 'I suppose it's not a bad joke as they go.'

'But old Bradders never tells the rest, y'know. Doesn't explain that the poor wretch in the nun's outfit had dysentery. Oh God, yes – the gallopers, poured out of him, blood and all the bits. Startled the life out of this French priest who'd taken "her" under his wing, and he nipped off to have the Huns find a doctor on the train and – well, the quack took one look and that was it. The whole lot of them were carried off, treated unspeakably, and then they were shot one by one, firing squad, y'know. Eight ack-emma each morning. Bradshaw might be a bit of a rough diamond, a bloody bolshy sort of cove, but that's what kept him alive. Those swines tried everything on him, kept him till last, but Trigger Stevens cracked under torture, spilled the beans about their escape route, then succumbed, all in the nick of time. The chaps say Bradders came back to the camp in a frightful state, and was chucked straight into the cooler for a month's solitary, while he licked his wounds. Came out very shaky but –'

'Shhhh!'

The night was deeply silent.

'Sorry, go on, sir. You were saying?'

'About prejudice. Got to be damned careful, y'know. Make sure you know the whole story. Isn't "Kramer" German?'

'Pardon?'

'Of course it's ruddy German!' chuckled Wilson, pointing

accusingly with his pipe stem. 'A name notorious in certain quarters! And there you are, you see – the weak link!'

Kramer forgot about the door for a moment. 'I'm not with you, Mr Wilson,' he said. 'You mean a weakness in my theory?'

'Look, old boy, your whole fanciful proposition depends upon the effect that a couple of harmless chaps could have on an eavesdropper by blethering on about blasting Jerry to bits. A thing I've done *dozens* of times! May I go on?'

'Oh ja,' sighed Kramer. 'But will you please try to keep your voice down a bit?'

Wilson laughed. 'There isn't anybody out there! Good God, that's what I'm about to prove to you.'

'Even so, if you don't mind, hey?'

There was a dull, metallic clunk some distance off.

'Didn't have a motive for the cowardly attack on poor old Bradshaw, did you? No idea what brought about Bonzo's wretched end? So what did you do? You decided to put yourself in the shoes of this murdering swine.'

'Ja, ja, obviously.'

'Young man, of distant Germanic extraction, tries to imagine motivation. Young man asks himself: Now what possible motive could I have for killing these men? What would make me feel justified in doing so? And with all that Hun blood in your veins, up popped the answer! Revenge, old boy; pure and simple.'

'Ach, who's showing prejudice now! Let me tell you that –'

'Prejudice! The very word! You're very obviously anti-Bradshaw even now, despite the fact he's been on the receiving end! Doesn't this tie in with that "feeling" you insist gives you the right to invade a chap's privacy? When did that feeling first assail you? Was it when you were first confronted by an ex-RAF –?'

'It was when I went to interview Bradshaw at his –'

'What did I tell you?' chortled Wilson, delighted with himself. 'As a former member of the RAF, it must now be very plain to you why *I'm* not so easily persuaded by this tommy-rot of yours!'

Kramer almost walked out then and went home. But his hunch had never felt stronger, and he dismissed Ernie Wilson's deck-chair psychology with the thought that, were carrots a less accommodating shape, then he'd have told the old bastard to stuff one up his cotton-tail.

CHAPTER EIGHTEEN

Zondi gradually allowed his taut muscles to relax again, fairly confident that there was nobody close at hand who might have heard the clunk of his gun barrel against an unexpected water pipe. Then he continued to crawl closer to the chicken house along a shallow, weed-choked ditch, pausing only when he had the door to the main rondavel in sight.

How heavy the Walther PPK always seemed at moments like these, and how slippery in his grip.

There was a shower of pebbles down the side of the ditch behind him.

A toad, most probably.

'Saved by the bell!' said Ernie Wilson, reaching his hand into a chipped water jug. 'Don't look so startled, old chap!'

Bleep-bleep-bleep

Kramer reholstered his Ruger magnum. 'Robert du Plooi?' he said, recognising the device.

'So you've met? You wouldn't have so much as a pencil about you? Whacko! I'll get this number down...'

The control-room girl's voice sounded eerily disembodied, and Kramer stole a quick glance out of the window. Still nothing.

'Ah, where were we?' asked Wilson, tearing the corner off the ancient copy of *Wings* that he had used for a note pad. 'That's right, talking about this thingummy. Being in cahoots with young Du Plooi, he lets me have one on the cheap – absolute ruddy God-send, as you can imagine. You don't happen to have a spare coin on you, do you? Here's the pen.'

'Hey, hold on a tick, Mr Wilson! You're not thinking of leaving this –'

'Only to pop up the road, old chap.'

Kramer blocked the gap leading to the door. 'I'm sorry, but

under these circumstances, I can't allow you to leave the rondavel, sir.'

'Good God, don't think you can come barging in here and start telling a fellow what he can and can't do! If I wish to leave, there's nothing you can do to stop me!'

'There's a lot I can do,' warned Kramer, 'and don't worry, I bloody will if you don't listen! Whose number is that anyway? What makes it so urgent?'

'I haven't the foggiest, to be honest. Now, if you'll be so good as to get out of my way, I'll –'

Kramer snatched the scrap of paper from him. 'You don't even know whose number this is?'

'That's what makes it so damnably intriguing,' replied Wilson, trying unsuccessfully to grab it back. 'It might well be that tragic young woman I met only last week.'

'Does she live in this area? Because the first digit shows it must be a phone on the west side of Trekkersburg.'

Wilson looked a little less cocksure of himself. 'Six Valleys and all that, do you mean?'

'Or very much closer than that.'

'Look, it wouldn't take me more than a minute or two to find out,' said Wilson, digging into his hip pocket.

Like one of those special colour slides, flashed for only a split-second on the screen at the police college, Kramer saw a fleeting tableau in his mind's eye : A Free State farmer and his family; an Israeli hitch-hiker; a hefty, fair-haired man with his back turned, who kept looking from his coffee to his newspaper to the clock to the telephones standing out on the forecourt.

'Wait here, Mr Wilson!' he said, edging towards the door. 'And don't you move an inch outside this rondavel, because that's exactly what he wants you to do!'

'Oh, what utter tripe,' snapped Wilson, whipping out a five-cent coin. 'I'm simply not going to be dictated to by a –'

Kramer heaved over a pile of egg boxes, blocking the exit, and then grabbed for the door handle.

Zondi felt the heavy footfalls through the ground before he heard them. He raised his head, looked quickly behind him, saw nothing, and turned in surprise to face the rondavels. A giant was heading straight for him, looming enormous against the scud of clouds across the moon. He aimed his pistol and curled the first squeeze on its trigger. He had to suck spit from his cheeks before his voice would work.

'Hold it right there! Police!'

'Don't be a bloody fool,' hissed the Lieutenant. 'The killer's that fair-haired bastard back at the café! But stay here and see this old fool doesn't try to come after me – use your cuffs, use anything!'

'But, boss, you can't go by yourself to –'

'Orders, kaffir!'

It would be a pity, thought Zondi, as he watched the Lieutenant sprint towards the service station, if those turned out to be his last words. Then he was distracted by a very agitated white man who skidded to a halt and wet himself.

Adrenalin gave Kramer his high and his cool detachment; while everything at the service station now seemed pricked out much clearer, sharper, brighter than before, it also appeared so unreal to him that he moved with the confidence of a dreamer in a dream world where nothing had the power to hurt him. He covered the last fifty yards without feeling his feet touch the uneven ground, then cut back his pace, slowed right down and came to a halt behind the His and Hers lavatory block, which stood at the abrupt edge of the spotlit set, an actor's stride away from the darkness.

Deception was the crucial factor in a one-man operation like this. First he removed his shoulder holster, being well aware that only police officers went about covered up in jackets on sweltering hot nights, and hid it behind a rubbish bin. Next he tucked his shirt in very tightly all the way round, which would give the impression that he had only just risen from a prolonged sitting in the gents'. He switched his watch from his left wrist to his right, a little trick that had more than once gained him a split-second's advantage when his opponent had mistaken him for a southpaw. He combed his hair, just as he might have done at the basin after washing his hands, and then, lastly, he slipped the Ruger magnum into a sleeve of his jacket, and arranged the folds so that he could carry it casually without any telltale lumps or bumps showing.

Action. Kramer slipped out from behind the lavatory block, sidestepped into the straight line leading from His to the café entrance, and fell into an easy stroll, fighting an inclination to up heels and run. Heavy traffic roared and flashed by across the back projection, divorced from what lay before him.

The Israeli hitch-hiker had moved on to the concrete apron in front of the pumps, his haversack at his feet and his thumb in the air. It was good to see him there : one less innocent bystander to be mourned if anything went wrong. Better still, as Kramer neared the café, the Free State family came solemnly from the side entrance, applauding the quality of drinking-water in Natal, and dispersed to their numerous vehicles. Circling them with a friendly smile, Kramer went to pretend a check on whether his car was securely locked – Zondi had forgotten to see to this, as it turned out – and to take in the revised tableau inside the glass-fronted café. The two black waiters were disappearing into the kitchen with trays of dirty plates, followed by the raven-haired manageress gesturing in their wake, and the fair-haired man was still at his table. But what made Kramer shudder was the scamper of young children that had since appeared, racing around all over the place, and plainly far beyond the control of their travel-weary parents, who sat studying the menu together right in the middle.

Realising that any form of direct approach was now out of the question, he took advantage of the fact the fair-haired man's back was still turned to beat a quick retreat behind the Chevrolet, there to reconsider his strategy.

The hitch-hiker came over. 'You gonna eat too? Or are you ready to blow?' He spoke with an odd American accent. 'I mean I could use a ride, man.'

'You must be tired,' said Kramer, trying desperately to think of a way to get rid of him fast without attracting the fair-haired man's attention – short of slugging the stupid bastard. 'You look tired,' he added, lamely.

'I'm dead,' said the hitch-hiker.

You could be at any moment, thought Kramer, and noted the very masculine, aggressive stance the youth had, which suggested that tough tactics wouldn't work too well on him. He also had a self-pitying sulkiness that didn't guarantee a polite rebuff any success, not without a long wheedling argument.

'Don't much care which way you're headin', man,' the hitch-hiker said. 'If it's back downtown, then I guess I'll find me a pad at the Y.'

Kramer decided it'd have to be done the other way round: the hitch-hiker would have to reject *him* – yet an outburst of rank anti-Semitism could backfire nastily.

'If you're so tired,' said Kramer, smiling like a toothpaste ad, 'perhaps you'd like a bed for the night at my place? I don't live far away.'

'You don't? That's great! And I'll get a chance to study your culture up close the way –'

'Shhhh! Not so loud, hey? Of course, you can study my culture! And this bed, it's a really big one, you know? Satin. All the sheets are satin. Not pink-for-girls satin, mind! Blue satin. Do you like blue things, my friend?'

'Sure, I like blue things. I sleep on anything.'

'So you'll sleep on mine?'

'Sounds really snappy.'

'Share and share alike, hey?'

The hitch-hiker's bloodshot eyes suddenly narrowed, and there was a horrifying moment when a small smile played about his thick lips – then those lips twisted down at the corners. 'Oh shit,' he said softly, 'and so butch with it. I thought this was gonna turn out my lucky night.'

'And so it could, my friend! Don't go!'

He went. Lock, stock and haversack, and never glanced back, which tended to prove two basic suppositions: firstly, that it was possible to lose the look of a police officer, and secondly, that every prejudice had its virtues, provided it was used correctly. Then Kramer forgot all about him and turned to face the café once more, having tried to keep half an eye on the fair-haired man throughout this bad moment.

The man was moving. He had stood up with the newspaper folded in his right hand, and he was going out towards the telephone boxes. The traffic noise made it impossible to tell at that range whether one of the telephones was ringing, but Kramer judged from his stride that he was in no particular hurry. The man went into the far box with his newspaper still clutched tight and closed the door. Vandals had kicked in its panes of glass, and someone had stuck a sheet of semi-transparent blue plastic in their place, which showed whether anyone occupied it but gave away no details of feature.

This made the far box an ideal place for a killer to hide himself

– but only up to a point. His intended victim might well not be able to see in, but how was the man going to see out? There would be no need for him to see out, Kramer reasoned, if instead of gunning Wilson down on his approach to the telephones, he shot him in the actual boxes themselves. The dividing wall was only a sheet of thick plywood, and a .32 could go right through that and still blow a hole in a war-surplus squadron leader. There was a snag, though. How would the man be able to know for certain that it was Wilson in the next box, and not some innocent member of the public? The traffic sounds were enough to blot out even the sound of Wilson's self-opinionated voice. But this wouldn't apply, of course, if the killer heard that voice over the telephone! And there might be a few words of hate he'd like to spew out before he pulled the trigger.

'Ach it's perfect . . .' murmured Kramer, admiring a mind which could think like that. 'Only I've got him like a dead duck!'

Kramer moved swiftly round in a wide circle, coming up on the pair of telephone boxes from behind. There were no sounds of speech coming through the rear wall of the far box, although he pressed an ear gently against it to check this. The bastard was just standing there, waiting for Wilson to step into the empty box and dial his number, and then he would plug him. The timing of the whole thing was pretty good too, considering how long Wilson would have taken to reach the garage, had there been nobody around to save his bacon.

As Kramer edged around the side of the near box, he saw to his annoyance that the hitch-hiker had returned, and was crouched about seventy yards away, taking something out of his haversack. The hitch-hiker had not noticed him, however, by all appearances, and so could probably be safely ignored.

The big problem was whipping open that far door fast enough to disarm the killer before he had time to react. Some sort of distraction would be the answer, but it wasn't easy to think of one which mightn't alert him. Then Kramer was seized by a sudden temptation to hear exactly what it was that he said to his victims before pulling the trigger, and just how this strange mixture of an accent sounded.

He paused, took out the scrap of paper with the number on it, memorised the digits, put it away and decided to kill two birds with one stone, as it were. Neither would this be anything as difficult as it might seem. The nearside telephone box had three things going for it : it was vacant, of course; the vandals had removed its door completely, so the killer would not be listening for any opening and closing; and best of all, it wasn't a large telephone box, which meant that Kramer could remain on the concrete outside – out of the firing line – while he put through the call.

Before stepping up to the front of the empty box, he glanced round to make sure there were no kids, petrol-pump attendants or other encumbrances who might either get hurt or precipitate the action by becoming nosy at the last moment. There was none. The hitch-hiker had settled down on a patch of lawn, and was connecting together what looked like one of those small, take-apart tent poles.

Kramer made his move. He reached into the telephone box, lifted the receiver, dialled the number with the muzzle of his magnum, and was not at all surprised to hear the ringing tone without there being a reciprocal ringing sound from the other box beside him. The killer would have anticipated what an immediate give-away this could be, and had no doubt disconnected the bell leads in his instrument. He had no need to be alerted by the bell, not when a hand, pressed against the plywood division, would easily pick up the distinctive vibration of the dial being turned and allowed to return to zero. After feeling the vibrations cease, he would probably wait about twenty seconds before lifting the receiver on his side. What followed after that would be the fascinating part. Kramer stood poised outside the box, ready to plunge his five-cent piece into the slot at the very moment the call was answered.

The delay was only eleven seconds.

This bastard, thought Kramer, as he jammed the coin home, is a man in a hurry.

The coin mechanism whirred and gulped.

Kramer whipped his arm out of the box, then almost lost his balance by stepping backwards on to a Coke can he hadn't noticed earlier. He teetered, caught a glimpse of the hitch-hiker advancing, and nearly let the receiver slip from his grasp.

'Who's that?' someone demanded distantly.

Recovering, Kramer brought the receiver to his ear and said,

169

'You tell me who you are first, hey? Fair's fair!' There was a thoughtful pause, then he started violently.

'You bastard!' exploded Colonel Muller. 'De Klerk worked out that was where you must have disappeared to, but I didn't want to believe him!'

'Sir? But why –'

'Because there's been another shooting, Lieutenant!'

'Hey? Not Bradshaw again!'

Colonel Muller laughed nastily. 'No, not Bradshaw again – nobody even remotely like Bradshaw! Do you want to know the name of the intended victim this time? She was a schoolgirl called Classina Marie Baksteen.'

And the fair-haired man came out of his telephone box muttering, 'Jesus Christ, it was only a trunk call – can't anyone get anything right these days?'

CHAPTER NINETEEN

Classina Marie Baksteen was a very sweet sixteen and had short-cropped blonde hair, big blue eyes, an unblemished, honey-coloured skin, and long, comely limbs. She lived at 33 Hiemstra Road, Six Valleys, with her mother, father, and two younger sisters. She was working for her Junior Certificate of Education, and went to the J. G. Strijdom High School for Girls, where the medium of instruction was Afrikaans. Classina was a model young Afrikaner, born of Afrikaner parents, reared in an Afrikaner atmosphere, and her worst subject was English. How anyone could invent a language where words like *plough, cough, through* and *though* each had totally different vowel sounds was beyond her. She was very pleased and proud that when Afrikaans had been invented in 1926, nobody had allowed himself to be so silly. Her mother tended to endorse her views, but her father gave her no encouragement – in fact, quite the reverse. Although Klaas Baksteen had a secret loathing for all things even marginally Anglo-Saxon, and had taken the Germans' side in every war film he'd ever seen, he was none the less aware that if Classina failed to improve her knowledge of the republic's second official language, then her hopes of becoming a psychiatric nurse could be dashed. And so, ever a conscientious parent, he had told Classina to sit at the desk by the window in the back room that night until she had finished her English homework. *One hot sunnie day*, Classina had begun, before running out of inspiration. The window had been wide open, and through it had come all sorts of tiny, distracting sounds from the wattle plantation behind her back garden. Chitterings and squeaks and the raark of frogs mainly, and then sudden ghostly hushes. From further away had wafted the bugle noises made by the English-speaking boy on the corner, who had recently joined his school's military cadet band. *a new and very sad case came to the hospital*, Classina had gone on, *and he*

171

was put with the other patience in the ward for people who's per-
sonalities were split up. After that she had managed an entire page
before the blank expanse of a new leaf in her exercise book made
her mind wander. Standing on the inner sill of the open window
had been a very big glass vase in the shape of a swan with its neck
tucked down as a sort of a handle. Classina's mother had arranged
five bullrushes in it that afternoon, and had been surprisingly
boastful of the effect. The arrangement was, she had told Classina,
based on an idea she had picked up from that snobby Mrs Drake
down the road, only she had greatly improved on it. The new
case, wrote Classina, *was a big worrie because he liked to fill his
water jug with all sorts of funnie things "There must be sum
hidden reeson behind this, said the Ward Sister, who was very
wise for her age and had lovely blue eyes.* From then on, the essay
had just flowed from Classina's fountain pen of its own accord
until she reached the middle of a sentence which began, *The new
case cried big tears when they said he was cured for ever and he
tried to kiss the Ward Sister's hands and*

'And then,' said Classina, retelling her tale for the third time, 'I
just screamed! It was amazing! The vase just blew up in bits all
over my exercise book!'

Kramer felt quite numb as he looked around the room, seeing
in the fragments of glass far more than merely a shattered vase.
He caught the triumphant gleam in Colonel Muller's eyes and
turned back to the young girl. 'Uh-huh? What happened next?'

'Pa heard me scream, and he came running in like a flash! He
started looking for the stone the boy must have thrown, because
he's always doing things like that, you know – the boy on the
corner with the bugle.'

'Uh-huh.'

'But instead he found this bullet lying on the couch.'

'Uh-huh.'

'He knew it was a bullet because my pa's in the Active Citizen
Force,' Classina disclosed proudly. 'He said it was a thirty-two
and he phoned the police.'

'Ah, that's an interesting point,' remarked Colonel Muller. 'You
say your pa is a soldier, but has he ever been in the air force?'

'Never ever. My pa says being a pilot is soft. He likes to push
his bayonet right into the terrorists and give it a twist.'

'Well, Lieutenant?' said Colonel Muller, turning to Kramer. 'Have you any further questions for this little girl before she goes to bed? Any comment to make?'

'Only that you and her pa would seem to have a lot in common, sir,' said Kramer, whose numbness was giving way to a sense of extreme irritation.

Colonel Muller responded with an angry look of his own. 'Okay, Classina, off you go then! Just thank God tonight in your prayers that you weren't hurt and –'

'Ach, I think it's exciting!' said Classina, and her big blue eyes sparkled. 'Think how jealous all my friends will be! I only wish there'd been some water in the vase, so I wouldn't have to hand in my composition tomorrow. Pa says I've got to get up at six to finish the last page.'

'I'll see what I can do to change his mind,' promised Colonel Muller, with an avuncular wink. 'Come, Lieutenant, if you've seen all you want to here, I think we might as well go through to the sitting room and see what Frans has organised.'

Kramer strode after him, his fists clenched, and found the sitting room filled with detectives and uniformed men. Bateman was interviewing the parents.

'But why would anyone want to murder my little girl?' Mrs Baksteen was demanding to know. '*Why*, for heaven's sake? That bullet couldn't have missed her head by more than an inch!'

'Half an inch, in my opinion,' said Mr Baksteen, a stern pedantic-looking man with translucent ears like a fruit bat. 'Half an inch higher and it wouldn't have been deflected by the vase – you saw where I found it lying spent on the couch, didn't you?'

'Ja, but *why*, Klaas? She hasn't an enemy in the world!'

'Can we just get back to whether you heard a shot or not?' Bateman asked patiently. 'Oh hullo, Lieutenant! Come to take over?'

Kramer ignored him.

De Klerk was seated at the dining table in an alcove, with the telephone at his side and a map spread out before him, looking like a hyena at an air crash.

'No hard feelings, hey, Tromp?' he said, grinning. 'Or did I interrupt them? Just thought you'd like to be where the action was, and Colonel Muller here –'

'Let's hear it, De Klerk. What's the position?'

173

'Well, sir,' said De Klerk, pointedly addressing his reply to Colonel Muller, 'I've had Botha dug out and he should be at Ballistics by the time the bullet arrives – say in about another ten minutes. Galt is here with a team of his men – he lives only round the corner, luckily – and they are at the back here, searching in the wattle trees for any sign of where the man stood et cetera. I've got men going along the road, asking house-to-house if anyone saw or heard anything, and –'

'Any results yet, Frans?' asked Colonel Muller.

'Negative, sir. Naturally, there are also uniformed patrols and dogs making an extensive search of the whole area, and we're picking up anybody who looks suspicious.'

'Any comment?' Colonel Muller asked Kramer. 'Anything you'd like to see us do that we're not doing already?'

Kramer could think of a number of things, but none of them were too polite or even practical. He shook his head.

'Our chief difficulty, Colonel,' De Klerk went on, 'is the access this bastard had to the plantation behind. If you'll look at this map, you'll see that he could have parked anywhere along the dirt track leading from the reservoir, and then cut up through the trees. Or he could have circled round into the trees on foot, supposing he lives in this district, which seems even more likely now. Either way, by the time the alarm went up, he could easily have got away long before we arrived.'

'You know what I think, Frans? I think he probably meant to strike again at the race-course, only we frightened him away by anticipating that and going there ourselves.'

'And this poor kid was just an easy target he found instead, sir?'

'Ja, everything seems to point to that,' agreed Colonel Muller. 'You know what these lunatics are like, they set their minds to do a thing, and especially after challenging us as he did, he had to find someone to do it to.'

Kramer let them babble on unheeded, and then decided to go and see what success Galt was having. He found the team from Forensic a short distance into the wattle plantation, in line with the window at which the girl had been working.

'A heavy man,' Galt was sighing softly, treading round in a circle on the soft earth. 'Very heavy – take a look under that branch there, Lieutenant Kramer. That's where he must have stood, you see. I'd say a man of at least two-fifty pounds.'

Kramer looked at the spot, and saw the earth deeply indented. 'These cigarette ends – are they his too?'

'Fresh as one could hope for,' confirmed Galt. 'If you take eight minutes as the average burning time for that brand – I'll double-check this in the morning – what you see there is about quarter of an hour's worth. It all fits in rather nicely.'

'Couldn't she have seen his cigarette from that window? There's not even a twig in the way, and the range can't be more than thirty yards.'

Galt smiled. 'Haven't you ever sneaked a smoke while you were in uniform?' he asked. 'There's not much of a trick to keeping – '

'Look at this, sir!' said one of his men. 'I found it stuffed inside a bush further along to the right.' And he held out a crumpled nylon stocking.

'Aha! I think somebody must have panicked a bit tonight!' applauded Galt, taking the stocking and unfolding it in the beam of his strong torch. 'If this was used for what I imagine it was, then we *may* find something if we turn it inside out.'

He did find something. A longish hair and a tiny smudge of pinkish cream, at which he sniffed cautiously.

'Pimple lotion?' guessed Kramer.

'It could be – then again, it might . . . No, I'd rather not say until I've had a chance to analyse it. What colour would you say this hair was? Reddish? Auburn?'

'Brownish – it's hard to tell in torch light.'

Colonel Muller made his way up to them and was shown these finds. 'Still very little to work on,' he observed. 'The cigarettes and the stocking tell us more about the man, but they don't point a finger at anyone in particular. Bradshaw's description of his build is verified, of course, by the depth of these footprints.' Then he looked up and said, 'Something else has been verified, by the way, which I'm sure both of you will be interested in.'

'Colonel?' said Galt.

'Botha has just been on the phone from Ballistics. The bullet fired here tonight is in every respect an exact match with those recovered from Bradshaw and Hookham.'

This came as no real surprise to Kramer, yet it proved the last straw. 'Ach, the hell with all this!' he grunted, and turned towards the house.

'Lieutenant?'

'I'm buggering off, Colonel. I've had a gutful.'

Miriam was surprised to hear the Chevrolet outside her house in Kwela Village at such an early hour, and reached the window just in time to see her husband jump out, give a wave, and then disappear in a cloud of dust as the car took off again.

'Hau, but the Lieutenant seems in a big temper tonight!' she remarked, as she welcomed Zondi at the door. 'Who is he so cross with, Mickey?'

'Himself, I think,' said Zondi, patting her behind affectionately. 'Where are the twins?'

'Out. They promised to be home before the curfew.'

Zondi sat himself down at the table and rubbed his knuckles in his eyes. 'Is there tea?' he asked.

'First there has to be hot water,' said Miriam, placing the kettle on the Primus stove. 'You seem very tired.'

'Tired? I'm nearly finished! Would you like to know what happened today?'

And while they waited for the kettle to boil, Zondi went over the main events, trying to sort them out in his own mind as much as anything. Miriam found it very hard to understand what had made the Lieutenant get such a fixed idea that he'd ended up making a terrible fool of himself.

'I have not recited all of it,' said Zondi, 'for truly, woman, it no longer matters, but I do think I know the reason behind it.'

'He is a good man, Mickey, so it must have been a good reason.'

Zondi smiled. 'Uh-huh, but he has his weaknesses, like all of us. His undoing was this Boss Hookham, for he was a brave man and a man of great spirit in the Lieutenant's eyes. Even though he is dead, I am sure he has taken a strong liking to him. That isn't all. Boss Hookham had this girlfriend from long ago, also a good person who had endured much suffering with courage, and the Lieutenant likes her very much – he even told me so. Do you see the dangers in this?'

Miriam picked a matchstick out of one of the lines she had scored in the rammed-earth floor to simulate proper floorboards.

'No, but you go on,' she said. 'I will smack that Gogo if she makes her mother's room untidy again!'

'To understand properly, you have to have seen the defiled body of Boss Hookham in the boot of the car. It was so small, so broken; the hands tied and the big hole filled with flies in the back of the head. Hau, it was not how a brave man should die! It was wrong! What happened, I think, is that the Lieutenant could not accept that Boss Hookham had died in this meaningless fashion, that he had been caught and tied up and shot by some crazy person for no reason at all.'

'But these things are not uncommon, Mickey,' said Miriam, filling her teapot. 'And did not the first boss get shot at for no reason? The young girl also?'

'No reason,' confirmed Zondi, 'except what a madman thinks is a reason. Only the Lieutenant doesn't care what anybody does to this Boss Bradshaw, you see, whereas Boss Hookham was different. So he tried to find some sense in such a terrible thing, and all that came to him was this bombing. It explained both shootings to him, giving him a strong feeling he had grasped a branch when it was not even a twig.'

After pouring two cups of weak black tea, Miriam clucked her tongue again and said softly, 'What a pity the Lieutenant has no belief in God, my husband. Only God can give any meaning to this life we lead.'

Then one of their children stirred in its sleep in the next room, chuckled happily, and they smiled at each other.

Vivid pink and blue lights flickered in the windows of the flat above the hairdressing salon, and sounds of heavy rock, laughter and hard drinking were clearly audible from the street.

'Well, I'll be buggered!' said Jonty, swinging wide his front door.

'Not a chance, cuddle bunny,' said Kramer. 'But can I come to your party all the same?'

Jonty feigned a knee kick and dragged him inside. 'Christ, you look shattered!' he said. 'That sort of day, was it? Never mind, pal, your troubles are over! Trust in Jonty!' He was really pretty drunk.

The main room of the flat was packed like a lift in a burning skyscraper, except the people crammed into it were having the time of their lives and were only too delighted to welcome another passenger aboard. Faces he had never seen before smiled at Kramer from all sides, a few pretty girls raised their eyebrows, and within moments he was engulfed in the deep belly-boom from the big speakers and the sheer warmth of so many sweaty bodies. Blue, pink, blue blue, pink, blue, pink pink pink, rattle, howling horn and guitar chords crashing – it was chaotic. He grinned : a splurge of senseless, mindless, meaningless chaos was just what he needed. And drink – lots of it.

'Booze is through in the kitchen,' said Jonty, anticipating his wish like a good fairy. 'I've got me a genu-wine Texas bartender tonight ! Yessiree, some fella one of the lasses from the varsity brought along. Just sing out yer order, pardner, and ol' Gene'll set 'em up ! There's somebody I need a quick word with . . .'

Kramer shouldered his way through into the kitchen and spotted the Texan easily enough : he had a tanned, pleasantly laconic face, and was wearing faded jeans, a checked shirt, a belt and rawhide shoes. He was also recounting some anecdote to a young couple in faultless Afrikaans. Not wishing to spoil the punch-line or to interrupt anything so comfortingly bizarre, Kramer helped himself to half a tumbler of neat brandy, drank most of it, topped up and joined the couple just as a laugh ended the tale.

'But why were you living in Hong Kong?' asked the girl.

'I was learning Mandarin Chinese – a very elegant language with only four tones. A dropping tone, a rising tone, a dropping-rising, and a fourth tone which is just a high flat note.'

'You can actually speak it?' asked the man.

The Texan smiled. 'One night I had some friends coming for drinks at the college, and I went down to the kitchen to get some ice from the big ice machine they had there. The old cook was slaving over the stove. I was aware that most people in Hong Kong spoke Cantonese, but I thought they'd probably learn some Mandarin at school – the Communist government is trying very hard to make it the national language.'

'Is that a fact?' said the girl.

'He was slaving away over the stove, and I said to him in Mandarin, "How are you?" – *Ni hao ma? Ni* is "you", *hao* is "well", and *ma* is a verbal question mark. He looked at me and his mouth fell open ! So I repeated myself, *Ni hao ma?* And then he started laughing, and he asked in English, "You speak Mandarin?" "Yes." He said, "Do you know what you say? Mandarin velly differlent flom Chinese." "No, I've no idea." "You say: 'You velly good lacehorse!' " '

That got an even bigger laugh, and someone just behind Kramer joined in with a throaty giggle. He turned to find the little red-head from the salon standing there, half-tipsy and dressed in a wine-coloured frock. She had a wide, quirky mouth, a neat snub nose, and cornflower eyes as round and as bold as her pair of high breasts.

'Hi!' she said, smiling. 'Remember me?'

'Even the parts I didn't see,' said Kramer. 'You work downstairs for Jonty, am I right?'

Her smile broadened. 'I do a lot of things for Jonty.'

'Oh ja? That sounds interesting.'

'Are you going to interrogate me?'

'Definitely,' said Kramer.

'When? Now?'

'No, first I've got to soften you up a little – can I fill that glass with something?'

'I'm not sure I like the sound of this!' she said, and her blue eyes twinkled. 'I can't help feeling we're talking at cross-purposes.'

'Ach no, all I'm going to do is probe your innermost secrets, hey?'

She laughed. 'We'll see about that! All right, I'll have another – a long Campari, please. Lots of ice.'

'One long Campari coming up . . .'

'I'm Tish.'

'Gesundheit,' said Kramer. 'I'm Trompie.'

It all went with dreamlike simplicity after that, and had Kramer not been drinking on an empty stomach, he might have had his suspicions. They moved back into the main room, found somewhere to balance their glasses, and joined the dancers. For an hour or more, pausing only for quick refills in the kitchen, they took their cues from the raunchy, strutting music, letting it become a bond which grew until finally, dazed and intoxicated, they sank down on some cushions in the corner. Her pupils were huge as his hand slid from her shoulder and down inside her dress.

Tish giggled. 'That's not going to soften me up, Trompie!'

'So it seems,' he murmured, feeling her left nipple swell up hard against his cupping palm. 'But what if I press this?'

'You mean like a "play" button? Ve haf vays of making you talk?'

'Uh-huh.'

'Press that and you just might start something you can't stop!'

'Should I, hey?'

'You have been warned,' she said, nuzzling his ear.

Kramer pressed the nipple, very gently, and started something all right. The kiss lasted until someone tripped over his legs, and he drew back astonished by her tongue.

'Shall I confess now?' she asked. 'Spill the beans on who had poor Bonzo to dinner? Tell you all that I know?'

'Hey?'

'Now don't start looking serious,' said Tish, pouting and tapping him on the nose. 'Not when we're having fun.'

'But if you've –'

'Oh dear, what have I done now? I haven't *anything* about the poor man, honest! Everyone's been talking about him and that horrible Archie Bradshaw, but it never gets anywhere. All that really seems to matter to most of them is that super-stud Darren hasn't been making the rounds of their daughters this time.'

'So young Bradshaw's a super-stud, is he?' muttered Kramer, finding another button to press. 'What does he specialise in? Lacehorses or polo ponies?'

'Velly lacey horses!' laughed Tish. 'You know, the pearls-and-purer-than-driven-snow set. Usually he's out every night on the prowl, so much so that last year a certain perfect young lady had to take a short trip to a London clinic, if you know what I mean! Hence the fact his dad banished him to Jo'burg, and why – Ooooo, that's nice . . .'

'And this?'

'Even nicer. Don't you think we – ?'

'No stalling, hey? You do that and I'll have to give you the full treatment.'

'Lovely.' Her hand grasped him. 'My God, a rubber truncheon! It's all true what they say! Big bright lights and hand-cranked generators!'

'That's nothing, lady – wait till you see what I do with my little plastic duck.'

They kissed again, then she pushed him away. 'But not here, Trompie,' she whispered hoarsely. 'Not out here, and I think there's someone already in Jonty's –'

'No problem,' he said, standing up and lifting her to her feet. 'Show me the bloody door then hide yourself for a minute.' Moving in a blur of flashing lights, throbbing sound, brandy and lust, he took out his Ruger magnum, burst open the bedroom door and strode in. 'Police!' he snapped. 'This place is being raided!'

And all three people believed him.

CHAPTER TWENTY

'But this is a horrific idea,' said Colonel Muller, glancing at the neatly typed report that De Klerk had handed him over his first coffee of the day. 'A *silencer*, you say?'

'I'm not so sure it is horrific, sir,' said De Klerk. 'In fact, I would go so far as to suggest it is merely in line with some of your own theories about this lunatic, and that we can probably rest assured that his experiments are over for the time being.'

'Really? What started you – ?'

'The trouble we had out at Six Valleys last night, sir, when nobody would swear to hearing a shot fired.'

'But there were reports of – '

'Oh, plenty of people thought they'd "heard a pop", and the kid with the bugle said it'd been two loud bangs, but what about Classina Baksteen? She never mentioned it.'

Colonel Muller shifted uneasily. 'That happens sometimes, as you'd know if you had worked in Murder and Robbery. People either take the bang for granted, or else the bullet seems to reach them before the sound does, which means – '

'True enough, sir! But what about her parents?'

'They had just started to watch that cowboy film which begins with all the shooting – nearly everybody was.'

'Even so, Colonel, it rang a bell with me.'

'It did?'

De Klerk removed Bradshaw's statement from the docket in front of him. 'I remembered that although Mr Bradshaw spoke of seeing a "flash" come from the gun, he hadn't mentioned a bang either.'

'But he does say he was temporarily stunned when the bullet hit him, Frans,' Colonel Muller pointed out. 'He could've been unconscious before he had a chance to hear it!'

'I considered that possibility myself, sir, but I thought it still merited a quick check. I called in on the Bradshaws on my way to work this morning, explained the position, and asked him to go over this point in his mind.'

'Oh, how was Mrs Bradshaw this morning?'

'I didn't have time for one, Colonel, but Bradshaw came up with the goods in the end. Ach, to begin with, he scorned the idea of a silencer, and asked me who would ever believe such a thing. Yet I could see something in his eyes, and gradually I forced an admission.'

'That stupid bastard again!' seethed Colonel Muller, rising in agitation. 'Don't tell me he'd withheld another piece of information because he was scared of appearing a bloody fool? Well, he *is* a bloody fool! – I might even charge him!'

De Klerk smiled placatingly. 'Would that be fair, sir? It could be a matter of approach. I find that if Mr Bradshaw's not being forced to live up to his image of a big, tough man, when you treat him nice and gentle, then he'll talk to you as freely as anyone. Here, in my hand, is his final statement, which includes the fact he heard no shot go off. Furthermore, I am confident we have all of it now.'

'What else is there?' asked Colonel Muller. 'Silencers! Criminal involvement! The mind boggles!'

De Klerk's smile held unwaveringly. 'I doubt that, sir. Firstly, what criminal would be interested in Classina? And secondly, no silencer has ever been found on a criminal in Trekkersburg – or anywhere else in Natal, for that matter. They're simply not sophisticated enough. But before outlining my personal theory, all that Bradshaw had to add was the fact he'd seen this tall young bloke with reddish hair on the race-course a couple of times. He never talked to him, but he'd seen him stop and pat his dog – didn't want to get into conversation, because even at a distance his manner seemed a bit strange. It wasn't until I'd picked this out of his casual chatter that he saw a possible significance, and then I told him about the hair that'd been found inside the stocking. That shook him.'

'I'll say! But why didn't Kramer get this? And where the hell is he this morning?'

'You did tell him to get a good rest, Colonel. Poor old Tromp, he was in pretty bad shape last night.'

Colonel Muller admired nothing more than loyalty among

fellow officers, and smiled his approval. 'You're quite right, I did, Frans. Now let me hear your theory. Is it straightforward and simple?'

'It's mundane, I'm afraid, sir.'

'Excellent!'

'But it is backed up by the blokes in Ballistics, on account of the *low*-velocity ammunition being used, which is imperative with silencers on conventional weapons. A thirty-two Smith & Wesson, for instance, which has fallen into the hands of an amateur gunsmith. I picture him as a very ordinary young man by all appearances, living in Six Valleys, on the quiet side, obviously not much of a shot, who none the less has this deranged side to his personality. A schizophrenic even, with paranoid tendencies, who gets his kicks from trying to match wits with us and –'

'Enough,' said Colonel Muller, quite confident that at last a reliable pattern had emerged from the shootings. 'I had a case not unlike it when I first started; a sixteen-year-old who killed four old ladies with a catty till I caught up with him. He would also ring me with messages, but where he went wrong was in first stealing this catapult from a friend of his, and then asking at his local garage for any old ball-bearings.'

'Fascinating, Colonel,' said De Klerk, producing another neatly typed sheet. 'My suggested plan for the day is outlined here, sir, and if you and Tromp think it's any good, then I'll be happy to –'

'I think it's a marvellous piece of work, Frans,' said Colonel Muller, giving the subheadings a quick glance. 'And I don't want us to waste any more time, hey? So off you go! Put your plan into action!'

'But, sir . . .' began De Klerk, looking appalled.

'You're worrying about your friend?'

'Tromp will probably go berserk if –'

'Leave that to me, Lieutenant De Klerk. I'll think of something, and there won't be any repercussions.'

De Klerk left, plainly reassured by the ring of command in Colonel Muller's voice, and the latter sat back well satisfied. It wasn't going to be easy dealing with Kramer, yet a speedy conclusion to this case would make it well worth it.

Kramer awoke to a new world that morning at a quarter past

nine, and to a ceiling he had never seen before, decorated with pretty paper daisies.

He sat up.

He was in a bedroom with whitewashed walls, black woodwork, an uneven bare floor and a little louvred door in one corner. The furniture in the room was all made of bamboo. There were three big pictures on the walls — some sunflowers, a red café with a billiard table, a man not dissimilar to Meerkat Marais with a bandage over his ear — and near the door stood an old-fashioned hat-stand, on which were draped his clothes and his shoulder holster. A note written in blue crayon was stuck to the end of the bed with a piece of Sellotape.

> *Some of us have a job of work to do.*
> *Your breakfast is in the warming oven,*
> *and your shirt and undies are drip-drying*
> *in the shower. See you at six? Tish*

Kramer flopped back and smiled at the daisies. Perhaps this is what it felt like to be born again, he thought, and considering his birthday-suit nakedness, an apt enough conclusion. He stretched, gathered the sheet about him like a trailing diaper, and went over to look out of the high sash-window. The flat was apparently part of an old house in the dip below the hospital, and faced the willows along the Umgungundhlovu River. Then he opened the little louvred door, discovered the shower, removed his things, and made good use of it. He would have liked to try some of the candy-coloured potions arrayed on a shelf above the tap, but wasn't too sure of their effects with a dodgy character like De Klerk around. The man protested too much. Tish had left out a proper Gillette razor with a badger-hair brush and a tub of shaving soap, slightly used; interesting and reassuring somehow.

Once he had dressed and hurriedly strapped on his holster, Kramer felt decidedly hungry. He went through into the next room and found it to be a large kitchen-cum-lounge, with huge cushions instead of chairs, venetian blinds over the windows, shelves stacked with books and records, and a number of expensive ornaments that didn't quite belong; interesting.

Your Breakfast said a second note on the warming-oven door, just in case he had missed the first one. It was a very good breakfast : four grilled lamb chops, six rashers of bacon, potato cakes, fried banana slices, egg-plant and mushrooms. Although usually a refueller rather than an eater, he sat at the chair marked *Your Place* and relished every morsel of it. His eye picked out another little notice propped against a glass bowl : *Your Bullets.* It didn't trigger off any memory of his arrival in the flat, nor of his condition at the time, but it was extremely suggestive. He put the dishes in the sink for the flat girl, reloaded his Ruger and slipped on his jacket. *Your Key* read the label on the Yale key hanging on a pink ribbon behind the door.

'Whatever you say, lady,' said Kramer, leaving the ribbon behind and sauntering out.

Zondi stood at the back of the briefing being held in the main CID office by Lieutenant De Klerk, and chewed on a matchstick.

'Now I want you Bantu to listen to this as well,' said De Klerk, pulling back his narrow shoulders, 'because the whole success of this operation depends on leaving no stone unturned. Those of you who are going into Six Valleys this morning must ensure that no property with a hobby workshop is overlooked. It is in this regard that the work of the Bantu officers will be most important : I want you to double-check with the servants at every address, just in case some householder, suspecting his or her son of illicit activities, attempts to mislead us.'

Zondi chewed on his matchstick.

'You will all be issued with a list, of course, which indicates what raw materials you should be looking out for. The same list will be carried by Group Two, who will visit metalwork classes, the technical college, and every other place of potential instruction in the skills required to build a silencer. Group Three, I want you to remember that you're checking out every sports shop in the province, not just the ones in Trekkersburg, and not just because they sell guns and may know of a suspect answering our description. They also sell skipping ropes, don't forget that ! Ignore no coincidence, however slight, that could point to the man's identity. And Group Four, as I said at the beginning, will remain here at headquarters and collate all the information coming in.'

A groan escaped Detective Sergeant Bateman, who had spent the previous day checking the gunshot reports.

'It's okay, Bateman,' said De Klerk with a neat, flashing smile beneath a precise moustache, 'those gunshot reports are no longer considered relevant, and will simply be processed in the ordinary way by the girls in the office. Any questions?'

'Yessir,' replied Detective Constable Van Rooyen, on loan from the Liquor Squad. 'Where exactly does Lieutenant Kramer fit into these arrangements?'

'Or do you mean *when* exactly?' quipped De Klerk, and got his roar of laughter. 'If that's all, men, you may dismiss.'

Zondi spat out the matchstick, turned on his heel and went to ground in the loft above the non-white lavatory. From there, through a chink in the red tiles, he could keep an eye on the vehicle yard.

Kramer arrived at the CID building at eleven o'clock, having found his car only after quartering the hospital area in a taxi. He loped into Colonel Muller's office and sat himself down on a corner of the desk.

' 'Morning, Colonel!' he said, winking an eye.

Colonel Muller looked up at him wearily. 'Is that what getting a decent sleep does for you?' he asked.

'Not exactly, but where's everybody, hey?'

'Ah.'

'Uh-huh? And?'

'And this,' said Colonel Muller, thrusting two neatly typed sheets at him, each initialled by his own fair hand. 'Cast your eye over these, Lieutenant – they'll give you an idea of the current position.'

Kramer took the sheets so obviously prepared by De Klerk and skimmed through them without feeling a thing; his night – or what he could remember of it – made their contents seem as remote as an item in one of last year's newspapers. As for any feelings of indignation, they were stillborn. Like Tish had said, locking her legs around him, all that truly mattered in the final analysis was that he enjoyed himself.

'Really first-class, sir,' he said, handing the sheets back, 'if it isn't impertinent of me to state an opinion. There's method there and there's imagination. This silencer idea of yours! Hell, I'd have written all that off to poor observation, as per usual.'

'You would?'

'It could be the answer, Colonel – but you know how it is, I've gone completely stale on that case. When did you get the inspiration?'

'Ach, it was more a combined effort in some ways,' began Colonel Muller, stopping to light his pipe. 'If you say you're – '

'One thing, Colonel.'

'Lieutenant?'

'Well, to be honest with you, I can't see where I'd be wanted. Frans de Klerk is your man, surely? I'm not enjoying it any more and there's one hell of a backlog to catch up – any chance of me coming off it for a couple of days?'

'Er . . .' said Colonel Muller, as though something had just been snatched from the tip of his tongue, then he looked at Kramer even more warily. 'Is this some of your sarcasm, hey?'

'Sorry, sir?'

'You know, maybe you're right, Tromp!' said Colonel Muller, offering him one of the tennis biscuits he treated himself to for his elevenses. 'Statistically, all we've got here is one murder, two attempted, and the dead man was virtually a foreigner. It must be more than a week since we added – '

'Then can I get weaving, clear up some of the routine stuff, sir?'

'Certainly! If you don't mind Frans – '

'Mind? To be honest, Colonel, I'm bloody relieved to get shot of it,' replied Kramer, truthfully.

'What have you first on your list then?'

'An easy one. I thought I'd help Zondi nail this Banjo Nyembezi for the fatal stabbing down at Mama Bhengu's.'

'Ah.'

For an instant, as he saw Colonel Muller stealthily slide a neatly typed memo slip under his blotter, Kramer felt his new approach to life threatened. Then he rationalised that there was nothing he couldn't achieve by picking his targets and keeping things light-hearted.

'You said "Ah", sir.'

'Well, Bantu Detective Sergeant Zondi is at present seconded to Frans' group, so he can keep an eye on him. I can put him back on general duties, naturally, but first I must satisfy myself about something. You know I'm prepared to overlook last night's unfortunate little incident on the grounds of the stress and strain you have been under these past weeks. But what was Zondi's excuse? Did he deliberately accompany you to that small holding in the knowledge you were contravening my strict instructions? Or was he obeying orders?'

Kramer got off the corner of the desk with a grin. 'Hell, Colonel, he's only a kaffir, isn't he? What do you think?'

They caught up with Banjo Nyembezi at four o'clock that same afternoon. His mistake was leaving a string of gambling debts behind him, and the word had gone out that he was no longer to be trusted. This meant that gamblers far and wide had been keeping a sharp eye out for him, and when they heard that Kramer and Zondi had a warrant for his arrest, they couldn't do enough for them. Flashy cars zipped this way and that in Peacevale, stopping at street corners, pausing briefly down alleyways, and much the same happened in Trekkersburg's two more recent black townships. Eventually Yankee Boy Msomi, a professional informer with sad eyes like two boiled eggs in black eggcups, pinpointed his position in a tin shack at the edge of the Baptist mission.

'You see how you add to the violence around here, man,' Yankee Boy complained to Zondi, from his customary seat in the rear of a rusting Plymouth in a scrapyard. 'Banjo never packed a rod till an hour ago, when he heard the whisper that you and Uncle Tom over there was a-gunnin' for him.'

'Banjo's got a gun?'

'Too right – already hurt a man bad to get it, only *his* name stays a secret with me, brother. But you dig what I mean?'

'What kind of gun?'

'Some kinda six-shooter, I guess. Ain't you pigs comin' a little heavy for a gamblin' debt?'

That made it Zondi's turn to smile crooked. 'What debt? The warrant we've got is for murder.'

'Oh, wow, man!' Had Yankee Boy's eyes had shells on them, they'd have cracked right then. 'If us cats had known it was a hangin' matter, why she-it, you'd notta heard a goddamn word!'

'We figured that,' said Zondi, who'd also read a few American paperbacks in his time. 'He's a bad bastard then?'

'He's *mean*, brother, really *mean*. Just see you don't goof this up and let him run free, 'cos Yankee Boy for one ain't ready to head for the hills yet! Maybe I should go hide down a big hole.'

'It'll be okay,' Zondi reassured him.

He couldn't remember when last the Lieutenant had been so relaxed or in a better mood, and that was half the battle when dealing with a desperate killer like Banjo Nyembezi.

The tin shack was poorly positioned. The only cover in front of it was an old oil drum filled with stagnant water, and that still left a ten-yard gap to the door. There was a low stone wall behind the shack, but between it and the small back window was a litter of fire-damaged cast-iron beds, almost as difficult to cross in a hurry as a barbed-wire entanglement. To complete the problem, down each side of the shack was a thick row of prickly-pear cactus.

'We'll give him a chance to come out with his hands up,' said Kramer, surveying the scene from a corner of the mission chapel. 'I'll get in behind the oil drum, and you circle round behind the wall at the back. Not used a gun before, you said?'

'So Yankee Boy tells me,' confirmed Zondi.

'Then he'll be a lousy shot. If he wants to play this one for keeps, how about trying the old up-and-under?'

'Sounds good, boss. All gamblers are pretty fast in their counting.'

The missionary tugged at Kramer's sleeve. 'Pardon me,' he said, anxiously, 'but I couldn't help overhearing. You're not contemplating dealing with this man on your own, I hope? I've got children all over the place, and if he – '

'They'll be all right, reverend, so long as you keep them behind the church like I said.'

'But it's still only a matter of a hundred yards from there to here,' protested the missionary, squinting at the shack through a pair of cheap, cracked spectacles, and the purple birth-mark on his blanching cheek stood out like an ink blot. 'He could cover that in twelve seconds!'

'Even ten seconds, reverend. Only he won't get the chance.'

'But how can you – ?'

'Watch,' said Kramer, 'and pray, if you like, but for Christ's sake keep your head down.'

Two minutes later, under a gloriously hot afternoon sun, Kramer crouched basking behind the oil drum, with the door of the shack in his sights He heard a shrill whistle, which indicated that Zondi was ready, and whistled back. A shot cracked out from the PPK, pinging harmlessly off the roof of the shack.

'Police!' Kramer called out loudly. 'That was a bullet from the gun of Sergeant Zondi, Banjo Nyembezi! He is behind you, I am in front of you, there is no escape! We know you have a gun — just chuck it out of the door, then come out slowly with your hands up!'

There was a bang and dust spurted up three yards to the left of the oil drum.

'So now you've only got five bullets left!' shouted Kramer. 'How many have we got, Banjo Nyembezi? There are still six in my gun! Yes, six! And Zondi has eight in his! What are the odds, hey? Can you win this?'

A torrent of Zulu obscenities came from the shack, and Kramer was amused to see the missionary regain some of his colour. 'Reverend?' he called back to him. 'Will you try telling him how hopeless his situation is? Swear on your bible oath everything you say is true.'

The missionary began pleading loudly with the fugitive in urgent Zulu from the corner of the chapel. Nyembezi interrupted him with a question, which he answered after some hesitation.

'What was that, reverend?'

'He asked if there really were only two of you, and I'm afraid I couldn't lie to him. I said, Yes, just the two, as God is my witness.'

'Just the job,' said Kramer, who knew the man's reputation for complete honesty among the blacks. Then he turned his attention back to the shack. 'Your last chance, Banjo! I count to five, and if you're not out, then Sergeant Zondi has my permission to kill you!'

The missionary gasped.

'One,' began Kramer. 'Two, Nyembezi! Three! Remember I have six bullets! Zondi has eight! Reckon the odds against you, Nyembezi! Four, Nyembezi! How many bullets have you got left, Nyembezi?' He waited for the man to surrender. 'Five!'

Two shots rang out from behind the shack in quick succession, followed by a louder bang from Nyembezi's weapon. Zondi screamed, and became visible to one side of the shack for a moment, staggering back, throwing his gun high into the air. Then he collapsed behind the low wall.

'For the love of God!' cried the missionary. 'Your African's been – '

Kramer fired six times at the shack door, shouting out, 'I've got you, you bastard! You'd never have got out that way!'

There was a scurry as Nyembezi crossed the floor of the shack, whipped open the door and came running straight at him, intent on closing the range to a dead certainty before he squeezed the trigger. Kramer hurled his empty magnum at him. Then he dropped into a crouch and shot Banjo Nyembezi with Zondi's Walther PPK, which he had caught only moments before, as it completed its lazy, carefully aimed trajectory.

'You look like a man who has just seen the light, reverend,' said Kramer. 'And don't worry, hey? Banjo's only got a flesh wound.'

'Mama, mama!' yelled the younger children, making Miriam hurry to the door. 'Mama, look! Our father is back and it is still daylight!'

'It's not even six o'clock!' she said, and her belly went hollow when she realised she'd heard no car draw up. 'Mickey?' asked Miriam, as she met him in the road. 'Mickey, what's happened?'

'We had a good day, that's all. The Lieutenant was in a bit of a hurry though, so he dropped me at the gates.'

'But when were you last home so early?'

Zondi shrugged. 'It is our new way of working.'

'Hau! Then please God that it lasts!'

'Oh, I think it will,' said Zondi.

CHAPTER TWENTY-ONE

Meerkat Marais was wasting away in the toils of a total obsession, and looked each day more like a mongoose than ever.

The nympho from the telephone exchange was wantonly candid in her reactions to this unappealing metamorphosis. She told him that his tiny red eyes would soon be so red and tiny through staring at the wall that they would glow in the dark. She said his thin cheeks were becoming so pinched with never eating that they made his teeth look like small yellow fangs which needed cleaning. Finally, she also remarked on how creepy his skinny, hairy little body was beginning to feel, and rashly added that perhaps his cobra was past it, because it hadn't raised its hooded head to her in a week. So Meerkat beat the hell out of her with the steam iron she was using, ironed her nipples flat, and took himself home to the scene of the crime above the dry-cleaning depot.

He had a vague description, that was all.

Vague because it had been given to him by an epileptic who also suffered from poor vision, and yet it did provide him with a basic impression of at least one of the two gun thieves. The man was white, he had darkish-brown hair, he was tall and aged somewhere between eighteen and perhaps as much as thirty. His clothes had seemed smart enough to suggest someone from a much better part of town, and they had included a dark suit, a blue shirt and a striped tie, the colours of which eluded her. He had carried a black briefcase and had walked with a spring in his step. He had knocked on Meerkat's door two or three times, before taking out a white card and disappearing into the flat. He had been there a very short time, and then had walked quickly away again.

'Come on, Dynamite! Let's hear the rest, hey?'

'Grrrrr,' said Dynamite, wolfing down the whole can of Kit-eez Delite that his provider had thoughtfully shoplifted on the way home.

'You're some watch dog,' grumbled Meerkat, not without a smidgeon of affection. 'What I want to know is which Monday was this? Is that too much to ask?'

'Grrrrr,' warned Dynamite.

The trouble was of course that Meerkat had been away for eight days before he discovered the outrage, and for several other days here and there before that, making it impossible to be sure when the thing had occurred. Not that this was all that important in the final analysis, but his mind had taken to worrying over every single detail. That striped tie, for instance : the only striped ties that Meerkat knew about were either the fancy sort or the ones schoolboys wore, and the description, vague as it was, certainly didn't describe a schoolboy. In fact the class of person it described was also bewildering, because smart young men never ventured down to his end of town unless they were selling insurance, and Meerkat had already pursued that line of enquiry to no useful conclusion. The other thing that sorely perplexed him was that the epileptic had seen only one person come to his flat, whereas the fingerprints on the tumblers indicated there must have been two.

Humming to himself, temporarily elated as always by a good beating, Meerkat decided to go back and take another look at those tumblers. It was just possible that one of them would provide him with the sort of a clue that Kramer went wild for – a missing middle-finger among the impressions, for instance. The tumblers lay broken on the floor by his bar, but in quite a short time he had managed to sort them into two piles of their respective pieces, some of which were big enough to examine. The fingerprints seemed much fainter than they had done originally, and no matter how he twisted them to the light, a clear image eluded him.

'Prrrt?' said Dynamite, coming through and settling on his jacket.

But Meerkat was lost in thought. The men from Fingerprints used chalk dust, he remembered, and wondered if talcum powder would work as effectively. Not that he had any at hand, but he could always whip down to the corner and steal some. They also used a black powder a bit like soot from an oil lamp. but he hadn't any of that around. They sort of puffed it on out of a rubber-ball thing, and then lifted the prints with a piece of Sellotape. He had Sellotape all right, five cartons of it. Then he remembered that he also had a puffer filled with graphite powder, which was marvellous for lubricating locks and allowing a key to turn without a sound. Perhaps that would do the trick.

'Stand aside!' he said to Dynamite, 'Sherlock Houses is on his way!'

Dynamite fell into a deep, digestive sleep, and paid no heed to the excited activities that filled the next five minutes. Fortunately there was nothing in Meerkat's jacket pockets that he wanted.

'Hell, look at that!' exclaimed Meerkat, as he peeled away the Sellotape and found on it a set of clear impressions. 'Now let's see what we can see . . .'

He screwed a jeweller's eyepiece into his right eye, having always believed that he would find a use for it eventually, and tried to detect what Fingerprints men detected in such circumstances. He was amazed by how distinctive the patterns were, with spirals on one finger contrasting with a sort of banana shape on another. He went on to make further comparisons with his own fingerprints, which had also been lifted by the Sellotape in his handling of it. But instead of his fingerprints looking entirely different, they looked exactly the same to him. His hands began to shake. He checked and double-checked.

'Oh no . . .' groaned Meerkat, 'one of those glasses was mine all the time!' And he should have realised this at the start, being hopeless at taking things through to the kitchen to wash up, instead of jumping to wild conclusions that had cost him weeks of fruitless endeavour. 'I'm looking for only one guy, Dyna, not a gang of two, and that makes all the bloody difference, hey?'

Or was the other glass marked with his prints as well? he wondered with a shudder. 'That would really put the cat in among the penguins, hey?' But it wasn't; those fingerprints looked to him entirely different.

'Now what?' said Meerkat, taking an unbroken tumbler and trying to find something left he could put in it. 'Where do we go from here?'

Before trying to sort that out, his mind went back to the smart young man and did some fresh reasoning. Maybe he wasn't a professional after all. Maybe those drawers had been pulled out, starting with the bottom one and working upwards so time wasn't wasted by pushing them in again, by Meerkat himself, acting through sheer habit and training. Maybe he was just a clown from the smart side of town who wanted a gun and had somehow heard that Meerkat was in the market. That fitted : only that type of person would be mad enough to come buying guns in broad daylight, carrying his briefcase full of used notes, and expecting to take the gun away in it afterwards. And then? No answer to his knock, and he had knocked again, needing a gun very urgently. So badly, in fact, that he had decided to break in, and had used a trick with a credit card that he had seen on the films, and which actually worked. Once inside, however, the baboon had started to panic, unsure of where in all the mess he would find what he was seeking. He had gone to the bar and steadied his nerve with a slug of Scotch. But why suddenly look in the fridge? That was simple : because he just might have seen the same television programme as Meerkat had seen – and now he came to think about it, fridges had featured more than once in such stories, making it not such a smart place to hide things. Anyway, the youngster had gone through, found the revolver in the ice compartment, which did look a little like a safe on reflection, had kicked Dynamite and hurried out, too scared by then to check that he had closed the door properly. No wonder the epileptic had said he'd had a spring in his bloody step !

Meerkat drank three fingers of crème de menthe and felt quite certain that this time he had it right; it was more than a hunch, it was a dead certainty. Then his mood changed abruptly frcm euphoria to a blind rage at the thought of having had something stolen off him by a brat whose parents had always given him what he wanted. Meerkat's parents had never given him a thing, apart from abuse, scalds, cigarette burns, fractured arms and a starvation diet, and the shrieking injustice of the crime made him clasp his hands to his ears, sob and sit on the floor rocking to and fro.

He was still rocking to and fro on the floor of his living room when he heard a cheery voice from above him.

'My God, Meerkat ! It must be some hangover you've got there !'

Meerkat looked up and saw Basil 'Silver Touch' Benson, a con-man who specialised in cleaning out stupid old women, in one of his best suits and happiest moods. 'Go,' said Meerkat, unable to trust himself to say more.

'Steady on, old thing,' murmured Benson, who also dabbled in porn films, dirty magazines and almost any other sudden yen felt by the mugs at his end of the trade, 'I do think I've been frightfully patient.'

'About what, hey? Because I'm not in a patient –'

'That spot of commission you owe me – y'know, young gent making vague enquiries about a shooter. Well, it has been well over a month since then, and I was getting just a little concerned about our – er, little arrangement? Been looking for you everywhere. Been holed up, what? Pretty young thing, was she?'

Meerkat sprang for Benson's throat and sank his uncut nails into it. 'You! You sent him here?'

'Ste-steady on,' gasped Benson, collapsing backwards on to the sofa. 'Not been involved in any jobs, y'know! Pure collector interest, every reason to believe – ugh!'

'Basil,' said Meerkat, very softly, and Dynamite fled the room. 'I'm not going to hurt you, Basil, but don't try biting me again, hey? Just tell me who wanted –'

'Gun-gun enthusiast, collects 'em, I only spoke to the chap in between, of course, very discreet, *very very* discreet, that I can assure you! Old ammuni –'

'*When?*' demanded Meerkat, breaking a standard lamp. '*And who?*'

'Mon-Mon-Monday just over a month ago! Oh God, I'm going to have a heart –'

'*Who?*' screamed Meerkat.

But Benson was out cold, blue-lipped and breathing like a pair of leaky bellows. Meerkat took his hands away, wiped them on the seat of his trousers, and picked up his jacket. He would have a cigarette to calm him down while the old fool completed his act. Once a con-man, always a con-man, and Meerkat Marais felt confident that his terrible revenge was only a matter of hours away now. He could afford to relax for a bit.

CHAPTER TWENTY-TWO

When Kramer arrived at the mortuary that afternoon a little
after four, he found Van Rensburg in such a deep sulk that he
was spared the usual smalltalk. They simply nodded to one
another, and Van Rensburg muttered, 'The so-called district
surgeon isn't here yet.'

'Uh-huh. I'll go through where it's cooler.'

There was a body waiting on each of the five slabs in the post-
mortem room. The nearest had to be very fresh, because the
sheet covering it was a sticky scarlet. He took a look at the white
male beneath it, saw a face mutilated beyond all recognition, and
decided these were probably the remains of some young motor-
cyclist who'd tried to take a bite out of a lamp-post. The three
corpses in the middle he ignored, and then flipped back the sheet
on the fifth, exposing a white female of about twenty who had
been murdered in the Blue Stream Motel the night before. What
made it a potentially fascinating case was the ligature used to
strangle her : a piece of knotted twine on which were threaded
113 keys. He had counted them personally.

A movement two bodies away made him glance up sharply.
There it was again. A bump in the sheet, which he had taken
to be a protruding naval, was moving towards the chest. He
approached the slab cautiously, half-amused by his own trepidation, and removed the sheet with one quick pull. It was a snail.

'Bloody hell,' he snorted. 'Come on, my friend, out you go !'
And he tossed the snail through an open fanlight.

'Hullo, Tromp !'

It was Strydom, bustling in cheerfully, followed by a heavily
built garden boy and Nxumalo, who were carrying four viscera
buckets covered by wet towels. 'Over there by the sink, Josiah,'
he ordered. 'Just put them down and wait for me by the car,

okay?' The buckets were deposited and the two Zulus slipped out.

'Having a busy day, Doc?' asked Kramer.

'Ach, no busier than you, I'm sure,' replied Strydom, carelessly, 'and you're looking all right on it! Have you been putting on weight recently, by the way?'

Kramer shrugged. 'Never fitter.'

'It was all that living on your nerves,' said Strydom, trotting over to see what lay in store for him. 'This bloke's still warm hey? Oh ja, this must be the lady with the faulty hair-curlers. And this?'

'Ja, I know about that one,' Kramer confirmed. 'Unidentified Bantu male, aged around fifty, found with his head on the main line this morning. Apparent suicide.'

'Really? No papers or anything?'

'He was in rags,' said Kramer, puffing a stray lash out of the eyesocket of the motel victim. 'If you look closely at her nose, she may have had plastic surgery. Do you think you might be able to give us some sort of lead from that? She's also unidentified.'

'Are you in a big rush? There's something . . .'

'Go right ahead, Doc.'

While Strydom was out of the room, Van Rensburg came in and glared at the buckets. 'Not more,' he muttered darkly.

'Not more what, Van?'

'You wouldn't believe me, Lieutenant,' said Van Rensburg, and went out again.

Kramer was about to go over and examine what was in the buckets, when Strydom returned, carrying an electric-kettle flex and with Nxumalo in tow.

'Now this won't take a minute,' said Strydom, baring the body of the apparent suicide. 'I've been waiting weeks for a chance like this – the last one I tried wasn't the right build or age, you see.' He lifted the arms, knotted the flex around the wrists and held out the ends to Nxumalo. 'You know what to do?'

'Two rand, my boss?'

'Four,' said Strydom.

'Ach, no!' laughed Kramer, realising what the district surgeon had in mind. 'Isn't it time all that was finished and forgotten? You know Frans de Klerk nearly ended up a basket case because of it.'

'This is something of a personal matter, Tromp – although not between you and me, you understand. Proceed, Nxumalo.'

The Zulu wound the ends of the flex around his fists, braced his massive shoulder muscles, and gave a sudden, sinew-cracking jerk. The wrists bounced on the abdomen and lay there, bound unbelievably tightly together.

'But the bones aren't bust,' observed Van Rensburg, who had joined them unnoticed. 'I've already said it a million times, Doc – it's bloody impossible.'

'What was that about the nose?' Strydom asked Kramer, turning to face the table behind him. 'Out you go, Nxumalo! This is a white lady here.'

Nxumalo left crestfallen, and Van Rensburg indulged a lofty expression until he caught sight of something on the spring-balance above the sink. Kramer noticed it too. It was a snail.

'Look at that!' protested Van Rensburg. 'I tell you, Dr Strydom, this can't go on! Yik!'

'Science doesn't recognise your petty prejudices, Sergeant,' said Strydom, taking up his biggest knife. 'If you organised things better, it wouldn't happen anyway.'

'Science, the man calls it!' said Van Rensburg, addressing a despairing appeal to Kramer. 'It's scientific to have slimy creepy-crawlies all over a State mortuary? Leaving their trails everywhere? That's not scientific! That's how mistakes are made!'

'Rubbish!' snapped Strydom, transferring his aggression by slitting the murdered woman open from pubis to mandible.

'Oh ja?' retorted Van Rensburg. 'And who was it last week who thought he found the glisten of semen stains on that poor income tax inspec – '

'De Klerk's back in Housebreaking, I hear,' said Strydom, changing the subject. 'I must say he did a first-class job on following all those early leads until they petered out, but his basic premise couldn't have been right.'

'Maybe he should have used snails, hey Doc?'

'Which theory was that?' asked Kramer, lighting a cigarette to ward off the smell of the motel's cooking. 'He went through quite a few near the end, hey? The best one was when he tried to pin it all on Digby-Smith.'

'Never!' gasped Strydom. 'What had Hans Muller to say to that?'

'He cried for a whole afternoon, Doc.'

Van Rensburg felt the edge of his bone-saw. 'If I could get them all in one long line,' he said, 'then maybe I could cut through the lot in one chop.'

'Quiet!' growled Strydom, snipping the ribs. 'But why? What happened exactly?'

'Well, for a start, he went out to Morninghill and challenged Digby-Smith to deny his allegations.'

'Before he'd consulted Hans?'

'I think he was hoping to surprise him,' said Kramer, smiling at the memory of that particular afternoon. 'Mind you, it was all fairly logical except for one or two details.'

'Go on.'

Kramer was bored with the story, having already told it to Tish and to the Widow Fourie, before she took her children down to the beach for their holidays, but felt the effort might be worth Van Rensburg's silence. 'Ach, De Klerk's basic theory was that Digby-Smith had suddenly gone snap, being a strange sort of bloke filled with "pent-up" emotions – his phrase. There was the resentment he'd felt for Hookham over the years, coupled with the humiliation he'd suffered at the hands of Bradshaw. It all began, De Klerk decided, when Hookham came back from the flying club social and, instead of being grateful to Digby-Smith for suggesting such a nice evening, he'd drunkenly teased him about Bradshaw – probably said far too much. Digby-Smith could have imagined, for instance, that Bradshaw had told Hookham how he'd rooked his stupid brother-in-law, and they'd been laughing at him behind his back. It's true enough that Digby-Smith said to me it was a pity the bloke hadn't emerged to shoot Bradshaw properly, and Colonel Muller had passed this on.'

'I see – so he just went on the warpath generally?'

'No, it was only Bradshaw to begin with, De Klerk worked out. A sort of blind rage made him want to kill him, even though he was a pacifist, didn't know anything about guns, and –'

'Was a terrible marksman,' chortled Strydom, catching the drift. 'After all, he did miss two times out of three in effect!'

'Uh-huh. Hookham may have told Digby-Smith about the conversation regarding walking dogs on the race-course, and so he found himself an old gun – probably a revolver left by his father or something – and went after him. He thought the first shot had killed him, left him lying there and rushed home, maybe already terrified of what he had done. What happens next? The paper the following day says that Bradshaw isn't dead after all! And Digby-Smith gets the shakes, thinking Bradshaw must have identified him.'

'But I thought it was Hookham who got the shakes?' said Strydom.

'Only according to Digby-Smith's evidence, Doc. Mrs Digby-Smith saw a reaction in her brother-in-law, and De Klerk ascribed that to the likelihood Hookham had half-guessed who'd done the deed.'

'You know something, Tromp? This makes better sense than anything I've heard so far!'

'It lacks one or –'

'No, no; you carry on, and I'll see if I can guess.'

Kramer lit a fresh cigarette off his first and wished he'd thought to bring a cigar along. 'Okay, so De Klerk puts himself in Digby-Smith's shoes and imagines what a hell of a time he had until the Sunday papers gave Bradshaw's description of a "giant". Digby-Smith is quite tall, but he doesn't look too well-built, and so he must have thought Bradshaw had failed to recognise him entirely.'

'Phew!' said Strydom.

'Ja, but what happened that night, Doc? Hookham starts to act strangely and suddenly wants to go home. He behaves like a man who finds himself in a nasty situation; he isn't sure of his facts, but just wants to have nothing mcre to do with it. Digby-Smith begins to feel certain that Hookham suspects him, and takes a look in his diary. Hookham has stopped adding comments. Why? Because he can no longer trust his thoughts to paper? Digby-Smith encourages him to leave. Then comes Tuesday night, when Hookham visited Mrs Westford, and said he'd go on a final "sortie" that would decide whether he stayed on or not. Was this a confrontation with Digby-Smith? More than likely, and Digby-Smith decided the time had come to rid himself of this terrible danger. He'd never liked the man anyway.'

'Good, good, good,' approved Strydom, peeling away the scalp to give Van Rensburg something to do. 'But this time he tied up the victim, so as to have a sitting target and to get his shots in from closer?'

'Uh-huh. Not only that, but De Klerk found that Digby-Smith

had a small workshop for his hobby of ship-modelling, and deduced he'd used it to make a silencer. By now, he said, Digby-Smith could afford to take no chances, and had to be extra careful with everything he did. Not knowing where to find Hookham when he went off at night, he'd simply hidden in the back of the green Rover until, reaching an isolated spot, he'd made Hookham stop by pushing the gun in his ear. After killing him, satisfied he had suspected him of Bradshaw's shooting, Digby-Smith had brought the car back home for three or more reasons : firstly, it would complicate the investigation; secondly, it would pay his wife back for years of the "blue-eyed boy"; and thirdly, how else was he to return from to-hell-and-gone without transport?'

Strydom looked up from the throat. 'Ah! But what about the schoolgirl? She doesn't fit into this!'

'You've got it in one, Doc.'

'Hey?'

Kramer shrugged. 'De Klerk actually gives me the credit for her role in all this, because of my obsession about the RAF. By another of life's coincidences – like Digby-Smith's mistake of sending Hookham to the social, which I'm sure was genuine – he had decided around that time to hire some bleepers from Robert du Plooi, thinking they'd be useful for keeping in touch with the office while out visiting sites. De Klerk discovered that Du Plooi had told him of my interest in what'd been said at the social, and Digby-Smith had seen how dangerous this could be, by way of providing a possible motive et cetera.'

'That also makes excellent sense,' remarked Strydom, 'but you still haven't – '

'Digby-Smith realised he'd have to destroy this link-up of mine. De Klerk had told Colonel Muller he was being tortured by hearing Mrs Baksteen saying over and over, why had anyone wanted to kill her little girl? And suddenly, instead of feeling bad about it, he'd felt marvellous. The answer to Mrs Baksteen's question was simple : nobody had tried to kill Classina – they'd just tried to make it look that way! Digby-Smith broke *two* links in this fashion : the incidental RAF link, much more important one, which made what Bradshaw and Hookham had in common – a man who hated them both.'

'Ah!'

'When he pulled the trigger out at Six Valleys, bang went any chance of the suspicion coming back to him. De Klerk was sure he could find out where the skipping rope came from, the stocking and everything else, once he'd seen that look of guilt in Digby-Smith's eyes.'

'All very plausible,' applauded Strydom, removing the hyoid bone, which was fractured. 'Especially the part about the schoolgirl.'

'I agree,' said Kramer, 'but what De Klerk should have done first was to ask the servants a question or two.'

'Their coons? Why?'

'Because they are able to provide Digby-Smith with a cast-iron alibi every time there was a shooting, never mind what Mrs Digby-Smith had to say after De Klerk visited them.'

'Yirra!' exclaimed Van Rensburg, smiling his evil smile. 'What a clanger to drop, hey? So he never got round to giants?'

'Oh, for heaven's –' Strydom got out.

'He did in the end,' said Kramer, smiling again. 'He rang Colonel Muller at his house at two in the morning, and said it was so simple he could kick himself. He was reminded he'd been put back into Housebreaking, and that the case was being stamped "unsolved", but insisted on having his say. The silencer was the key, he told Colonel Muller, and pointed out that Digby-Smith was easily rich enough to buy expensive skipping ropes *and* to hire a Jo'burg hitman to do his dirty work for him. A real pro, who not only used a proper silencer, but had a build like a giant, which explained the fractured wrists that he'd not been able to fit into everything before. Clearly a foreigner with a funny accent, and Digby-Smith had taken the precaution of telling me that –'

'Oh no, I can't take any more!' laughed Strydom. 'Poor old Fransie, hey? That's always the trouble with these loony cases: there *is* no shape to the thing, just a lot of bits and pieces, and the imagination runs riot trying to fit them together. By the way, did Galt ever find out what that pink stuff inside the stocking was?'

'Some kind of complexion cream,' said Kramer.

'Ladies' complexion cream?'

'Ja, but people also use it for sunburn, apparently. I don't think they'll be reopening the docket to look for a six-foot-four lady wrestler with paranoid schizophrenia.'

'God forbid!' said Strydom, taking up one of his knives. 'Isn't it about time you got sawing, Sergeant?'

'Even a wrestler couldn't do it,' mumbled Van Rensburg. 'Not even *two* wrestlers trying their –'

'There's a thought!' said Strydom. 'Would you mind, Tromp?'

'Be my guest,' said Kramer.

But try as they would, Nxumalo and Josiah could not synchronise their separate tugs into one simultaneous, bone-shattering explosion of force, and a great deal of time was wasted on several other improvisations. Kramer suggested what was missing was the sort of surge of adrenalin that gave housewives the strength to carry washing-machines out of blazing kitchens, then lost all interest when his offer of inducing such a surge in Van Rensburg was rejected.

'But I've proved something at least,' said Strydom. 'It could be achieved only by one person, co-ordinating his movements with a single impulse from the brain. Have you ever considered the idea that the "giant" might be a real giant? Much, much *bigger* than Bradshaw described him?'

'From a circus or something you mean?' asked Kramer, keeping a straight face.

'Why not? You could try the shoe shops, see if anyone around takes a specially big size. In tending to belittle Bradshaw's evidence, you could have made the mistake of literally belittling the suspect.'

'Hmmmm.' Another snail had made its appearance, and was crawling across the face of the electric wall clock. 'Doc, I must be off – got someone to pick up.'

'Hey? But what about this nose? It's only five-past five.'

'You know my philosophy: tomorrow's always another day.'

'That's *your* philosophy?' asked Strydom, in surprise.

'Uh-huh.'

And Kramer was gone, leaving Strydom to put down his knife, blink a couple of times, and turn to Van Rensburg. 'That's a bit of luck,' he said. 'Just put those others back in the fridge for me to see tomorrow, and then you and I can get on with my little experiment. It's getting to the interesting stage, isn't it?'

Zondi did not wait to hear Banjo Nyembezi remanded in custody for trial on a charge of murder. He slipped out of the preliminary examination at the Regional Magistrates' Court at a quarter past five and headed for the main street, intent on buying his children a present before closing time. They had all received excellent end-of-term reports, which made him a proud if apprehensive parent : doing well at school was one thing, finding them an outlet for their talents afterwards was quite another.

He dived into the biggest bookshop in the centre of Trekkers-burg and searched hurriedly through the textbook section. His chief difficulty lay in deciding which book – he could afford no more than one – would be of some assistance to them all, and he had already bought him their Zulu, Afrikaans and English diction-aries, as well as a couple of comprehensive works on mathematics and Zulu history. Finally he hit upon an atlas that was going cheap because its cover was slightly torn, and took it to the pay desk, delighted by his luck.

'Are you quite sure you want such a big book?' asked the kindly faced shop assistant with plastic teeth that whistled. 'It is rather expensive, you know, and all it's got in it are maps.'

'Please, madam.'

'You made certain by looking inside it?'

'Hau, me not look inside, madam. My boss say to buy him atlas cheap, and that is all.'

'Oh, that's fine then, isn't it? Ten rand, please ...'

Zondi smiled his thanks for her concern as ne handed over the carefully hoarded notes; it wasn't a very honest way of going about things, but often it was much simpler.

'Carry it nicely now !' she said.

'Yes, madam. Thank you, madam.'

Half-way back to Boomplaas Street, he could no longer resist temptation, and sat down on the grass outside a public building to unwrap his purchase. He removed the brown paper without tearing it, and raised the atlas to his nose for a good, long sniff. There was nothing like the smell of a brand-new book for making him feel as fortunate as any man. Then he began turning the pages, relishing the sound of them parting for the first time, and worked his way through small maps of the world until he reached the first proper section, which was on the British Isles. With very little trouble, he found Hookham's village near Southampton, and felt reassured that this must be a very fine atlas indeed. France began the section on Western Europe, and again he paused, intrigued to discover the Picardy across which Hookham and his fellow prisoners of war had escaped from Germany. The distances involved were all far less great than he had imagined, and he traced his finger this way and that, guessing at the probable escape route through the more thinly populated areas. He was just passing north of Amiens when there came an unwelcome interruption.

'Pssst!'

It was none other than Jiji Govender, working as a street cleaner. Zondi was in no mood for any more of the Indian's grovelling gratitude, and shooed him away with his free hand.

'But I have tiding of great importances,' whined Jiji. 'You hear me telling of mysterious gentleman with request to buy thirty-two size volovolo?'

'I remember.'

'The same has been seen this very day, Sergeant – am I hearing this from brother street cleaner working that side.'

'What side?'

'The side where abodes a man whose name I can only say and tremble : Mr Meerkatty Marais.'

'Meerkat?' Zondi lost his place in the atlas. 'Go on, Jiji. What is the name of this gentleman?'

'At luncheon I am partaking of this informations,' confided Jiji, crouching beside Zondi. 'No word of the gent's name is undisclosed, but Sammy Panjut, who working that side, he say he observing same personage diverge into flat of Meerkatty.'

'How long was he in there?'

'Much shouting, and Sammy says gent not seen again. He came away to cater for the needs of the belly – we have timing off from one to two o'clockies.'

'So this gent could have left while Sammy was away having his lunch with you and the other street cleaners?'

Jiji nodded, and plucked a trophy from his left nostril, studying it intently.

'If Sammy didn't know the gent's name, what did he say he looked like?' asked Zondi.

'Just a white gent, that's the lot, Sergeant,' said Jiji, adding the trophy to his main collection on his broom handle. 'I must treading like fairy for Sammy not know I work as undercovers intelligent man.'

'So you didn't ask for more details?'

Jiji shook his head but stayed smiling. 'Is it not a great favouring I perform for you, Sergeant?'

'I'm not sure,' replied Zondi.

It was such a long time since he'd last thought about the shootings case, and so many other more interesting things had happened since then, that he needed a moment to get back into the required frame of mind. The likelihood of there being some connection between the shootings and Jiji's mysterious gent seemed more than tenuous, while to suggest that Meerkat Marais had been involved was a total non-starter. Why was that? Because the Lieutenant had given Meerkat a good grilling the day Hookham's body had been found, and not once had the man shown any of the tiny telltale signs that indicated he was lying when he denied having supplied the weapon. In fact, the Lieutenant had been so sure that Meerkat was in the clear that they hadn't bothered to search his place or keep an eye on him. Some time factor or other had come into it as well, with the offer of good money for a .32 revolver having been made after Bradshaw had already been gunned down . . . And yet here was Jiji Govender with a piece of half-baked information that seemed to suggest that it could all be reconciled somehow. Perhaps the dates were wrong, but what about Meerkat's patent innocence? As he couldn't have faked it that well, thought Zondi, then the only explanation was that Meerkat had played an unwitting part in all this. He might not have liked that, which would in turn explain the shouting.

'Where's Sammy Panjut now, Jiji?'

'Till five-thirties, he still that side, then we knocking off. You go see him?'

Zondi looked at his watch. 'Who knows?'

'Always such a pleasuring,' said Jiji, cupping a hand, 'to do great favour for Number One Sergeant of All Time.'

'And it's a pleasure to do you one in return, Jiji,' said Zondi, who wasn't going to part with a cent until having satisfied himself as to the strength of this tip-off. 'If you go back ten yards, you'll find some orange peel you missed.'

Then he strolled away, carefully returning the atlas to its brown-paper wrapper, and wondered why an early entry in Hookham's diary had been hovering before his mind's eye ever since that interruption. What had triggered it off? And why had he the feeling it held the key to the whole affair? On May 27th, Bonzo Hookham had still been in England.

CHAPTER TWENTY-THREE

Tish Hayes was not waiting on the corner of Alemap Avenue and Reid Street when Kramer drew up punctually in the Chevrolet at five-thirty. He cut the engine and settled back to see what associated ideas he could find for 113 keys on a piece of knotted twine. He started by considering the possibility that 13 was significant, in that it was an unlucky number, but soon abandoned such fanciful nonsense. These were 113 small brass keys, smaller than door-size, and widely varied in shape. The next thought along was that they belonged to the keeper of a safe-deposit vault, but that received an instant thumbs down; twine, knotted or otherwise, just didn't have the style to go with the job. He toyed with the idea of a locksmith, rejected it as too obvious, and went on to the notion that the keys belonged to a collector of old shop tills. Too fanciful again. Then Tish came out of the front of Jonty's, and work was forgotten.

'Home, James, and through the park,' she sighed, flopping into the seat beside him. 'God, I'm exhausted.'

'Has that bastard been giving you a tough time, hey? Maybe I should – '

'Don't be horrid, Tromp. Jonty's very sweet and he's very hardworking, which is more than you can say for most bosses. I couldn't just walk out and leave that old bat for him to finish off, you know. And besides, what about your undying gratitude to him?'

'Huh,' said Kramer, and swung into the traffic.

Tish smiled and put a hand on his knee. They drove like that for a dozen blocks, just pleased to be in each other's company. And for a gentle joke, Kramer took a detour through a small park, skirting it under an avenue of oak trees.

'Tromp?'

'Mmmm?'

'You never did tell me what made you suspect Jonty and me were – y'know,' murmured Tish, giving his knee a squeeze. 'Come on, what was it? I thought our little affair had been ever so discreet.'

'Aren't you also from Southampton?'

'But you didn't know that until our second night.'

'Those ornaments in your flat. They were expensive, very classy, intellectual – none of them was you.'

'Well, thanks a lot, Lieutenant Kramer!'

'You're welcome, lady.'

They joined the rush-hour traffic again, but turned away down a quiet side street at the next intersection.

'What else?' asked Tish.

Kramer wished she hadn't started this. One of the joys of being with her was that they had always lived in the present, making no mention of past or future, and simply savouring what each moment brought with it. Once begun, however, it was an inevitable conversation to be concluded as quickly as possible.

'Before we met,' he said, 'there was that time right at the beginning when Jonty told me in the gym that you had the hots for me.'

'He didn't!'

'Oh ja, and then he laid it on thick he was after the Swedish popsie, just so I'd feel free – if you see what I mean.'

'He's got a cheek! I'd not said a word to him about you at any stage, and anyway I'd only seen you once in the salon, hardly even noticed you.'

'That wasn't how it felt to me,' said Kramer, grinning at her. 'Why, for instance, did he rush off to tell you I'd come to that party?'

She gave her throaty giggle. 'What arrogance there is in the man! I took myself into the kitchen because that Texan fella seemed rather juicy.'

'You're denying that Jonty practically threw you at me?'

'No,' she admitted, in one of those sudden turnabouts that made her mind so attractive, 'he'd probably become as bored in bed as I was, and he probably thought, in his big-hearted way, that you were sorely in need of a distraction.'

'Some distraction!' Kramer laughed. 'But – ?'

'But I still retained the right to choose for myself – he'd been fobbing me off all night, you know. I saw this great boorish Boer standing there, the first I'd ever seen from close up, and thought to myself, Well Tish, how do you fancy a bit of rough? It must've been the booze and not having had it for a week.'

Kramer shook his head, still amused by the forthright way truly English girls appeared to talk, forsaking the salacious prudery of their South African cousins. 'Are we still working on that backlog, hey?' he sighed. 'Only I wanted to ask you if I could have a few nights off once we catch up.'

'Knackered?'

'If that means what I think it means,' replied Kramer, stopping the car outside her flat, 'yes.'

But they were making love again within three minutes of getting inside, and it was a slow, sweet and quite effortless thing. The sunset came to pink the bedroom walls, a light breeze carried the scent of magnolia through the open window, and somewhere along the river bank a black man was playing a penny-whistle, soft and wistful. They dozed for a while, her small head resting beneath his chin, then stirred in the last of the twilight, refreshed and ready to lose themselves utterly in a closed world of their own making. Kramer had never asked her the reason, but he sensed in Tish a great hurt somewhere.

'Your turn to count the daisies,' she whispered, rolling over on him, and bending forward to kiss his mouth, 'I've been thinking. Wondering, really.'

'Tish?'

'Why don't you ever ask me anything? You haven't even asked the usual questions people ask about Jonty. Is he queer? – and all that.'

'But I know he isn't queer. It's all an act so the husbands don't suspect the way he flirts with their wives, and it's his sexy approach to them that keeps them coming.'

'No pun intended?'

'Hey?'

Tish laughed. 'Never mind, my grizzly Boer . . . Some husbands aren't so thick, though! There was one dowdy little thing with the most fabulous figure who – wait a moment, Tromp, I'm still talking.'

'I know : that's what I'm trying to put a stop to.'

'But it's *my* turn to – '

'Shhh,' said Kramer, touching her lips. 'It's our turn, let's put it that way.'

'No, wait, I'm being quite serious.'

'What more must I know that I can't see for myself?' he asked, looking up at her.

She was so frail and light on his loins, fragile almost, and yet fully a woman, with breasts that swayed heavy and ripe above his lips, inviting him to taste their strawberry-tipped sweetness; breasts with character too, one nipple an extrovert, the other turned in on itself until coaxed out gently, and both aware of the mutual pleasure they could bring. Her copper-coloured hair, mussed and tickling, curled down over her thin shoulders, fragrant with her own special smell, and to the left of her navel, neat as a button, was the largest of her freckles, shaped like a butterfly's wing. He kissed it, and entered her as she sat back again.

But Tish made no movement. 'Why won't you ask me anything?' she repeated. 'Wouldn't you like to know, for example, what gifts I bought Jonty in exchange?'

'Ja, I have a question.'

'Which is?'

'How is it that your freckles stop when they get to your face and your hands?'

'I put some stuff on my skin,' she said crossly, and tried to roll off. 'I really don't think you're interested in me as a person at all!'

'Ach no, you're just a distraction,' said Kramer, holding her hips tightly, imagining he was pinning a butterfly to a cork board, making himself laugh. 'You're just *you*, woman! Can't you understand that? You're not parts of Jonty's life, your uncles', aunts' and sisters' lives. You're everything, nothing further is needed! You're Tish! Finished en klaar!' He had never spoken to anyone quite like that before in his entire life.

Tish stared down at him. 'Do you know,' she said, 'that's the sort of adolescent thing a boy comes out with the first time he falls in love.'

'Perhaps that's it,' said Kramer.

'But then surely I'd be part of your life, wouldn't I? And wouldn't the most important part of you be mine too?'

'Isn't it already, hey? How can you sit there and ask such bloody silly questions? Can't you feel it?'

Then Tish began to grin as well. 'Oh, sit *here*, you mean?'

Their laughter set them in motion, bringing with it purely mechanical responses, and then a new wild joy took over, building its own steady rhythmn. 'One daisy,' counted Kramer. 'Two daisies. Three daisies, four daisies, five dai – six! Seven! Eight! Nine!'

'Ooooopsy-*daisy*!'

And they fell out of the bamboo bed just as the telephone in the other room started ringing.

Zondi, watched by Sammy Punjat, and holding Meerkat Marais' receiver in a clean handkerchief to safeguard any fingerprints that might be on it, waited impatiently for someone to answer. At their feet lay the dead body of a smartly dressed, grey-haired man who had fingernail marks in his throat, but seemed to have actually died of a heart attack. The flat was a shambles.

Rrrrr-rrrrr

No answer. Zondi looked at his watch. It was almost six-thirty. Perhaps he should try again in another five minutes.

'Hullo?' said a breathless voice. 'Tish – Tish Hayes, speaking.'

'Sorry to disturb the madam,' said Zondi, 'but this is Bantu Detective Sergeant Zondi here. Is it possible for me to speak with the Lieutenant?'

'How did you know this number, Sergeant?'

'The Lieutenant gave it to me to keep for emergency uses only, madam. Many apologies, but –'

'Just hold on will you? I'll see if he's available.'

Zondi smiled. The Lieutenant had told him it was the telephone number of a flat down near the hospital, and flats didn't have stairs that made people breathless. She sounded very nice, younger than he'd expected, and she'd not called him 'boy'. Then the receiver at the other end rattled as it was snatched up.

'Christ, kaffir, this better be bloody good, hey?'

And Zondi's smile faded.

'Did you have to speak to your colleague like that?' remonstrated Tish, when Kramer stumped back into the bedroom. 'He did say it was an emergency.'

'Another bloody wild-goose chase, that's what! Why are you getting dressed?'

'Because I thought you might be going out, and I'd love to come with you – can I?'

'I'm not sure I'm going to go anywhere,' said Kramer, and sat down on the bed.

Tish laughed and pointed at him. 'My God, what would that sergeant have thought if he could have seen you like that! That's my petti you've got keeping you decent – may I have it back?'

Kramer stripped the petticoat from around his waist, and tossed it over to her, giving in to a small smile. 'Mickey's had worse shocks in his life.'

'So that was Mickey! Why didn't you say so?'

'I don't remember ever mentioning him.'

'Oh, but you do quite often,' said Tish, disappearing inside her dress, 'while you're asleep.' Her head emerged from the neckline and she shook her hair free. 'Has he discovered the secret of the hundred and thirteen keys?'

'No, he's found a man dead on the floor – but only of a heart attack.'

Tish raised her eyebrows inquiringly.

'A confidence trickster and jack-of-all-trades called Silver Touch Benson,' said Kramer, lying back. 'An old rogue I've not had much to do with, but it's where he was found that makes the difference.'

'Go on.'

'I'm thinking.'

'Think aloud then, let me share.'

'It's back to the shootings case, hey? What a pain in the arse – and this only makes it even more mindbending. Mickey heard late this afternoon that somebody who'd been trying to buy a thirty-two around the time of that affair had been seen paying a call on a certain Meerkat Marais – Mongoose Marais to you, and a complete little psychopath who deals sometimes in firearms. Even though I'm sure Meerkat wasn't implicated, Mickey now thinks it could have been unwittingly. Anyway, he decides to check out this tip-off, and he speaks to a street cleaner, name of Sammy Punjat, who witnessed this visit. Punjat tells him that the visitor was a grey-haired, well-dressed-looking white male, carrying a brief-case. Mickey doesn't connect the description with any of Meerkat's known associates, which Silver Touch Benson wouldn't rate as, and decides it warrants further investigation – in fact he admits he thought it could have been Digby-Smith.'

'Just what I was thinking!' said Tish, hopping on one foot as she fastened her other sandal. 'And then?'

'He gets Sammy to go with him back to where Meerkat lives, they wait for a while outside in an empty lot, then Mickey goes up the fire escape and sees a cat walking out of the front door, which is standing open. He gets Sammy to call out like he's a pedlar selling fruit, and when there's no answer, he slips in and finds Benson lying there, dead as a doornail with scratches in his throat.'

'From the cat?'

'From its master more likely,' said Kramer, wiggling his toes. 'Anyway, as soon as Mickey sees Benson, the nickname Silver Touch brings Bradshaw to mind, because there was once a dubious bit of business with some silver at his shop. That's a possible three-way link, in his opinion, with a suggestion of the motive, so he rings me up.'

'And this Mongoose fella?'

'Gone. Sammy tells Mickey that Meerkat's been hunting some youngster lately, who is probably also connected. Maybe it's him he's gone after. This Sammy hadn't a description though.'

Tish threw him his trousers. 'Get weaving, Tromp! This could be the break you've been waiting for! You're not thinking of passing it on to Frans de Klerk, are you?' And she smiled openly at her piece of blatant manipulation.

'Ja, I am as a matter of fact,' he replied. 'Wild-goose chases are just his line. You and me were going to that new restaurant tonight.'

'Here's your shirt, and your holster – by the way, you do realise you left your bullets in the bowl in the sitting room last night? Or this morning, rather?'

'I was that drunk again when we came home?'

'I'm afraid so. Now come on, you can't leave Mickey to cope on his own.'

'He's not even on duty himself,' said Kramer. 'I'll ring the duty officer and get him to turn someone out.'

Tish came and stood over him with her small fists on her hips. 'You're not a sleuth, you're a sloth,' she said. 'Do you seriously think Mickey would dare ring you here unless he felt he had an overwhelmingly good reason? Even to a layman, this sounds just as though – '

'Look,' said Kramer, sitting up and reaching for his trousers, 'I honestly couldn't care less about that case, it sort of sickens me with all the – '

'But what about this fresh angle?'

'Is it one, Tish? Or is this fight between Benson and Meerkat something else entirely? Mickey's only guessing that Benson was involved in that silver deal, because we never got to the bottom of that one either.'

She shrugged. 'But isn't that how it's done? By chasing up even the most unlikely possibilities?'

'While the answer lies under your nose all the time?' said Kramer, pulling up his zip. 'Is that your advice?'

'I think you'd be very silly *not* to,' said Tish.

'Not to what?'

'Well, follow your nose,' she quipped feebly. 'Just try not to think it all out in advance, and see where this leads you. I want to see how – '

Kramer smiled indulgently and tugged on his shirt. 'Fine. I'll compromise then,' he said. 'We'll drop in at Meerkat's, have a quick look at the picture, and if I don't think it's worth taking up, then we'll go on to that restaurant – okay?' He strapped on his shoulder holster and gun, then did up his shirt collar. 'Have you seen my tie?'

'You dropped it just inside the front door,' said Tish, looking pleased and excited. 'Come, I'll put it on for you – bring my handbag.'

Kramer followed her through, had his tie tightened and neatly adjusted, then stepped aside gallantly as he swung open the door. 'After you, lady!'

'Thank you, my man,' said Tish, bowing slightly. 'Mongoose Marais' residence, if you please, and don't spare the horses!'

Zondi had not wasted the time he had spent waiting for Kramer to arrive. He had cleared a space on the living-room floor, and had piled it with stolen goods that he'd recovered from a large number of poorly considered hiding places. There were boxes of shirts, cartons of Sellotape, half a dozen stereo systems, and a great many other disparate items, but most pertinent of them all were the forty-one cartridges for a 9 mm pistol that he had found in a cheese tray in the refrigerator.

'No gun anywhere to go with them?' asked Kramer.

'Not that I can see, boss. Nine from a box of fifty looks like a full magazine.'

'Uh-huh. What's he up to? Making a last stand like Banjo? Or is it something else?'

Zondi glanced down at Benson's body. 'If he had killed this man, he would not have left him lying here, Lieutenant. I don't think he has any guilt to make him run. It must be the youngster he is after.'

Tish was also looking at the body, staring at it in morbid fascination.

'What youngster?' asked Kramer, rounding on Sammy Punjat, who jumped slightly. 'What do you know of this matter?'

'Mere rumour, sir! Idle gossipings! Only that Boss Marais seeks some young fellow to exact justice for wrongdoings.'

'Is that all you know?'

Punjat nodded nervously, and Kramer marked him down as a man as honest as his lowly position in life would allow. It was amusing to note how like De Klerk he looked, were the latter to lose an eye and be given a good rub down with brown boot polish.

'But you said,' grunted Zondi, 'that Meerkat had been spreading a description round among his intimates.'

'That is only my belief,' explained Punjat.

'Where's the nearest intimate?' asked Kramer. 'Fat Solly Wynberg?'

'There is still somebody at the back of the shop,' said Zondi.

'Fine, I'll have a quick word.'

Tish hurried after Kramer. 'I thought dead people were ghostly white,' she said, taking his hand. 'That man is almost purple.'

'Uh-huh.'

'It's funny,' she went on, 'but I don't really *mind* him being dead, if you know what I mean. It didn't frighten me. Too unreal.'

'Dead people are never the problem in this business,' said Kramer. 'It's the living.'

They descended the fire escape in silence, found the backdoor of the dry-cleaning depot slightly ajar to let in the cool night air, and surprised Fat Solly Wynberg at his desk. He had a plastic bag of rice pudding for a head, and through two puffy gaps in this pudding his wet, coal-black eyes looked out, alighting lecherously on Tish.

'Yisss, my dear?' he wheezed. 'What can I do you for?' And he poked his fountain pen into his shirt pocket without fitting its cap first, so the ink spread suddenly like a premature ejaculation. 'In fact, what wouldn't I do you for!'

Kramer moved himself in front of her, sickened. 'Murder and Robbery Squad,' he snapped. 'Lieutenant Kramer.'

'Kramer?' Fat Solly's eyes flicked momentarily in the direction of the flat above his head. 'Of course, Lieutenant! Anything, anything! But who is this gorgeous young lady?'

'I'm asking the questions, Wynberg – one question, one damned fast answer required. I've got a table booked.'

'I'm sorry, I don't –'

'This is it, Wynberg: I want to know all about this young bloke Meerkat has been looking for recently, his name and why. Got it?'

'I don't know what you're talking about, I'm afraid,' replied Fat Solly, breaking into a sweat. 'I don't have much to do with my tenants, you will appreciate, and so –'

'There's a stiff lying dead upstairs,' cut in Kramer. 'Am I going to have to bring you in as an accomplice?'

'For pity's sake! I know nothing about it!'

'Then what *do* you know?'

Fat Solly squirmed as though he had the horns of a dilemma through each sagging buttock, and his sweat smelled sickly and fecal. 'It isn't I don't want to be of service, believe me . . .' he said hoarsely.

'Last chance, Solly. Let's hear it.'

Still no reply. That was the trouble with Meerkat Marais' friends, relatives and acquaintances: they all thought his anger was the most horrifying thing that could ever happen to them. So Kramer asked Tish to go out into the corridor, and to count up to sixty before coming back in again. When she returned, having heard not a sound, Fat Solly Wynberg was sitting bolt upright in his chair, whiter than a tea towel in a detergent ad, and talking nineteen to the dozen.

CHAPTER TWENTY-FOUR

'Now *that* frightened me!' said Tish, as she and Kramer went back up the fire escape. 'Whatever did you do to him?'

But Kramer was too preoccupied to reply. 'Mickey!' he called out down the passage of Meerkat's flat. 'Send that Sammy bloke on his way, and then come and hear the latest.' He went into the kitchen and had a quick look at the refrigerator's ice trays.

'The latest, boss?' asked Zondi, a minute later.

'Don't ask me what this means,' warned Kramer, whose head was swimming with contradictory pieces of information. 'But more than a month ago, according to Fat Solly, someone broke into this place and stole a thirty-two with a faulty barrel out of that fridge. This someone was allegedly seen by a cripple living in the weeds out there, and she gave him a vague description of a smartly dressed young white male. Meerkat swore revenge and has been out looking for this bloke ever since. Then this morning Fat Solly heard a ruckus going on up here, and did some eavesdropping from the balcony. From what he could make out, our late friend Benson had acted as a sort of middle-man, he'd tipped off a gun collector about the thirty-two Meerkat was holding, and something had gone wrong. He didn't learn anything else until around five tonight, when Meerkat came down to the shop and asked to borrow fifty rand. He told Fat Solly that he'd discovered who the thief was, and had plans for him.'

'So I was right, Lieutenant? That is where Meerkat has gone?'

'Uh-huh, it certainly looks that way,' agreed Kramer, sitting down at the kitchen table. 'But by the same token you are wrong in thinking this has anything to do with the shootings case. The thirty-two's barrel was lethal, Fat Solly tells me, so it couldn't have been used without the gunman blowing his own head off the first time he pulled the trigger.'

Zondi shrugged and smiled. 'A feeling in my bones, boss. Can a barrel not be changed?'

'Why go to all that extra effort, man?'

'True, Lieutenant.'

'But what,' said Tish, stroking a friendly ginger cat with a white tail, 'if Mongoose lied to Fat Solly about the barrel? You know, as a way of protecting himself? Making it seem impossible that his gun was used?'

'Uh-huh, you could have something there,' conceded Kramer. 'Marais comes home, finds the gun's been pinched, puts two and two together, and decides to put himself in the clear . . .'

'Meaning it could be the same gun as used on Boss Bradshaw and Boss Hookham and the little missus,' said Zondi.

Tish opened the kitchen cupboard and found a dusty tin of sardines. 'This poor creature seems starving,' she said. 'Well, what next? Surely you'll have to establish things one way or another.'

'By getting hold of Meerkat Marais, you mean?' said Kramer.

'Or the smoothy who stole it,' suggested Tish. 'Which amounts to the same thing, I suppose, if Meerkat – is that how you pronounce it? – is after him. Wouldn't it be marvellous catching the two of them together? Then you'd be bound to get the whole story!'

Zondi moved restlessly.

'I know what you're thinking,' said Kramer. 'You're worrying we'll be too late, and Meerkat will have taken care of any evidence.'

'It is two hours' start he's got, Lieutenant.'

'Ja, and we haven't the faintest where he's gone. You see what I mean about wild-goose chases, Tish?'

She was shaking the sardines into a saucer. 'There, kitty! Try those for size . . .' The saucer was placed on the floor and immediately pounced upon. 'If you could work out who the smoothy is, then you'd at least know what direction to go in.'

'Some chance! The description doesn't ring a bell with anyone I've ever set eyes on.'

'Are you sure? What about Sergeant Zondi?'

Kramer turned to him. 'It's as vague as hell, Mickey. The suspect is aged between eighteen and thirty, tall, has a noticeable spring in his step, and wears good clothes – a dark suit. He was carrying a briefcase, and had darkish-brown hair. Oh ja, and his tie had stripes on it a bit like a school tie or one of those rugby club things.'

'Fat Solly also said that Meerkat had proof he was a nervous type, probably unused to breaking into people's homes,' added Tish.

'Hmmm.' Zondi closed his eyes.

'He's checking his memory bank,' said Kramer, winking at Tish. 'Any moment now, the first bit of rubbish he can think of will pop up. Once we were –'

'That tie, boss,' Zondi interrupted. 'Like a school tie maybe?'

'Ja, only I don't –'

'"And an Old Boy of Trekkersburg High,"' quoted Zondi. 'Don't you remember? The article in the *Gazette*?'

Kramer went tense for a moment and then relaxed with a scornful laugh. 'Ach no, you've got Bradshaws on the brain, man! And besides, there's millions of kinds of striped ties you can get.'

'Darren Bradshaw?' said Tish, catching her breath.

'Yes, madam,' confirmed Zondi. 'Do you know what the young boss looks like?'

'Look, I've –' began Kramer.

'Yes, he's tall, darkish-brown hair, goes in for Old Boys' ties and good suits to impress the customers when he's helping with the family business – and God, yes! Once you come mention it, he does have a slightly unusual way of walking: a bouncy, cocky sort of step.' She turned to Kramer. 'Why no reaction? You've seen him too, haven't you?'

Kramer nodded slowly. To be sure he had met Darren Bradshaw, only he'd been swimming not walking, clothed in no more than bathing trunks, and his height had been distorted by the refraction of the water. Apart from the darkish-brown hair, he had no personal observations to corroborate her claim – nor to deny it.

'Boss?' prompted Zondi.

'He was in the pool at their house.'

'Hau! Getting sunburnt?'

Tish clapped her hands. 'Marvellous! That pink stuff on the tights you found in that forest.'

'Not tights, stockings,' corrected Kramer, pedantically, wary of how quickly everything was fitting together.

'Stockings?' said Tish. 'That's interesting! They must have

222

been thrown away by an older woman. I'd imagine. His mother?'

Zondi grunted his approval.

'Ja, his nose was red and it was beginning to peel a bit,' recalled Kramer, getting to his feet. 'But this is crazy! Why shoot his father? Why Hookham? Why Classina?'

'Detective Constable Schoeman told me that they had many arguments while he was guarding Boss Bradshaw,' said Zondi.

'Yes, and his father had banished him, remember,' Tish went on. 'With two nasty pieces of work like that, who knows what bad blood there was between them?'

'But Bonzo Hookham?'

'Perhaps . . .' said Zondi, pausing to find an answer. 'Perhaps Boss Hookham was down at the race-course with the dogs that night, and Small Bradshaw feared he'd seen him!'

'And the same with the schoolgirl,' blurted out Tish. 'She might have noticed something without realising it, but Darren didn't want to take any chances.'

'Opportunity?' objected Kramer. 'So far as I know, he was up in Jo'burg at the time of the first shooting.'

'Which *is* only as far as you know,' Tish pointed out.

'Ring the Kritzinger Business Studies College, boss, and see if he was registered there that day,' suggested Zondi.

'What, at this time of night?'

'Then try and find out where he was the other two nights,' urged Tish, moving forward to stand beside Zondi.

'On the night Boss Hookham died, Lieutenant, Boss Darren went to fetch his father from the fishing cottage, but I think you said he arrived there very late.'

'He certainly didn't look all that strong to me,' muttered Kramer, still trying to pull all the different strands together.

'Why not start with the night the schoolgirl was shot at?' suggested Tish. 'Your policeman at the Bradshaws' house should have some idea of Darren's movements.'

'Where does the strange accent fit into all of this?' asked Kramer. 'And am I also being asked to believe that Bradshaw wouldn't have recognised his own son?'

Tish lost patience. 'Look, will you stop all this pondering and *do* something? What on earth's holding you back?'

Kramer nearly said the feeling in his bones was wrong, but

answered instead, 'Okay, I'll ring Schoeman – that can't do any harm.'

The telephone was on the tawdry bar in the living room, balanced on the open telephone directory. Kramer dialled the CID number, asked for the Murder and Robbery extension, and found himself in luck.

'Can I help you, Lieutenant?' asked Schoeman.

'I hope so, Stormtrooper. You know the night Classina Baksteen was given a fright? Where was Darren Bradshaw?'

'Oh, you mean the – let me think. I've got it : that's the night I finally got him to get out of the house and go to the drive-in.'

'How long was he gone?'

'About three hours. He left at a quarter to seven, and came in around ten with lipstick on his shirt. God, there was so much of the stuff you'd think he'd been smearing it on himself!' Stormtrooper Schoeman laughed. 'I said something to him about it, just as I was knocking off, and he nearly bit my head –'

'His mood then?' asked Kramer. 'What was it like?'

'Very agitated, sir. She probably hadn't let him finish the job properly. Why, don't tell me he's finally got a parent to make a formal complaint against him!'

'There has been some talk,' said Kramer, evasive and still unsure of all this. 'Anyway, thanks for the help, hey? I'll probably need you tomorrow to help with the keys.'

'Fine, sir. Good night, hey?'

Kramer replaced the receiver and stood staring at it. Then he could not help noticing that the directory had been left held open for easy reference by the weight of the telephone at a page that began with Bradnock, J. F. and ended with Branch, P. C. Somewhere in between would be an entry for Bradshaw, A. M. – and suddenly that was one coincidence too many.

Zondi and Tish waited in the Chevrolet outside the house in Kitchener Row, and kept their eyes on Kramer who had just knocked for the second time on the Bradshaws' front door.

'I wonder why they had their telephone disconnected?' murmured Tish.

'Maybe cranks are still worrying them, madam.'

'Please, Mickey, don't call me that! It makes me feel as though

I'm running a brothel! Now we know each other, plain Tish would be fine.'

Impossible, thought Zondi. 'The Lieutenant's going to try round the back,' he said. 'It could be they are out.'

'There isn't a car parked outside.'

Zondi nodded, and took another surreptitious sniff at his atlas.

Mrs Bradshaw was listening to the radio under a mulberry tree by the swimming pool. She had on a long black evening dress which went well with the music, classical but romantically light, and the garden itself seemed twice as enchanted, being lit here and there by carefully placed floods. She was so much in a world of her own making that it took a few seconds for her to notice she had a caller.

'Lieutenant Kramer!' she said, smiling a welcome. 'How awfully nice! I didn't think we'd be meeting again now that horrible business is over.'

Kramer shook her languidly extended hand. 'I wouldn't be worrying you, Mrs Bradshaw, only I couldn't get through on the phone.'

'Archie had it disconnected you-know-when and has decided we probably didn't need one at home anyway. It saves quite a few pennies, you know!'

'Uh-huh. Is Mr Bradshaw in?'

'It's his Masonic night, I'm afraid.'

'And Darren? I suppose he's back in Jo'burg?'

Mrs Bradshaw turned her radio down. 'He went back weeks ago, but this weekend he'll be at our fishing cottage near the mountains. We're driving up to see him and his new girlfriend tomorrow. We were going to go up tonight, actually, to have a supper waiting for them, but as I say, it's Archie's Masonic night and – '

'He never misses one?'

Her smile tried to be bright, but had that sadness which Kramer had noticed before. 'Never, nor a flying club social. Have you time for a drink?' And she uttered the trite phrase earnestly, the way lonely people often do.

'I can sit a minute,' said Kramer, taking the other deckchair. 'So Darren is up at your fishing cottage tonight?'

'Well, not quite yet, I shouldn't imagine,' Mrs Bradshaw

replied, trying to see the time on her tiny wristwatch. 'They were driving down from Jo'burg after lunch. He doesn't have any classes on Friday afternoons, you see.'

'Oh ja?' Another piece in the jigsaw had just gone click.

'Goodness, it's later than I thought,' said Mrs Bradshaw. 'Eight o'clock – is that right?'

'Uh-huh. Where is the cottage exactly? Very far off the national road?'

'It's on a farm in the Dargle area – Twin Falls Farm, owned by a dear old couple we've known for years. They divided it up, gave one half to their son, and are really in semi-retirement these days. They're wonderful people; polite, warm, terribly friendly and yet they leave one alone to enjoy the blissful isolation. When Archie and I are up there, we sometimes pop over for tea on Sunday morning, but otherwise that part of the valley could be all our own. Darren should be almost there now, as a matter of fact, and I can just imagine his new girlfriend's excitement when they come to the end of our little track and she sees what a sweet little thatched cottage it is. Exactly like a piece of Old England, you know, Lieutenant Kramer – I copied the design from one of the antique magazines Archie subscribes to, and we found a terribly clever native builder who put it up. I do hope she likes it.'

'Mrs Bradshaw,' said Kramer, 'why sound so anxious?'

'Well, Darren's been so unlucky with so many girls he's fallen in love with,' she said, reaching for a long gin and tonic that had been hidden by the radio. 'Every mother has the same sort of hopes and ambitions, I suppose! You do so want your children to marry the right person, and not to . . .' She gave a light laugh that tinkled like a broken champagne glass. 'I'm hoping that this time he'll be lucky, that's all. Sonja sounds an absolute poppet.'

Kramer watched her drain the gin and tonic right down to the ice cubes. 'Ja, I'm sure you're no different to any other parent,' he said. 'They all have their worries. How well does he get on with his dad?'

'Marvellously well. They had their differences, of course, but when all is said and done, those two are very close.'

'Uh-huh? Serious differences?'

Mrs Bradshaw shook her head. 'Nothing that couldn't be sorted out. Archie did become a little worried by some of the friends Darren had at one stage, although it was only to be expected that such a manly, daredevil sort of boy would attract all sorts of people to his leadership, but that was solved when we decided to send him up to the business college in Johannesburg. He's very happy there and doing frightfully well, he tells us. He's been there almost a year now – how time flies!'

Another click. It was almost a year since the suspect silver had been discovered in Bradshaw's antique shop.

'What was he doing before then?' asked Kramer, relieved that it took very little to keep a proud parent talking about her child. 'Was he on the business course at the tech?'

'Oh no, Archie had him in the shop, showing him the ropes, but it really was more sensible to give him this proper grounding in commercial techniques first. Are you sure you wouldn't like a drink? Not even a teeny-weeny one? Because I –'

'Let me get it for you,' said Kramer, standing up and taking her glass. 'Where do you keep your – ?'

'It's all in the fridge, but –'

'Sit and relax,' said Kramer. 'Look at the lovely big moon there is tonight.'

He needed a moment to think. But his concentration was broken when he reached the kitchen and saw, left on the draining board of the sink, a short stubby spirits glass with a heeltap of whisky in it. Bradshaw, he remembered, had been a beer man – and then, almost unbidden, like one of Zondi's pop-up ideas, he recalled something Tish had said about Jonty and a dowdy little woman with a sexy figure. Jonty liked nothing more than a neat tot of Scotch after dark. He refilled Mrs Bradshaw's glass, also remembering now how Jonty had denied ever having had her in his salon, and made his way back across the lawn.

'It's a double,' he said, handing the glass over. 'I see I'm not your first caller tonight, hey?'

She gave a surprised little laugh. 'However did you – ?'

'There's another glass on the draining board, ready to be washed up.'

'You're as bad as Detective Constable Schoeman, Lieutenant. Although he never *said* anything, I always had the feeling he was deducing things about us – and I know it made Archie very edgy at times! He was terribly polite, but it was a relief when he and the others left.'

'Ah well,' said Kramer, sitting down again. 'You know how things become a habit?'

'Actually, I'm glad you reminded me it's there – I'd better get rid of it before Archie gets back, or he mightn't be too amused.'

'Mrs Bradshaw, you surprise me!' Kramer said with a wink. Even in the moonlight, it seemed that she blushed. 'You are being naughty!' giggled Mrs Bradshaw, shocked but pleased. 'No, it wasn't anything like that! It was simply that one of those awful old friends of Darren's popped in, hoping he'd see him this weekend, and I was able to tell he'd be up at our cottage, thank goodness.'

'Did you know him?'

'Not from a bar of soap, but he obviously knew Darren, and was so eager to hear all my news about him, that I couldn't be rude and shoo him away. A nervous, twitchy little man, probably a year or two older than Darren, but really quite sweet despite his appearance. That's where I think Archie is sometimes wrong, you know, he *will* be such a snob about certain classes of people, but I suppose that comes with dealing with the Morninghill set and the – '

'It sounds like Wee Williams,' said Kramer, making the name up. 'That bloke who plays the guitar?' he added. 'Long fingernails?'

'You are clever!' said Mrs Bradshaw, toasting him with her glass before taking a quick sip. 'He didn't tell me he was an entertainer, or even his name, but I did notice the fingernails. Oh yes, *and* the cat fur on his jacket! Musicians are often scruffy, aren't they? It's odd; I can remember when they played in tuxedos and wore black bow-ties.'

Kramer was back on his feet, feeling sick at the time he had wasted – he'd never supposed for an instant that Meerkat Marais would risk making an appearance at the house, but it just showed how hellbent the bastard had become on exacting his vengeance.

'Now I'll tell you what *I* deduced!' said Mrs Bradshaw, with a very slight slur. 'I worked out that he must own *two* cats. How? Because the light in Archie's study was good and strong, and I could see that some of the fur was white and some was ginger. You don't often get them combined in one animal, do you?'

'I'm sure you're right, Mrs Bradshaw,' said Kramer, as he began to edge away, utterly convinced now that his guesswork had proved correct. 'Enjoy the moon and the music, hey?'

'You're not going?'

'Well, I thought you might be wanting an early night,' he replied, trying to find the right feedlines without sounding too clumsy. 'It must take you how long to drive up to the cottage?'

'Oh, only two hours or so. But isn't there some message for Archie? Here I've been yattering away, not giving you a chance to explain why you called ! – please forgive me.'

'Ach, nonsense,' said Kramer, 'it's been a pleasure, and my errand can wait until another time. Or can I get your husband on the phone tomorrow at the cottage?'

'I'm afraid we like to cut ourselves off from the world while we're up there, and the farmhouse is so far away that –'

'Never mind then, another time, as I say. It was just I was hoping to sell him a few tickets to our dance next month.'

She giggled again and looked archly at him. 'I know a funny story about holding a policeman's ball – not that I could tell it to you *or* Colonel Muller !'

'Mrs Bradshaw, you surprise me,' said Kramer, who hadn't intended that as a feedline as well. 'In fact, being with you out here has been one tingling shock after another.'

She loved that, poor woman.

'But this means you're in one hell of a fix,' said Tish, as Zondi drove away from Kitchener Row after a quick résumé of the situation. 'You can't possibly hope to make up the hour's start he has on you, Tromp – if it isn't much more than that ! I don't understand why you didn't use Mrs Bradshaw's phone to ring the local police and get them to –'

'There's something you don't know about Meerkat Marais,' interrupted Kramer. 'Going on his past record, when he's in this sort of mood, he doesn't like to rush things once he gets his victim in his sights. He enjoys savouring the –'

'Even so, boss,' Zondi cut in, picking up speed on the main highway back into the city centre, 'one hour is a long time. It'll have to be Uniform from Dargle that takes the first action.'

'No, kaffir. Those two bastards are mine.'

'Mickey, pull up at the next public phone box you see,' ordered Tish, leaning forward in the back seat to tap his shoulder. 'You're just going to be sensible about this, Tromp. That girl's life is also in danger.'

'Ach, I don't think Meerkat's going to *kill* anybody – he isn't that much of a fool. His style is to leave them so they'll never dare to cross him again, which is why we've never got a conviction on any of his – '

'Why are you being so pig-headed?' Tish demanded angrily. 'Why? When you can see Mickey's as – '

'Because I'm not sure yet it's impossible to get there in time,' said Kramer, shrugging, 'and because I don't want a crowd of trigger-happy country cops cheating me of knowing the truth by starting a shoot-out.'

'Huh! Who didn't want to go on a wild-goose chase tonight? What do you call this then? It's completely crazy!'

The Chevrolet braked sharply and Zondi brought it to a halt beside an empty phone box.

'Thanks,' said Kramer, and climbed out.

'Tromp!' Tish called to him. 'Tromp, promise me you'll do the right thing now!'

He smiled, felt for some change, and went into the phone box where he made two calls, one long and the other quite short. When he returned to the car, Tish and Zondi were looking at the map of Natal in an atlas that had appeared from somewhere.

'How far is it as the crow flies?' he asked them, slipping into his seat again.

'About seventy miles, boss, but there are all these foothills of the mountain range to go around,' replied Zondi. 'Is Dargle alerted and setting up a road block?'

'Ja, it's alerted.'

'But what about the road block?' asked Tish, looking at him suspiciously. 'You didn't do any more than alert them, did you? I can see it! Just what else have you been up to?'

'Getting myself a wild goose,' said Kramer. 'They're a bloody sight faster than any crow, you know.'

CHAPTER TWENTY-FIVE

At 7,000 feet on a clear, moonlit night with scattered cloud and not much turbulence, the four-seater Cessna droned steadily towards Dargle at well over 100 miles an hour, making very little fuss about it.

Kramer watched the landscape become progressively more like a lumpy eiderdown in silvery-grey silk, patterned by dark patches of wattle and stitched this way and that by long barbed-wire fences. It was a dreamy, rather unearthly sight, and he wished Tish were at his side to share in it. But young Robert du Plooi had been adamant about whose lives he was willing to risk, and hers hadn't been one of them. Zondi was missing out on the view as well; he had never been in the air before, and lay curled on the double seat at the back with his hat over his face, giving an unconvincing display of extreme nonchalance.

'We're mad,' muttered Du Plooi, for about the twentieth time since take-off. 'Quite mad. You can't judge ground-to-air distances in this amount of light, not when we come in for the landing.'

'Surely it's nearly as bright as when you're wearing sunglasses?' said Kramer. 'Look how the moon is shining on the nose there.'

'How many cars are they arranging to light up this farmer's air strip?' asked Du Plooi.

'Ach, they're turning out the whole district.'

'When did you have time to arrange that?'

'I delegated.'

'So you're not certain of the –'

'I told Stormtrooper Schoeman to fix up the best that could be arranged at such short notice.'

'Now he tells me!' exclaimed Du Plooi, and the plane yawed slightly.

But for all that, he seemed to be enjoying himself. It was the hunt, thought Kramer, the thrill of the chase; the challenge of something unexpected and dangerous. Du Plooi had been playing with his little son on the nursery floor when he'd phoned him.

'Boss?' said a strained voice from the back seat.

'We're making good time, man,' Kramer said over his shoulder. 'Murray Dam is coming up now, and once we're over that, it'll be about another five minutes to touchdown.'

'*Touch*down?' echoed Du Plooi. 'You'll be lucky if they don't have to dig us out!'

'It'll be fine, you'll see,' Kramer reassured him.

They began to lose height, and the huge expanse of Murray Dam spread out across their flight path. Kramer pressed his head against his side window and saw the land end abruptly and the water begin. His stomach hollowed a little and his pulse rate stepped up, just as Bonzo Hookham's must have done each time he crossed the Channel. The rippled surface below seemed to last for an eternity. Then just as abruptly they were flying over land again, and now there was something hostile and menacing in the deep shadows that filled the gullies, flooded the valleys, and cupped the round mud huts, making them look like pillboxes. The plane began to shake and tremble, buffeted by the flak of thermals coming up off the foothills, and Du Plooi's ankle squeaked as he compensated on the rudder pedals.

'Target area coming up,' he said, picking up the line of a wriggling dirt road. 'Would you like a look at it before we go in?'

'Please,' said Kramer.

A minute later, Du Plooi pointed down at a homestead set back about 200 yards from the road. 'Twin Falls Farm – we'll follow the river now.'

They were down to about 600 feet above the ground now, and still losing height. Things were coming up very fast, making Kramer anxious he'd not miss any important details when the fishing cottage came into view. The first intimation he had of it was a track leading down from the road into a valley which had been dammed to provide irrigation water for surrounding dry grasslands. Then he saw a small stone dwelling with a thatched roof, so like a model of an English cottage it seemed possible to reach down and pick it up between finger and thumb. There were two cars parked outside the front porch, a large American sedan and an MG sports, and a light was showing from the windows of the main room. Just at the point where this light faded into the night, another light was burning on a little jetty sticking out into the dam. Beside this light, which probably came from a pressure lamp, a man was crouching, while a second man stood over him and held a female figure by the hand. All three glanced up at the plane, then returned their attention to whatever they were doing. And just as they flashed from sight, Kramer saw that the crouching man reflected the lamplight as though he were very wet.

Du Plooi began muttering to himself again. 'That surely can't be the strip,' he said, nodding to a straggle of orange pinpoints ahead of them. 'I've seen more candle-power on a birthday cake !'

'It's two straight lines though,' remarked Kramer. 'What more do you want?'

It was a lucky landing. As the Cessna came swooping in, the double row of farm labourers, each equipped with a paraffin lantern, suddenly decided that discretion was the better part of valour, and took to their heels, running in every direction.

Kramer left Robert du Plooi looking pale but proud on the edge of the air strip, being fortified by the farmer's hip flask, and climbed into the cab of a waiting police Land-Rover with Zondi. The driver of the Land-Rover was a beefy, red-faced sergeant in off-duty shorts, sandals and a blue singlet.

'Mok Grobbler, sir,' he said, introducing himself with a shake that implied he did quite a lot of milking by hand in his free time. 'Is your boy to come too?'

'Uh-huh – I need him to identify the suspect. Shall we go? You can brief me on the way.'

'There's not much I can tell you, sir,' grunted Grobbler, starting the Land-Rover with a jerk. 'Six men is all I've got on tonight, and I've got them sort of circled round the cottage on Uncle Pretorius's place, keeping their heads down as you instructed. The trouble is mainly our walkie-talkie's on the blink again, and we haven't got a replacement from you blokes down in Trekkersburg. You don't know what it's like being out in the sticks like this; just one damn requisition after another, but nobody ever seems to take any notice.'

'Well, I had a look at the place a few minutes ago myself,' said

Kramer, 'and things seem pretty quiet at the moment.' Then he described what he'd seen, chiefly for Zondi's benefit.

'Can you tell me exactly what this is all about, sir?' asked Grobbler, in the same aggrieved tone as he used when mentioning requisition forms. 'Your youngster Schoeman just said it was a murder job.'

'No, Sergeant, I can't,' said Kramer, quite honestly. 'If you'd asked me half an hour ago, I might have had a go but from the behaviour of these people now, I'm flummoxed. I'll just have to go in there and find out.'

The road dipped and climbed, edged round steep slopes and dived between deep cuttings, and finally plunged into a long straight section that had a small concertina wire gate half-way down it. Grobbler, who had maintained an aloof, sullen silence for the last five minutes, throttled back.

'This is the track to the cottage?' said Kramer.

'This is the one, sir. Do we go in with the headlights off?'

'No, I want you to park across the gate, blocking the exit.'

Grobbler did that and killed his engine. 'Now, sir?'

'You've got a gun on you?'

'Of course.' Grobbler took a .38 Smith & Wesson out from under the dashboard. 'I've also got a Sten in the back. Is this the same case you wanted reports of gunshots? You know how it is, Trekkersburg headquarters never bothers to explain or acknowledge any –'

'Fine,' said Kramer. 'You sit tight here and see nobody gets out this way, okay?'

'But can't your – ?'

'Look, Mok, I'm making you the kingpin in all this, hey? Neither of the vehicles at the cottage is a jeep, so this is the only escape route if anything goes wrong. Or would you rather a Bantu from Trekkersburg takes the biggest responsibility?'

Much mollified, Mok Grobbler climbed out of the Land-Rover, armed himself with the Sten gun as well, and wished Kramer the best of luck.

'Not long now, boss,' whispered Zondi, as they moved away from the gate down to the cover provided by the plane trees along a little stream. 'Soon all will be revealed . . .'

234

'I hope so, Mickey,' Kramer murmured.

The curious thing was that the feeling in his bones still said, Hmmmmm.

Stormtrooper Schoeman drew up alongside the big Chevrolet at Trekkersburg's small aerodrome, and was surprised to see it was empty. His last little job of the night, after arranging the reception party for Kramer at Dargle, and seeing to it that Colonel Muller was kept in the dark for as long as possible, had been to pick up some lady friend his superior left behind in a vehicle she was unauthorised to drive. Kramer had warned him that she'd declared her intention of waiting out at the aerodrome until the plane returned, but that he was to ignore this and return her to her flat.

'Ach, she's probably in the ladies',' sighed Schoeman, who was in a state of some need himself.

He got out of his car and walked across to the small brick building where Trekkersburg Air Services was based. It was locked although, for security reasons no doubt, all the lights were on. The outside doors to the lavatories were also locked. Then a stout Zulu nightwatchman, armed with a knobkerrie, came round the corner of the building.

'Hau! Po-eese?'

'Police,' confirmed Schoeman, then slipped into Zulu. 'I'm looking for the lady who was waiting in that big car. Do you know where she is?'

'She's gone, sir,' said the nightwatchman. 'She ask me to let her inside to ring some man, and then he come in another car and fetch her.'

'What? A taxi?'

'No, sir. Just a car. At least I thought it was a man; his hair was very long and curled like a lady's.'

'Strange,' said Schoeman. 'How long ago was this?'

'Half an hour,' replied the night watchman, after consulting the large timepiece on his watch-chain. 'The lady put a note in the big car.'

'Oh, really? Thanks, hey?'

Schoeman went back to the Chevrolet and saw the note on the steering wheel. It had been folded several times, and had *Tromp* written across it. He reached through the open window and took it to glance at, being idly curious to know her name and why she had decided to pack in her vigil. Then Schoeman saw that the note also bore a kiss mark in red lipstick.

'No, you mustn't,' he told himself, replacing the note where he'd found it, and then he went back to Boomplaas Street.

By keeping to the bank of the stream and sometimes even having to wade into it, when dry bracken on either side made a stealthy approach impossible any other way, Kramer and Zondi moved like two shadows through the moonlight. The trunks of the plane trees began to thin out, and ahead of them they could see the glint of the small dam where Archie Bradshaw caught his trout. The pressure lamp had moved from the end of the jetty, and had been left still burning on the doorstep of the cottage. Everything was very quiet.

'Well, both cars are still here,' whispered Kramer. 'I just hope the silence isn't as ominous as it bloody sounds.'

'Shall we close in, boss?'

'Ja, we'll get ourselves behind that pine tree on the little lawn. I'll cover you – run!'

Zondi broke from the rushes at the side of the jetty and made his way safely up the bank and across the grass. Kramer dallied a moment, looking at the mud and puddles on the jetty, and then at the little rowing boat moored to it, before slipping his magnum back into its holster. Crouching low, he followed swiftly in Zondi's footsteps, and lay still for a minute with his back against the pine trunk, listening.

'Still so quiet – can you see into the house, Mickey?'

'No, boss. We are too low here, and the windows of the main room – '

'Try a quick climb then. You're the lighter.'

Zondi handed him his hat, put away his own firearm and stood up slowly. He reached into the branches, got a grip and pulled himself out of sight, making only the faintest of crackles as the smallest twigs snapped off. He was gone for long enough to set Kramer's heart beating harder and harder. Then there was a shower of pine needles and more twigs, and he dropped silently to the ground again. His expression was most peculiar.

'I have seen many things, Lieutenant,' he began, shaking his head.

'Just one at a time will do,' snapped Kramer, only just keeping his voice down. 'Come on, Mickey, let's hear it!'

'The woman is in the bedroom where a small lamp is burning. She is lying on the bed with her hands and her feet tied to it.'

'Raped?'

'No, boss, her dress is down and she looks not so bad, but she has a gag in her mouth.'

'And the others? How many are there? Just the two?'

'Just Meerkat and a boss who answers the description of Darren Bradshaw.'

'And they are where?'

Zondi shook his head again. 'They are in the sitting room, sitting top and bottom of the long eating table. And you know what? In front of each is lying a gun.'

'Hey?'

'They're not talking, just sitting there. Meerkat is smiling, and Boss Darren is looking very frightened.'

'Christ, it sounds like a bloody duel! Are there any marks on Darren?'

'No marks I could see, Lieutenant.'

'Then what is Meerkat up to? Why has he let the kid have a gun? He'd never risk his own skin like that!'

'Shhh! Not so loud, boss.'

Kramer looked up into the pine tree to see if there were enough branches to bear his weight. Then he had another idea. 'Come, Mickey, if they're so wrapped up in each other as you say, and if we keep low enough, we can get under the sitting-room windows without them noticing. But before we go, did you see any way we could enter the premises?'

Zondi's teeth flashed a quick smile. 'The front door is standing open, boss, and the door to the sitting room must be about three paces inside it to the right. Are we going to listen?'

'Uh-huh. See what's going on, then pick our moment. One last thing, Mickey: I don't want any dead bodies, hey? These two have a lot of explaining to do before the night is over.'

'Check,' said Zondi.

By going down on all fours, and making good use of a long shadow thrown by one of the porch posts with the pressure lamp behind it, they crossed the remaining twenty yards between the pine tree and the cottage. It was something of a shock to hear Meerkat Marais' voice hissing so close to them.

'But it can go on all night,' Meerkat was saying. 'It won't though, because your nerve will crack. For one of us, this is his last night on earth, hey? Who will it be? Who will be the faster?'

'It's just a joke,' Darren Bradshaw blustered. 'The same as me taking your gun was meant to be a joke.'

'Some joke,' Meerkat observed bleakly.

'Well, you weren't in, as I've already explained a dozen times over. I had the cash with me then, honest! I was going to pay for it later, give the money to Silver Touch even, but my old man sent me back to Joey's and –'

'You stole my gun, little rich boy. You didn't leave any money in the fridge. You stole that gun which is lying in front of you. You tried to cheat me. That was a big mistake. Nobody does things like that to Meerkat. You ask anyone you like.'

'I was going to pay you this weekend for it!'

'You're lying,' said Meerkat, unmoved.

Darren Bradshaw began to whine. 'Please hear me out, hey? This bloke who wanted a small revolver never came back into the shop. It was my dad's money I'd taken from the till to pay you, and when he didn't come back –'

'I'm not interested in all this,' sighed Meerkat.

'But I've got you the gun again! It's just as good as when I took it – it's never been used!'

'I believe you, Darren.'

'You do?'

'But that doesn't change things,' Meerkat went on. 'You must still be punished for what you have done.'

'Be fair! Let's stop this crazy –'

'But I am being fair,' said Meerkat. 'I'm offering you a sporting chance, *Mister* Bradshaw. I've promised I won't go for my gun until you do, and then let the best man win. Isn't that what you were taught at that posh school of yours?'

Kramer nudged Zondi. He had been right, it was some sort of duel after all – although he'd never seriously considered the idea for a second. It didn't fit in with Meerkat's strong sense of self-preservation. Zondi raised his eyebrows, indicating that he was equally perplexed by the bizarre confrontation.

'Listen,' said Darren Bradshaw, hoarsely, 'I don't want to hurt

238

you – I don't want to *try* to hurt you! Isn't that obvious? You can't really want to hurt me either, not over a thing like this. Why don't we – ?'

'No, I don't want to hurt you, Darren. I want to kill you.'

'But – but *why*, for Christ's sake?'

'I hate you,' said Meerkat Marais.

Kramer shuddered involuntarily and the hairs at the back of his neck rose. Meerkat's voice had sunk very low, it was purring and soft, and conveyed far more than even the terrible words he uttered. The psychopath was in the grip of a compulsion, and what made it worse was the hint of grim amusement, as though he was enjoying a private joke which had still to reach its punch-line.

There was despair in Darren Bradshaw's voice when he began talking again, trying for the conciliatory tones of sweet reason. 'You're obviously very angry with me, and you've got every right to be, Mr Marais – you feel I've made a fool of you. But don't let that anger run away with you. If you kill me, then Sonja will be able to tell the police – '

'You must really think I'm a fool,' said Meerkat, almost inaudibly. 'If I win then I'm going to shoot Sonja, put my pistol in your hand and make it look like a double suicide.'

'What?'

'I tell you, Darren, this is for keeps hey? But to make it easier for you I'll put my hands on my knees. That way you'll stand a better chance of grabbing and aiming before I do.'

Kramer motioned Zondi to take up a position where he could train his Walther PPK on Marais. Zondi gestured back, concerned that he would not be able to see Darren Bradshaw from that angle. That was all right, explained Kramer, with a zigzag movement of his hand, because he would be coming through the passage door behind Marais, and he'd have the youngster in full view.

'When?' mouthed Zondi.

Kramer tapped an ear, and mimed turning a door knob. Then he gave Zondi a light touch on the arm and made for the porch.

From inside the room, Meerkat's voice could just be heard saying. 'I'm tired of waiting, little rich boy. I'm going to start counting up to ten.'

He had reached three when Kramer, tugging his magnum

239

from its holster, twisted the door knob and stepped suddenly into the room. Zondi came into sight at almost the same instant, with his pistol pointing at Meerkat's head.

'Freeze!' barked Kramer. 'Police! Don't try anything!'

Meerkat froze, but Darren Bradshaw made a move to grab up the .32 revolver lying in front of him.

'Hold it, Darren – or you're dead, hey?'

The hand remained poised an inch above the weapon.

'You first, Meerkat,' said Kramer. 'Bunch your fist and knock that gun off the table. Zondi's got you covered from the window.'

'I can't see anyone.'

'Do it!'

Meerkat's narrow shoulders shrugged in contemptuous indifference. He clenched his fist and sent the pistol clattering under a sideboard.

'Now you do the same,' Kramer ordered.

Darren Bradshaw looked back at him, white-faced and panic-stricken, gulping hard.

'There's only you here,' said Meerkat.

'Shut up! Come on, Darren – take it easy now.'

'Get him, Darren!' shouted Meerkat.

Kramer pulled his trigger as Darren Bradshaw snatched up the .32 Smith & Wesson. It went click.

He pulled it again as the muzzle of the .32 Smith & Wesson levelled with his chest. It went click.

Darren Bradshaw was grinning.

Click, click, click!

Kramer saw his cartridges lying forgotten in a glass bowl on the shelf above the record-player in Tish's flat, and was certain he would never count daisies again. Even so, in that same frantic second, he tried to throw himself sideways, but collided with the open door.

The .32 went off with a hell of a bang.

Kramer felt nothing, although it had been pointing straight at him. He stood stunned. Then Zondi came rushing through the doorway behind him, and stopped and stared too.

Darren Bradshaw was crouched at the far end of the table, looking in astonishment at where his right hand had been only a moment before. The hand had been blown apart, leaving only a tatter of tissue, bone splinters and a spurting stump. Then the

.32 Smith & Wesson's hammer, which protruded from a small hole in his skull above the right eyebrow, sagged and fell out, and he followed it to the floor, stone dead.

How Meerkat Marais laughed. 'You can't say that *I* did a thing to him!' he gasped, and then delivered the punchline of his terrible revenge. 'You see, Lieutenant Kramer, there was no way I could lose! That bloody thirty-two was *lethal*.'

CHAPTER TWENTY-SIX

They took off again an hour after dawn, climbing slowly into a dull grey sky as leaden as Zondi's mood.

Kramer finally twisted round in his seat beside Robert du Plooi and demanded to know what was eating him. 'Is it because I was proved right after all?' he added. 'That wasn't even a wild-goose chase – it was a hunt for a bloody red herring!'

'Maybe I am just tired, boss,' murmured Zondi, yawning.

'But you can't dispute how wrong you two were, hey? I knew from the start that Meerkat wasn't involved in those shootings, and now we have proof positive. Not only couldn't that have been the gun used, but Darren was nowhere near Trekkersburg at the time his father was shot. Furthermore – '

'How do you know that?' interrupted Du Plooi, who had spent the night swapping flying stories with the helpful farmer.

'The girlfriend told me,' explained Kramer. 'She's been going steady with him for two months, and he was at her parents' place in Jo'burg when he received the news of his old man having been shot.'

'What sort of state is she in?'

'Shock like a rape case. She's talking calmly and coldly, but tonight I reckon she'll really crack up.'

'Poor kid . . .' said Du Plooi, levelling out.

'Ja, they'd only just arrived at the cottage, and had opened all the windows to air it properly, when Meerkat arrived in that hired car. Darren went out to see who it was, and came back with a gun in his back. The rest you must know.'

'Except for the bit about how the gun ended up in – '

'Ach, Darren chucked it in the dam the night he came to fetch his father,' said Kramer. 'Meerkat insisted he got it out again, and that was what they were doing when we flew over.'

242

Du Plooi shook his head. 'Stupid little idiot getting mixed up in things like that,' he said.

'I think he must have needed the extra cash. You should have seen the girl, this Sonja – very expensive piece of goods. The temptation must've been too great when the offer was made for a small revolver.'

'Not specifically a thirty-two?'

'No, Zondi and I heard Darren use the words "small revolver" – but they're not much use under a thirty-two anyway.'

'All nice and neatly tied up then?'

'Uh-huh, except I've got to do the informing of next-of-kin.'

Du Plooi pursed his lips sympathetically. 'Rather you than me, friend! Darren may have been a proper little bastard in many ways, but he was the light of his mother's life, you know. I bet she was behind him getting that brand-new sports car recently. And Archie's going to take this pretty hard as well. They may have had their rows, but that's only because they were as alike as peas in a pod those two. Don't like the look of that cloud up ahead.'

Kramer saw what he meant, and looked at his watch. 'How much longer to go round it?'

'Why?' chuckled Du Plooi. 'Are you thinking of the welcoming arms of your lovely lady friend?'

'Ach, no,' said Kramer. 'It's just I'm knackered.' And his smile lingered for quite a while.

The plane began to wallow and make complaining noises with its engine. Du Plooi altered course, steering thirty degrees further to the south, and kept checking the map on his knees. The plane settled down again.

'Another twenty minutes,' he said. 'Sorry, but it can't be helped.' His eyes were red-rimmed, and his shoulders sagged a bit.

'That's fine,' said Kramer, growing weary himself.

For ten of those minutes, nobody spoke.

'I suppose what's giving the glooms to our black friend back there is the fact you're back at the start again. Must be very disappointing.'

'I'm not with you, Du Plooi.'

'Who *did* do the shooting and all that.'

'Ach, life's too short for that, hey?' replied Kramer, lighting a cigarette.

243

'But doesn't it annoy you to think he's out there somewhere? Laughing at you up his sleeve?'

'He can laugh all he likes, man, just as long as he doesn't interfere directly with my life.'

There was a sound of stirring in the back seat, and Zondi sat upright to look out of his window. 'Hau! Where are we now, boss?'

'On the approach, Mickey – relax.'

They were banking slowly to the left and losing height over the yellow thorn scrub which stretched to the south-east of Trekkersburg. Kramer found no difficulty in picking out the bungalow and garden where Mrs Westford lived with her big son Timmy: it looked like a green trading stamp stuck to a sheet of creased brown paper. He looked away again.

'May the twenty-seventh,' mumbled Zondi.

'What was that?'

'Nothing, Lieutenant. Soon, you say?'

'Very soon!' said Kramer, and skipped his visit to the Bradshaws, imagining instead the shower he would take first.

Trekkersburg was becoming real, and no longer seemed no more than a collection of pebbles and parsley in a hollow. Houses stood out, trees, street lamps, people.

Du Plooi sighed. 'Pity it had to work out like this,' he said. 'Is it true that the most you can hit Meerkat with is a couple of assault charges and possession of a stolen weapon? I would have thought that the fact he shouted at Darren to shoot made a difference.'

'It did,' agreed Kramer. 'But what does Darren become if Meerkat is an accessory before the fact? A co-accused? I think Mrs Bradshaw will have suffered enough. I'll get Meerkat another day, don't you worry.'

'He's certainly a sly one.'

Zondi leaned forward against the back of Kramer's seat. 'Boss,' he said, 'I think that is what's worrying me: why did the young master try to shoot?'

'Because he was urged to in the heat of the moment!' Du Plooi retorted. 'You were there, for Christ's sake! You don't think he'd do it off his own bat, do you?'

'The boss misunderstands me,' said Zondi, politely. 'As the

Lieutenant first reported to me, Boss Darren tried to grab his gun before Meerkat said anything.'

'Instinctive if someone comes barging into a room waving another gun around,' commented Du Plooi, lining up for his landing.

'Yet the Lieutenant shouted at him that he was from the police, Boss Du Plooi. Would not a policeman be his rescuer in such a predicament? It was not as though he didn't know that the Lieutenant was truly a police officer – he had been introduced to him at his parents' house.'

'Phew! You've really got yourself one here, haven't you?' Du Plooi remarked jokingly to Kramer. 'A properly perverse little – '

'Perverse?' echoed Kramer, determined that his homecoming was not going to be soured by an argument. 'Christ, Mickey here is the head of our Bantu Perversions Squad – am I not right, hey?'

Zondi turned away from their laughter and gave an extra tug to his seat belt.

Then the world fell in on Kramer, and he didn't have so much as a smile left in him. The note lying open on his lap behind the wheel of the Chevrolet was hurried and brief.

> *My Darling Tromp,*
> *I want to thank you for more than you will*
> *ever know. You made me come to my senses*
> *tonight. It was the face of that poor man*
> *and how utterly, utterly dead he was. I*
> *can't fully explain what I realised then.*
> *Realised about me and Jonty. I also realised*
> *I didn't fit here. And that there was a part*
> *of you someone had that I could never share.*
> *Give my love to Mickey and tell him to look*
> *after you. Don't try to contact me. I'm going*
> *home, and that's a long, long way.*
> *With fondest memories, Tish XXXX*

'I want to thank you for more than you will ever know . . .' he repeated aloud, trying to make the words have some meaning.

The passenger door opened and Zondi ducked his head into

the cab. 'I have telephoned your message to the duty officer, Lieutenant, and Colonel Muller is being informed about last night at the earliest – '

'I've got a message for you too,' said Kramer bitterly.

'Boss?'

'She says – no, come on, kaffir! Get in!'

Zondi slipped into his seat and closed the door. 'What is wrong, Lieutenant?' His voice was very concerned.

'It's nothing,' said Kramer, crumpling the sheet of paper in his fist. 'It's bugger all!' Then he laughed as a white rage burst deep in his belly, barging aside the sob that had been building up there. 'Let's get going to the Bradshaws', hey? I feel just in the mood to grind that bastard's face in what he's done!'

'Done, boss? Done how?'

Kramer knew he was being irrational, but even that had its bitter-sweetness. He started the Chevrolet and swung it hard out of the car park, clipping a bollard and almost running down Robert du Plooi, who was returning to his own vehicle from the flying club's hangar. No, he was being quite rational in another way, Kramer told himself, as he opened up down the still sleepy streets of outer Trekkersburg. Almost from the moment the call had come through about Archie bloody Bradshaw being shot, his life had never been the same. One failure on top of another, one humiliation after another – and finally this. The bastard had left him nothing; little wonder he had produced that feeling of revulsion in him. But now the boot was on the other foot, and with Mrs Bradshaw out of the way, he would relish the impact of what he had to say. God, he would be cold. Hard. Ruthless.

'Like father, like son, hey, Mickey?'

'I'm not sure what you are talking about, boss,' said Zondi, flinching as a milk-float nearly turned into Cleopatra's bath-tub. 'Do you speak of Boss Bradshaw?'

'Right! And of what you were saying on the plane – you know, how that little bastard had still gone for me when he could hear and see my gun was empty.'

'Did I say that?' queried Zondi.

'It's what you were leading up to, only Du Plooi was too thick to see it.'

Zondi received this oblique apology with a small smile. 'I don't think Boss Du Plooi was too thick, Lieutenant. I saw a very

246

troubled look come into his eyes, and that's why he made a joke. He did not want to know more.'

'Well, I do. What else were you going to say?'

'Only this, Lieutenant : what instinct makes a boy like that see a police officer as an enemy?'

'A criminal instinct, man – and that can be taught.'

Zondi nodded. 'That is so, boss. I do not claim to have found any big answer, but I think we have now come right round to the place we started. Perhaps it was for a criminal act that Boss Bradshaw was marked down to be killed – and Boss Hookham plus the schoolgirl were only for a cover-up when we came too close to the persons responsible. I have also been pestered all night by a page from Boss Hookham's diary for May the twenty-seventh.'

'He was still in England then.'

'True, Lieutenant. He took his wife to hospital in Southampton.'

'Uh-huh? But what does that connect with?'

'Hau, if only I could catch again what gave me this picture of the page so vividly,' sighed Zondi, scratching the side of his head. 'I can see it all – the appointment, and where he speaks of the suffering of Albert, her family and then of herself.'

'We'll have to leave that for now then,' said Kramer, and dropped his speed abruptly, bringing the car under icy control. 'What I'll do is use this message I've got for the Bradshaws to see whether, without breaking any rules if you're wrong, it could make him open up. Logically, if he committed some crime against his attackers, he ought to know who they are – right?'

'Check, boss.'

'Lucky I got Grobbler to give me some Polaroids of the body, wasn't it?' Kramer added wryly, still so angry it was like being drunk. 'And it was only out of the kindness of my heart, you know; I thought Doc might like them for his collection.'

At 7.55 a.m. that dreary morning, Zondi climbed back into the Chevrolet outside the Bradshaws' undistinguished property in Kitchener Row. He had just seen the Lieutenant give the front door a miss and go straight up the side entrance with a pair of fingers crossed behind his back.

For a moment or two, Zondi stared at the Audi saloon owned by Archibald Meredith Bradshaw, which was parked hard into the kerb just ahead of him, and then he reached for his atlas, disturbing a crumple of paper that was lying on top of it.

'Poor Lieutenant,' he said to himself, without opening it out, 'but the Widow will be pleased.'

Then he turned to the map of France once again, and gave a snap of his fingers.

It was nothing like being drunk, Kramer corrected himself, as he reached the wooden gate into the Bradshaws' back garden. It was simply the effect of the adrenalin still coursing through him that made him so clinically detached, and instead of things being hazy and vague, every detail of his surroundings imposed itself on his mind with vivid clarity.

'Tish,' he said once, as a cynically administered booster to his contained rage, before lifting the latch.

Looking back on that moment an hour later he would be tempted to dismiss the extraordinary sequence of events which followed as simply a case of arriving at the right place at the right time. And yet he would have to admit that almost everything he sought had been there from the very beginning, and what had made the real difference was his state of mind.

The gate swung back, and through the mulberry trees he glimpsed a bikini-clad figure. He closed the gate and walked towards Mrs Bradshaw, who was engaged in arm-swinging exercises that undoubtedly did her magnificent breasts a great deal of good. He stopped beside the first tree. Totally absorbed, Mrs Bradshaw tossed aside the pair of old Indian clubs she had been using, then stooped and picked up a skipping rope. It was no common or garden skipping rope, but a properly professional length of blue cord that had varnished wooden handles. She began to skip, counting the number of times she left the ground, and her finely turned thighs took each successive shock on landing with barely a tremble. Then the skipping rope was also tossed aside, and she placed her hands on her hips to begin rotating her torso. A body like that was no accident of nature, certainly not in a woman of her age, but the result of regular, carefully planned routines, carried out until she dripped with perspiration. Round and round her head went, showing glimpses of the plain little face she could do nothing about. All the clues had been there that first day, mused Kramer, the problem being that he had not seen a physique but what the Widow Fourie called a sex object. Mrs Bradshaw turned and dived into the swimming pool, swam two fast lengths and climbed out.

'Why, Lieutenant Kramer!' she said, squinting at him with her weak blue eyes. 'Back so soon again?'

'What do you mean by back so soon?' rumbled her husband, tipping himself out of a hammock, where he had been reading the morning paper.

Kramer saw that the hammock had been drawn up by a system of crude pulleys.

'Keeping fit, Mrs Bradshaw?' His voice was frozen over.

She giggled nervously. 'Well, I do think one should, don't you? I've been doing it for years! Haven't I, Archie? I even tried to get you to join me! And Darren! But you're both such naughty boys! Do you know, Lieutenant, I bought Darren everything he would need when I was last in Johannesburg – granted it was in a sale, and it didn't cost the earth – but has he used it?'

'Some of it,' said Kramer.

'Look here, Lieutenant,' growled Bradshaw, 'have you any idea of the time? Do you usually barge in on people before they've had their breakfast?'

Kramer stared at him, interested in the effect this might have.

'I know what it is!' said Mrs Bradshaw. 'Lieutenant Kramer has tried to be here early to sell you some tickets. He came last night while you were out and we had such a lovely long chat about Darren. You asked me all sorts of questions, didn't you, Lieutenant?'

Bradshaw shot a worried glance at his wife, and began folding his newspaper up very tightly.

'Can I see that?' asked Kramer.

'What? The *Gazette*?'

'The *Gazette*,' said Kramer, taking it from him. 'What's on the front page this morning? Any news of Basil Benson being found dead in Meerkat Marais' flat?' There was in fact a small paragraph in the stop press – all it gave was the flat's address. 'You know Marais, don't you, Mr Bradshaw? Skinny, nervous type with long fingernails?'

'No, I don't,' replied Bradshaw.

'Long fingernails? But I thought Darren's friend was called Wee Willie something-or-other?' said Mrs Bradshaw gaily, then

249

brought her fist to her mouth as she realised the slip she'd made. 'Oh dear, don't be angry, Archie!'

Bradshaw looked from his wife to Kramer. 'What the hell's going on here?' he asked. 'I haven't understood a word of this conversation, and I don't like the attitude you're showing, Kramer!'

His wife tittered. 'You're dreadful in the morning,' she said. 'Now don't take on so, Archie! The nice Lieutenant looks like he's been up all night, so you can't expect him to be bright and breezy either! Shall we get tickets for Sonja and Darren as well? It would be nice if we could make up a little foursome for the policemen's ball.' She flushed slightly as she said that.

'So that's it? said Bradshaw. 'You've come to sell tickets to a ball?'

'No, I haven't.'

The Bradshaws looked at one another.

'But you said last night,' Mrs Bradshaw began.

'I was lying,' said Kramer. 'I came here with only one purpose: to discover the whereabouts and associates of your son.'

'What?' exclaimed Bradshaw, trembling. 'My God, when I get hold of Colonel Muller, I'll have him –'

'I thought then that his life was in danger.'

'Oh!' Mrs Bradshaw clasped her mouth. 'But is he all right? Whatever was the matter? Why couldn't you tell me?'

'I didn't want to embarrass you, Mrs Bradshaw. I'm afraid the news I bring this morning isn't good.'

'Didn't want to embarrass me? I don't understand!'

Kramer felt his icy edge in danger of being blunted. 'I wonder if I couldn't have a word with your husband first?' he asked. 'Perhaps you would like to go and put some clothes on.'

'Yes, Myra, I think you'd better,' said Bradshaw going over to her and touching her arm. 'Please, my love.'

She started slightly and looked at him in surprise, as though unused to any display of tenderness. 'But not till I know Darren's safe!'

'He's safe and sound where he is,' said Kramer, wishing she would get the hell out before he damned his soul any further. 'I think what I've got to say is man talk.'

'Man talk? Oh, he *hasn't*! Is her father – ?'

'Your husband is the only father involved,' Kramer assured her.

'Thank goodness!' sighed Mrs Bradshaw, giving one of her scatty smiles. 'Yes, it is rather chilly, and I'm in need of my cup of tea. Will you call me when it's over?'

Kramer nodded, then turned to Bradshaw. He was not watching his wife's retreat into the house, but staring at him, grey about the cheeks.

'Do I gather it's bad news, Lieutenant? Is that why you've been acting so strangely?'

'I wanted to find some way of getting Mrs Bradshaw out of hearing.'

'I've realised that. How bad is it?'

'From your point of view, Mr Bradshaw, I don't think it could be worse. But don't you think we'd better go inside as well? Into your study, maybe?'

'But you've got to – '

'Please,' said Kramer firmly.

Bradshaw led the way, walking in a swift stumble. He was cracking badly, as might be expected of any man fearing the worst of his son, but what was interesting was the fright there had been in his face before Darren had become the focus of the conversation. There were yellow daisies in the lawn.

'My study?'

'That would be the ideal place,' agreed Kramer, playing all this by instinct and letting the vicious juices run.

'Step inside, man! Step inside!'

But Kramer wanted him right on the edge before he said another word, so he paused to wipe his feet on the doormat just inside the covered-in verandah. He did this meticulously, and while studying his shoes to gauge the effect, he noticed, as distinctly as green confetti on a black-tile floor, the little leaves of a water plant stuck to his shoe leather. He looked up with something close to murder in his eyes.

'We've got Darren, Mr Bradshaw,' he said.

'Meaning?'

'We've got him at Dargle police station. He's locked in a small brick building round the back.'

The truth, phrased carefully, could be a terrible weapon, and it was satisfying to see the way it made Bradshaw sag at the knees. He shuffled into one of the leather armchairs. Kramer entered the study and perched on a corner of the desk. His phrasing probably no longer mattered, for he felt certain Zondi's insight would carry the day without any complaints being made to higher authorities, but he couldn't resist breaking Bradshaw with a few more slaps of the velvet glove.

'Last night, Mr Bradshaw, acting on information received, and with the inadvertent help of your good wife, I went in the company of other police officers to the fishing cottage you own on the farm Twin Falls. There we found your son Darren in conversation with a known dealer in illicit arms. They were having an argument, a quarrel – you could even say a bitter engagement. It would appear that your son went to purchase an illicit firearm from this dealer, and finding him absent from his flat, he forced an entry and stole the – '

'The fool! I gave him plenty of – '

'Sorry, what was that, Mr Bradshaw?'

Bradshaw was greyer than grey now, and trembling. 'Nothing,' he mumbled. 'I gave him plenty of warnings about . . .'

'I see, so he had been warned? I thought you were going to say you'd given him plenty of money, but he must have stolen the gun instead and kept the money for himself.'

'*He did what?*'

'It's the way it looks, Mr Bradshaw. But don't worry, in no way are you implicated in these matters. How could you be, when you yourself were a victim of the shootings?'

'You believe Darren – '

'Ach, I know it must be hard for you, hey? But do you see the water plant on my shoe here? Just the same as that found on Bonzo Hookham's shoe? And the revolver in the dam? No, you wouldn't know what I'm talking about, but Darren helped us a lot last night to finally bring the case to a satisfactory conclusion.'

Bradshaw staggered to his feet. 'My God, what did you do to my boy? He would never – '

'It wasn't so much what we did, Mr Bradshaw. I regret to say that this illegal arms business has its own methods when it comes to dealing with people who try to cheat it. He lost a lot of blood.'

With a groan, Bradshaw buried his head in his arms and stood rocking. Then he looked up. 'You've got it completely wrong,' he said. 'I never thought the boy would have it in him, but he's been lying for my sake. Oh sweet Jesus!'

'I'm sure Darren hasn't told me any lies,' said Kramer. 'Not one.'

'But he *must* have done! If I prove it to you, will you let him go? I'll give you the whole story!

'It better be good,' said Kramer.

CHAPTER TWENTY-SEVEN

Colonel Muller tapped on Zondi's window. 'Where's your boss?'
he asked. 'What the hell went on up at Dargle last night? Why
wasn't I informed from the – ?'

'The Lieutenant is breaking the news of Boss Darren's death
to the parents,' said Zondi, getting quickly out of the Chevrolet.

'Really?' Colonel Muller scanned the front of the house. 'Oh,
there's Mrs Bradshaw!' She was waving to him, and he waved
back. 'Doesn't look to me as if she's had bad news!'

'I think the Lieutenant wanted to first tell Boss Bradshaw,
Colonel.'

'I'd better go and see how he's taking it.'

Zondi risked catching him by the sleeves. 'Excuse me, sir, but
the Lieutenant asked me to get your urgent opinion about a fresh
clue to the shootings. Here, he left an atlas for you, and I will
explain the full details.'

'A fresh clue? I thought the case was dead? And what the hell
has an atlas to do with it?'

'You ll find it interesting, sir.'

'Ja, but –'

'Will you look at it, please Colonel?'

'On second thoughts,' said Colonel Muller, glancing again at
Mrs Bradshaw, 'perhaps Lieutenant Kramer is welcome to what
will happen to that poor lady's face any minute now. Come,
we'll sit in my car.'

After a prolonged, agonised silence, Archibald Meredith Bradshaw began to talk. He did so without fuss or preamble, just as a
man might speak who simply couldn't care less what he said any
more.

'I killed Bonzo Hookham, Lieutenant Kramer. I did the deed –
nobody helped me.'

'Rubbish!' said Kramer. 'Your one hand wasn't working at the time, and that was a medical fact. How could you tie the rope like that? How could you –'

'I will explain everything, I promise you.'

'Huh! What was your motive?'

'Revenge, I suppose you'd call it.'

'For what?'

'Hookham had first tried to kill me.'

'Hey?' Kramer's head jerked back. 'When was this? In the war?'

Bradshaw smiled a ghost of a smile. 'No, here in Trekkersburg just over a month ago.'

This was too much to absorb immediately. Kramer took out his cigarettes and lit one, noticing that his fingers shook. He looked back at Bradshaw. The smile was gone.

'I was walking my dog when I heard someone call out a name – not my name, a man's name. I turned and saw him there against the sunset, with the gun in his hand. I couldn't believe it. I took a step towards him and he fired. The bullet smacked into my shoulder and I went arse over tip. I may have fainted for a second. The next thing I knew was that my whole shirt on that side was soaked in warm blood. He was trying to get near me, trying to see where the bullet had gone, but all the blood must have hidden the little tear eight inches above my heart. My dog was keeping him off, it was going for him. Jesus, I thought, if he sees I'm still alive, I'll catch another one. It was amazing how clear my thoughts were. I realised he must be able to see me breathing, so I gave this choking sound, went tense then flopped. I held my breath and my dog went on barking. I heard him saying something to himself that gave me a sudden insight into what was going on. Then, just as my lungs were bursting, I heard my dog's barks getting fainter, and I raised myself just a fraction to see him running away. Then I fainted properly, and when I woke up again it was dark and the dog was licking my face. It just shows you what life is like, Lieutenant: three days later that same dog, a loyal friend, was hit by a car and died in my lap.'

'And then? You crawled to your car?'

'I hobbled – it was agonising. Once I had managed to make myself believe what had happened, I started becoming very angry

255

– furious! Outraged is perhaps the word I'm looking for, and I made up my mind to take my revenge.'

'Stop,' said Kramer. 'Already you're lying, Bradshaw. I thought this story was meant to be the truth?'

'It is the truth!'

'Revenge of that kind is police business, Bradshaw. Why didn't you come and tell us all this?'

'Because you would have arrested him, and have found out his motive. I didn't want you to do that.'

Kramer blew a smoke-ring. 'What was his motive?'

'Do you need to know that? So far as I know, Lieutenant, the prosecution doesn't have to prove the motive, and I don't intend revealing it to you.'

'Why not? Was it based on another of your deeds, hey?'

The ghost of a smile came back. 'I gathered so, although it's not one which I'll ever feel any personal guilt about – it occurred under unusual circumstances. None the less, it isn't something I'm proud of, and if people knew about it, I'd be ruined at the very least.'

'We'll leave that for now, hey?' said Kramer. 'So far you have said nothing that convinces me that Darren –'

'Then listen, damn you!' growled Bradshaw, gripping the arms of his chair. 'The crux of the matter was that I knew I could never feel safe again. Hookham would either make another attempt on my life, or he would spill the beans – something like that. There was a terrible light in his eyes, and he'd been made unstable by his wife's death. I am certain he was in a state of not caring very much what he did any more.' The grey cheeks puffed out for a second. 'Huh! My first reaction, I remember, as I was driving home, was based on some kind of stupid guilt, I suppose. I remember thinking he must have some kind of divine guidance on his side, which had made our paths cross as they did. But once I rationalised, it was almost natural that they should at some time or other. He was one of those typically "English" types that only Trekkersburg seems to produce – you know the kind I mean? The ones who call England "home" in conversations, even when they've never been there? And I had moved here after the war for that very reason: "English" types don't only "dote" on antiques, but they provided me with plenty of untapped sources of their own stuff to flog around the country to other dealers.

Then again, we were both ex-Raf, so it wasn't a freakish chance that we should bump into each other at a flying club social. Once I got rid of those stupid fears, I decided the most sensible thing would be to kill him. God, I must have killed thousands with my bombs, people who'd never done a thing to me directly, and one more wasn't going to make much difference to my immortal soul – certainly not when he was a murderous bastard to boot! I had no need of moral scruples, and besides, I've never let anyone push me around without me getting even.'

'You're a bastard,' said Kramer, 'I know that. But forget all this philosophy crap! Facts are what are needed to save your son's reputation.'

'Listen!' Bradshaw urged once again. 'Here are the facts! Fact one is that I decided to wipe him out. But I needed to think first, make a plan. Until I'd done that, I made up my mind to remain silent, to fake amnesia, deep shock, whatever you like. So when I got home, I said nothing, and I said nothing that night in hospital either. By the morning I knew what I had to do first. I had to take Hookham right off his guard – I could imagine what must have gone through his mind when he saw the paper that Saturday morning, when he saw I was still alive! That was the worst day of all : dreading he would come to you and give himself up. His only other alternative, as I saw it, was to get the hell out back to England.'

Kramer nodded. From the evidence, that's exactly what had passed through Hookham's mind.

'So what did I do?' Bradshaw went on, and despite everything the braggart came close to the surface then. 'I turned the little runt into a sodding giant! I fed you a whole lot of total bullshit about the "looming figure against the sky", I think the *Gazette* called it, and that wasn't all. I knew that a hard case like yourself wouldn't take that kind of story too seriously, and would think me an idiot, while trying to find better things to do.'

'You are an idiot, Bradshaw. Go on.'

'Yet you still need me to tell you what happened!' Bradshaw shot back, almost cocky with it. 'Be careful who you call an idiot, Lieutenant. You never stood a chance.'

'Right, you'd put Hookham off his guard – although let me tell you he probably had his suspicions – and now you made your plan of attack.'

'Correct, and that included the possibility that Hookham wasn't completely fooled, but in no position to tell anyone else this. I decided to use the fact he would most likely come after me again – and where was he most likely to do this? I couldn't go walking round deserted parts of the race-course until he pitched up! Obviously, he'd known about that habit of mine from our conversation at the social, and so I decided to let him use something else he had picked up, when I'd described the whereabouts of our fishing cottage to him. Again the *Gazette* did the work for me there, and published the story about me going trout fishing. Have you got the picture? I had set my lure for him.'

Kramer nodded. That story had appeared at the beginning of the week, and coincided with the night Hookham had got very drunk with his friends on the lawn in Morninghill.

'My next concern was *how* to kill him,' said Bradshaw. 'It's so easy to make mistakes with a murder, and leave clues that lead straight back to you. Ah, I thought, I will leave clues deliberately; nice big clues that will stand out in front of any I overlook myself – that water plant gave me a nasty moment when I read about it, I can tell you!' He was almost enjoying this recital; like the perpetrator of any 'perfect crime', his only disappointment had been making do without his rightful share of applause. 'Then I took it a step further. I reasoned that, rather than a ragbag of mixed-up clues that could lead anywhere and might even backfire on me, they should point in a specific direction. Where better than at a giant I knew didn't exist? That was brilliant, I told myself, because if it seemed that Hookham had been murdered by the same person who'd tried to kill me, then I would be the last ever to be suspected!'

Uh-huh.' Kramer could not but concede that.

How would I achieve the impression of a giant? Well, what we were really talking about was strength, and so first off I made a fist out of an old golf club, holding the thing in a vice and rubbing with a rasp in my left hand. That was another nasty moment, by the way – when that fool De Klerk started going mad about home workshops! I covered the club with its leather hood, and tried a swing with it – plenty of leverage, you see, and I burst a pumpkin in bits. But I needed more than that. The skipping rope occurred to me, as it was bound to send you running round all the gymnasiums in town until you'd had a gutful. Myra had given it to me some months ago, after visiting Jo'burg, and I'd told her I'd accidentally thrown it away, not wanting to join in her bloody nonsense every morning. It looked too obvious with the handles on, so I cut them off and burned them, fairly sure your forensic experts wouldn't let me down. A good tight knot, tighter than any normal man could manage, was my next idea. I tried the pulleys I've got outside for my hammock, attaching extra rope on either side, but it was too cumbersome, so I left it for the moment. What would really clinch the whole thing would be if I could fake a bullet to match the one found in me, but I knew that was impossible. For one crazy moment, I thought of burgling the Digby-Smiths' house, to see if I couldn't find the actual gun Hookham had used – he must have borrowed it from someone without their knowing. Then I had to accept that it wasn't likely to be that poof's weapon – he's a pacifist, you know – and that Hookham must have snitched it somewhere else.'

Kramer nodded. Dear God, Mrs Westford had said that her husband had left behind everything that a woman needed to protect herself when living almost alone in the country, and this would no doubt have included a lady's handgun, a .32 probably kept on top of the wardrobe or beside her bed. On that last night, just before deciding to go on his final sortie, Hookham had been alone in the bedroom for some time, while she calmed Timmy down. From the rest of what Hookham had said, just before leaving her, it was now fairly plain that he intended to kill Bradshaw and possibly stay on.

'Well, now I'm going to admit something to you,' said Bradshaw, leaning forward and raising a finger, 'that you've got to accept for my Bible oath. It concerns Darren.'

'Of course – and you're going to say you'd not made him aware of any of these plans when he came down to help out in the shop.'

'Exac ly ! And that *is* the truth !'

Bradshaw was lying, Kramer could see it in his eyes, but decided to let it pass for the moment. Like father, like son, and two peas in a pod. If Bradshaw had gone to the wall, then the shop and young Darren's future would have gone with it.

'You're satisfied it's the truth?' Bradshaw demanded.

'Uh-huh. Go on.'

'I had another brilliant idea,' continued Bradshaw, and without any attempt at humour. 'The snag about the bullet was the scratches left on its surface by the barrel – but what if there was no bullet? What if it passed right through and disappeared? Then all your district surgeon would have was the hole made by a thirty-two, and he could use that to put together the two and two I wanted. Quite without Darren knowing what was happening, I fixed up with Silver Touch Benson for him to get hold of a thirty-two for me. It was to be brought to the shop, and Darren was to pay for it from the safe. Despite anything you have heard to the contrary, that is what happened.'

And he believes that part, thought Kramer. He believes that Darren didn't try to cut in on the action, perhaps with the hope of beating Meerkat down, and pocketing the difference in the price. He had taught his son the tricks of the trade too well.

'Darren didn't know it was a gun he was buying?'

'No idea,' said Bradshaw. 'He brought it home to me in a shoe box that was still taped up. Then I went up to my cottage and waited for Hookham to appear. Nothing happened Monday or Tuesday night. On Wednesday, when lack of sleep was beginning to get me, I rang the Digby-Smith house, putting on an accent, just to see where he was. Or was that the Tuesday? Never mind, the accent came in handy later on.'

'Ja, let's not bother with the details, Bradshaw. That was the night Hookham arrived?'

Bradshaw grinned. 'At about ten. He left his car up near the gate, and took the obvious route down along the stream. I had the thirty-two stuck in my belt, and I was down by the jetty, listening to his progress, when the thought occurred to me that, unless I could get very close and surprise him, then it was still possible he might get a shot in -- and I didn't like the thought of that.'

'Uh-huh. Not many would.'

'The boat, I thought. If I take the boat out, then I can catch him sideways when he reaches the rushes. But the distance was the problem. I had it! Back in the cottage was my Marlin Century, which I kept for buck. You know, a lever-action thirty-thirty! The trouble was I'd had revolvers on the brain, and had missed this easy answer. I just had time to double back, grab it and get behind the pine tree by the time Hookham appeared, creeping up the bank.'

Bradshaw's eyes had a gleam in them now, which Kramer found decidedly sick. But he went on listening, fascinated.

'The boat still served its purpose. Have you seen it? It's white. Against that background, even in moonlight, Hookham's head looked like a black bull's eye on a target.' Bradshaw paused to moisten his thick lips. 'Like I said, I keep the rifle for buck, shooting them by torchlight, and its foresight has a luminous bead. As Hookham's head was raised slowly to look at the cottage, I waited until the bullet would end up in the middle of the dam, and then squeezed the trigger. Bam! I got him first shot, right in the forehead, and the hole was perfect for being mistaken for a thirty-two.'

Oh Doc, thought Kramer, just wait until Van Rensburg hears this . . .

'The rifle shot was loud, naturally, and I knew it would be heard up at the farmhouse, so I couldn't waste any time. I was about to pick up Hookham though, when the revolver in his hand slipped from his fingers, and I saw then that my wishes had all come true. I would put a few more shots into him, angling them so they wouldn't come out. The gun had a hell of a kick for its size. The first bullet went into the soft mud beside him. I was more careful with the next two, getting him nicely in the chest, and I checked his back for exit wounds – none. Before anything else, I threw his own revolver as far out into the dam as I could, keeping the other one in my belt so I could tell the Pretoriuses I was just taking potshots for fun if they came down.'

'You went for the car?'

'Naturally, Lieutenant. He'd left it parked in an odd place. I drove it down to the front of the cottage, dragged him up to it, and decided to ring Darren to fetch me – he could drive Hookham back to Trekkersburg unwittingly, while I could use my own car, which had automatic.'

Kramer stubbed out his cigarette. 'So Darren was on standby all this week? Not going out because he didn't know when you would ring him to stage a rescue operation?'

'He was very happy just being with his mother!' snapped Bradshaw, lying again by the look of him. 'And he was exhausted by his long day in the shop.'

'Uh-huh. Then you had him help you tie up the wrists? You pulled with your strong left, and he put his muscle –'

261

'Jesus!' exploded Bradshaw. 'I've told you the boy didn't have any part in it! I was fiddling with the skipping rope by the porch – all right, trying hard to get it tight like you've said – and a very simple solution occurred to me. I took out the long tow rope in the back of Hookham's car, and used it to attach one end of the skipping rope to the Rover's bumper and another to one of the porch posts. All I had to do then was ease the Rover forward and it did the pulling for me. Frankly, I thought I'd overdone it a bit when I saw the bones smashed, but thank God that didn't seem to worry your forensic so-called experts. Did it?'

'One of them was a little doubtful,' admitted Kramer, 'but he has been distracted by other things lately. Slimy things in hard shells like yourself, Bradshaw. Tell me the rest.'

'You are beginning to believe me now?' asked Bradshaw, showing his relief in a weak smile. 'My boy's going to be released from custody? All charges dropped?'

'Darren's not got a thing to worry about,' said Kramer.

'Thank God! Well, the rest must be fairly self-evident to you. The point is that Darren had no knowledge of what lay in the back of that car when he drove it back to –'

'Ach, come on, man! Doesn't he read the newspapers?'

Bradshaw was trapped, and his cheeks went grey again. 'All right, I'll tell you what actually happened. I drove the Rover myself – I left before he arrived, and he found a note saying I'd got a lift from someone.'

'Rubbish, Bradshaw. He drove the Rover, you waited round the corner for him, and then you two went home together. That fits in much better,' Kramer lied glibly, 'with what he's –'

'Then why hasn't he anything to worry about?' asked Bradshaw, glancing up at footsteps on the floorboards above his head.

'Because I think Mrs Bradshaw is going to suffer enough,' said Kramer, and began to make a plan to really spare her all he could; with Bradshaw's help, it would be easy to fiddle the evidence and yet still leave sufficient to hang him with. 'Please speak freely from now on.'

'You mean that, don't you?' remarked Bradshaw in surprise. 'I can't understand why!'

'Perhaps that's because you can't see your wife as a person,' said Kramer. 'Where does Classina Baksteen figure in all this?'

'You should know!' snorted Bradshaw. 'You were the one

digging your nose into the last thing you should have done! Why did you latch on to the RAF angle like that?'

Kramer glanced around the room. 'It was in here I first got that feeling,' he said. 'Here in your study. Mrs Bradshaw was talking about Bonzo Hookham and – ' A sudden flash of hindsight brought it back to him. 'Ja, I know where that feeling came from! It was when, from what Mrs Bradshaw was saying, I must have felt surprised you'd not spoken to her about Bonzo since the party – funny behaviour for a veteran, hey? And where were all the old mementos? The sort of things an ex-RAF bomber pilot would have on view in his own private room. Why weren't they there? Had you tried to cast them out of your mind too? And yet, socially, you still had to play the part, you couldn't get round it without avoiding – what? Suspicion?'

'I can see,' said Bradshaw, 'that I wasn't wrong in trying to mislead you and get you away from digging into that too deeply.'

'I might have found Bonzo Hookham's motive?'

'You stood a very fair chance. But weren't you interested in Classina? The idea came to me when you and Colonel Muller came here, and I could see how obsessed you were with the Raf. Luckily, that "strange accent" nonsense I'd planted in Myra earlier put up a bit of flak, distracting the Colonel, and from what he said I had to break the pattern before it got any further.'

Half a mark to De Klerk, thought Kramer; maybe even eight out of ten.

Bradshaw had his braggart's glint back. 'It all came to me in a flash. Colonel Muller seemed dead set on the race-course being the scene of the crime, so I made a phone call that I knew would get every available patrol down there, clearing the rest of Six Valleys for a young bloke I'd hired. It had to be Six Valleys, of course, because that would support your pattern. I was also getting a bit sick of making up stuff I'd "forgotten to tell you", and wanted the investigation to die a natural, so I made it fit Muller's prediction of one last attack.'

'It sounds to me,' said Kramer, 'as if Stormtrooper Schoeman needs a kick up his arse.'

'No, you can't blame him for missing me making the call,' said Bradshaw, smugly. 'I suggested to Myra that she should invite him for a swim, and he seemed quite transfixed by her. Anyway, do you remember the first shot I'd fired with Hookham's revolver?'

'Uh-huh.'

'I'd recovered that bullet, naturally, and I'd hung on to it, the way one does with something that might come in useful unexpectedly. I gave it to this youngster, who I paid good money, and told him to go round the back of Six Valleys and take a look at these Afrikaans addresses I'd picked out of the Kelly's directory. If he saw something harmless he could shoot at, using the bullet for a stone in his catty, and preferably with someone near it, then he was to have a go. I made the stipulation about a harmless shot because I didn't want – '

'Ja, I've got the picture,' said Kramer. 'You didn't want the innocent to suffer? Not after all those bombs you dropped?'

Bradshaw appreciated the irony. 'A very nasty moment,' he admitted. 'I equipped this kid with some more false clues, a bag of cigarette ash and cigarette ends, told him to stand under a branch in these big shoes, and by pressing upwards, really make some deep impressions, and so on. He was meant, however, to light a firecracker and fire his catapult when it went off, but the cracker was a dud and made hardly any noise at all. Again, very fortunately for me, the imaginative geniuses in the police force put forward a theory to cover that, and as De Klerk explained it to me before asking any questions, I was able to play him along nicely.'

'That wasn't just any kid,' said Kramer. 'It was Darren. Detective Constable Schoeman is not all tiptoes and tinkling laughter, Bradshaw – he made his observations.'

'What? Then why didn't you – ?'

Kramer shrugged. 'Why didn't we try for you before? Ach, it was simpler to let you think the whole thing had been forgotten, and then to wait until one of the pair of you made his fatal error. That's what Darren did last night, Mr Bradshaw, when he pulled a gun on a police officer. You are not the only man in Trekkersburg who can use elements of the truth to keep the pot boiling.'

That dropped not so much a bombshell as a blockbuster on Bradshaw. He went rigid. He probably died a little in that moment.

'Fatal error?' he forced out, his voice quavering. 'You mean somebody shot him? Who?'

'Totally fatal, but nobody shot him.'

Bradshaw started to come out of his seat at Kramer, his great arms ready to claw at him. A push on the chest sent him reeling back.

'Jesus Christ Almighty! I must know what's happened!' Bradshaw bellowed. 'Tell me, you bastard! Tell me!'

'Calm yourself, Bradshaw, and I'll do better than that,' said Kramer, in a soft voice like Meerkat had used, 'I'll actually show you. But first I want to know why you killed a true man like Bonzo Hookham – and why he wanted to kill you.'

'Oh no, no more tricks!'

'It all began at the social, didn't it? You said something to him that tore the lid off, ripped open an old scar? You gave yourself away somehow, even though he'd never seen you in his life before? What was it? Come on, you must have guessed long ago!'

'Get stuffed! Go and –'

'What was it? A name? The name he called out at you? Was it your nun joke? You tell that to everyone, don't you?'

Bradshaw actually shrank back, and Kramer knew he had him then. 'Just tell me about my son,' he whimpered.

'We'll play swaps, Mr Bradshaw. You tell me what really happened when the Gestapo caught you, and I'll tell you what really happened to Darren. Okay?'

Bradshaw looked up at him with tears beginning to stream down his gross cheeks. 'We were not just father and son,' he said, lost from the reality of the moment, 'we were –'

'Ja, I know,' said Kramer, 'two of a kind. But that's Snap, and swaps is played this way.'

Then he began to deal out the Polaroid pictures of Darren Bradshaw's mutilated corpse face down on the study desk. For every print Archie Bradshaw turned over, he would have to pay a forfeit of the truth, the whole truth, and nothing but the truth. Kramer felt sure he would catch on very quickly.

A slight shadow fell over the atlas on Colonel Muller's lap, and he looked up to see Mrs Bradshaw trying to smile sweetly at him, but her eyes were frantic with worry. 'Please,' she whispered, 'can you tell me what's happening? I can hear Archie crying like a baby in his study, but I'm not really supposed to go in.'

'Er, there's some bad news, Myra,' mumbled Colonel Muller, handing the atlas back to Zondi. 'Um, an accident. Sergeant, will you take yourself – '

'On my way, Colonel,' said Zondi.

He retreated to the Chevrolet and slipped in behind the wheel, propping his atlas against it. The rear-view mirror on the right wing showed Colonel Muller helping Mrs Bradshaw into his car. They spoke for less than a minute, and then Mrs Bradshaw threw her arms around the Colonel's neck, and buried her plain little face in his big broad shoulder. Her own shoulders shook and shook. Then the Colonel's arms came up and wrapped comfortingly around her, while he bent his head to say soothing things in her ear.

'Hmmmm,' said Zondi, opening his atlas to stare at it for inspiration.

At the same moment, the front door of the house opened for the first time. The Lieutenant stepped out, leading a shambling, shrunken figure tightly by the right arm.

Zondi gave a final glance at the map of Picardy. There, just above Amiens, was a town called Albert. Knowing this, it was possible to give a fresh interpretation to the entry in Bonzo Hookham's diary for May 27th: *Dear God, hasn't my poor Alice suffered enough in her life? Albert – her family, now this!* Albert lay on what seemed a likely escape route from Germany, and Alice's family had been betrayed to the Germans. A motive for murder if the traitor were discovered? Colonel Muller had been impressed by the idea, but neither he nor Zondi had been able to decide quite what to do with it.

CHAPTER TWENTY-EIGHT

Everyone seemed to be in the Supreme Court on the balmy summer's afternoon when Archibald Meredith Bradshaw, aged 56, of 19 Kitchener Row, Bullerton, Trekkersburg, was sentenced to death for the murder of Edward 'Bonzo' Hookham, aged 55, of Forge Cottage, Little Bowerby, Hampshire, England.

The Widow Fourie was there, sitting in the front row of the public gallery on the side reserved for whites, and she caught Kramer's eye with an understanding look as Mr Justice Willoughby-Evans, an Oxford Blue, began to intone the formula.

Archibald Meredith Bradshaw, the sentence of the Court is

Miriam Zondi was there, seated in the middle of the public gallery on the side reserved for non-whites, and gazing proudly at her husband, who had just received a special commendation in the judge's speech for the assistance he had given the arresting officer. Zondi, squirming a little on the wooden bench beside the Lieutenant, kept his eyes averted in embarrassment.

you shall be taken back

Colonel Muller was there, hunched forward in the disused jury box, watching Bradshaw's face with a curious sort of satisfaction, for all the world as though his bachelor days were numbered. It was already known there would be no appeal.

to the place of custody whence you came

Three former members of the French Resistance were there, having been flown out specially to confirm beyond any reasonable doubt that the prisoner in the dock was the selfsame bullnecked, toadying airman glimpsed pointing out the 'safe house' in Albert where young Alice Hookham had once lived with her family.

and that you from there, on a day to be appointed

Six former prisoners of war were there, also having been flown out, to testify that the prisoner in the dock had not been seen for a month after his return to camp, by which time he claimed to have recovered from his injuries by torture. None of this was essential to the case, but the Attorney-General had left such a show trial required the proper embellishing.

by the State President

The widow of Trigger Stevens was there, having travelled the 6,000 miles at the expense of a British Sunday paper, to see her husband's name cleared at long last.

shall be brought to a place also appointed by him

Mrs Sophie Pritchard, the late Alice Hookham's dearest friend, was also there, having testified that on countless occasions the dead woman had described the coward who had looked up at her bedroom one day, pointed, and then had been led away by a friendly, chattering group of Gestapo officers.

and that there you be hanged by the neck

Classina Marie Baksteen was there, loving every minute of it. A busty girl with frizzy hair sat beside her balding fiancé.

until you are dead

'Thank you, my lord,' said the prisoner.

Oddly enough, Dr Christian Strydom and Sergeant Van Rensburg were not there. Kramer found them engrossed in a corner of the post-mortem room at the mortuary when he called in just after five. They had scores of test-tubes, flasks, beakers and lengths of glass tubing arranged about them, and were communicating in pleased little grunts.

'My God,' said Kramer, stopping short. 'What is this? Dr Jekyll and Mr Hyde?'

'Ah, Tromp!' said Strydom, turning round with a test-tube of blood in his hand. 'You've solved the one with the keys?'

'No, I've just been in court to hear your friend the jolly green giant being sent for the chop.'

'Oh,' said Strydom. 'Was that today?'

'Shall we show him, Doc?' whispered Van Rensburg.

'Show me what?' asked Kramer.

'What we can do with our extract of slime,' replied Van Rensburg, proudly. 'Man, it's like a miracle! For instance, what colour of blood do you think that is in Doc's hand?'

'Red,' said Kramer.

Van Rensburg frowned. 'Ach no! Is it white blood, or is it

268

black blood? If you found that at the scene of a crime, would you know?'

'I'd taste it for purity,' said Kramer, grinning and moving over to the bench where they were working. 'Is this what all those bloody snails were for?'

'Let me show you!' enthused Van Rensburg. 'It's a question of a protein action, hey? You just put a drop of our extract in the sample, and then it precip – er, precipitates according to whether the blood is white or not.'

'Hey, Doc! That's not bad!'

Strydom flushed slightly. 'Not entirely original, I should point out. Pioneer work in this has been done in Port Elizabeth, using the snail Helix –'

'No, don't start being too scientific with me, please!' begged Kramer, looking round him. 'I'm just a layman, remember?'

'Ja, Doc, we must make allowances,' said Van Rensburg. 'Have you lost something, Tromp?'

'Uh-huh, an unopened letter I brought in here this morning in the mad rush before court. It's got "air mail" on it and English stamps.'

'Oh, of course, I picked it up and I've been keeping it for you,' said Strydom, fishing the envelope out of his apron pocket. 'Where will you be tonight? The farmhouse?'

'Uh-huh.'

'Only I'll be able to give you some results on the Bantu midget job.'

'Fine – well, keep up the good work, hey?' said Kramer from the doorway. 'There's just one thing : what happens if you find a sample of Cape Coloured blood? Mixed blood – you know?'

'Yirra!' said Van Rensburg, turning in alarm to his mentor.

Zondi discreetly stayed outside the car, chatting to Nxumalo and sharing a cigarette with him, while Kramer read the letter he had opened with some trepidation.

Dear old Tromp,
Excuse the handwriting, but I'm doing this in the waiting room of Southampton General maternity section – need you ask. Tish is having to have special tests or something. She wanted me to let you know how well everything has worked out since we got

*home, and to pass on her best wishes. You really taught us both
a lesson, you know. I never thought I'd get her back — day after
day I begged and pleaded with her. I even dragged old Smorgasbord along from the gym to swear blind we hadn't been
having it off in the sauna room. No more of that for me. Not
only that but as Trish says, there's no place like home in the
end, and the hell with la dolce vita, matey! By the way, you
may be interested to know that I've Gone Straight with my new
salon. I have my reasons of course. What if a few months from
now a* very *butchy babe is born in Southampton town, scream-
ing for its bottle in Afrikaans? I suppose I'll have to learn the
lingo and in the meantime, old pal, there's something for you
to think about. Many thanks!*

> *Yours sincerely,*
> *Jonty Hayes*

'Hayes!'

'Yes, Lieutenant?' asked Zondi, coming to the window. 'You're ready to go?'

Kramer nodded, laughing and looking again at the letter, which had a lot between the lines. 'Now there's a typical example of how prejudice doesn't help in this job,' he said, as Zondi got behind the wheel and started up. 'You never stop to think that a poof hairdresser might have a second name, do you?'

'Boss? Have you slipped up somewhere?' Zondi said with concern in his voice. 'Is this letter – ?'

'No, it was just as well, I suppose,' said Kramer, putting the letter in his pocket for the Widow Fourie to read. 'Kwela Village, please, Mickey, through the park, and don't spare the horses.'

AUTHOR'S NOTE

Sailor Malan, Dr LeMoyne Snyder, the Texan and all but one of the epileptics are or were real people; the blood test is also quite genuine. All other characters are fictitious, although the names of two South African policemen have been used as a reminder to them that they are not forgotten. Finally, I would like to thank Joe Connolly for his part in the initial stages of this book.

PANTHEON INTERNATIONAL CRIME

Now Available in Paperback

Laidlaw by William McIlvanney
0-394-73338-X $2.95

"Everything in *Laidlaw* rings true. It is a tough novel, with an exciting ending, and it is superbly written. You should not miss this one."—Newgate Callendar, *The New York Times*

"I have seldom been so taken by a character as I was by the angry and compassionate Glasgow detective, Laidlaw." —Ross MacDonald

The Blood of an Englishman by James McClure
0-394-71019-3 $2.95

"This well-plotted, well-written mystery is exceptional… sometimes grim, sometimes comic, always shocking." —*Atlantic Monthly*

"An altogether superior piece of work."—Newgate Callendar, *The New York Times*

The Steam Pig by James McClure
0-394-71021-5 $2.95

"A first-rate mystery with a solution that is a shocker. The pace is relentless, the prose riveting, and the pair of detectives remarkable. Not to be missed, it is the essence of what the best of the genre aspires to be."—*Saturday Review*

The Poison Oracle by Peter Dickinson
0-394-71023-1 $2.95

"If you have time for only one mystery this month, better make it *The Poison Oracle*."—*Chicago Sun-Times*

"*The Poison Oracle* is a fascinating suspense story. A clever mixture of psycholinguistics, anthropological adventure, and detection."—*Psychology Today*

Coming from Pantheon International Crime

The Thirty-First Floor by Per Wahlöo
Caterpillar Cop by James McClure
The Lively Dead by Peter Dickinson
A Killing Kindness by Reginald Hill
The Eurokillers by Julian Rathbone